ALSO BY ANNE RENWICK

Venomous Secrets

THE ELEMENTAL WEB CHRONICLES

BOOK 4

ANNE RENWICK

To all the scientists who worked countless hours to bring us the scientific triumph of today's vaccines.

THANK YOU TO...

My husband. Your help was above and beyond. From plotting and medical science to support and encouragement. Without you, this book would never have seen the light of day.

The Plotmonkeys—this one was a long time in the incubator.

Sandra Sookoo, my brilliant editor who mercilessly ferrets out weaknesses and sets my work on a better course.

My two boys and my newest nephew.

My mom and dad who made reading and science priorities.

Mr. Fox and his red pen.

CHAPTER ONE

London
May 1885

ANY MINUTE NOW.

The steam orchestra played the opening bars of a Viennese waltz, turning all eyes away from the magnificence of the refreshments table.

All save his.

Jonathan "Jack" Tagert kept the ice sculpture of a phoenix rising from its ashes at the edge of his vision. An extravagant artistic display that presented an easily exploitable weakness. Odds were low that anyone would notice when hydrogen gas began to slowly drift upward from beneath the fragile icy feathers constituting its base.

"Isn't Lady Mildred perfection?" Beside him, his mother's lips curved into a smug smile as her oldest son led his bride-to-be and future viscountess onto the ballroom floor. "With her heart-shaped face and rosebud mouth, she could grace a postcard in a bookseller's shop window." Her chin lifted. "Their wedding will be the talk of the *ton*. It's a shame your sister fell victim to temptations presented by the duchess. Angela would have done much better with one of Lady Mildred's discarded admirers."

He flattened his lips. On the first point, they agreed. His sister's impulsive wedding was ill-conceived. Not that he could discuss Angela's motivations. Or presumed whereabouts. As to Lady Mildred's other suitors? Milk sops, all of them.

"An appealing visage," he answered his mother. "But it's her curves that won her a proposal. She appears fertile enough."

Strip away her clothing, and a dank, dark hole of a shop on Holywell Street would sell you the same image at a considerably higher price point. A fact that explained a certain predatory gleam in his brother's eyes.

Thwack. His mother snapped her fan down upon his wrist. Built with iron staves, it was rather more sturdy than it looked. When she was truly mad, hairline fractures of the wrist became a decided possibility. "We do not utter such words aloud!"

Unflinching, for he would not give her the satisfaction of a reaction, Jack stared out over the whirl of colorful ballgowns and black dress coats, irritated that the faulty peripheral vision of his left eye made tracking familiar faces more difficult. He closed his eyes for a moment, took a deep breath, and returned to needling his mother. "Is that not what precipitated his reform?" he asked. "The quest for an heir?"

His brother, Viscount Aubrey, was her favorite, absorbing all her love and devotion, no matter how often he tempted the grim reaper. He was the handsome one. The charming one. The amusing one.

Mother stiffened. "It is his duty."

"One my brother has spent a lifetime avoiding. Why the sudden turnabout?"

Spoiled rotten, his mother's beloved child had reached adulthood and embarked upon a life of self-absorption and debauchery. Until a few months past, his every action seemed aimed at accelerating his trajectory into a coffin.

Not even the death of their father a few years past—revealing the dismal state of the family finances—had slowed the pace of Aubrey's revelry. He'd been content to let Jack wrestle with outstanding debts and mismanaged investments while their mother, dismissive of her spare's efforts, worked to acquire a wealthy young American bride for her eldest. A well-established technique to buttress the deterioration of funds and smooth the cracking veneer of a family's genteel façade.

When orders to depart for Austria arrived, an assignment that would occupy him for several months, Jack had dropped the account books on his brother's lap, frustrated, irritated and expecting catastrophe.

"Perhaps it is because he is now free to choose his own bride," Mother suggested on a huff.

"And how is that, exactly?" For Jack had returned to London to find the family coffers were once again full.

How else to explain this ball or his brother's bride-to-be? English, possessed of an impeccable family tree and, to all appearances, raised in the countryside on milk and honey. Sweet. Young. Innocent. And in for a world of disappointment.

"It is none of your concern." His mother's gaze remained fixed upon the waltzing couple. "Suffice it to say Aubrey has come into his own."

"Mmm." Jack harbored serious doubts.

Outwardly, nothing seemed amiss. Aubrey behaved exactly as society expected of a lord. But taking a wife was merely a bit of novelty. A distraction. Once the shine wore off, tried and true patterns would reassert themselves. They always did.

Especially when his brother's old school chums were about.

Dr. William Oakes might hold a medical degree and project maturity and dignity, but he was no stranger to the hedonistic. Though not *ton*, he moved among the self-important by virtue of the successful medical practice he'd built by catering to their every need and whim. Even now, he lurked about the edges of the room, ingratiating himself with mothers of unsuccessful debutants in hopes of plucking low-hanging fruit to secure himself a blue-blooded wife.

At the other end of the spectrum was Stephen Carruthers, son of Lord Saltwell. Married. Father. A second child on the way. Yet Jack could not recall a single time when the man was fully sober. Even now, he kept his feet beneath him by propping himself against a column, his only ambition in life to ensure the flask tucked in his pocket never ran dry.

Together, the three of them rarely found their beds before dawn.

Jack let his gaze drift back to his brother's waltzing form.

Maintaining an outward guise of respectability was too much of a struggle. Any day now, Aubrey would lose the fight, reach for a brandy tumbler, another man's wife, a morphine-filled hypodermic syringe—possibly all three at once—and the façade would come crashing down.

Such self-indulgent behavior would not only estrange his new wife, but Aubrey would ignore whatever hare-brained financial scheme propped up his current lifestyle and the estate's coffers would suffer a sudden and precipitous decline. One which Jack would, yet again, be called upon to repair. Venting his simmering frustration was pointless as it would only be met by denial.

Naturally, he'd attempted to investigate the estate's current condition. Forewarned was forearmed. Yet he'd arrived at the study's door to find a new lock. Not something a simple set of lock picks would open, but a new, shiny, firkin cincture bolt.

Insulting, really, that his brother believed such a contraption could stop him. The corner of his mouth kicked up.

Still, uncovering family secrets was not a project to undertake with steambot staff monitoring his every move, ready to sound the alarm.

Hence the need for a disaster.

Had he over-coated the sodium pellet? By now, it ought to have reacted with the ice melt. Did he need to engineer another distraction to allow him to slip, unnoticed, down the hallway and into the study?

The couple spun, and Lady Mildred glanced in their direction. Briefly, but long enough for Jack to note vacant eyes and a fragile smile, one that threatened to crack at any moment. Had she pried back the edge of Aubrey's veneer and glimpsed the shallow emptiness of his existence beneath?

His mother's lips pursed. "Tell me you did not attempt to dissuade Lady Mildred from this engagement."

"What if I did?" An advantageous match made so early in the Season cast a pall of disappointment over mothers and debutants—one less title on the market. With Aubrey unavailable, the question became: who to pursue now? Already, a few speculative glances had been cast in his direction. If not the heir, what about the spare?

He hated that term, value measured in increments of perceived societal status.

"She's in his arms, is she not?" For all the usual reasons, he presumed, for Lady Mildred had been incapable of speech in his presence.

He *had* tried. But how did one explain the profligate life his brother led to a lady with delicate sensibilities? Or convince her, when she clung to the idea of a title like paste to the wallpaper she dreamt of installing in the townhouse, that it wasn't worth the price she would pay?

The engagement had been announced. A date set.

Aether help her, Lady Mildred would need the yards of pink ruffles and lace in which she was wrapped to weather the crushing blow of inevitable humiliation.

Beginning with tonight's small disaster.

There was a soft pop.

Finally.

A small, bright orange flame erupted at the base of the phoenix. A brief hiss accompanied each tiny spark of molten sodium that leapt away, all combining into a brief, hot flare that wrought irreversible damage to the ice sculpture.

Though the initial incendiary event went unremarked, there was a loud, audible crack as the ice sculpture broke free. For a moment, the bird teetered upon its pedestal, then dove—beak first—into the champagne fountain. Crystal shattered. Ladies screamed. And a torrent of golden liquid gushed over snowy white linen, flooding sugary delicacies before cascading to the gleaming marble floor beneath.

His mother threw him a brief, narrow-eyed glance before springing into action, clapping her hands and issuing orders. Damage control was her forte. With children like hers, how could it not be?

As steam footmen abandoned their posts to rush to the scene of the disaster, Jack backed away, sliding down a now unguarded and shadowy hallway off limits to guests.

Captain Jack's Tension Torque popped the lock in a matter of minutes and a moment later, he'd located the ledgers. He shook a Lucifer lamp to life, noted the time on his pocket watch, then bent his head over the columns of numbers, not caring at all for what he found.

Expenditures were up, alarmingly so. Most of them upon luxuries. Not unexpected, but what income covered their costs?

There.

An impressive sum deposited on a monthly basis for—he flipped backward through the pages—the past three... four... five months.

At the sixth month mark, Jack swore under his breath. No income. Instead, expenditure. Upon the construction of a building. A retreat for the wealthy. In Yorkshire.

Had Aubrey lost his mind? He must have, to invest such a prodigious amount on the Grand Menwith Hotel and Spa. A Turkish bath? Massage therapy? Recouping the outlay alone would take ages.

Spa.

Jack growled. He would bet long odds that Dr. Oakes' influence lay at the center of this madness. Who else could convince his brother to bankroll a luxurious hotel where he might offer—in addition to mineral waters—a variety of dubious medical treatments of the snake oil variety?

A glance at his pocket watch told him that the few minutes he'd allocated to his investigation had elapsed. Time to return to the festivities before his absence was noted. He slammed the ledgers closed and exited the room, re-engaging the lock.

Fuming, he stalked down the still-deserted hallway. Paused. He wasn't the only one to have taken advantage of the phoenix's plunge. The library's door was ajar. Enough so that a faint moan emerged.

Rolling his eyes, he turned away. If one dragged a paramour into a deserted room for clandestine activities, the least one could do was close—

Gaahhh. A strange, strangled cry.

Jack hesitated. *Not* a sound he would associate with an enjoyable moment.

Bang. Crash. The sound of furniture toppling. Of a lamp shattering.

Thud. Thud. Thud. Heels drumming on the floor.

Such were the sounds of an assault.

Jack flung the door open.

A dark-haired woman in a white gown crouched upon Lord Saltwell, pinning his bucking and thrashing form to the floor. Long white fingers grasped his head, tilting the gentleman's pale and shocked face away, her mouth latched upon his neck.

His breath froze in his lungs. Ice ran down his spine. Impossible. And yet, the evidence lay before him. The London Vampire in a scene straight from the gossip rags.

Had eyes finally betrayed him? He blinked.

No.

Sense returned.

"Stop!" he cried, rushing forward, ready to pry the woman from the lord's throat.

But she sprang away, hissing, her face all but hidden.

He dropped to the floor beside her victim, not at all reassured by the man's shallow breaths and twitching limbs.

"I didn't know. I swear it." Lord Saltwell's words were the faintest of whispers. "She is evil. Her blood polluted."

"Hang in there." Jack pulled back the man's collar. Two puncture wounds. Red and raw was to be expected from a so-called vampire. But the tissue surrounding the bite was rapidly swelling. That suggested poison. He shifted to keep the woman within his sights. "Help!" he yelled. "We need some help here!" He dropped his voice and spoke to the woman. "If he dies, you'll hang."

As he straightened, shifting his weight in the attacker's direction, she leapt into an open window overlooking the garden. Moonlight cast her body's curves into dark shadow against the thin, white material of her gown as a gentle breeze fluttered the ruffled lace about her wrists. A thin trickle of blood ran downward over her chin. Were those fangs?

Fine hairs upon the nape of his neck lifted involuntarily, and his heart pounded. Anyone with superstitious inclinations would think her a vampire fresh from the grave.

"It's an end he deserves," she hissed. Crouched upon the sill, her hands gripped its frame. With gold-rimmed gray eyes, she cast a long, seductive glance over her shoulder.

"Why?" He took a step toward her, hands upturned—a gesture offering an innocent, but false, chance at reasonable discourse. "What has he done?"

Footsteps thundered in the hall.

He lunged, grasping. But the silky hem of her dress slipped through his fingertips as she jumped.

The door slammed open. His brother barely glanced at the body upon the floor before hurling an accusation. "Jack! What have you done?"

Did his brother never tire of casting him in a bad light? "Not a damn thing and you well know it." He made a decision in the space of a heartbeat. "Call Dr. Oakes. Lord Saltwell needs attention. I've a—" What exactly? "His attacker to catch."

Turning, he jumped through the window, landing hard upon the ground. Less than fifty yards away, his quarry climbed the garden wall with surprising agility given her billowing skirts. He took off at a run, drawing his TTX pistol from its holster. He fired, but missed. Branches caught at his coat along the winding garden path, but he was gaining on her.

Until his traitorous vision concealed the uneven pavers beneath his feet. Cursing, he stumbled, just managing to stay upright.

Heart pounding, he flung himself at the stone wall and scrambled over its summit. A flash of white caught his eye as she turned a corner, dashing down a covered arcade.

Ha! There would be no escape from such a venue at this late hour. He would catch her. If not, the Beadle would. The uniformed patrolmen of the Burlington Arcade were forever present ensuring standards of propriety were met even when the stores were closed.

He rounded the corner, plunging into the arcade.

Arches overhead supported dark panes of glass that would flood the space with sunlight during the day. At night, globes of white-blue Lucifer lamps counteracted the London gloom, all reflected in the curved glass bent about the various store fronts to display the wares within.

Yet nowhere was there a fleeing female garbed in white.

Impossible. He spun, searching above and behind him. He pinched the bridge of his nose, cursing his vision. Slowly, carefully, he paced the length of the arcade, inspecting each doorway, every possible nook and cranny. Nothing.

Then he drew up short. A ventilation grille mounted between the pavement and a shop window was askew. *Dammit.* She'd dropped into the basement, a space where rooms led to a tunnel that shop boys might deliver parcels as no high-ranking customer was permitted to carry their own packages in this venue.

He pried the meshwork free and quickly followed, ignoring the irate Beadle's shrieking whistle blasts and calls to "stop!"

Musty underground smells assaulted his nose as he tripped and careened around worktables, knocking shadowy contents to the floor as he raced into the tunnel. Alas, there were no fluttering white skirts to point his way. He ran its length, bursting onto the street. Gentlemen and their ladies stared, jaws agape.

"A woman," he demanded, ignoring the insistent pounding of his head. "In white. Has anyone seen her?"

A question met by denial and apprehensive looks. No one had seen anything unusual. If the woman was loose upon the streets, she was long beyond his reach.

He punched the wall, cursing. Those few pointed words exchanged with his brother might have cost him the time needed to catch Lord Saltwell's assailant. Grinding his teeth, he turned back into the tunnel. There was nothing else to do but rattle door handles in the hope she'd hidden somewhere within the basement rooms.

Alas, an hour later, he admitted defeat. Grim, he ducked out onto the street and pointed his scuffed shoes back toward his childhood home. Questions he couldn't answer would await him. Rumors and gossip would fill the void. He would do what he could to mitigate the disaster for, if Lord Saltwell had met his end at his brother's engagement ball, there would be hell to pay.

With all due haste, the Duke of Avesbury must be informed of tonight's incident. And of his agent's failure to secure the murderess.

CHAPTER TWO

THE CRANK HACK CLATTERED to a stop.

Holywell Street.

Two long rows of crooked, timber-framed houses stood shoulder to shoulder, hunching over the narrow street. Secretive, furtive. Casting storefronts and pavement into half-shadow beneath the anemic light of a gray sky.

And enticing a small crowd despite the early hour and a persistent morning drizzle.

A knot of men gathered beneath black umbrellas upon the street. Didn't most men pursue their vices under the cloak of full dark? What illicit amusement pried them from their warm beds? The promise of a new, risqué postcard? Did she dare sidle close enough to find out?

Cait mentally slapped at such ill-bred curiosity.

"No one must recognize you," Janet had warned. Repeatedly and at length. A steam maid would fuss less. Neither, however, would a mechanical servant provide critical tips and hints as to the many shadowy secrets London hid in plain sight. "That's no place for a lady of quality to be spotted. Indecent images propped up in the windows of those so-called bookstores. All those gaping men offering uncouth opinions about women's unmentionables." Janet's voice dropped to a whisper. "And there's worse, I hear tell, inside. Photographs of a pornographic nature."

A detail that failed to deter Cait the slightest bit.

"I'm not a lady, and I won't linger," she'd promised Janet. Though if postcards were scattered across a nearby surface, she'd certainly satisfy her curiosity with a quick glance. Growing up with brothers who dabbled in the medical sciences and no supervision over her selection of reading materials, she doubted anything of an anatomical nature could shock her—much as she'd enjoy learning otherwise. "A few minutes to chill the snake, then back to the carriage, safe and sound."

For Logan would kill her if he ever found out she'd ventured here, unaccompanied no less. Not because he believed her of naïve and virtuous character, but because such a street presented a physical threat, especially for a young woman with *exotic* features.

How she hated that term.

With such in mind, she'd chosen a dress of dull gray. There were ruffles and lace aplenty, but the cut was more severe than most of her gowns, displaying little more than her hands and face. Any remaining modest displays of flesh were addressed with gloves and a wide-brimmed hat complete with a veil. Like low-hanging fog, she planned to drift down the street, a sober, unremarkable matron.

Was there still risk? Certainly. But Cait's actions were entirely justified. The study of bacterial exotoxins was all well and good. An excellent professional pursuit. But ever since Mother's tipsy revelation a few months past, a corner of Cait's mind would not stop turning over her unguarded words and the possibilities such a revelation suggested.

"You wish to know of your true father?"

"I do." She'd pressed for years, only to be met with denial after denial.

Mustering resolve, her mother had splashed a generous amount of whiskey into her teacup, a vast deviation from the norm, for Mother frowned upon ladies who imbibed. But Cait's announcement had ripped a ragged hole in her mother's over-inflated plans to secure her daughter a respectable husband within Glaswegian society. Perhaps the indulgence could be understood.

"Very well, you are of age. I'll tell you."

And she had.

So much clarity from the briefest sentence. It explained much, especially her affinity for snakes.

But the final proof, the final test?

Cait had yet to manage that.

First she needed to procure a live cobra. Not the easiest of tasks. Not even in a city such as London.

The zoological gardens would possess one, certainly, but staring at a reptile through glass was not her aim, no matter how fascinating. And as her brother refused to accompany her to the Reptile House, let alone put in a word for her with the London Zoo's research committee, she was on her own.

It hadn't taken her long to locate a pub housing a suitable snake, but the owner was disinclined to part with his serpent. "Keeps me in business, it does. Nothing better than a live feeding on payday to keep the ale flowing. But if it's a private viewing you're after," the man had leaned closer—his hot, fetid breath threatening to gag her, "I'll arrange for an innocent white rabbit to be delivered."

"No thank you." She'd backed away. "I'll find another."

Her inquiries had finally borne fruit. A photographer thinking to boost sales with a racy depiction of Eve—an image involving a half-eaten apple and a snake twined about her neck—had found himself in possession of a venomous creature instead of the harmless grass snake he'd been promised. Understandably, his model had balked. For a price that smacked of extortion, he'd agreed to sell the serpent to Cait. She was to collect the cobra today.

Excitement skittered along her each and every nerve.

The crank hack's door swung open and the driver held out a palm. She accepted the assistance, careful to keep a tight hold of her refrigerated carry case and its precious contents. This expedition would drain the last of her funds, but it would also accelerate her personal research program by leaps and bounds. That or land her in a coffin, six feet under.

Risks to which she was accustomed.

But first things first.

Cait hurried down the street under her own umbrella,

hunting for the correct address. There. Number thirty-seven, a secondhand bookshop, lay just past an alley that reeked of urine and beneath the figure of a golden crescent moon with a long, sullen face.

Keeping her face turned away from the crowd that gathered next door, she ducked inside.

Dark and musty, the interior was mercifully devoid of occupants, save the lone shopkeeper who eyed her and her case with decided suspicion.

"I'm here about Mr. Dryer's snake," she stated. Direct and businesslike, yet the man sniggered.

"Whatever you say, miss. Stairs are in the back."

Though she lacked the nerve to inquire about any titles secreted behind the counter, she slowed her steps as she passed a prominent bookshelf, scanning the titles. *The Lustful Turk. Colonel Spanker's Amatory Exploits. An Erotic Philosopher's Lectures.*

Goodness. Perhaps she *could* be shocked. *If* she dared lay as much as a finger upon a book's spine. But not now, not here.

In and out.

She located the stairs and climbed upward. Beneath her feet the treads creaked and shifted in a manner that did not inspire confidence in the building's timber-frame construction.

"Mr. Dryer?" Cait called, pulling back the annoyance of her veil as she stepped into a narrow hallway. Its walls were papered from floor to ceiling with photographs and drawings, including a number of charcoal sketches of a nude woman wearing a cobra about her neck. She traced a circle in the sand at her feet while a cauldron bubbled over a fire.

She squinted. Was that snake the one she intended to purchase? Could be.

"Up front!"

In a small room, two people stood with their noses pressed to the rain-streaked glass panes that overlooked Holywell Street. "It can't be Molly," argued a woman wearing little besides stockings, boots and a thin satin wrapper. "I spoke to her this morning at the tea shop."

"Lucy, perhaps?" the man answered. This, presumably, was Mr. Dryer.

Long drapes hung from overhead rods, cascading into a pool upon the floor. A low sofa was positioned among their folds. A camera stood upon its tripod, waiting for its subject, for its photographer. Leaning against the walls and stacked upon simple shelving were numerous props. Feather boas. Silk flowers. Leather riding crops.

And one spectacled cobra, *Naja naja*, in a small, barren and miserable cage upon a wobbly table. A risky setup. Cait reached out and tapped a finger upon the glass. The snake spread its hood and lunged. No surprise to find the poor thing stressed by its current environment, what with no source of warmth and not so much as a branch upon which it might coil.

"I'm so sorry," Cait whispered, leaning close. "You'll not enjoy the trip home, but I'll take far, far better care of you. Fat mice can be found around every corner in the Lister Institute." Feeding the snake would be the easy task, not so preventing Mother from evicting such a creature from their rented townhome.

She set down her case and unfastened its latches. Sliding metal tongs from an inside groove, she grabbed a lump of dry ice and dropped it inside the snake's cage. Once a mild torpor was induced, she would transfer the cobra into the carry case. Cold, the venomous snake would be safe to transport through the streets of London.

"Goodness, did you see how the bobbies all stand straight and tall now that new man's here?" the woman exclaimed.

Time to announce her presence.

"Excuse me." Cait cleared her throat. She opened the purse hooked to her belt, withdrew a pouch heavy with coin and held it out. "I'm here for the cobra."

The man turned. "Well, now." His eyes raked over her from hat to hem. "A young, slim beauty. You've gloomy taste in clothing, but if we peel it all away..." He ignored the bag of coins she held. "Exactly how handy are you with such a snake?"

"Very," Cait answered, confused as to why her answer sparked a speculative light to flare in his eyes. "Else I wouldn't take the risk."

"You promised." The woman stuck out her lower lip. "Only me today."

"Hush, Louisa." Mr. Dryer flapped a hand at her without breaking his intense appraisal of Cait's form. "Keep an eye on events below. See what you can make out. We wouldn't want to end up like the others, would we?"

"No," Louisa pouted. "But…"

"Opportunity like this rarely presents itself. With those dark eyes and lashes…" Slowly, the photographer paced about Cait. Ought she be offended? It was difficult, given his open admiration. As a rule, people who looked closely ended up commenting upon her complexion, one that whispered of the Indian subcontinent, in a rather negative and suggestive manner. "One photograph. Nothing but you and the snake twined about your neck." He tipped his head toward the waiting sofa. "What do you say? Will you pay for the snake with your image?"

Heat rushed across her skin. Her? He wanted to photograph her *naked*? Holding the cobra? Pass her likeness into the hands of men who would gawk, objectify and…

No need to explore *that* thought further. One did not grow up with three brothers without being peripherally aware of what lustful men did behind closed doors.

"Absolutely not." Private romantic liaisons were one thing, but indecent exposure? Not a scandal in which she wished to feature. Easier to accomplish her goals by remaining *out* of the public eye. She set the coin pouch upon the low sofa. "But thank you for your generous offer."

"Pity," Mr. Dryer said.

Ignoring his disappointed sigh, Cait again tapped the glass cage. This time, the cobra barely blinked. Sufficiently cooled, the snake would be easier to manipulate. Less of a threat.

"If you'll both remain quiet and calm," she requested, "I'll transfer the snake and be on my way."

She positioned her case upon the ground, withdrew a collapsible snake hook and extended its telescoping handle, all oft-practiced wrist movements with her pet adder, Willy, had honed her skills. A bite would not be as much a threat as a disappointment. After all, one only encountered a new venom once. This time, she wished to document her every reaction in the laboratory where she could easily collect a multitude of samples.

She drew on thick, padded leather gloves and—slowly, calmly—set aside the top of the cage. With the hook, she gently lifted the cobra and guided its head to the gathered neck of the linen sack. Without protest, the snake slithered inside.

"Most impressive," Mr. Dryer breathed.

She sealed the opening and slipped the bag into the cooled carry case.

Done.

"A steam wagon!" the woman exclaimed, turning away from the window. A hand flew to her mouth. "Oh. Sorry. Did I—?"

"I'm done," Cait said simply, choosing to ignore the woman's idiocy. She latched the case, collapsed her hook, and stood. Time to leave. In and out, just as she'd promised.

"Reggie?" Louisa beckoned the photographer toward the window. "They're lifting out a stretcher. It *is* Lucy! The London Vampire's killed one of our own! What if he comes back?"

A victim of the vampire? Here? The men Louisa watched upon the street were clustered about a dead woman? A frisson of fear mixed with excitement ran down her spine. Her brothers were forever getting mixed up in strange situations. Ones exactly like this.

She resisted the urge to join them at the window where the photographer and his model once again had their noses pressed to glass.

"Goodbye!" Cait called as she stepped into the hallway, picked her way down creaky stairs and strode past musty shelves. Even the shopkeeper now stared out his window, barely glancing in her direction as she exited.

She ought to lower her veil, open her umbrella and walk away. Hail a crank hack and direct the driver straight home.

Except.

Cait found her feet glued to the stoop, unable to turn away, adding her face to those others that gaped at the tragedy.

A litter had been slid beneath the dead woman, and they were lifting the body. Wet, muddy skirts clung to striped stockings and buttoned boots. Frayed cuffs wrapped about the wrists of pale, limp hands. A blood-stained cloth covered the victim's head and shoulders.

Hiding what?

Stretching her neck, she leaned forward, trying to see more of the vampire's latest victim.

"What are you doing here?" her brother Logan barked from beside her, nearly shocking her from her skin.

Cait turned, swearing. Heart in her throat, she glared into his eyes as she set her jaw. "I'm about Lister business, if you must know." An equivocal answer tinged with the hint of a lie, but she'd learned the technique from the best.

Logan's gaze dropped to her carry case. "Aether, Cait. You had to find one *here*?" Suspicion twisted his lips. "Did Dr. Whitby actually grant you permission?"

She shrugged one shoulder. What she did after hours in the laboratory was her own business.

"A woman at loose ends often finds herself forced to take certain steps..." She let that settle into his mind. A warning. After all, he had flat out refused to aid her when she announced an intention to hunt for poisonous snakes. And where had that led? To the simmering start of an argument on an infamous street before a dead body. Best to redirect his grousing. "Perhaps if you'd taken my request more seriously..."

"Cait." His voice held a note of warning.

"I don't know why you fight it. I've every intention of securing a meeting with the Duke of Avesbury." She eyed the weapon holstered beneath his jacket. "Eventually, one of my letters will reach him. Or my work will draw his attention." Covert poison experts couldn't be thick upon the ground.

Logan closed his eyes and tipped his head back, inhaling deeply. "I've explained the requirements for a female agent time and again."

"I must be married," she said. "Either to another agent or to a man of the duchess' choice." As she'd no intention of playing the perfect wife to snag a man under suspicion of disloyalty, she would avoid the Duchess of Avesbury and her machinations at all costs. Quite simply, she needed to find herself an unmarried Queen's agent. A task which, given that her brother refused to provide her with a convenient list of unwed agents, was proving difficult.

As if that would stop her.

Cait did her best not to smirk as Logan attempted to calculate how he might tuck her back into a laboratory where she could play safely with her various poisons.

Dismay, then resignation crossed his face.

She'd won. He only needed a moment to come to terms, to accept the inevitable.

"You're determined to join the family business?"

She nodded.

"Then there's no reason not to start your training now." He waved a hand, an invitation to view the corpse before them.

"Don't tease." An offer to contact the Duke of Avesbury on her behalf would have sufficed. Unless... "Vampires aren't venomous."

Logan let out a long, beleaguered sigh. "And yet there's something you might be able to explain." He raised his voice. "Hold!"

What? She hurried after him. What about the murders had yet to reach reporters' ears? Curiosity spiked her pulse.

Men parted, clearing a path without so much as a word from Logan, though their frowns carved deep lines into their faces as he led a woman to stand beside the chuffing and hissing steam wagon that would carry the dead body away.

"Are you certain you're up to this?" Logan asked.

"Of course." Never would she admit that her stomach gave a twist at the metallic scent of blood curling into the damp air, that she was glad her breakfast had consisted of only tea and toast.

"You'll speak to no one of this without permission, or you'll never work for the Queen's agents. Understand?" At her nod, Logan peeled back the ragged cloth.

Cait found herself staring into the sightless eyes of a pretty young woman. Thin streams of blood trickled from her nose, marring the soft curves of her cheek.

Her brother directed the beam of his decilamp at the woman's throat.

She gasped. Two puncture wounds were sunk deep into musculature and surrounded by inflamed and necrotic tissue, consistent with a venomous bite. Were the marks not approximately one and a half inches apart, she would have wondered what serpent had taken to the streets of London to find its prey. "It's not the mark of a vampire," she informed her brother. No such thing existed. "But what?"

Logan's lips twisted. "A question I was hoping you might help answer."

CHAPTER THREE

"Apologies for the intrusion in the wake of your loss." Jack stood, declining the offer to sit. He'd not cultivate an illusion of amity with his brother's friends. "I'll be brief."

Stephen Carruthers, the new Lord Saltwell, slumped in a wingback chair before a cold hearth. An empty decanter rested upon the floor at his feet. His eyes were distant and devoid of expression as he stared into a cut-glass tumbler, swirling a final half inch of brandy.

Yesterday, Carruthers could barely stand. Today, sitting was a challenge. Tomorrow, a fainting couch?

The censure written on his face caused the new Lady Saltwell to leap to her husband's defense. "We all have our own ways of mourning."

She stood behind her husband, already garbed in flat black, her hands spread over the gentle swell of her stomach, the reason for her absence from the ball. Despite her words, a deeply ingrained sense of propriety, stock and trade of the *ton,* drew her lips into a frown at the brightly embroidered blue and red stripes of her husband's smoking jacket.

"Won't miss the old bastard," Carruthers muttered. "Nothing I did was ever right."

A complaint often lodged by many sons.

"Nonetheless," Jack said, "his death will be investigated. A task which I will handle personally." As of this morning, it was agreed. The London Vampire would be hunted by the Queen's agents of the Lister Institute.

A late-night flurry of insistent messages between Lord Thornton, Mr. Black and the Duke of Avesbury himself had won Jack the right to take the position of head agent. Not only had a man died in his family's townhome, but his background was well-suited to such a case.

Local authorities had no leads and bodies were piling up. Lord Saltwell's death brought the total to five. All known victims were male. That was, until early this morning, a final skeet pigeon tapping on his apartment window had brought news of the creature's first female victim.

At dawn, the body of one Lucy Cooper had been found in a Holywell Street gutter. Another mysterious death, this time involving a woman involved in the pornography trade. Facts that thrilled and inspired reporters as they composed their titillating headlines, intent upon causing the London elite to sputter over their morning tea.

Cold calculation or sloppy mistake, the London Vampire had broken pattern, a misstep that Jack hoped would ultimately lead to her capture.

He needed to conduct this interview quickly and adjourn to the morgue.

"You work for the Crown?" Contempt flashed in Carruthers' eyes. "Ought to have guessed. Always prowling about the edges of the room."

Jack ignored the dig. "Did your father exhibit any unusual behaviors recently?"

"Aside from dying?" Carruthers snorted. "We did our best to avoid each other." He tossed back the last of his brandy, frowned at the empty glass. "Though perhaps you'd find it unusual that he often visited his grandson in the nursery? Easier to avoid me, his heir, to focus on a more distant and promising future for our family." The corner of his mouth kicked up. "Wasn't too happy when he left."

"I'm afraid our son is teething," Lady Saltwell explained. "Bouts of crying have unsettled his stomach, the contents of which he emptied onto his grandfather's trousers."

"Otherwise, my father spent his days at the club, his nights chasing pretty things wearing skirts into shadowed corners. Hardly unusual." Carruthers lifted a finger. "Save the final part where he was bitten."

"You mentioned the attacker was a woman." Lady Saltwell tilted her head. "You're certain?"

"Absolutely. I found her bent over him, mouth at his throat. Before I could catch her, she leapt from a window and escaped via the garden."

Lady Saltwell frowned. "While wearing a gown?"

Pride stuck in his throat, but facts were facts, regardless of the damning implications. "Yes."

"Sounds like your investigation is off to a running start." Carruthers snorted. "But you'll pardon me if I question your interpretation of my father's death. Aubrey saw no such figure fleeing the scene and is convinced you chased after some imagined specter. There must be a more logical explanation. Perhaps my father suffered an apoplexy?"

Jack's eyebrows rose. "Involving puncture wounds to the neck?"

A pained look crossed Lady Saltwell's face, but she held her tongue. It was clear that Carruthers cared neither who—or what—might have perpetrated the crime.

"Yes, well, for all we know the marks were made earlier during overenthusiastic role play on the part of his mistress. My father was both a lusty and wealthy man, Tagert. His mistresses were keen to retain his favor. If that's all," Carruthers waggled his empty glass, "I've other matters to attend to."

Jack ignored the dismissal. "As relates to your father's death, I will keep you informed. However," he held up a finger. It was wrong of him to let personal matters intrude, but the three school chums often shared a single brain. He'd not waste this chance. "Unofficially, I would appreciate any information you can provide about the Grand Menwith Hotel and Spa."

"I'll wager you would." Carruthers squinted. "Predictable. Digging into Aubrey's finances, unable to accept his success. Envious, are you?"

Lady Saltwell laid a hand upon her husband's shoulder. "Perhaps—"

"No. Absolutely not. The answer is a firm no. We are not interested in another investor." He snapped his fingers at the steam butler. "No worries, Tagert, if you fail to catch this vampire. My father sucked the life from me and many others, so it's a fitting end. He won't be missed."

JACK TOOK a deep breath and climbed the broad, stone stairs that lead to the entryway of the Lister Institute. He crossed black-and-white checkered tiles beneath a bright, new Lucifer lamp that replaced the one shattered by the Christmas Eve explosion. Though months had passed, a respectful silence endured in the space where a fellow agent had lost his life to the machinations of a jealous colleague.

No trace remained of the scorched pits that had marred the walls, ceiling and floor save those upon a single floor tile —formerly of smooth, white marble. There, the blemishes served as a memorial. A silent reminder that sometimes betrayal came from within.

Much like the tumor that threatened his vision. His own cells conspired to grow into a small but stubborn mass within his skull, pressing upon the optic nerve. Not life threatening, but career ending. First Jack would lose vision in his left eye, then possibly his right. Worse symptoms would follow if the pituitary adenoma continued to grow unchecked.

But to remove it? To date, physicians had only speculated about how such a surgery might be accomplished, none yet willing to attempt a feat with a high likelihood of mortality.

All save Thornton—neuroscientist, surgeon, fellow agent and friend—and even he had reservations. "Blindness and headaches aren't life ending," he'd objected.

"If it leads to sexual dysfunction as well," Jack replied, all grim determination, "it might as well be."

"I'll need to consider the approach—transcranial or transsphenoidal—there are risks to both." Thornton had rubbed the back of his neck. "*If* I agree to carry out the surgery, you'll need to have your affairs in order."

"Done. In the event of my demise all I possess is willed to my sister."

Thornton had sighed at his eagerness. "There's no rush. For now, we'll track the progression of your symptoms, but Mr. Black needs to be informed."

"No." Jack had snatched away his medical chart. "I'm fine."

"For now." Thornton frowned. "When your symptoms worsen—"

"I'll let you know." He wouldn't. Lest Black use the information to relegate Jack to a desk job. "Please. You said yourself it would be months before my vision worsens."

"One month, Tagert," Thornton had grumbled. "If there's any change, I will place it on record and inform command."

A fortnight remained. He hoped it was enough time to hunt down a murderess.

To that end, he strode down the hall with a newfound

sense of purpose, winding his way through a maze of corridors. Summoning the ascension chamber. Standing inside the metal cage as it lowered him into the bowels of the building. The door slid open and he turned a corner to face the autopsy suite.

Would this be his own endpoint?

It might well be, unless Thornton pulled off a miracle.

Since the diagnosis a certain detached numbness had clouded his mind, leaving him adrift with nothing to dwell on save his brother's suspicious good fortune. But now excitement curled through his veins and fired his pulse. A small explosion, a moonlight chase and murders headlining newspapers to investigate.

Chance might have brought him eye to eye with the murderess, but the next time they met, it would be no accident.

This was why he'd become a Queen's agent, why he'd first abandoned medicine, then research. Nothing compared to the thrill of fieldwork. He'd damn well enjoy it while it lasted.

He pushed open the door and stepped into the morgue. Lord Saltwell lay upon a metal gurney, reduced to a rotund, cloth-covered lump, yet not alone in death. Upon the central table beneath harsh, bright lamps lay the slight form of a young woman.

Thornton himself was bent over the body. Black was also in the room—an unnecessary, supervising evil. Jack supposed it was inevitable. But as there was a third individual present, an unfamiliar woman, he clenched his teeth preventing the obscenities that burned in the back of his throat from escaping.

Instead, he let the metal door slam closed behind him.

"There's a neurological component?" he asked Thornton, abandoning any pretense of greetings and focusing on the business at hand. There was only one reason the man would be roped into this investigation.

"So there is," Thornton rumbled.

Black's head snapped up to meet Jack's gaze. "It's about time you arrived. Lingering over your eggs and bacon when you have such a new and interesting victim?"

"Not at all how I'd have you introduce me, Logan," the woman chided with casual familiarity as she turned, pushing a cart toward the female victim's side.

A jolt crackled down his spine and heated the air in his lungs, halting any words he might have formed in response. She was stunning, her beauty unmuted by the dull gray gown she wore or the refrigerated storage chambers that served as a backdrop.

"You must be the infamous Jack Tagert, Jack of all trades." Unless he was much mistaken, he detected a hint of a Scottish accent.

"Master of none." He grinned. An epithet he'd earned by refusing to sit the medical boards in favor of working in the Department of Cryptobiology, before abandoning medicine and research altogether. It was rare for an agent's reputation to be known to a lady. "So I am."

She glanced from Mr. Black back to Jack, both expectant and assessing. "Does the chill in the room always extend to such proceedings, or do the two of you have something you'd like to get off your chests?"

Her dark eyes flashed, and her wide mouth hinted at a suppressed desire to laugh. *At both of them.* An unusual reaction.

Cautious deference had always colored the manner in which women approached him, be they Lister employees in awe of a Queen's agent, or calculating debutants who simpered and giggled, trying—and failing—to entertain a man who, with a sudden stroke of mortal luck, might become a viscount.

He couldn't recall the last time a woman addressed him with such brazen overfamiliarity.

Was Black growling? His gaze flicked sideways. Indeed, a dark cloud had descended upon the man's face.

"Oh, for aether's sake." The woman exhaled, stepping around the body to extend her hand. "Allow me to introduce myself. Miss McCullough, venom expert and sister to the mute Mr. Black who rather grudgingly permits my involvement."

Sister? Black had *family?* His eyebrows shot up. Jack would have been less surprised to learn that the man was raised by a pack of wild wolves.

"A pleasure to make your acquaintance." Jack bent over her bare fingers, lips twitching at this opportunity to vex Black with situationally inappropriate ballroom behavior. He did, however, wish to live. And so, the kiss dropped harmlessly into the air above her hand.

When he straightened, Miss McCullough's gaze momentarily alighted upon his lips. Was that disappointment in her eyes?

It was.

He imagined Black's sister was as much trouble as his own—a thought that had him fighting a smile.

Ah, how the tables had turned.

"A venom expert?" he repeated, ignoring Black and forcing his mind back to the task at hand. "To examine the bite of a vampire?"

Miss McCullough all but snorted. "A rumor we can now dismiss." She peeled back the cloth cover, revealing two puncture marks in the dead woman's swollen throat. "The bite to Miss Cooper's neck pierced the external jugular vein, a poor choice for a vampire, who would presumably target the carotid artery, harnessing the victim's own blood pressure for feeding purposes."

Black sighed. "Is such speculation necessary?"

She smiled. "Not strictly so, but given the tabloid headlines—"

"Venom?" Jack prompted in an attempt to refocus their squabbling, much as the idea of watching Black engage in a sibling spat appealed.

"The tissue damage surrounding the wounds is consistent with illustrations drawn by experts who have studied the venomous bites of elapid snakes, such as the cobra or krait." Lifting a cotton-tipped stick from the cart, she carefully swabbed the region around the bite marks, dropping it in a glass test tube. "However, caliper measurements of the distance between the puncture marks of both victims are twenty-four millimeters, consistent with the maxillary inter-canine distance of humans."

Black sighed. Heavily.

Thornton's lips twitched, but he withheld any comment.

"Such are facts, Logan," she said. "You've either a venomous human prowling dark streets or an extremely large reptile, one that could not possibly function with vigor during our cold nights. A snake that size would hail from the tropics." A faraway look entered her eyes. "Though with a knowledgeable handler..."

Black snapped his fingers. "Stop daydreaming."

She shot her brother a narrow glance. "Fine. To summarize, the swollen tissue surrounding the wounds is consistent with illustrations drawn by experts who have studied the venomous bites of elapid snakes, such as the cobra or krait."

"Illustrations?" He looked at Black. "You said your sister was an expert—"

"She's plenty of experience," her brother grumped, "with all manner of toxins and poisons."

Miss McCullough gave her brother a worrisome grin. "If not with serpents, a deficiency I intend to correct as soon as the London Zoo agrees to allow me to—"

"Not now," Black interrupted, giving his sister a pointed look.

"Fine." She lifted a syringe and expertly drew blood from the corpse. "I'll run a few immunological tests, pass samples through the Ichor Machine to see what might turn up, but between protein degradation rates and the length of time her body is presumed to have been in the rain, there's little hope of positive results. I have to admit to a certain disappointment that you," she glanced at Jack, "failed to collect fresh samples from Lord Saltwell."

The truth of her words burned. "An inexcusable oversight on my part not to carry laboratory paraphernalia with me at all times."

"No need to snipe," she said, repeating the same procedures upon the second corpse. "I understand this man died in your brother's library during his engagement ball. Likely you were overwrought. You have my sympathies."

Disappointment.

Overwrought.

Sympathies.

Pandemonium clanged inside his head. Was Miss McCullough deliberately needling him?

He began to understand the pained look on Black's face. He'd been in Miss McCullough's presence for all of ten minutes, and Jack wasn't sure if he wanted to strangle her or kiss her.

Kiss her?

Where had that come from?

No. *No, no, no.*

Not Black's sister.

Absolutely not. Though it was rare to find beauty and accomplishment in one forthright and confident bundle, Miss McCullough was not for him. No matter how much satisfaction he would derive from annoying both his mother and Black by marrying a venom expert.

Marrying?

What was wrong with him?

They'd never make it to the altar. From the glare Black had shot him earlier, Jack would find himself strung up in a noose if he so much as laid a single finger on Black's sister.

He had no business making *any* woman his wife.

"Not overwrought, Miss McCullough." Why did he feel the need to defend himself in her presence? "I interrupted the attacker and was forced to give chase."

"Interrupted?" Miss McCullough's face lit with curiosity. "You saw him?"

"Her," he corrected. "I lost the murderess when she slipped into a ventilation shaft."

Miss McCullough's eyes widened, then grew distant as she contemplated the implications. "A venomous female..."

Black cleared his throat. "Not information to be shared, Cait." His words were stern and full of censure. "With anyone."

"Please," she huffed. "Spare me the lecture. I know the family business well enough."

Black fixed Jack with a glare as he delivered yet another warning. "She's a venom expert, Tagert, not an agent. I've read your report and we'll discuss it *later*." His expression promised Jack a world of pain should he dare utter another word about his encounter with the woman in white in the presence of his sister.

Not that there was much more to discuss. He brushed his thumb across the torn skin of his knuckles and redirected his attention to the dead woman. "The blood escaping Miss Cooper's nose?"

"Extensive trauma to the nasal septum and deeper still," Thornton said, bending over this newest victim. "See these small punctures at the edge of her hairline?"

Jack nodded. "How many?"

"Six," Thornton answered. "We might speculate that something gripped her face while the damage was done. Hand me the crystal visilux scope, and we'll have a closer look."

Jack slid back into the role of medical student, aiding those he had shadowed. Together, they snaked the long, thin jointed device into a ragged, bloody hole that had been a nose.

"Interesting." Thornton waved Jack forward to peer into the oculus.

"All soft tissue damage appears to terminate at the sphenoid, where a circular orifice has been drilled into the bone." Jack straightened, his mind whirling as he contemplated the implications.

Thornton fixed him with a piercing stare. "And the significance of this bone, Tagert?"

Black glanced between them, forever suspicious of unspoken words.

"Well?" Miss McCullough prompted, eyebrows raised.

The sphenoid was a bone that formed part of the skull base, lodged between the two cerebral hemispheres. Rumor maintained that a hard, sharp blow of the elbow between a man's eyes could thrust the bone into the brain, an instant kill.

Not, however, the significance Thornton referenced.

"The sphenoid bone houses the pituitary," he answered. Of late he'd devoted an excessive amount of attention to studying its various hypothesized functions. "A complicated gland thought to regulate water and mineral metabolism, along with growth and reproductive functions."

A gland which appeared to be missing.

Not that a definitive diagnosis could be made from this angle.

Thornton cleared his throat. "It appears our murderess may have collected a rather odd souvenir. To be certain, we'll need to remove her brain."

Most would have paled at such an announcement. Instead, Miss McCullough brightened. "An autopsy?"

"A partial one, yes." Thornton, already garbed in a canvas apron, lifted a scalpel, and raised an eyebrow. "If anyone cares to make an exit, now is the time."

Black reached for his sister's elbow, but she side-stepped his grasp with practiced ease.

"Not a chance," she snapped at her overbearing brother. "I'm not leaving until I know what happened."

Black sighed and dropped his hand.

Jack blinked. Not only had Avesbury's top agent been defied, he'd accepted it without resistance. So many questions ran through his mind. Were he to catch Miss McCullough alone, would he dare ask them?

Thornton made an incision, peeling back Miss Cooper's scalp to reveal the skull beneath. Jack pulled on a thick, canvas apron, then passed around safety goggles before handing Thornton a vibration knife.

With the flip of a switch, a loud mechanical buzz filled the air and Thornton set to the task of cutting through bone, but not brain. A few minutes later, he set aside the knife and removed the skull cap. Lifting the brain free, he placed it in the ceramic bowl Jack held out.

Together, they stared at the inside of Miss Lucy Cooper's skull, at the inferior surface of her brain.

"As suspected," Thornton pronounced. "No pituitary gland."

"But most expertly removed." Jack studied the smooth tunnel drilled into the sphenoid bone, one that ended at the sella turcica, the depression in the sphenoid bone that housed the pituitary gland. The dura mater, a tough membrane surrounding the brain and spinal cord, had been sliced and the delicate stalk connecting the pituitary to the brain severed. "One can only hope the venomous bite rendered her unconscious before an as-yet-unknown device penetrated her nasal cavity to remove a portion of her brain."

"How awful." Miss McCullough shuddered, lifting a hand to her mouth as she contemplated the horror of this woman's death. "But how, exactly? And why would anyone wish to harvest such an organ?"

Thornton caught Jack's gaze. Held it a fraction too long.

Black's eyes narrowed.

"Excellent questions, Miss McCullough," Thornton replied, crossing to the sink. "Prior to this moment, I would have told you no such surgical device existed. Not even within the halls of the Lister Institute. However, answering such questions is a task now set before Agent Tagert."

She looked to Jack. "Have any of the other attacks involved organ theft?"

Such was the very next thing he intended to discover. Until this morning, the London Vampire attacks had been under the purview of the Metropolitan Police. But given the deadly glare Black directed at him, he dared make no comment.

"I know that look," Miss McCullough declared, hands on hips, the faintest curve of a smile at the corners of her mouth. "You don't know. Any of you."

Black glowered. "The Queen's agents don't, as a matter of form, investigate London homicides—"

"Unless they directly threaten national security or involve preternatural elements," she finished. "I see. Rumors of a roaming vampire wasn't of particular concern given they don't exist." She rolled her eyes. "But now that there's a dead lord and a venomous woman involved, we're taking over the investigation."

Jack suppressed a snort.

Thornton didn't. "Direct and to the point."

"There is no *we*." Black planted both hands on the metal table, leaning across the corpse, his gaze humorless. "Listen carefully. You are not a Queen's agent, simply an expert consultant for this case. Analyze your samples and report back. Agent Tagert will handle the investigation."

She crossed her arms and lifted her chin, looking as if she'd like to add her brother to the body count. "I wish to speak with the Duke of Avesbury."

"No. I'm serious, Cait," Black warned. "Stay out of this."

He could swear Thornton's lips were twitching. Jack struggled to suppress his own amusement.

With a huff that did not at all concede defeat, Miss McCullough swept up her samples. "I'll be in the laboratory. I did, after all, put other projects on ice in order to assist you." She stormed from the autopsy suite.

Black muttered under his breath. A long string of unfamiliar words, but their essence was plain. His sister possessed talents he wished to tap. But at the same time, he hoped to keep her safe.

A situation quite familiar to Jack, and the top agent knew it.

Black pointed a finger at him. "Under no circumstances are you to permit her further involvement."

CHAPTER FOUR

"How dare he?" Cait fumed, glancing out the window yet again. The entire day had consisted of low-level torment, all orchestrated by her brother.

"Mr. Black does enjoy his games," Janet agreed.

What was taking the messenger boy so long? He'd left to follow Mr. Tagert hours ago, long before she'd left for the zoo. Time was running out. A decision must be reached and soon. There were only so many nights she could cry "ill" before Mother would insist upon sitting by her bedside, and she did not wish to squander them.

"My brother invites me into an active investigation. Avails himself of my knowledge." She swatted at the air. "Then shoos me back to the laboratory as if my presence was nothing more than an inconvenient nuisance."

Her maid had heard such tales of woe before. Logan

wasn't the first sibling to bleed Cait for useful information before cutting her out of the ensuing excitement.

"To keep me off balance and out of the way, he proceeds to arrange a private tour of the Reptile House at the London Zoo, dangling promises of groundbreaking research in his note." She threw up her hands. "But saddles me with a tour guide so ossified that the man can't countenance the idea of a woman stepping into the behind-the-scenes space of the Reptile House." Cait turned. "What kind of twisted apology is that?"

"A poor one, miss." Her maid spread a bright, aniline purple ballgown across the bed. "Nonetheless, a tour is a step in the right direction. Were you able to learn anything?"

Cait huffed. "Very little." To gain even that had required batting her eyelashes and smiling at a distinguished gentleman—one she'd caught eyeing her décolletage—before attempting to follow him through a door marked "private".

The tour guide had stopped her with a raised hand and a frown. "I'm sorry, my dear. Research staff only. They're not to be bothered."

Bothered!

Because a woman couldn't possibly engage in deep, reasoned scientific conversation with zoo curators. She rolled her eyes. Next time she visited the Reptile House, it would be without an escort. Easier that way to gain access to the inner sanctum.

"And your mother, did the visit to the zoo inspire her to share any more information about your father?"

"Not a peep." Cait sighed. "Though my inquiry about

the past performances of snake charmers did have a rather satisfying effect." Unkind of her to relish another's irritation, but the tour had left her in a sour mood.

Mother's face had turned puce as she'd hissed under her breath, "This is neither the time nor the place."

But their guide, standing before the plate glass window displaying a despondent puff adder from Sub-Saharan Africa, had a ready answer. "A popular attraction when the Reptile House first opened, but I believe Jabar and Mahommed returned to Egypt shortly thereafter."

"The timing is wrong." Cait twisted the poison ring upon her finger. "Neither of the men could possibly be my father."

The Reptile House had opened in 1849. Over thirty-five years ago. More than a full decade before Cait's birth and, if Mother was to be trusted, both men were of the wrong nationality. It had been wrong of her to step outside her marriage, even if Father had broken his vows. Yet what was done could not be undone. And Cait did not regret her existence.

Janet squeezed her shoulder. "Perhaps it is for the best."

Save that past formed the core of her research. But the precise origins of her strange biological gifts remained an enigma. At least for now.

She dragged in a deep breath, slowly exhaled. Nodded for her maid's sake. Putting a name to the itinerant carnival man who had once charmed her mother might gain her no more than that, a name.

Time to refocus upon her future.

"You're right," Cait said. "I did not come to London to

reprise my role in Glasgow by hiding away in a windowless laboratory."

To escape, she would have to marry. The sooner the better. A fact she'd shared with her mother some two weeks past.

Mother, momentarily struck dumb by her daughter's stated intention to marry, had wasted no time shredding the cobwebs that cocooned her former *ton* connections. Alas, such was a task in frustration as she'd managed only to secure a small handful of invitations, most of which were deemed socially unacceptable.

Almost as if her mother was being punished for a past misdeed. Likely, but what daughter wished to learn any more than she must about the indiscretions of her parents?

While Cait regretted her mother's social misery, teasing out potential husbands from the general pool of eligible *ton* men would prove difficult given the precise qualification parameters she required.

If not outright impossible.

A better strategy was to wheedle her way into the company of Queen's agents by insisting she be included in the current investigation. A plan she would have to set aside —at least for the evening—if her messenger did not return with news, and soon.

She'd stated her intentions upon arriving in London. But, as of today, it was clear Logan would not aid her quest to advance her career beyond laboratory assistant.

So be it.

But if Logan thought he could keep her out of the field

by relegating her to the position of consultant, he was badly mistaken.

The so-called vampire was venomous. She was certain of it, even though she'd been unable to confirm the presence of venom due to protein degradation. Too much time had elapsed from their deaths. She required fresher samples.

By now, Mr. Tagert must have interviewed the coroner. Why had the messenger boy not sent word of the man's name and address? At this very moment, the agent might be interviewing those who witnessed the victims' deaths.

She paced back to the window.

The torment of being excluded was too much to bear. What if he missed some key detail that only she could unravel?

"London will be safer in the morning," Janet warned. A Greek chorus predicting doom. "When pickpockets and thieves and all manner of reprobates have crawled back into their holes."

True.

But patience was not Cait's strong suit.

"In and out," she said. "A crank hack to the man's office door. A few minutes of conversation. Then I'll have information upon which I might formulate my next move." Cait waved a hand at the glass terrarium housing her new snake where, wary of its new environment, the serpent had yet to uncoil. "Easily accomplished. Less trouble than collecting an unwanted cobra."

Janet's lips twisted. "Until you stumbled upon a dead body lying in the street."

"Most fortunate, indeed." Cait threw her a saucy grin. "Not only do I possess unique insight into the exact nature of the so-called London Vampire, but I have the name of an *unmarried* Queen's agent."

"Handsome, from the spark in your eye."

"I won't deny it." Dark and brooding with a roughness to his jaw that suggested he'd not managed a smooth surface since leaving boyhood behind, the man had refused to smile. But she'd seen his lips twitch, seen his eyes flare with interest.

Jack of all trades.

Memories of the details her brothers had shared of the man's exploits—however scant—whetted her interest.

Her status as sister to the great and powerful and much feared Mr. Black was not a point in her favor. Finding an agent willing to cross her brother to tie the knot might present a significant problem. But if she could manage a few moments alone with the agent, the hostility that bubbled and simmered between her brother and Mr. Tagert might work to her advantage.

The urge to tease the man into a smile was overwhelming, and Cait looked forward to cracking through the thin coating of ice that surrounded his demeanor. She'd work the case, worm her way into Mr. Tagert's presence, take a closer look. Assess matrimonial possibilities.

"He has the most curious background," Cait mused aloud. "Medical training, but no acknowledged degree. At one point, he assisted cryptozoologists. Some undisclosed problem regarding foreign pteryform species." Then her brothers had left home, cutting her off from a regular source of agency gossip.

"A mystery and a challenge," Janet deadpanned. "Aether help him, he has a target painted on his back." Her maid lifted a pair of thin satin slippers that matched the purple ballgown. "The hour grows late. Time to decide, miss."

Already, Cait's hair was twisted and piled upon her head. Pearls dangled from her ears and encircled her neck. She wore all the compulsory undergarments of a lady about to attend a ball. Combinations. Corset. Corset cover. Wire bustle. Petticoat upon petticoat. Silk stockings.

Pacing, she plucked at the bandage wrapped about her wrist. Earlier, when the Ichor Machine indicated the presence of no foreign proteins in her samples, she had proceeded to nick her skin, to touch the swabs to small cuts. A—completely unauthorized—technique she'd used before to reveal faint traces of biological toxins. Alas, the attempted inoculation had failed. No redness or tenderness developed.

Cait needed a non-compromised, non-degraded sample of venom to establish herself as essential to the case. Something she could not accomplish at a ball.

She pressed a hand to the cool glass of the window, staring down at the busy street beneath, relieved—even as her heart jumped at the danger—to see a boy darting between steam cart and crank hack, zigging and zagging to avoid steel hooves and rubber-rimmed tires.

"He's back," Cait announced.

Excitement electrified every nerve as the boy vaulted

over an iron gate and dropped into the sunken service well to knock upon the kitchen door and deliver his message.

"A walking dress, not the ballgown." She plucked the pearl drops from her ears. "The copper one with blue accents and skirt hikes." Nasty liquids pooled on London streets and, despite her outstanding immunity, she did not wish to return with hems soaked in gutter fluids teaming with microscopic life that might herald the next great plague. "And boots. Sturdy ones that lace to the knees."

Janet turned back to the wardrobe. "Will you at least allow a footman to accompany you?"

"Absolutely not. For a shilling, James will rat me out and Mother will have a fit." She stripped off extraneous petticoats, leaving a single ruffled affair draped atop the wire cage of her bustle. Too many flounces would catch at her ankles and hinder her ability to move. "Convince my mother I'm ill. Possibly contagious. Bar the door and refuse to open it until my return."

Boots on, Cait lifted her arms. Janet dropped a copper skirt over her head, topped it with a simple blue, bustled overskirt. A fitted copper bodice with velvet-covered buttons followed. She'd chosen this ensemble because of the matching jacket. Certainly its lapels and turned-back cuffs were fashionable, but its true appeal lay in the hidden pockets. Sewn into the lining, they allowed her to secrete coins, keys, and an assortment of various vials along with the means to collect samples of blood and—dare she hope—venom.

On the whole, her appearance in the mirror brought pirates to mind. A gleaming saber strapped to her side was all that was missing. Alas, the wide leather belt fastened about her waist was largely decorative, save for the skirt hikes that lifted her hem to expose what some might consider an indelicate amount of ankle.

Fingerless gloves concealed the bandage at her wrist, and a matching hat with an arcing feather completed the ensemble.

"Fancy for a visit to a coroner." Janet clucked her tongue. "One might expect you plan to stumble upon a certain gentleman."

She grinned. "One can only hope." Locating Mr. Tagert out and about in the wild, so to speak, would open a world of opportunities.

"Hurry back," Janet urged, opening the servant's door, one that blended seamlessly into the wallpaper.

Cait hurried down the stairs and burst into the kitchen. All about, steambots whirled and chugged, performing their evening duties while Cook bent over the sink, washing up. A job best performed by human hands lest the mechanical kitchen help find their joints frozen by rust.

"Miss!" The messenger boy leapt to his feet and held out a grubby slip of paper. "He's only just on his way to the coroner's now. Got the address from a man in the mews."

"Coroner Baxton," she read aloud. "A lawyer with his firm on Cannon Street near St. Paul's. A respectable address. Good work." She slipped the boy a coin and pushed a plate of biscuits in his direction with a knowing smile. "Carry on."

The crank hack delivered her to the solicitor's door in a building situated between those of a bookseller and a bootmaker. The district hummed with wholesalers and tradesmen of all kinds, men and women who took little notice of her as they hurried along the pavement.

A bell above the door jingled as she entered.

"May I help you, miss?" A young man in a mud-brown suit rose from his seat. A perfectly polite greeting, but an unconcealed glance at a wall clock made it clear her presence was an imposition. "We're about to close, but I'm happy to schedule an appointment."

From a back room, she heard voices—if not exact words—one of which belonged to Mr. Tagert.

Success! Like a glass of champagne, excitement bubbled and went straight to her head.

The lie leapt from her lips. "No need. I'd meant to be here earlier, to prevent my husband, Mr. Tagert, from working himself into a flap." Wives rolled their eyes, right? "I'll join them. See if I can soothe his ruffled feathers and steer this meeting to a swift conclusion."

Conflicted, he cleared his throat. "Errhmm—"

Lest the secretary choose duty, Cait darted down the hallway before he could formulate an intelligible response. Then stopped short.

A door ajar. How very convenient.

No stranger to male dismissal or how a female's presence might smother a candid conversation, she stood back to the wall, listening to the unfiltered exchange. During the few minutes Mr. Tagert had preceded her own entry, her not-a-husband had managed to inflame Mr. Baxton's ire.

"I must insist," he said, interrupting the coroner's tirade.

"No reason exists for the Queen's agents to interfere," the coroner barked. "None. No foreign nationals are involved and the victims are of no political or social consequence."

"I am not at liberty to discuss the details that draw this investigation into our sphere." Mr. Tagert's voice was calm, steady and unyielding. "Suffice it to say that, in the past twenty-four hours, new information has surfaced. You may, of course, continue your own investigation into these murders. In fact, we encourage it. Nonetheless, you must relay any information uncovered directly to me."

"Yet *I* am not to be afforded the same consideration?" Mr. Baxton retorted, apparently itching for a fight. "The Metropolitan Police are doing all they can with the conflicting reports of those who, unconvincingly, claim to have seen this vampire. We suffer nothing but public ridicule and unreasonable demands that we immediately apprehend the perpetrator."

Mr. Tagert invoked the one name that would make any London coroner shake in his shoes. "You are, of course, welcome to lodge a complaint with the Duke of Avesbury."

"Now, now." The coroner's voice took on an altogether different tone. Cait imagined his hands lifting, palms out. "There's no reason to involve the duke himself."

"I'm glad we agree." Disdain dripped from Mr. Tagert's tongue. "Tell me, what *facts* have you collected regarding the attacks of this eponymous London Vampire? Begin with autopsy results."

"None were necessary. Damage to all four bodies was superficial."

"*Four* victims?" Mr. Tagert snapped, as if the coroner's failure to immediately inform him of an additional victim was a personal affront. "Not three, as reported by the press? Or do you include this morning's victim in that count?"

"I do not," Mr. Baxton groused. "All were male. By the time my men and I arrived to view the female, your agents had taken charge. We were waved off."

"Perhaps you had best start at the beginning," Mr. Tagert growled. Not a request, but an order. "With all the newspaper men milling about, reveling in sensationalism, accuracy is in short supply. I will need, of course, copies of all official documents related to all *four* incidents. For now, if you will provide a brief, oral summary that I may begin my own inquiries."

Perfect. Cait edged a bit closer, not wanting to miss a word.

"Very well," Mr. Baxton said. "Each victim sustained two punctures to the neck. Swollen and red tissue surrounded the bite marks. Certainly, a trail of blood oozed from the wounds, but they were not—as the press would have their readers believe—drained dry, leaving behind naught but desiccated husks of men." The man forced a humorless laugh. "Yet something about the bite killed them and quickly, though our laboratory technicians have found no trace of any poison. Finally, ribald speculation aside, we have no evidence as to why the murderer chose to remove certain," he cleared his throat, "organs."

"Organs?" Irritation threaded through Mr. Tagert's voice.

Did Mr. Baxton refer to the pituitary? Was such a term applicable to an organ?

"No one—er—interfered with the woman discovered this morning?"

"No. Do enlighten me as to which body parts were removed."

"Yes, of course. Though discovered fully clothed, all the victims were found to have been gelded. Brutally so."

Cait's hand flew to her mouth and her eyes threatened to pop from their sockets. *Castrated!*

Mr. Baxton continued. "The one man who survived claims to have no recollection of the attack. I expect his lips have been sealed by the humiliation of waking to find his testicles removed in their entirety."

Exasperated, Mr. Tagert focused in on this particularly relevant point. "There's a survivor?"

"Indeed. An empty shell of a man now. He'll refuse to speak to you," the coroner warned.

"Ma'am," the secretary murmured at her side, his eyebrows drawn together in confusion. "Is something amiss?"

Kraken. Intent upon what they were discussing, Cait had failed to keep an eye out for him whilst eavesdropping. She pressed a finger to her lips and flapped a hand at him, indicating that she wished to be left alone, that he should return to his desk. It *might* work. After all, he'd been remiss in not announcing her presence.

"Nonetheless, I'll need his name," Mr. Tagert said. "His address."

Mr. Baxton hesitated, realizing that the final tidbit of privileged information was about to be ripped from his hands. But there was no arguing with a Queen's agent. Without grace, he capitulated. "William Acker. Proprietor of The Hissing Cockatrice, a pub in Covent Garden on Rose Street."

"Have you managed to find *any* leads?" Mr. Tagert's voice rose. "Uncover any connections?"

"I'm sorry, but I cannot allow this," the secretary hissed, cupping her elbow and exerting a gentle pressure to draw her away. "Please come with me."

She resisted. "In a moment," she breathed, keen to hear Mr. Baxton's response.

"None." The coroner's admission grated over his vocal cords. "Save one possibility. All have fathered multiple children. A publican who is father of five, a shopkeeper with six daughters, a robust dock worker leaving behind a family of seven, and a banker, a known philanderer who supports, in total, twelve offspring—four of whom are legitimate."

Goodness, but that was a lot of children. At a head count of four, her own family often felt too large and confusing.

"Our best guess," the coroner finished, "is that the murderer seeks to make a statement about irresponsible reproduction and/or a need for the reduction of population growth in our burgeoning cities."

Without releasing her elbow, the secretary glared at her and pulled open the door, exposing her presence. "Mr.

Baxton," he intoned. "Mrs. Tagert has arrived to join her husband."

Coal gas and corpse candles.

"I don't—" Mr. Tagert caught sight of his not-a-wife. His mouth snapped shut. A hard-edged gleam sliced across his eyes. Then he smiled.

Over the years, Cait had been the recipient of a wide variety of smiles. From polite and indifferent to indecent and speculative. This one was the first that promised a retaliation of dark, unspeakable things.

Warmth washed over her, settling low in her stomach.

Another woman would have quaked in her boots, fearful of the repercussions. Cait, forged in fire, tossed back her own grin, daring him to do his worst.

Aether, she hoped he would.

This, her body insisted, was a man worth having. Worth keeping.

Could it be done?

She looked forward to the attempt.

CHAPTER FIVE

O F COURSE BLACK'S SISTER was a problem.

She'd shed her earlier morgue-drab attire and stood before him transformed. Luminous copper skirts—hiked to display a flutter of petticoat ruffles about leather-clad ankles—shifted and changed color in the faint gaslight while the soft, velvet nap of her bodice absorbed all. Including his attention.

A beautiful, interfering handful who knew all there was to know about venom. Add to that a poison ring that he very much doubted was empty, and she was downright deadly.

So very cavalier around most women, Black would burst an artery if he learned his sister had claimed to be the wife of an aristocratic gentleman in a prominent lawyer's office. But the duke's right-hand man was deluding himself if he'd expected her to follow orders, to not forcibly insert herself into this investigation. Anyone who met her could tell she had a rebellious streak a mile wide.

He was in so much trouble.

Jack had kept an eye out all day, waiting for her to materialize beside him. He'd expected her hours ago. Tempting as it might be to invite her to join him, to go against direct orders meant he'd risk losing the case.

Not that Black would learn about his sister's attempt from him.

And she knew it.

In a move calculated to provoke, her hands went to her hips and a smile curved the edges of her soft lips.

Soft?

He gave himself a mental shake. He had no way of knowing that. And finding out would end with Black burying his body in a location that wouldn't be found for over a hundred years.

Neither, however, could he deny her present claim on his person. Not if he wanted to remove her without incident from the coroner's office.

He'd play along.

If only for the moment.

"Ah, Mrs. Tagert." An odd sensation, to hear himself speak such words aloud. He drew out his pocket watch. "It does appear I'm running late. My apologies." He nodded to the coroner. "Thank you for your time, Mr. Baxton. I'll be in touch." With that, he donned his top hat and strode from the coroner's office, snatching up his not-wife's hand to anchor it to his arm. The mannerly method of dragging about a headstrong woman, assuming a minimum of cooperation on her part. At least she hadn't heard—

No. Scratch that.

From the guilty look on the secretary's face, she'd heard plenty.

Dammit.

The building's front door slammed behind them. The last of the evening's light had fled, and the streetlamps cast bright pools onto the pavement with dim edges that merged at intervals to create dark and dangerous recesses against unlit doorways.

He kept his hand pressed firmly upon hers. An unescorted and untrained lady would be at the mercy of the perils of such shadows. Not that it was a chore to have Miss McCullough at his side, bumping against his frame, all soft curves and swooshing satin. Impossible not to admire a woman brave enough to ignore Black's direct orders.

For that alone, she'd won his regard—and Black his sympathies for the impossibility of managing such a sister who thought nothing of traipsing about London in the evening unescorted.

How had she found him? He'd not detected anyone—

"The boy?" he mused aloud. "A new addition to the mews..."

She smiled. "I find it worrisome that it took you so many hours to finally question Mr. Baxton in person."

"Various family members required my attention." More accurately, he'd been delayed by futile attempts to question the various members of his family.

"A most fanciful account." His brother had dismissed the oddness surrounding Lord Saltwell's death as one would a child's fantasy, choosing instead to rant about the blow such a public death dealt his wedding plans, to complain about Jack's insistence that the dead man's body be transported to the Lister Institute. A viewpoint his mother shared, judging by her decision to blur the sharp edges of the nightmare with a few drops of laudanum.

Not a single mention of his friend Carruthers' loss had been made. The dead Lord Saltwell, it would appear, was beneath contempt.

That alone raised questions.

"Next stop, The Hissing Cockatrice." Miss McCullough's pronouncement yanked him back to his current predicament. She walked at a fast clip along the street, lifting her free hand to hail a cab.

Presumptuous of her.

"I've heard tell that some pubs pickle their mascots after they die," she chattered on, "keeping them in vats of alcohol upon shelves. A Cockatrice. How do you arrange for a most impressive hoax? Foot of an ostrich. Tail of a python. Wing of condor. Which leaves the question of a head. Roosters do have a rather distinctive wattle."

He drew her to a halt and lifted an eyebrow.

She tossed him a smile. "Agreed." Mischief glittered in her eyes. "Body parts in three jars, then, and a clever story about how the head was stolen one dark and stormy night."

Amused, he snorted. A shame, really. She would make the perfect accomplice, a bubbly foil to his gruff demeanor. Amidst merrymakers abandoning the theaters mid-performance, they might pretend to indulge in each other's charms whilst listening for gossip about the London Vampire. "It won't work, Miss McCullough." A statement made to himself as much as her.

Her lower lip protruded in a pout. "I thought it was rather clever."

"Your over bright chatter," he clarified, dropping his arm and setting her free. "You were given very specific instructions not to pursue this case external to Lister Institute. Then arrived, unchaperoned, at the public offices of a prominent lawyer claiming to be my wife. That alone will cause you grief. Even if I overlook all that, there is no chance that Mr. Acker will ever speak about his... injuries in the presence of a woman."

She huffed. "One doesn't have to be married to know how testicles function."

Heat gathered beneath his collar. Book learning or personal experience, he did not wish to know. Did he? For he caught himself looking at the lace that covered her hands and thinking about how they might feel upon his—

Absolutely inappropriate. He needed to send her safely away. Home. And away from him.

A crank hack rattled to a stop. Jack pulled open the door and held out a hand to assist her ascent. "Your address?"

Miss McCullough laughed. "That you might come calling tomorrow? Let's not pretend, Mr. Tagert, that I'm not going to redirect this conveyance directly to Covent Garden." She patted the seat beside her. "You might as well join me, dearest."

He gave her a quelling look, but climbed inside to sit across from her. "I'll see you home."

She sighed. "It won't work, this attempt to shepherd me about." She gave him a pitying look. "I know the address, and I will attempt to speak with the victim. If not tonight, tomorrow, or the next day. You'd have to stay glued to my side to stop me. As we're not actually married, I'm not certain how you could accomplish such a feat."

"I could summon your brother." A comment made to study her reaction.

Amusement danced in her eyes. "But you won't. Most agents would kill for a chance to work with my brother, but you don't want him involved. Distaste is written all over your face." She leaned forward. "What did he do to irritate you so?"

"Irrelevant."

The fine arch of an uplifted eyebrow expressed doubt. "Hence your sullen response."

She was right. But Jack wasn't about to dip into the tangle of his emotions to detail how he'd begged Black not to allow Angela into the societal liaison program. Unfair, perhaps, to hold such a grudge when his sister had been adamant about serving the Queen. What was a few years married to Icelandic royalty, Angela had argued, when afterward she would be a young, wealthy widow of considerable status?

A valid defense.

Until the North Sea wedding disaster had marooned her on the Faroe Islands with a husband of questionable morals.

Now Black's own sister sat before him, hell bent on opposing her brother's plans.

Was turnabout fair play?

No, not for the purposes of revenge.

"Your brother is uncharacteristically protective." A flat statement. An acknowledgement that to take her side was to oppose Black. Not a position one undertook without careful consideration.

She glanced out the window, tugged at the cuffs of her jacket, then met his gaze. "Because he can guess my agenda."

"Which is?"

"The list is long." Her steady gaze grew calculating. "Refusing to be confined to a laboratory ranks at the very top."

She was an acknowledged venom expert. If Miss McCullough believed she had something of value to add to the investigation in the field, ought he not dismiss her out of hand as her brother had done? Some agents partnered with others to achieve specific ends, why not him?

Aether. What was he thinking?

This would end badly.

Yet failing to hear her out might be worse.

"Fine," he surrendered. "Why exactly do you wish to interview Mr. Acker in person? Why won't a detailed list of his symptoms suffice for your work?"

As if she held the winning cards, she smiled. "Relying on secondhand reports prevents me from examining the bite marks and asking appropriate follow up questions. There are any number of direct observations a non-expert might fail to notice." She turned back the label of her jacket to reveal hidden pockets. "And I want a sample of his blood."

"A syringe and vials?" Really, he ought to stop being surprised.

"Among other items. Always on hand, much like an agent carries his TTX pistol." Her gaze fell on the edge of his coat where the familiar weight of his weapon lay. "One never knows when the opportunity to study a new toxin will present itself," she added.

An offhand comment that caught his full attention. "Has it?"

"Upon occasion." Her grin widened, as if recalling stories that could only be shared with trusted confidants. "When one has brothers who work for the Queen in one capacity or another, certain opportunities present themselves. One learns to be prepared."

An evasive answer. *Wait.* "Brothers? Plural?"

"Alec made a bit of a splash in certain circles recently." She tipped her head, waiting while he assimilated that tidbit of information.

"Alec McCullough?" he asked. "Member of the BURR team based in Glasgow?"

"The very one."

Her brother had played a key role in saving the floating castle from collapsing into the icy waters of the North Sea and killing all aboard. Including Angela. Rumor was he'd married a selkie. And Alec had a brother, Quinn. An agent no one had laid eyes upon in quite some time.

They were both brothers to Black? Yet they did not share a surname. Curious.

Jack pondered the implications. Had Black been involved in the North Sea incident? Was he partially responsible for preserving Jack's sister's life? He shifted uncomfortably.

Which brought him back to Miss McCullough. She was not a Queen's agent. Yet. Though the title was clearly in her crosshairs. With persistence and time, she might manage it—despite her brother. Talent lay in her lineage.

"Mr. Acker was attacked over a week ago," he pointed out, not quite ready to concede. "Any toxin will be no longer detectable."

"Agreed. But my studies indicate that, in response to exposure to a biological toxin, the body will produce small, soluble proteins—antibodies—designed to neutralize future exposures. He's the *only* known survivor. The only one who has lived long enough to produce these proteins. With a sample of his blood, I can test several known toxins in my collection. If there's a match to the venom used by this woman, I'll find it."

In her collection.

There was a phrase to strike fear into the heart of a man. As was a madwoman with what appeared to be poisonous fangs. One with a nasty habit of castrating her victims with a sharp knife.

"Sir?" the driver called, impatient. "A direction?"

Anything they could discover would help, and Jack was in charge of this investigation, not Black. But aiding and abetting Miss McCullough's first foray into the field was bound to have unpleasant consequences. "The Hissing Cockatrice. Covent Garden, Rose Lane." The carriage lurched into motion, and he pinned her with a look. "Don't make me regret this."

"Most men find they regret *not* letting me accompany them." She fell back against the straw-filled squab. Her smile grew cunning. "Like the times my brothers left me behind to sneak out of the house in the middle of the night. After all, men gadding about Glasgow couldn't be seen in the company of a girl." A certain bitterness crept into her voice. "Not one expected to redeem her origins by marrying well."

"As the spare of a wild heir, I sympathize."

"Wild?" Her eyebrow quirked.

"Most likely to ride a clockwork horse over a cliff following a drunken bacchanal?"

Her laughter sent zings of pleasure zipping down his spine. There, it coiled and tightened into desire. Instinct told him he played a dangerous game, letting this woman into his life.

"Yet here you are," she said, "pursuing interesting and necessary work while he frets about the newspaper's reporting of the great ice sculpture's punch plunge and a cooling corpse upon his carpet. He drains a decanter while you track down a murderer."

"Not inaccurate." How long had it been since his face had stretched into a such a wide grin? "But working for the Lister Institute comes at a cost."

"Such as the lack of a wife?" She reached out to give his

starched cravat a tug. "You're wealthy enough, handsome enough. It can't be for want of attention from the ladies."

"More a lack of *engaging and intelligent* ladies." Someone like her might have tempted him to matrimony. Miss McCullough was an original. Would he dare court such a woman? And how had she loosened his tongue so? Marriage was not a topic he cared to discuss. With anyone. "I've time yet to find a bride. What of your excuse?"

"You need to ask?" She gave him an odd look. "I'm a difficult woman. I refuse to settle for any less than exactly the right man."

What about me?

No. He wouldn't rise to the bait and ask, lest he find his own flaws and deficiencies disqualified him. *Not* that he was in the market for a wife, or wished to wed a woman who wore a poison ring. The last thing he needed was more trouble in his life, no matter the appealing trappings in which it was wrapped. Time to move the conversation back to safer footing.

"You didn't say," he nudged her knee with his, "why your brothers regretted leaving you at home."

"So many reasons." A mischievous light danced in her eyes. "But one particular exploit rises to the surface. If you ever feel the need to stretch your neck out on a block, ask the great and mysterious Mr. Black about the tattoo on his hairy arse."

"I can't imagine wanting to know." He grimaced. "Or see. Would you have stopped him?"

She snorted. "I would have advised him against his

chosen image. It's a clear illustration as to why such permanent body art ought not be selected while under chemical influence."

Laughing, he crossed his arms and fell back against his seat. "But you've no objection to making an impulsive, if sober, choice."

Her sly grin slid back into place. "What makes you think I haven't done exactly that?"

His heart gave a great thud, then picked up its pace as his mind peeled back layers. Envisioning the curves of her backside wasn't at all unappealing. What would he find? Not a delicate flower or a sweet songbird. A honeybee? A diaphanous jellyfish with barbed tentacles?

"Mr. Tagert!" Miss McCullough pressed a hand to her chest, feigning insult even as her eyes laughed and her voice teased. Had his expression given him away? "Such loud and personal thoughts! Think twice about that inquiry. You might like my answer."

He might indeed.

She nudged his foot with the pointed toe of her boot. "But now you know too much about me, and I very little of you. Time to even the score. Share a secret."

What made him wish to match her daring statements with one of his own? He should confess to nothing, but found himself admitting to the calculated sabotage of his brother's engagement ball. After three tortuous months of listening to his mother plan the centerpiece, its dramatic destruction had been deeply gratifying. "I myself set the fuse that melted icy feathers and precipitated the newly risen phoenix's punchbowl plunge."

"You?" This time it was Miss McCullough's mouth that fell open. Satisfaction, primitive and warm, spread through his limbs as her eyes widened. "A magnificent distraction allowing you to..."

"Investigate my brother's imprudent use of funds. As I left the study, I noticed a door ajar and found—"

"A murderous woman in white bent over the neck of Lord Saltwell." She leaned forward. "Tell me. Was there anything about her that struck you as unusual, something that others might call supernatural?"

The crank hack slowed, turning the corner onto the narrow street where they would find the only man to survive the London Vampire's bite. All levity fell away as he contemplated his response. "Her agility was... exceptional. Leaping from a window, scaling a wall, diving into a ventilation shaft to disappear in an underground tunnel."

"And her teeth?"

"Sharp. A trickle of blood upon her chin."

"Then fangs are a decided possibility." Miss McCullough hummed as their conveyance drew to a standstill.

A gas flame burned steadily inside an overlarge lamp that illuminated the hanging pub sign of a strutting cockatrice. Gold-painted letters confirmed arrival at their destination. Beside the building ran a narrow alleyway, connecting Rose Street with another. When Mr. Acker had stepped into its passageway, someone—or something—had been lying in wait. Had he been a specific target? Or merely a ready victim?

"Anything is possible." Jack eyed a poster nailed to the front door advertising tonight's bare-knuckle fight. Soon, spectators would flood the pub. They needed to be quick. "It's merely unlikely. Shall we see what we can convince the publican to share?"

He needed to leave this pub with a tangible lead, with more than a newfound appreciation and regard for Miss McCullough. Otherwise, Black might realize Jack's interest in his sister was more than academic and decide to unman him.

CHAPTER SIX

THE INTERIOR OF THE PUB was a sad disappointment. Though the dark wooden paneling, sputtering gas jets, and the pulsing red glow of hot coals in a grate yielded a sufficiently mysterious atmosphere, not a single anatomical specimen floated in a glass jar upon a shadowed shelf.

With a resigned sigh, she allowed Mr. Tagert to tug her toward the bar.

"A nice downy bit." A man hunched upon a stool with his fist wrapped about a beer glass shot her an ill-mannered glance, then turned his bloodshot gaze upon her companion. "But if it's a room you're after, turnabout and leave. Your cracked pitcher isn't welcome here."

Chatter among men scattered about at tables quieted.

Mr. Tagert returned the man's stare. "You'll be polite to my *wife*, or the fight will start early."

Had the man called her a whore? Cait's cheeks heated.

He must have. It was the only explanation for Mr. Tagert's continuation of their charade. Why else stake a public claim in a questionable establishment?

She slid a narrow glance at the man and lifted her chin ever so slightly.

"What can I get for you?" asked the bartender.

"We need to speak with Mr. William Acker," Mr. Tagert replied.

"Will's not up for any more prying," his eyes narrowed as he spit out the last word, "visitors. He's said all he has to say."

"Not an option," Cait piped up. "He survived. Others did not. We need to know why."

"You've a bare-knuckle fight scheduled to raise funds." Mr. Tagert dropped a sovereign into a large jar. "For Will" read the hand-lettered paper pasted to its surface. "Shame to cause a scene." He let his coat fall open to reveal the handle of the Queen's agent's trademark TTX pistol.

The bartender frowned. "Ten minutes." He jerked his head. "In the back room."

They walked the length of a hall, stepped into a room empty of all but one occupant. A man of considerable size sat, hunched and forlorn, tin cup in hand.

All tables and chairs were pushed against the wall. Across the floor, a layer of sawdust in anticipation of blood and sweat. Rarely, tears.

"Mr. Acker." While Cait elected to stand, Mr. Tagert lowered himself into an empty chair beside the man. Without preamble, he said, "Two more fell prey to the

London Vampire last night. A man and a woman. Both dead."

"A woman," Mr. Acker repeated, voice flat, eyes downcast. "Was she robbed of her..." The man blinked as Cait's ruffled hem came into focus. "Female bits?"

"Worse. A portion of her brain was removed."

"Brain?" His eyebrows drew together. "Whatever for?"

"We'd very much like to know, though preventing another death is top priority. Our search for clues, however minor, led us to your door. I understand your disinclination to speak about your encounter, but there are questions we need to impose upon you."

Mr. Acker glanced at Cait. Squirmed in his chair. "They were cut clean off. Not tied or bandaged. I was left for dead."

As an almost undetectable shudder ran across Mr. Tagert's shoulders, Cait picked up the conversational thread. "We're more interested in the initial attack." Fascinating as was castration, there was nothing this man could tell them about the why. Better to focus upon the attack, upon the bite. "There's reason to believe the bite of the vampire is poisonous."

"Poisonous?" For a long moment, Mr. Acker fell silent, considering this new notion. "Well it did hurt something vicious. So bad I heaved up everything in my stomach. Couldn't breathe. Everything went blurry. Then I collapsed." He closed his eyes. "That's the last I remember, until I woke up."

More consistent with venom coursing through his bloodstream than mere blood loss. "You didn't see—" Cait hesitated, not wanting to lead him to a gendered pronoun.

He shook his head. "The creature leapt upon me from behind. Sunk his teeth into me." He ran a hand through his hair. "Dark hair and pale skin? Black clothing. Maybe a cape. It isn't well lit, the alley beside my pub."

"Murderers do prefer the dark," Cait sympathized. "Did you feel a pair of hands? A mouth? Knees?"

Silent, Mr. Tagert lifted an eyebrow, inviting her to continue.

Mr. Acker tossed back the gin in his cup, swallowed. "Unnaturally strong hands. Clawed fingers dug into my coat as it bit down." He pulled his collar from his neck to expose an angry scar crawling—red, ropy and gnarled—across his shoulder and neck. "Fangs tore through both my collar and cravat."

"A nasty bite," Cait hissed in sympathy. "Your outerwear might have been what saved you, might have prevented the creature from discharging the entirety of its venom into your bloodstream. Incomplete envenomation. Or, possibly, the quantity of venom was lower because the creature had," she cleared her throat and adjusted her term to meet the man's expectations, "fed earlier."

Close enough, though Mr. Tagert tossed her a curious glance. Had she overstepped with such an opinion? Or was it her use of the word *creature* after they'd agreed nothing supernatural was in play?

The agent's expressions were hard to read, though she was beginning to recognize a few. Hard to miss the tell-tale heat of desire in his eyes as his gaze skimmed over her curves the moment before he'd addressed her as Mrs. Tagert. Her body grew warm at the memory. What would it be like to kiss such a man?

But she forgot herself. Again.

"Poison?" Mr. Acker asked.

"Of a kind." Cait nodded, then groomed his ego. "It would certainly explain how a man of your considerable size fell so easily. A mere bite could not accomplish such a feat. How tall are you?"

"Over six feet." Realizing he'd not stood much of a chance against so deadly an attack, the man straightened as his self-confidence struggled back to life.

Mr. Tagert gave her the slightest nod of approval. They could prove nothing, but the average woman would need to leap onto the back of a man Mr. Acker's size and cling tightly to sink her teeth into his throat.

"My colleague studies the effects of venom upon humans." Mr. Tagert lifted his hand, tapping the lapel of his coat. She reached inside her own jacket to withdraw a syringe, a rubber-corked test tube, and a vial of ethyl alcohol. Now was the time to press their advantage. "If you'll permit her to draw a sample of your blood, she has access to technology that might inform us what kind of poison was introduced into your blood."

Wary, Mr. Acker shifted upon his chair.

"It's a tiny needle," she said. "A small prick of the skin, easily tolerated by the *only* survivor of the London Vampire." The awe she injected into her voice was not at all manufactured. She was keen to learn all about this woman who walked the streets of London at night. To trap her in a cage where she might be safely studied. "Will you help us catch the creature?"

Her compliments tipped the balance. With a sigh he rolled up his sleeve and placed his arm on a table.

Cait moved quickly, lest he change his mind. "If you'll make a fist?" She drew a length of rubber tubing from her pouch and wrapped it about his arm just above his elbow to raise his veins. A splash of alcohol dabbed into the crook of his arm with cotton lint, and she was ready. No need to inform the poor man that he was her first patient. She'd practiced the technique one-handed upon herself for years, and the needle slid in quick and sure.

Blood spurted into the glass barrel of the syringe, and she unwrapped the tubing. A few seconds later, she pulled the needle free. Tucking the ball of lint into the folded crook of his arm, she transferred the blood into a tube. Fast and efficient. If life had taught her anything, it was to act decisively.

"Thank you, Mr. Acker."

"Mrs. Tagert, will you wait for me in the bar?" A hint of color darkened Mr. Tagert's cheeks. "I've a few more questions of a sensitive nature."

"Of course." She fought the roll of her eyes as she turned away. Really, men were so sensitive about the soft and squidgy dangly bits between their legs.

She opened the door and was met with a burst of male laughter. In the scant time they'd spent with the proprietor, a crowd of spectators for the bare-knuckle fight had gathered.

The tables were full, the bar surrounded. Commerce was lively. Every man held a glass as did the few women mixed in among them.

Those assembled were divided into two distinct groups, each taunting the other with—mostly—good-natured jeers. Two men, one per group, wore tight trousers and a loose, untucked shirt. The fighters? Given their brooding expressions and the dagger-sharp glares they threw at each other, she'd put good money on it.

Instinct told her to hang back. Curiosity made her jostle her way through the crowd, intent upon bellying up to the bar and ordering a pint, something positive to offset the certain misery her brother's wrath would force her to endure.

"Is this what's keeping us from the fight?" A man tugged at the flounce of her jacket as she passed. "A pretty piece in the back room?" He shifted, blocking her progress. "Will has no use for the likes of you anymore—they're not going to grow back. But me?"

"Try it," she retorted, "and I'll remove your full set."

His nearby friend laughed.

"A dangerous woman." He stepped closer, forcing his ale-addled breath upon her and blocking her path. "I'd like to see you try."

Really, it was a wonder so many men managed to keep their parts intact. But as knife skills had yet to be crossed off her list of accomplishments, she applied sharp elbows to the situation and left the lowlife behind.

Alas, his friend trailed behind her. "Nice moves," he commented. "Name's Rob. Can I buy you a drink?"

"No, thank you." At the bar, where the lights were brighter, she dropped a coin upon the polished wood and ordered herself a pint.

"Who're you for?" A woman with ink-stained fingers and a rough demeanor slammed down a ledger beside Cait. She held a fountain pen, waiting. "Murphy or Gibson?"

Cait blinked. "Um."

Still at her elbow, Rob raised an eyebrow and clarified. "The fighters?"

"Of course." Lay a bet? Why not. Maybe she could convince Mr. Tagert that they ought to linger, a most excellent chance to learn more about the rougher aspects of London. "Murphy." Cait handed the woman a coin.

"Name?"

"Katherine Black." No need to leave a written record of her presence.

The woman scrawled Cait's nom de guerre in her betting book then, coin pouch jingling at her hip, turned to accost another.

"So, Kathy." The irritation named Rob seized opportunity, sliding closer to bump his hip against hers. "If not the fight, what brings you here?"

She climbed onto a barstool, lips twitching as her now-scowling companion arrived at her side. "Not what, but who, would be the better question."

"The answer is, her husband." Mr. Tagert pressed a possessive hand to the small of her back.

"Erhmm. I see." Pint in hand, the man found something to interest him on the far side of the pub, then fled. It was an annoying truth that the death stare of a robust man would forever eclipse a woman's rebuffs, verbal or otherwise.

"Are you always so protective?" It ought to have sounded more like a criticism, except the warmth of his hand sank through layers of cloth and reached her skin, muddling her mind and stirring desires.

"I take care of my own."

"Not to mention presumptive?" Lifting her glass to sip at the frothy brew, she slid her gaze sideways, enjoying the buzz of attraction that simmered between them. "Your intervention is appreciated, but he was harmless enough."

With her brothers rarely about, she was accustomed to looking after herself. Self-reliance was critical, was it not? Despite the ridiculous stipulation that a female agent must be married to a male agent, there was no guarantee husband and wife would always work side-by-side.

Not that she'd object to spending copious amounts of time with a gentleman such as Mr. Tagert. Multiple possibilities of how they might enliven the inevitable long, dull hours of a mission sprang to mind.

A keen intellect. A willingness to partner with a woman. An undeniable physical appeal. She ached to skim her fingers over the rough scrape of stubble along the hard angle of his jaw. To tug at his cravat. To press her lips to his.

Did similar thoughts run through his own mind?

His considering gaze suggested they might.

What would it be like to belong to such a man? For such

a man to belong to her? She winked. Only to be disappointed when his hand fell away.

Alas, she might never know.

Their marriage was but a game of the evening, a convenient cover. Reality was a wet blanket. He was the second son of a viscount with an older brother who was as yet childless. Far too close to the title for a Scottish woman of mixed ancestry. His family would object. Vociferously. Better to set her sights on an agent more solidly middle class.

"Time to go." He took the half-empty glass from her hand and set it upon the bar. "Your samples require processing."

"They'll keep a few hours." She didn't want the evening to end, so when the door to the back room opened and excited patrons surged forward with an excited roar, she slid from her stool and flashed him a bright grin. "We should join them."

"No." His lips pressed into a flat line. "I did not promise you an evening of entertainment, only an interview. We're leaving. Home or Lister?"

"But my bet," she objected, moving toward the back room. "I want to watch."

"Cait." His pronunciation of her name was filled with dire predictions. Had she given him permission to address her so? Well, she *had* claimed him as her husband. "Have a care for your reputation."

And wasn't that always the refrain? She ignored him.

A side door opened, one that led to an adjacent alleyway,

and a rather odd assembly of men entered, each grasping long, sharpened sticks.

"Shit." Mr. Tagert's arm snaked about her waist. He spun her about and hurried her toward the front door.

"Who are they?" Cait craned her neck, trying to see past his broad shoulders.

"He who survived the bite of the London Vampire!" one of the men bellowed. "We must speak with him!"

"No one you wish to meet." His grip tightened.

But there would be no easy escape, for the pub door flew open. "Someone called for a priest?" A man wearing a long black robe blocked their exit. About his neck hung an overlarge, silver cross. His hand gripped a leather case.

Cait broke into a broad grin. Ridiculous, certainly, but vastly entertaining. Gossip over tea and cakes could not hope to compare. Confined to parlors, parks and laboratories, she missed out on so much.

The barkeep waved a rag at the men, annoyed. "Off with you. There's a fight on, and he's no time for such foolishness."

Mr. Tagert cursed again. He dropped into a chair at a nearby empty table and pulled her down beside him.

"Why, yes, I'd love to stay," she mocked. Such bad manners begged for immediate disobedience. "Please, do continue to treat me like a sack of potatoes."

"Will you be serious?" he hissed. Strong fingers gripped her chin and forced her gaze upward. "This is not the time for antics, not the time to fan flames. Do. Not. Engage."

"You forget I've a passel of troublesome brothers myself.

I can handle them." Leaning forward, she slid her hand over his cheek, delighting in the rough prickle that met her palm, and gave in to impulse. She pressed a kiss to his lips.

For a heartbeat, the world receded. Soft. Warm.

Unmoving.

Her stolen kiss was not reciprocated.

Humiliation burned.

Cait stood and, with effort, sauntered back to the bar to stand beside the self-styled, ale-chugging priest who had cracked open his leather case for all to admire.

Within lay a bible. Another cross. Vials of holy water. Bulbs of garlic. Pointed stakes. A wooden mallet to drive them home.

"Is that a vampire-hunting kit?" she asked.

"Indeed," he proclaimed, making the sign of the cross, all false piety. "Tonight we put the London Vampire back in his grave."

She laughed.

"You doubt us?" A question directed at her by a gentleman with wild, feverish sparks dancing in his eyes. Ones she suspected might be fueled by a chemical aid. "You're a pretty one." He crooked his finger. "Come closer and I'll tell you a tale that will curl your hair."

"Leave her be." Jack shoved himself between them. "Take this madness home before someone innocent is injured."

"That's Lord Aubrey, you wet horse blanket of moth-eaten wool. You're the one who claimed a vampire ruined my engagement ball, so I'm here to help put the undead back in its grave before dawn." He gave a snort, then spun about, hands wide, to address the room at large. "Has anyone with long, pointy teeth entered this evening?"

A few sniggered. Many looked away.

Corpse candles and grave gas. This was his brother?

Was their cover blown?

No, not yet. She had never met the viscount before. No reason for him to think her anymore than—what had that man called her—a cracked pitcher.

Cait tugged at Jack's coat sleeve. The moment called for a swift retreat. But he shrugged her off and hissed, "Stay out of this."

It's a family matter.

The words were unspoken, but hung in the air nonetheless. A sharp reminder that she would never count herself among them. She dropped her hand and backed away.

Lord Aubrey turned back to his brother with a shrug. "Perhaps your hallucination has moved on to fresh hunting ground? Shall we try another pub?"

Mr. Tagert's hands fisted.

"I dare you," the viscount taunted. "Go ahead. It'll be worth it, just to show the world what kind of man you are."

Better that she depart. That her presence was forgotten.

While they glared at each other, Cait spun about and slipped out the front door.

She'd lost her taste for a fight.

CHAPTER SEVEN

OUTSIDE, PLENTY OF PEOPLE moved about beneath bright streetlamps despite a gathering damp chill. Or had the weather been cold all along, her awareness of it driven away by warmth generated in Mr. Tagert's presence?

Best to stick with formality. Her mistake.

She huffed and set off toward the main road. No use in grieving the impossible. What the evening lacked in terms of matrimonial prospects was offset by the samples tucked into the pockets of her jacket. Properly leveraged, they could win her access to the world of Queen's agents where there were bound to be better unmarried alternative prospects.

To that end, her first stop would be Lister Laboratories. Anticipation swelled in her chest as she imagined processing the vials of blood and testing them against her collection of venom samples and—

Kraken.

With the chaos of the day, she'd milked the spectacled cobra but hadn't yet transported the venom to Lister.

She chewed on her lip. Every sign and symptom of the so-called vampire's bite matched those of the *Naja naja*. With one in her possession, she would be remiss not to include its venom in the evaluation panel.

Home first?

She sighed, resigning herself to the sensible decision. Refrigeration would hold the samples overnight. A good night's rest, then directly to the laboratory at dawn.

At the end of the short road, a gentleman alighted from a crank hack. He hustled past with a muttered, "Good evening".

The burly-armed driver jumped down to wind the mechanism of his crank hack. "A ride, miss?"

"Please."

She stated her address and climbed inside.

Moments later, the hack lurched into motion, clacking down the street at a swift clip. Only then did she realize she was not alone.

A pale, oval and vaguely familiar face stared at her out of the darkness. "You're a friend of the viscount's brother?" The woman's voice was a sibilant whisper.

"I beg your pardon?" Cait blinked. Had they been followed? If an audience with Lord Aubrey was her goal, why had this woman not exited with the gentleman?

She rapped the ceiling and called to the driver to stop. But the vehicle didn't slow.

Shivers of alarm rippled over Cait's skin.

"A colleague, perhaps?" The woman, wrapped in a dark, blood-red cape, crossed the hack to sit beside Cait. Strange gray eyes rimmed with gold edges peered at her. "Either way, you're a lovely diversion. An unexpected stroke of luck."

Cait dove for the door, for its handle, but the woman leapt, sinking razor-sharp teeth into the muscle of her neck. Pain lanced through her, rippling outward from the bite in waves. In a crush of satin and petticoats, she fell to the floor.

This wasn't happening.

Yes, it was. There was no denying it.

How could this be happening?

She could feel her body shutting down. A neurotoxin. Paralytic. In moments, she would be helpless.

"You should be dead." The woman reared back, hissing as she dug into an overlarge velvet bag and withdrew a monstrous, gleaming device. Hinged legs ended in claws. Its body, a solid brass core, terminated in a gaping circular mouth filled with sharp teeth. "Why are you not dead?"

A whirring sound filled the air.

It took every ounce of Cait's remaining strength to lift her arm, to wrap her fingers about the cool metal of the door handle.

This was her chance. Her only one. Else she would be found tomorrow sprawled in a gutter, the latest victim of the London Vampire. Quite probably missing a pituitary gland.

A twist, a push, and the door swung open. Pavement whipped past.

"No!" the woman cried.

There was no other option. Cait heaved herself from the crank hack, careening out onto the street.

Splash! Muddy water sloshed about her. She'd landed in a puddle. Alive for the moment, though she might yet meet her end beneath iron wheels and steel hooves.

The crank hack never slowed as a scream pierced the air. Not one of horror, but of incredible anger.

The frantic blowing of a whistle took its place. Was help on the way? She couldn't turn her head to find out. All she could do was stare, limp and unblinking, into the blurry sky of London as cold water seeped into the fabric of her clothing.

Survival wasn't a given, even if it was a high probability. Luck wouldn't factor into it. If her inborn immunity could carry her past the initial effects of the venom, her blood would answer many questions.

So many questions.

But darkness gathered in her vision and tied the drawstring tight.

WHERE THE HELL had Cait disappeared?

It had been all of five minutes.

Jack pressed his hand against his jaw as he staggered out onto the street, gently opening and closing his mouth to assess the damage. A few passersby eyed him warily and steered clear, believing drink the cause of his unsteady steps.

She'd wanted to see a fight. He'd given her one and come

out victorious, even if soft food might be a requirement for the coming days.

He'd knocked out Aubrey on his third swing. A punch that had been a long time coming. If Jack's exit from the pub held a touch of a swagger, it was earned. By morning, the jackass that was his brother would be nursing a black eye. A most satisfying way to put an end to Aubrey's ridiculous plans for a vampire hunt.

Alas, Cait had not remained to witness his victory, his own rude words the cause. He owed her an apology.

He glanced at the inky shadows of the alley that ran alongside The Hissing Cockatrice, but refused to believe Cait would be so stupid as to venture there alone. No, she would have made her way to the end of the street and hailed a hack.

Compelled to ensure she safely reached her destination, be it home or Lister Laboratories, he followed. As he turned the corner onto Garrick Street, the sound of blasting whistles pierced the air.

Shit.

He broke into a sprint. Most wouldn't worry. But this was Cait. Reckless and brave.

In the distance, traffic flowed around a crumpled form in the street. A nearby streetlamp cast its soft glow over shimmering copper and blue fabric. Onlookers gathered, barely heeding the constable's orders to step back.

Lungs heaving, Jack pushed past them all, dropping to his knees at Cait's side.

"Sir!"

"She's my wife." Once again, he staked claim for the sake of expediency. As the constable backed away, he ran his hands over her body, searching for broken bones and, thankfully, finding none.

Her eyes flickered open, shut. "Bitten," she whispered. Her head lolled away, exposing two red and angry puncture wounds.

Hunted and brought down by the very creature they stalked this evening? The coincidence was too strong to dismiss, but one he was not interested in exploring at the moment. All but one victim had died.

He gathered her limp form—wet and muddy—into his arms and stood. "A crank hack," he ordered the constable. "Now. I'll see her to the hospital posthaste."

"Yes, sir!" With a nod, the policeman set about flagging down a vehicle.

"Not Lister." Cait dragged in a shallow breath and wheezed her next words on an exhale. "Must stay secret. My bite."

"Not possible, Cait." He gave the Lister Institute's address to the wide-eyed driver with instructions to hurry, then heaved them both into the crank hack. "Lister provides the best care in all of London."

"No. Please, no."

The hack turned a corner on two wheels, and her head flopped against his chest. He cupped her head with his hand, gathering her close while trying his best to remain calm, to slow the wild beats of his heart as it slammed against his rib cage.

"You're not thinking clearly."

"No cure," she gasped. "No treatment. I'll be fine. But must stay secret. Can't let them know my secret."

"No secret is worth risking your life."

A tear slid from the corner of her eye. "No. Please, no. Many poisons, always fine. Just need time. Secret."

"Are you telling me that you're immune to poisons?" he asked.

"Not all. Biotoxins."

"How?"

But she'd lost consciousness.

His mind raced. How could she possibly know she wouldn't succumb to the creature's venom? Were these delirious ramblings? Or was there reason? Lister medical staff were not unaccustomed to cryptic medical matters. Why such objections?

Shit.

It wasn't impossible. Torrington, another Queen's agent, was married to a woman whose eyes appeared to glow in the dark, a feature that had brought her much grief this past February.

Cait's pleas might have cause. But if not Lister, where?

He patted her cheek, willing her awake, worrying at the coldness of her skin. "Does Black know your secret?"

"Yes." The word was slurred.

"Does your family?" But the second question came too late. She'd slipped back into unconsciousness.

Dammit. That left him only one option.

He banged on the roof.

The crank hack slowed and a small panel slid open. The driver's face appeared.

"Change of plans," Jack called. "We head for the Albany with a brief stop at the end of Trinket Alley." The Roma were always about, peddling their ingenious contraptions, and the fastest way to find Black in London was to send a gypsy boy.

When the hack stopped again, Cait had been unresponsive for far too long. Moreover, her breaths grew ever shallower, her pulse slower. Classic symptoms of a neurotoxin. He tamped down rising panic. Fought against a heavy dread that gathered in his chest.

Though he'd abandoned a formal practice of medicine, he had trained as a physician and had years of experience handling medical emergencies in the field. He could breathe for her, if it came to that. Could even force her blood to circulate for a time. The same care any Lister doctors and nurses would provide.

Not that telling himself such things did anything to loosen the fear gripping his heart as he laid Cait upon the bench of the hack.

He leapt down, spotted a likely child. Holding up a silver half-crown, Jack beckoned.

The bright-eyed boy drew close, keen to display his clever wares, chief among them the kinetic sculpture of a dragon who flapped his wings as it rode upon his fingertip.

"Best of them all," the boy touted. "Unless you're shopping for a lady?" He plucked a metallic, blue rose but from the hawker tray that hung from a strap about his neck.

"Watch," he said. With the twist of a wrist, it began to bloom.

"I'll pay for them both," Jack spoke quickly, "if you'll also carry a message to Logan Black. He'll pay twice this when it's delivered."

The gypsy boy's eyes widened. "Yes, sir!"

"Good. Tell him Tagert sent you. That his sister's life hangs in the balance. He's to come immediately. Number B6, the Albany." He searched the boy's face as the child repeated the information. Perfect recall. Jack dropped two coins into his waiting palm. "Hurry."

He jumped back into the hack. "Double fare if we arrive in five minutes," he called to the driver. He'd pay any price to see her safe.

Gears shifted and the cab shot forward at a breakneck pace, not slowing until it approached the courtyard of the Albany. Here, quiet discretion ruled, a fact that would safeguard Cait's reputation.

As the nearby clock chimes of St. James' Church sounded the hour, Jack strode into the building with Cait in his arms, pausing only to inform the porter—who held the door open with practiced disinterest—"I am expecting a Mr. Black. Please show him in with all due speed."

The man nodded.

In his apartments, Jack stretched Cait out upon his bed, once again checking her vitals. Heartbeat a touch irregular. Breathing shallow. Temperature far too low. He called her name and received no response.

He touched a match to the fire laid in the nearby grate.

As the flames caught, Jack hurried to remove the many layers of Cait's clothing. Wet and muddy, they would only chill her further, perhaps precipitate a fall into shock. Satin, silk, then cotton—all landed on the floor in one heap.

His breath left him in a rush. *Aether.* Hers was a figure worthy of adoration and soft caresses. Would that circumstances were different.

Jack shook his head, refocusing on the looming catastrophe that confronted him.

The corset and its restrictive bands of steel had to go. No impediment to respiration could be permitted. The swift application of a penknife to corset laces released her from its bonds.

He carried a clean cloth, water and soap to her bedside, then froze. A conscious Cait would scream at him to preserve any evidence. Hastily, he dragged a ball of lint over and around the skin surrounding the puncture wounds sunk deep into the musculature of her shoulder. Tucking them into a small jar, he screwed the lid in place and set it aside. That would have to suffice. Gut roiling, he bent over her to clean the swollen and blistering and—he leaned closer and swore.

A small area of skin darkened before his eyes—a sign of necrosis.

But so soon? Tissue death usually took hours or days to develop.

Time. She'd begged for time.

Could her immune system be so very powerful?

For the first time in over a year, he wished for Black's presence.

Nothing save to wait and watch.

He dropped into a chair beside the bed. Pressing two fingers to the inside of her wrist, he fixed his gaze upon the faint rise and fall of her chest, waiting.

Her life hung in the balance. Surviving the next few hours would be critical, and there was little that he—that anyone—could do. A heart that stopped could sometimes be jolted back into motion. Breathing could even be supported for a short period of time. But those were all solutions to an acute event when a potent neurotoxin might sustain its effects for hours. Days.

The carefully constructed shell about his life had begun to crack.

He pressed a free hand to a jaw that screamed in pain. Finally, a woman who roused both his body *and* his mind. So, naturally, on the very day they'd met, not only did he learn that she was related to Black, but she invited herself on an impromptu mission wherein his brother and friends materialized. Then, after freezing beneath her touch, he'd treated her to a spectacle of misplaced emotion, letting anger and irritation goad him into a public fight with his brother.

While she faced down a venomous vampire, unaccompanied.

So very unprofessional. There was no excuse.

He huffed out a hoarse laugh.

And now she lay half-dead in the bedchamber of a bachelor.

Jack wondered where Black would bury his body.

Cait woke to the sound of a fierce argument outside her room.

"...should have taken her straight to Lister."

"...begged...secret...tell me..."

"...followed..."

The room was cast in the gray glow of dawn. Firelight flickered upon the wall, mixing with the anemic dawn of a rainy morning. Not home, for both the fireplace and window were in the wrong location. Cool air caressed her bare shoulders, underscoring the fact that she wore little more than a chemise. A vague scent hung in the air that hinted at leather, spice and smoke.

Was this Jack's bed?

The beginnings of a smile turned into a grimace.

Aether, it had been ages since a venom had affected her with such vigor. It was as if a lance pierced her shoulder, pinning her to the mattress. And that wasn't the worst of it. Half her body was on fire, throbbing and burning. Her arm, her throat, the vast majority of her face and chest. Even her toes felt puffy and tender.

The symptoms did indeed bear a resemblance to those she'd read about in a book about cobras. Yet her tongue felt thick and her head pounded, venom characteristics generally attributed to sea snakes. Moreover, extrapolating from Mr. Acker's scars, the not-a-vampire's venom contained a proteolytic element that would lead to necrosis. Not a happy thought. How badly would she scar?

She tried to bend her elbow to touch the crook of her neck—and failed. Her arm had barely shifted. Given it was dawn, some eight hours had passed, yet the paralytic effects had not fully worn off. The potency of this venom was extraordinary.

She tried to call out, but only managed a strangled moan.

A dark form bent over her, and a cool cloth was pressed to her forehead. "I blame myself for this incident."

Kraken. It was her mother.

And if Mother was here, that meant Mr. Tagert had first summoned Logan.

He was going to rake her over coals for disobeying orders.

"This is what comes of strong drink loosening the tongue. Better I had never spoken of your true father. It's clear you're on some quest to explore your heritage. First you make an adder your house pet. Then we visit the Reptile House to inquire about snake charming. Now there's a cobra in your room." Mother tsked. "What were you handling last night? A black mamba?"

Far, far worse. She'd been kidnapped by a mysterious creature with an unknown venom and a hidden agenda.

If only she'd had time to experiment with the *Naja naja*, to administer small, increasing doses of the venom over several days, she might have been able to blunt the effects.

"Water," she croaked. First things first.

Mother stuffed pillows behind Cait's head, then held a cool glass to her lips, not that such activities slowed her words of censure. "Mr. Tagert insists we ought not move you, that all night you teetered on the very edge that separates life from death. Mr. Black is also concerned. But I cannot allow you to stay. Word of your misadventure cannot be allowed to leak. The Melbourne Ball is in five days. I've already promised a number of your dances to a number of eligible young men. If anything, this misadventure makes it all the more necessary to find you a husband."

Absolutely not. Cait would sooner die an old maid than marry a man of her mother's choosing. A fate easily avoided in Glasgow. Whenever Mother attempted to pass the problem of her daughter on to another man, Cait would lead them to the parlor and stand beneath the portrait of her legal father. Most quickly made the correct assumption and excused themselves.

Here, she would require a new tactic.

Light flooded the room as Mother threw open the curtains. Cait wrenched her head away, and every muscle in her neck screamed in pain. But her misery wasn't yet over, far from it. Cold air rushed over her as her mother tossed covers aside, revealing nothing but thin undergarments and sheer stockings.

"Aether," Mother gasped. "You're all but naked! Up. Up!"

Her body screamed in protest. Every movement a struggle, each limb as cooperative as that of a rag doll, all while her mother muttered about needing to haul her daughter home and see her safe in her own bed.

Mother's fingers faltered upon the buttons beneath

Cait's chin. Wide eyes met hers. "You were bitten upon the *neck?*"

"So I was."

"It wasn't a snake at all, was it?" Her voice cracked. "He sent you on a vampire hunt?"

"I fought free, Mother. I'll be fine. I always am."

"Nearly naked in a strange man's bed and barely able to move. You call that fine?" Her voice rose with every word. "That gypsy boy is culpable. Again."

"No. It was my—"

Mother held up a hand. "Please. No more lies on his behalf." She spun on her heel and stalked to the door to throw it open. "Mr. Black! We must speak. Now."

Outside the room, the contentious voices fell silent.

Logan appeared in the doorway holding a rolled newspaper. He tapped it against his palm, casting a sharp and pointy stare in her direction as red-hot, thermal waves of anger distorted the air about him. "Miss McCullough, are you ready to depart?"

"I am." Her stomach flipped, then crawled into a corner. What fresh hell had broken loose while she... slept? Had he taken steps to arrange for her dismissal from Lister?

"In a moment," Mother snapped, holding up a hand. "First things first. You *encouraged* my daughter to hunt the London Vampire—"

"I assure you, I did no such thing." His expression hardened.

But Mother wasn't finished. Her eyes narrowed. "That gentleman out there," a hand flapped, "the one whose bachelor's quarters my daughter now occupies, you claim he's one of yours?"

"Is Mr. Tagert a Queen's agent?" Logan clarified. "He is, but—"

"This is not the first time you've encouraged her to sneak from her home, to prowl city streets at night." Mother's stare was lethal. "I will hold you personally responsible should word of this incident reach the ears of—"

"Too late." Logan snapped open the morning newspaper. Or, rather, a gossip rag. One with an extensive readership.

The headline was typeset in bold lettering:

VISCOUNT SHOCKED TO LEARN OF BROTHER'S SECRET MARRIAGE

Cait's mouth fell open. "No. He didn't."

"I assure you, he did." Logan's lips twisted. "Boots on, little sister. The sooner you're under your own roof, the better. And congratulations. No doubt you've achieved your aim. I imagine the Duke of Avesbury will wish to have words. With *both* the newlyweds."

CHAPTER EIGHT

"How dare you!" Jack shoved past Emsworth. The steam butler's arms might be made of steel, but they were no match for his anger.

His brother sat behind his desk, one hand holding an ice-filled sack to his eye, the other scratching lines of text onto paper. After a prolonged exhalation, he set his pen aside.

"You wear righteous anger so very well," Aubrey drawled. "Did you think you wouldn't have to pay the piper? You sabotaged my engagement ball for your own amusement. I can't prove it, but I know it was you." A sly smile stretched his lips. "So when word reached me that you were at our favorite pub asking questions, I couldn't let the opportunity pass. Did you not like our staging? Carruthers went above and beyond, dragging that costume out of a theater's closet."

Jack swore. There were no depths to which Aubrey and

his friends would not stoop to amuse themselves. "I was on assignment."

"Were you?" His brother's eyes lit up. "Hard to tell, given the woman on your arm. In a pub no less. How many years since you last unbent enough to enjoy female company?" He snorted. "I'm going to enjoy watching you wriggle and twist as you try to escape the hook upon which you are caught."

"It's not only me who will suffer, but the woman you maligned." He and Cait were already in a heap of trouble. The last thing they needed was public scandal.

"Only if they learn her name. Which they won't." His brother's smile grew cold. "You're far too honorable, and for that you will suffer."

Goddammit. That Aubrey thought Cait no more than a piece of fluff was surprisingly irritating. Much as he wished to defend her, he couldn't. To do so might goad his brother into further action. "Is that what this is? Revenge?"

Aubrey shrugged. "And a bit of boredom. It's been a trial, these past weeks, courting a sweet young thing like Lady Mildred. But now she's won, and there's the wedding night to anticipate." He waggled his eyebrows.

"You grow overconfident," Jack growled, remembering Lady Mildred's pinched expression at her own engagement ball. "She may yet cry off. I do believe she's marrying you for your money as much as your title. How stable is the former? And where is Menwith, exactly?"

Shock rippled over his brother's face. "You wouldn't dare." Tossing aside the bag of ice, he narrowed his one good eye. The other was, much to Jack's satisfaction, dark purple and swollen shut. "Stay out of my business."

"As you've stayed out of mine?"

They glared daggers at each other, and a flicker of worry traversed his brother's visage. Something was afoot, something more than business as usual. Which meant Jack would make it *his* business to get to the bottom of this.

He crossed his arms.

A spa implied healing, possibly one that offered cures of the medical variety. His brother and Carruthers were up to something. Moreover, they always moved in lock step with Oakes, a most convenient physician.

Hell, were the three of them in cahoots to peddle snake oil to the gullible?

Another responsibility was not what he needed, but it was impossible to ignore his brother's misdeeds. Before he lost access to far-reaching contacts within the agency, it would be necessary to invest a bit of time investigating the Grand Menwith Hotel and Spa. He would launch a few skeet pigeons bearing inquiries.

"Boys!" Hand pressed to her forehead, their mother strode into the room and slapped a newspaper against Jack's chest. "Have you not cast enough of a pall upon your brother's impending marriage? What is this nonsense?" She glanced from one son to the other. "Explain."

"We encountered each other last evening at a public event," Aubrey said. "There was an altercation."

"With the press in attendance?" his mother cried, then caught sight of her precious child's eye. "Aubrey!"

"Jack threw the first punch." His response was petulant.

"I was provoked." Scowling, Jack peeled the gossip rag from the front of his shirt and began to read. Though the last article he'd read had been based on malicious pub blather, *this* reporter had done his legwork. Three times Jack had claimed Cait as his wife. At the lawyer's office. At the pub. Beneath a streetlamp. And this newsman had traced their path, spoken to witnesses at each scene and tracked down the driver of their crank hack.

The beginnings of a headache nagged, helped along by renewed problems with his vision. He pinched the bridge of his nose and closed his eyes for a moment. Tormenting his younger brother was a pastime of which Aubrey never tired. It was, however, the first time he had taken personal grievances into the public arena.

"None of this would have seen print if your cherished viscount hadn't given my name to the press." Jack addressed the comment to his mother, but locked eyes with his brother —who bared his teeth in the mockery of a smile, pleased to have thrown a wrench into spokes.

There would be no escaping the newspapermen now. With their stubby pencils and dingy notebooks, they would hound Jack's every step during this investigation, all in an attempt to learn the name of the "dark-haired mysterious woman that brought brothers to blows".

"There is no secret marriage." Bitterness seethed beneath the surface of his words. Nor could there be a secret partnership. Not now. Any contact between them within the walls of the Lister Institute might be remarked upon, passed along, or otherwise spoken of within range of the sharp ears of newspapermen. It was too much of a risk. If Cait was identified, her reputation would be shredded in black and white for all of London to read.

His brother's interference had compromised plans to catch this venomous creature and put an end to the ghastly murders. Hell, the duke would be wise to assign another agent to this investigation, though Jack would do anything he could to remain in charge.

Which might prove an impossibility, what with Black's wrath fully unleashed.

In the small hours of the night, well past the hour when Jack had most feared for Cait's life, Black had slammed into his apartments. "Where is she? What happened?"

Holding his hands in the air, Jack opened with, "Your sister was attacked by the London Vampire. But she's going to be fine."

A minor miracle, that. The fine satin jacket she'd worn was a flimsy barrier, easily peeled aside to expose the smooth column of her neck. And, given the deep puncture wounds and the rapid onset of paralysis, the creature had delivered a deadly dose of venom into Cait's bloodstream. Yet—against the odds—she'd survived.

Jack's contribution to that was, in the scheme of things, minimal. A few moments of rescue breathing when her chest had ceased to rise and fall. She'd rallied, heart and lungs returning quickly to normal function. Not so his own. A full hour had passed before his own racing heart had settled from the scare.

Bedside, Jack had issued a detailed report while Black peeled back the covers, staring at the irrefutable proof of said attack.

"It was necessary to remove her corset to allow her to breathe," Jack had hastened to point out, choosing to omit any mention of assisted respiration.

"I'll allow that, but why is she *here*?" Black had asked, his eyes steely. "In the Albany, in *your* bed. She ought to be in her own."

Wary, Jack had chosen his words carefully. "She refused transport to Lister Hospital, insisting they could not be allowed to learn her secret."

Of an extreme tolerance for poisons.

Would the top agent elaborate?

No. Black's impenetrable stare had volunteered nothing, save a promise of extreme pain should he find the slightest impropriety in her treatment.

"She indicated you were aware of her... condition, then lost consciousness." Jack had tossed his hands in the air and given an exasperated huff. "Without knowing her address—"

"You sent for me. And brought her," Black's lips had twisted, "here."

"The Albany is known for its discretion," Jack had stated. "I feared for her life. By rights, your sister ought to be dead."

"A thousand times over," Black had groused.

Regardless of how or why the creature had come to be outside The Hissing Cockatrice, to put a final end to Mr. Acker or by stalking Jack, she'd found Cait to be a convenient target, and laid hands and teeth upon a woman who was supposed to be under his protection.

Memories of a moonlit chase through a garden flooded back. The poisonous female had outmaneuvered him. Easily. She was not some mindless monster, but cunning, clever and quick. A predator undeterred by pursuit.

Jack had opened his mouth. Shut it. His suggestion would be unwelcome. If Black wanted his sister properly trained for fieldwork, he would have seen it done.

"The reports of castration are fascinating—and likely relevant." The agent had thrown him a dark glance that promised Jack the same, should Cait—upon awakening—claim he had taken any liberties. "But we have a new and more pressing issue. This not-a-vampire will be angry and vindictive when she learns her latest victim has survived."

All of London would know, for the great printing presses had been hard at work, churning out news of the attack, of Jack's secret marriage.

Nothing good would come of this. Personally or professionally.

Scowling, Black had given him orders through a clenched jaw. "You'll take no further actions until I've discussed the situation with the duke."

Confronting his family didn't count, for it resolved not a single thing. Antagonism. Opposition. Outright conflict. All normal family relations. Once, his father and Angela would have stood in his corner, but his father's fondness for the opium pipe had landed him in an early grave and his sister was trapped by the North Sea.

He glowered at the paper his mother had slapped against his chest, wondering if Black had managed to bundle his sister onto a steam train bound for Glasgow.

"Really, Mother, this is the perfect opportunity." Aubrey stood, circling around the desk.

Jack didn't like the unholy gleam in his brother's eyes. "No."

Nothing good ever came from one of Aubrey's offhand suggestions. Such as the time he and Angela had been caught smoking cigars. The blame had landed squarely on him—and Aubrey had suggested the punishment.

Weeks, near to an entire summer, locked inside with a tutor learning Greek that he might read Plato's work in the original. Torture, even if it was a skill that later served him well upon his application to the Lister School of Medicine.

Mother brightened. "A swift marriage," she eyed her spare son sideways, "has always been the preferred solution to a sullied reputation."

Aubrey grinned. "How many dark-haired, young eligible ladies do you know, Mother?"

She sniffed. "Precious few who would be caught at a notorious pub. But we only need find a single lady willing to claim she is ready to accept the consequences of her actions."

"Wonderful." The word tore from between his gritted teeth. "What man does not wish to be painted in such dark shades for his wedding portrait?"

His mother sent him an arched look. "Like oil on canvas, if the hue fits... And it's time you were wed. You're far past your prime."

"I'm three years younger than Aubrey!" Though he might well be dead—or worse—inside a month. But that was a weakness he refused to touch upon. Of late, he'd pushed the idea of taking a wife from his mind—until he'd caught sight of Cait sprawled across his bed.

Mother snorted. "As I said, aging. Any day now, your hair might recede and damage your physical appeal." She pulled Debrett's from the shelf and carried it to a writing table, where she began flipping through its pages. "This will require some thought."

"Stop right there." He refused to allow them to provoke him further.

His mother scratched a name upon the paper before her. Aubrey sniggered.

"You're wasting your time." Jack tossed the newspaper aside. "I will not be forced into an arranged marriage."

"Married to your work, are you?" His brother called as Jack stalked from the library.

He was indeed. Unless—or until—the Duke of Avesbury issued an official decree of divorce.

Muscles whimpered in gratitude and joints moaned in relief as Cait lowered herself into the warm, welcoming water of a deep, porcelain tub. Gravity ceded its grip and moist heat worked its magic, all aided and abetted by the handfuls of magnesium salt crystals Janet tossed into the bath. Sighing, she closed her eyes.

Not that there was to be any rest and relaxation for the newly bitten. She was in a pickle and could not see her way out of the barrel.

Slap! A soggy mass landed upon her shoulder at the crook of her neck.

Cait dragged a sharp breath in through her teeth as the contents of a poultice wrapped in damp cheesecloth seeped out over the still raw skin surrounding the puncture wounds. "Ouch! What's in this one, stinging nettle?" She sniffed. "Do I smell garlic? She's not a vampire, no matter what that horrible woman wishes people to believe."

"A little faith," Janet scolded. "Keeps the scarring to a minimum, does it not? Spiders, vipers, jellyfish and snails were too prosaic? You thought to add a venomous human to the list of creatures who've left their mark, yet not managed to kill you?" The maid poured warm water over Cait's hair, rinsing away the dirt and grime of last night's mud puddle before applying a generous amount of soap. "Secure I am in my employment, for I know I'll be following you to your new home."

Cait had gasped when she'd caught a glimpse of her neck in the mirror. Though the swelling had already subsided, it had left behind angry, ulcerated tissue an inch in diameter. Poultice or not, there was certain to be an ugly scar.

She cracked an eye open. "If I'm going anywhere, it's back to Glasgow."

"Not if your mother has her way. While you slept, she penned a dozen missives and sent them winging across London." More water poured over Cait's head. "Given

Cook's mutterings as she fired up the pastry automaton, I expect you are to be auctioned off to the highest bidder at tomorrow afternoon's tea."

"Determined to push, pull or drag me to the altar to see me safely shackled to a gentleman before the press uncovers my name?"

"Indeed, miss."

Her mother's various plots and schemes to marry off a troublesome daughter were old hat, easily foiled and unworthy of concern. Who and when and *if* Cait wed was not something she would let one or both of her parents direct.

Such was not the cause of her mind's mad scramble.

Cait had read the newspapers and gossip rags over tea and dry toast. It was all she'd been able to force down her throat, dropping into the pit of her stomach like a lump of wet cement.

One particular reporter had traced "Mrs. Tagert's" every step—from the moment she'd arrived at the coroner's office until her "husband" had scooped her from the London streets and whisked her away. As yet, the newspaperman hadn't been able to locate the crank hack driver who had conveyed her to the coroner's office. Her identity was safe. For now.

Did it matter anymore?

An unnatural heaviness settled upon her despite the buoyancy of the warm water. Years of intense study, hard work, and exertion to move against society's unrelenting current, one that sought to keep women out of academia and the Queen's service—yet her progress? Barely measurable.

It was only a matter of time before she received a summons to appear before the Duke of Avesbury. Logan had promised her as much. Rather than advancing in her desired profession by showing initiative, Cait feared she'd damaged it beyond repair.

Jack, however, might survive her blunder by throwing his hands in the air and recounting her obstinate insistence that she visit the pub. Only a foolish woman would exit such an establishment—alone—storming off into the dark of night in a fit of temper where any number of dangers lurked, including a venomous creature.

Already a Queen's agent, she predicted he would suffer no career-ending sanctions.

Unfair, really. Had she not convinced a reluctant victim to part with several vials of blood? Flung herself from a moving carriage? Suffered through the horrible effects of a deadly venom to awake with thoughts of how she might study the anomaly that was her own plasma for the benefit of others?

Had Alec or Quinn disobeyed orders yet pulled off such antics, there would have been a slap on the wrist, grudging praise, and a casual "carry on" dismissal whereupon they would return to duties as usual. All while their superior contemplated how to better employ such bright, new stars.

Not so for a woman. Instead, everyone pretended their greatest concern was for her so-called reputation. Such double standards.

Pfft. As if her character mattered in the eyes of London society.

The daughter of a baron, her mother had debuted in *ton* society and made her curtsy to the queen but, to date, all her mother's attempts to ingratiate her daughter among the city's elite were for naught. There was, of course, the nature of Cait's questionable heritage—always a topic for speculation. Nor did it help that her legal father, the wealthy Mr. McCullough, was chronically absent. But she suspected that, here in the Big Smoke, it was the whispers about her mother's past that caused the lords and ladies to distance themselves. Something to do with a footman and a linen closet.

Cait shuddered. She didn't wish to know anything more about *that* incident.

"I've a conundrum, Janet." She flexed her joints, working to stretch and massage stiff muscles back into compliance. Discouraged as she was, laying about the townhome accomplished nothing. Time to take action. "If there's to be any hope of remaining in London, of continuing my work at Lister, I need to return to the laboratories."

Before someone revoked her access to the Ichor Machine. Only there could she test both her blood and the tavern keeper's against the creature's venom. Thank aether the vials had not shattered during the attack.

Jack, as brilliant as he was handsome, had swabbed the bite wound at her neck before rinsing it clean. Eyes filled with burning questions, he'd slipped her a note along with a corked vial holding a ball of absorbent cotton—all while Mother and Logan bickered over the merits of exiting via the front of the Albany versus slipping out the back via the ropewalk.

A Queen's agent and trained physician, he'd been quick to take decisive action. The man would have made a wonderful partner. Husband. She ran a hand over a dull ache that lodged itself beneath her ribcage and sighed. There was no hope for it. He was beyond her reach. Not only was she not his social equal, but her attempt to arouse him with a kiss had been a miserable failure.

Still, he'd honored her wish to avoid a hospital, even if he had summoned Logan. There was no choice but to forgive him for that decision. With her stuttering breath and near-paralysis, the venomous woman had brought her to the perilous edge of death and given her a push.

Janet lifted the edge of the poultice and frowned. "The tissue surrounding the wound is red and angry. You need to rest. Let it heal, or you risk infection."

"I'll be fine." She set aside the poultice and stood, letting water stream down her body.

"You were unconscious and at the mercy of others." Janet handed her a linen towel as she climbed from the tub, then followed Cait back into her bedroom. "If Mr. Tagert hadn't come to his senses and followed you—"

"But he did."

For her maid's sanity, for her mother's and Logan's and—quite frankly—her own, she refused to recount a blurry memory of Jack bent over her prone body, lips sealed to hers as he forced air into her lungs. Of her lurching upright only to vomit over the edge of his bed before sinking back into unconsciousness.

Humiliation burned. But Janet was right. He'd saved her life, earning her undying gratitude and respect, however grudgingly she might bestow it.

Disconcerting to realize there was a limit to her tolerance of biotoxins, but lesson learned. Next time—should there ever be one—she'd proceed with more caution.

Never before had she been reliant upon another for survival. Under normal, experimental conditions, Cait increased her dose of poison by small increments. This was the first time she'd experienced a complete envenomation by a predator intent upon killing its prey.

The closest she'd come to crossing that line before was the night she'd managed to slip Logan's TTX pistol from under his pillow. Loaded with darts laced with tetrodotoxin, the weapon was standard issue for Queen's agents, and she couldn't help but wonder how *her* immune system would react to the poison.

While he'd slept, she'd shot herself twice in the leg. Three darts would kill a man and, therefore, most certainly a woman.

Stopwatch in hand, she'd spent the night flat on her back, cold and alone. Staring at the pipes and cobwebs that hung from the ceiling of her basement laboratory for hours, waiting for her body to clear the toxin, for her limbs to work once more. By dawn, she'd recovered.

Six hours from inoculation until recovery.

She'd recorded the time in her notes. Then shot herself with the remaining dart.

Much to her delight, she'd experienced not even the slightest of effects, and now counted herself immune to the effects of her brother's favorite weapon.

Logan hadn't been as pleased with the results. There had been much yelling.

She smiled at the memory.

Then sobered. Last night's experience had been terrifying.

Yet she'd survived. And there was every reason to believe that she was now immune to the creature's bite, even if the act of slipping on a clean chemise made the muscles of her arms groan in protest.

"A corded corset will suffice today," Cait said. "No boning."

"I should think so." Janet slapped lint and sticking plaster onto the dressing table, her disapproval clear. "The purple gown with the high neck and the simple bodice."

"A few hours in the laboratory is not overly taxing."

"As you say." Janet might not stop her, but neither would she condone such an imprudent decision.

But if Cait wished to retain her position at the Lister Institute, to remain—however peripherally—on the case, she would need to generate compelling data. Prove her value. Demonstrate that she was irreplaceable. A shrinking window of opportunity existed that would close the minute the duke issued his summons.

"The vials," Janet said, accepting the inevitable, "of both blood and venom, are in the kitchen icebox."

"Beside the cobra venom we collected?"

"Exactly so." Swatting aside Cait's unsteady hands, Janet swept her hair into a simple chignon. "Promise me you'll be careful? This venomous creature is bound to learn you've survived and is certain to attack again."

Cait grinned. "I'd like to see her try."

If luck was with her, she might well prove immune.

Still, fangs could rip and tear a person's throat. Next time she encountered the creature, she wanted a TTX pistol pointed at the woman's chest—even if it was a nearby agent who took aim.

CHAPTER NINE

"Miss McCullough," Dr. Whitby greeted her with a tight smile, "while I appreciate that any tasks assigned to you by your brother, Mr. Black, must take precedence here at the Lister Institute, I do expect you to inform our technicians. Someone must feed and water the laboratory rats in your absence."

"My apologies, sir." Cait struggled to keep her feet still. Every toe twitched with the need to be at her research bench, working with the samples tucked deep within the embroidered, tasseled reticule clipped to her belt. Impatient, she rubbed a finger over the black stone of her ring. "It won't happen again."

Assuming she lasted through the day.

"In the next two weeks, I expect you'll wish to begin hematological analysis."

Sooner, really. But not on the rats. On herself. "Yes, of course."

"Before I can authorize your use of the Haimatos Separation Machine," Dr. Whitby continued, "we'll need to schedule a meeting to review your progress and the next steps you plan to take regarding your proposed TTX project. My office, tomorrow at ten?"

"Certainly." She gave a polite nod, took a step sideways. She would be there. If Logan hadn't revoked her access to the laboratory altogether.

Dr. Whitby's frown followed her across the room and, even after he'd turned away, a guilty residue hovered over her as she lit her Bunsen burner. She ought to be preparing dilutions of tetrodotoxin for her neglected rats in preparation for a second round of exposure. Instead, she intended to pour biogel plates to analyze an unknown venom.

She tugged at her collar, pulling it away from the bandage at her neck and told herself that subverting Lister resources without approval was for the greater good.

Her brother was an efficient agent. She could not afford to delay.

With that thought at the forefront of her mind, she donned a laboratory coat and focused on the task before her.

While the liquid media she'd poured into two Petri dishes cooled and solidified, Cait turned her attention to extracting venom residue from the gauze Jack had passed her. Next, she loaded samples of both her blood and that of Mr. Acker into the centrifuge that she might collect serum samples from both.

An hour later, Cait bent over the Petri dishes—one for each of the venomous creature's victims. To set up the double immunodiffusion assays, she punched a cluster of three wells into the now-solid biogel, one set per plate. Then, with a steady hand, she lifted her pipette and filled the wells.

Plate one received ten microliters of venom residue from the creature who had attacked her, ten microliters of cobra venom as a control, and ten microliters of her own serum. Plate two replicated the first, save she used Mr. Acker's serum.

After she sealed the plates with wax—to prevent both contamination and desiccation—there was nothing to do but wait. She lowered herself onto a stool and stared at the deceptively simple experiment before her.

Results might take up to twenty-four hours, but if both serum samples reacted with that of the creature's venom, she would have proof of her own immunity, proof that the same creature had attacked both her and Mr. Acker. Proof that the woman in the carriage was not a vampire, but some strange and poisonous human hybrid.

Cait rolled her shoulders. While she waited, it was time to address her official research project. Developing an anti-toxin to tetrodotoxin. She reached for a bottle of sterile saline—

Only to have it snatched from her hand.

Logan set the flask upon the countertop. "While your mother is much distressed to find you already out of bed, she is not surprised." His eyes bored holes through her skull. "Nor am I."

Crumbling mummies and shrunken heads. She was officially out of time. The next few hours were bound to be pure misery. "I had samples to analyze. Besides, sneaking out of the house is a skill you helped hone. You ought to be proud." A weak argument tossed out in a last-ditch effort to deflect Logan's wrath.

And a failure, judging from the disappointment that rippled across his face, an expression that now hardened into iron resignation.

"Proud?" His eyebrows lifted. "You ignored direct orders, put lives at risk and compromised an investigation. I could go on, but why waste perfectly good air?" He handed her a paper-wrapped package. "From Janet. She implores you to change the bandage and reapply the ointment."

"I will. As soon as I—"

"You know I'm not here to play delivery boy." He jerked his head. "Let's go. Your presence has been requested elsewhere."

"The duke?" She hated the faint tremble in her voice. For years she'd dreamed of meeting him, but now and under such circumstances? Cait's stomach flipped and dove to her knees.

"Did you really think to escape?"

"No." The admission escaped on an exhale. She tucked the Petri dishes into the depths of her reticule, added Janet's packet and turned to a laboratory technician. "I'll be away..." She looked at Logan.

He glowered. "Indefinitely."

The technician sighed.

Outside, the clouds were gray and somber, determined to add to her misery by blotting out the sun with a steady drizzle. Worse, she rode to her doom in a rickety gig driven by her brother and drawn by a clockwork horse—a vehicle that did not possess a hood.

Pride compelled an attempt at preserving her appearance.

Cait opened her parasol—a purple, ruffly affair that did little to keep the uppermost feathers of her hat dry, let alone the rest of her. Though a short cape fell to her elbows, the lace and velvet points of her skirts would never recover.

Their route was scenic and took them through Hyde Park along West Carriage Drive and over the Serpentine. Alongside the road, spring flowers hung their heads, bowed over by the rain. But she refused to take her cue from the colorful blooms. There was every reason to hope that the duke would be amenable to reason.

She lifted her chin. "Am I to return to Glasgow via train or dirigible?"

Logan pushed a lever and the mechanical horse picked up its pace. "You could stay, evaluate the gentlemen who come calling. One or two might have central heating with a warm furnace." He lifted an eyebrow. "Perfect for indulging a reptile collection in an underground lair."

It wasn't the worst idea, save there were precious few potential husbands who would willingly allocate space for their wife to set up a laboratory, let alone permit her to gather a collection of venomous beauties within the walls of their home. Which was why she'd hoped to focus her courtship efforts elsewhere.

She huffed. "If you'd provided me with a list of eligible agents as I asked—"

"Reveal their identities? Their locations?" His narrow glance severed any hope of such an occurrence. "Always impatient. That's why you're in this mess. Not content to earn the trust of my men over time, you forcibly inserted yourself into an investigation against direct orders. How did that work out?"

"Quite well," Cait snapped. She missed the easy amiability they used to share. Once her brother would have championed her cause and laughed away her late-night antics. Annoying to find Logan's new position had turned him staid and proper. "As you've no doubt been informed, I collected blood samples of the only man to survive the predator's bite. Moreover, she was stalking us. Had that woman bitten Mr. Tagert on the neck, he'd be dead." She smirked. "Instead, he's alive and I'm immune."

"You can't know that." He slowed the clockwork horse, took a hard left and bumped the gig off the drive onto a gravel-strewn path.

"Can't I?" Her gaze slid to the lump made by the TTX weapon hidden beneath his coat.

Logan's jaw clenched. Referencing that incident never failed to find its mark. He drew the gig to a halt and jumped down. "The duke will meet you in the Italian Gardens. He wishes to speak with you privately."

The only structure in the gardens was the pump house. It did, however, possess a small terrace. She could see its roofline, a short, if muddy, distance away. Shelter from the unrelenting rain if not the chill that steadily crept its way through the various layers of her clothing to nip at her skin.

"Aren't you even the slightest bit interested in the experiment I set up this morning in the laboratory?" Cait asked as he handed her down.

His lips twisted, but she caught a flash of uncertainty. "You've already claimed immunity."

"So I have. But you haven't asked for proof." She lifted her arm and let her gaze drift to her reticule. Soon, the two biogel plates inside might tell a curious tale to anyone with the patience to listen. "Perhaps this duke you worship will be more interested in what I might have to say about the predator who stalks upon London's streets."

Without waiting for a reply, she turned on her heel with enough speed to smack him in the face with the fringe of her parasol.

The wet slap might just turn out to be the most satisfying moment of her day.

⸻❖⸻

APPREHENSION CURLED IN HIS GUT. So much for a private audience with the duke. These past few months, life was determined to be difficult. Today, it conspired to include the very woman who refused to stay out of his thoughts regardless of the tasks to which he set himself.

Against a backdrop of water lilies, glistening paving stones and the distant Tazza Fountain, none other than Cait

—Miss McCullough, he reminded himself—climbed the stairs to stand beneath the stone arch of the portico.

In retrospect, he ought to have known a meeting held in the Pump House at the Italian Gardens in the midst of a persistent drizzle would not proceed with anything resembling normalcy.

"Good morning, Miss McCullough." He doffed his top hat. "You look well." Stunning, really. Especially for someone who had nearly died in his bed last night. Color had returned to her cheeks. Spark to her eyes. Spring to her step. How on Earth had she made such a rapid recovery? "No ill side effects?"

"Ill?" She collapsed her ornamental parasol and gave it a brisk shake. "A touch of lingering muscle stiffness. A wound that promises to develop into an unsightly scar. But, as you see, I am quite well." Glancing about the portico and finding them alone, she stepped closer to place a gloved hand upon his wrist. "I must thank you for your swift and decisive actions." Her cheeks grew red. "It's not everyone who can share the breath of life."

His gaze fell upon the bow of her lips. A jolt crackled down his spine and heated the air in his lungs. There it was again. That inexplicable attraction. But she was thanking him for medical services, not inviting his touch. Or his kiss. No, he'd had that opportunity and let it slip past, unanswered, in a mistaken bid for privacy and propriety.

And it wasn't one that could be corrected now. Not with the duke's imminent arrival.

"You're very welcome. Your brother received a complete

report of the attack and its effects, all save that particular detail. Self-preservation, really. The sight of your corset upon my floor nearly had him calling for pistols at dawn."

Her breath caught. Did she too imagine their evening with an altogether different outcome?

Dark eyes flashed, and a laugh escaped her lips. "A wise choice. My brother is, as noted, overprotective of his sister." Her hand fell away and he mourned its loss. "I do hope the newspaper headlines haven't caused you much grief?"

Jack forced out a slow, controlled exhalation. "They might yet," he admitted. "The Duke of Avesbury is an efficient man. Given our summons, we're likely to both lose our positions this morning."

"That remains to be seen," the gentleman himself said, shattering their intimate tête-à-tête. They jumped away from each other. "A pleasure to finally meet you, Miss McCullough. I do apologize for the damp setting, but I judged it best to hold this conclave in a location the newspaper reporters would be unlikely to discover." The duke set his briefcase upon the stone floor.

Out in the gardens, a man and a woman strolled amidst the water gardens beneath black umbrellas. Waiting. Watching. He recognized them both. Mr. Black and the duke's wife, Lady Avesbury. Nothing good could come of their combined presence. This was no mere dismissal. Something more was afoot.

Suspicion planted itself beneath the portico and dug in its roots, fully prepared to burst into catastrophic bloom.

The duke glanced from Jack to Cait, then cleared his

throat. "I have been appraised of the eventful evening the two of you spent in each other's company. Of the gossip that nips at Mr. Tagert's heels, of the continued efforts by reporters to discover Miss McCullough's identity. A most unfortunate situation. Abilities aside, I cannot have so much public attention directed at those who are in my employ. Mr. Black and I agree that the termination of both your positions is the logical decision."

"Even if I could produce new information shedding light upon the case?" Cait's words tumbled forth in a rush while Jack drew breath, ready to lodge his own objection.

The duke lifted a hand. "Let me finish." Cait sagged. "I will hear you out momentarily, Miss McCullough."

Gritting his teeth, Jack held his tongue.

"Fortunately for you both, my duchess has the honor and duty of leading her own team of informants, one of whom is Mr. Tagert's sister. As such, she is sympathetic to your quandary and has proposed a solution that will permit you both to continue your work on behalf of the Queen and Lister Institute."

Wonderful. Meddling on the highest level. Blessing or curse?

"With both of you now under extreme societal pressure to select a spouse," the duke continued, "the problem can be reframed as an opportunity."

Jack's heart stopped, fell to his feet, then jumped into his throat. Where it stuck, leaving him mute. The duke could not mean—

"If the two of you agree to marry, confidentiality within

the relationship will be assured, rendering most of our concerns moot. You'll let it be known you are indeed man and wife. That a quiet ceremony was performed with only three individuals as witnesses, Mr. Logan Black and the Duke and Duchess of Avesbury."

The duke nodded toward the gardens where a third individual approached the Queen's agent and former societal liaison. An officiant of the church, no doubt, bearing a special license upon which both their names would be inked.

"Backdated, I presume?" Jack's wry comment belied his pounding heart.

"Of course."

Cait's gaze jumped from the duke to Jack and back again. She took a step away. Turned and came back. Breathless, she asked, "A real marriage?"

The prospect of a precipitous marriage had rendered her... excited?

He frowned, uncertain.

"Quite." The duke cleared his throat. "You will both live and work together. Beyond that, I won't presume to dictate the particulars of your arrangement. Take a few minutes to consider if we should proceed." He snapped open an umbrella and joined the others beside the fountain.

A wife. This was a bad idea, given the status of his health. Even before his diagnosis, he'd not thought to take one so soon, if ever. Did he even want one? Not particularly. Did he wish to continue his work as an agent? Yes. And that meant taking a wife. One in particular.

At least the proposed bride appeared amenable.

Miss Cait McCullough. A woman in possession of a perplexing secret. A woman Mr. Black called his sister. A woman from a complicated and tangled family. She wouldn't make life easy, that was certain.

Not that his contributions to the marriage would be sunshine and roses.

Cait herself was a curious contradiction. All that was fashionable and stylish, her attire called attention in the right ways to her slender figure, to its gentle curves. As did the feathered hat situated upon a mesmerizing twist of upswept hair.

She could flash a disarming smile with those wide, full lips and throw him off balance. All while her dark eyes sparkled with mischief and plans and purpose and drive.

Life with her would be anything but dull. Both a concern and a temptation.

But when was the straightforward path ever interesting?

"They'll say I trapped you." Cait met his gaze, daring him to disagree.

"Yes."

"Though it was not my intention, it will be, in part, true." She threw a hand in the air and began to pace, a swirl of purple silk and black velvet as she assessed their circumstances. "Had I not taken it upon myself to personally visit the coroner where—"

"You took my name for expediency," Jack finished. "You'll also recall I allowed the claim to stand unchallenged. Then invoked the convenient lie yet again as the evening progressed before sweeping you away to my apartments."

She turned. "A mistake."

"Was it? I made what I believed to be the best possible decision in the moment." He caught her wrist. Stopped her where she stood. "Regardless, let's not make another."

"A hasty marriage, for example?"

"I'm not so certain. Is it such a bad idea? Queen's agents are often called upon to make snap decisions based upon the limited facts available to them."

She gaped. "You're sincerely considering this?"

Was he?

"Yes. For entirely selfish reasons." He had to tell her. Any decision reached needed to account for the possibility that their marriage might be a brief one.

"As am I." Contemplative now, she circled him. "You're handsome. Intelligent. Second in line for a title. All reasons other women might rank you above other men. Each are points in your favor, but my top priority is to expedite the process of becoming a Queen's agent."

And he was a convenient steppingstone. An honest answer. "No interest in becoming a societal liaison?"

She rolled her eyes. "As if such was an option for me. I possess none of the social qualifications."

All unfortunately true. He gave an understanding nod.

"And your selfish reasons?" she asked.

He took a deep breath. "I've a tumor lodged within my skull." He'd begin as he meant to go on, with honesty. It was only fair to give her this chance to walk away, even if it ended his career as an agent.

Her lips formed a soft "oh". She glanced away, then back. "I'm so very sorry. I presume it's deadly?"

His laugh was rueful. "Not exactly." He took a deep breath. "It's a benign pituitary adenoma. Imminent death is not a worry, though there are—and will be—significant side effects. The primary and direct threat is to my eyesight, a complication I find difficult, no, impossible to accept. For now, it largely impacts only a portion of my peripheral vision. Lord Thornton is exploring survivable surgical options on my behalf."

Understanding filled her eyes. "Hence your interest in the venomous woman's extraction device."

He nodded. "It appears to be an advanced device..."

"You wish to catch the not-a-vampire so that you might examine her device, the one used upon that poor woman, in hopes that it might be modified to suit your needs?"

"Stopping the murders is my central goal, but any technological revelations would be welcome." From the corner of his eye, he caught the duke and duchess glancing in their direction. Sand ran quickly through the hourglass. There was no help for it. Courtship reduced to a few blunt sentences. "Regardless of the duration of our marriage, I've considerable resources to offer. You're beautiful, brilliant and well-connected. It would be an be honor to call you my wife."

"Beautiful?" She hesitated, frowned, then began to turn away. "Perhaps this is a bad idea."

She doubted his attraction? There was no avoiding it then. He caught her elbow. "Is this about the kiss?"

Scowling, she yanked her arm away. "Of course it's about the kiss. Beautiful, yet somehow not appealing? The half-truth trips easily from your tongue. I want a partner and a husband, not a disinterested man prone to extramarital affairs. Trust would be compromised. I won't have it, not to save my career or yours."

"Disinterest?" A glance toward the garden informed him that their audience had once again turned their backs, but this moment of privacy would be fleeting. "That's your sole objection?"

Her jaw jutted, obstinate. Willing to burn both their futures to the ground because she believed he wouldn't honor his vows. "It is a valid concern."

One that was easy enough to address.

Was he really going to do this? Commit to a lifetime—however long or short that might be—with a woman he'd known for less than thirty-six hours?

It seemed so.

"I count myself an honorable gentleman, not one who lightly breaks promises or abandons his responsibility." He dropped his hands to her hips, onto the points of the soft velvet belt encircling her waist, careful to keep his grip light. "An entire life spent observing the proprieties," he pushed, forcing her to take a step backward, "does not lend itself to easy displays of affection in a Covent Garden pub."

A faint smile teased her lips now. "Performance anxiety?"

He scoffed. He'd been as stiff as an iron poker against her hip and struggling for control. How had she not noticed?

"Rather a preference for keeping private matters private. Especially in front of family members prone to indiscretion."

Another step—one she took with him—brought them into the corner of the stone shelter. So close that the silk of her skirts folded about the wool of his trousers, close enough for her soft breath to mingle with his own. He lifted his palm to her smooth cheek and traced the fullness of her lower lip with his thumb.

She nipped at it. "You're wasting time." She slipped her arms about his neck, fingers dancing along the edge of his hair. "You should know I'm no innocent. Your display of gentlemanly restraint won't convince me of anything."

Her declaration did not surprise him. Cait was a woman who would investigate anything that intrigued her, all to satisfy curiosity. Why not sexual relations?

"I don't care about any men in your past."

"No?"

"No. So long as they stay there." But she was correct. He'd been holding back. "I find you intensely attractive." He nibbled at the lobe of her ear. "Fascinatingly intelligent." Then trailed his lips over the edge of her jaw, inhaling the scent of her skin. "Imagine what we might accomplish together as partners."

"As Queen's agents in the field?" Her breath was a soft exhalation, but no less demanding because of it. "Or as husband and wife?"

"Both, as that's what you wish." Envisioning how they could pass the duller hours of such work had portions of his lower anatomy once again standing at full attention. He pressed her against the stone wall, letting her feel his desire. "I look forward to exploring the possibilities of what we can achieve together, both in the proverbial marriage bed, and out of it."

Beneath her cape, he palmed the softness of her breast, reveling in its delicate curve before dragging the pad of his thumb over its tip. Teasing. Delighting in a primitive satisfaction as a moan caught in her throat.

"I begin to think we might suit, yet I've still not been properly kissed." Her hands pulled at the base of his skull, urging his face closer. "And, therefore, remain unconvinced."

"Very well." With that, he brought his lips down upon hers, pouring passion into his kiss as if his life depended upon her pleasure. And as flames ignited in his blood and rushed through his veins, he rather thought it might.

CHAPTER TEN

IS KISS WAS EVERYTHING and more.

Both hard and soft at once, both a rebuke and a caress.

Her fingers spiked into the soft waves of his hair, then tightened, crushing his mouth to hers, opening and welcoming the invasion of his most talented tongue as it drove the breath from her lungs and set her heart pounding.

The rigidly contained passion she'd glimpsed as they rode through the streets of London broke free and ignited, sparking desire wherever they touched, burning away any doubt that he found her less than desirable.

Only the cold stone at her back anchored her in the present. An existence altered in a heartbeat with the duke's proposed solution. One which would soon present an officiant, a marriage license and witnesses—then demand an answer.

This had to stop before the last of their good sense burned away. Cait shoved hard at his shoulders.

For a long moment, they stared at each other, chests heaving, struggling to regain control. His eyes searched hers, betraying a note of vulnerability she suspected he rarely permitted anyone to glimpse.

"Very well," she managed. "I'm persuaded of our physical compatibility." Slowly, higher brain centers engaged, insisting there was more to discuss. "If we speak vows, you'll honor yours?"

"I will," he breathed. "And expect the same of you."

"Agreed. But we both have pasts, complicated by secrets that are bound to tangle and tug."

"Along with difficult and often irritating families." He reached out to tuck a loose strand of hair behind her ear.

"A multitude of problems will arise." She turned her face into the roughness of his palm, wondering if she'd feel his touch across the whole of her body tonight. "It's a lot to ask. Of both of us."

"It is."

Was that doubt that crept into his voice?

Footfalls sounded on the pavement. Their time alone together was almost at an end.

"Tagert!" her brother barked. "Step away from my sister."

There was a clatter, the sound of umbrellas tossed aside as stomping feet approached.

"Do see reason, Mr. Black," a higher, yet no less commanding, voice chided.

Jack winced. "Have you met the duchess?"

"No, but her reputation precedes her." Her stomach quaked. "The repercussions of our night together must be numerous and far-reaching if the duchess herself is here to champion our marriage."

"You can be certain at least a half-dozen motivations drive her interest." His fingers brushed over the velvet edge of her sleeve. "The moment of truth has arrived. Will you marry me, Miss McCullough?"

There would be no going back. Only forward. For better or for worse, however long or short their time together.

"Yes, I accept." She swallowed and attempted to lighten the moment. "A quick ceremony ensures your body will not be found floating, lifeless, in the Long Water while I live out my existence locked in a tall tower."

Jack huffed a laugh. "Nonetheless, I expect your brother will make this difficult. Time to face the music." In a single smooth motion, his arm wrapped about her waist and spun her about. "Perfect timing. Miss McCullough has just agreed to become my wife."

"Absolutely not." Logan scowled, trying to break free from the vice-like grip the duchess had upon his arm. An arm that ended in a tightly balled fist. He glared at the duke. "Is it my resignation you're after?"

"Don't be melodramatic," the duke answered. "If Mr. Tagert does not marry her, it will ruin them both. Besides, your sister has all but buried my desk with missives imploring me to allow her to become a Queen's agent. Marriage is a necessary first step."

Beside her, Jack stiffened. His arm fell from her waist, and her stomach did a slow turn as a cool gust of air swirled between him. Had she intended to set out lures? Yes, of course. Not for him in particular. Many agents might have fit her needs, but she did have standards, ones he met and exceeded.

Why was this a problem? Would he back out? She hoped not. She clasped her hands and pressed them to her midsection, urging her stomach to settle. He was a man of reason. Any misunderstandings could be addressed later. Her course was decided and she refused to turn back. But she could not force Jack to her will.

The Duke of Avesbury placed his umbrella upon the floor beside his briefcase. "Lady Avesbury, allow me to present Miss McCullough, sister to our Mr. Black. Miss McCullough, my wife, the Duchess of Avesbury."

Cait dropped a curtsy. "I'm honored."

"As you should be," the duchess said. "Shall we proceed?"

"No." Logan barked. "I forbid it."

"You cannot." Cait scowled at her brother. "I'm of age."

"Had I known why the duke insisted I bring you here—"

"Which is exactly why you were left uniformed, Mr. Black," the duchess snapped.

"If you wish, you may excuse yourself from the proceedings," the duke said. "Otherwise, stiff upper lip. We've other matters to attend to this day, and the newlyweds will have a train to catch."

"Wait." Jack held up a hand. "A train?"

She quite agreed with his objection. Trains led *out* of London.

"On a honeymoon," the duchess stated. "To Menwith."

Where on Earth was Menwith? Did it matter? It wasn't in London, and they needed to be in London to hunt the not-a-vampire.

Jack pinched the bridge of his nose. "You intend to send us to the Grand Menwith Hotel and Spa under the guise of a honeymoon? Now?"

Guise? The word burrowed beneath her skin in a most irritating manner.

"Exactly so," the duke said.

"What of the investigation..." Cait trailed off. She wanted this case. Badly. And with the dark cloud that had descended upon Jack's visage, she was no longer quite so eager to find herself alone with him. But one did not challenge a duke's decree.

Yet Jack did just that. "What business has the Crown delving into my personal concerns?"

"It's your own fault, Tagert, sending out personal inquiries by bird." Black crossed his arms. "Ones which tapped into agency resources." He tipped his head toward the duchess. "An intercepted skeet pigeon was brought to her attention."

Confused, Cait asked, "Inquiries about?"

"My brother," Jack answered without so much as a glance in her direction. "Concerning a worrisome business venture in North Yorkshire. One not linked to the attacks."

"Or is it?" The duchess' smile was long-suffering.

"Finding it curious, I penned my own questions. That's quite a sum that Lord Aubrey and the new Lord Saltwell invested in a friend's venture. Everything appears above board with regards to the hotel and Turkish baths, but smiles grew strained and conversation terse when I inquired as to the precise nature of the special services offered by our good doctor, Mr. Oakes. All I could ascertain was that one patron was heard to joke about therapy being 'a pain in the neck'."

"A tenuous connection to the venomous creature at best," Cait pointed out.

The duchess lifted a silk-gloved finger. "*And* the deceased Lord Saltwell recently took an extended trip north. Shortly thereafter, he met an untimely end at the hands—or fangs—of an as yet unidentified, bloodthirsty creature. In your family's townhome."

After a long few moments of stunned silence, Cait turned to Jack. "Is it possible your brother's arrival at the pub was not unconnected with the venomous woman waiting in the carriage?"

Unwilling to concede the point, his mouth flattened into a grim, flat line. Finally, he gave a tight nod. "With Aubrey, anything is possible."

"Well then," Cait said, "the duchess has presented us with opportunity. A precipitous marriage followed by an immediate honeymoon signals romance, and we want to throw a wet blanket over any gossip, not fan the flames." She laid a hand upon his arm. "Any possible connection merits further investigation, if only to allay your fears that he acted rashly by investing in this hotel and spa."

The duchess gave her an approving nod. "Moreover, it's the only lead we have."

"Two birds, one stone," the duke said, delighted with the plan.

"And when the creature strikes again?" Jack dug in.

"It's nothing that Mr. Black can't handle while you're gone," the duke said.

Logan bared his teeth in the facsimile of a smile. Already overworked, her marriage and sanctioned involvement in this investigation meant her brother was about to blow a gasket.

"Now that we're agreed," the duchess' eyebrows arched, her expression making it clear that she would hear no further objections, "there is one final detail."

Jack's arm tightened beneath her palm.

"I've some expertise in the expectations of *ton* matrimony and my network is wide." The duchess' expression grew cynical. "Rumors suggest that the Menwith Spa provides treatments aimed at improving virility and, ultimately, fertility. Men will go to ridiculous lengths and costs to ensure their legacy. Use this detail to your advantage."

Jack sputtered and Logan growled while an embarrassed heat prickled Cait's skin.

She dropped her hand. "You want us to... We're to..."

"Pose as newlyweds who wish to conceive as soon as possible," the duchess finished. "Yes. Partake of the recommended therapy and discover—"

"Therapy? There's nothing wrong with my—" Jack choked.

The duchess turned toward her husband with a frown.

"I do not often find myself in the wrong, but these two seem ill-suited. For each other and the assignment. I rescind my earlier recommendation." She released Logan's arm and turned. "Dismiss them both and send Lord and Lady Thornton."

"Absolutely not," Jack said. "I refuse to pass this investigation to another. We'll go."

"Only if you are both agents in good standing." The duke stood firm. "A category into which neither prospective bride nor groom currently fall as unmarried individuals. Shall we amend that?"

Jack huffed a breath. "Fine."

Not a trace of his former enthusiasm for their nuptials remained, and the weight of his irritation dimmed her hopes for their future. She twisted her poison ring, conflicted. This might be a mistake, marriage for the sake of her career. For his.

But no other path forward within the Queen's agents remained. If she refused, she would be sent away from the Lister Institute in shame. What then? A prosaic life. London or Glasgow, married or an old maid, she would find herself working, as she always had, in a laboratory alone.

The duke looked to Cait. "Train tickets and a room reservation have been made under the names of Mr. and Mrs. Tagert. No point in pseudonyms when we wish to establish the veracity of a love match. Many guests are of a high rank. You will be under scrutiny. Do you feel up to the role, Miss McCullough?"

Agents often assumed identities. Could she portray a

young woman in love? Smiles, blushes, discreet touches. The occasional stolen kiss when prying eyes were upon them. Her gaze slid sideways and caught upon Jack's own intent stare.

Dangerous eyes set in a face of hard planes that promised no leniency. Easy to see how he scared away young ladies. But beneath the wide breadth of his chest beat a romantic heart.

Foolishly, she still hoped to lay a claim upon his affections.

No, it would be no trial to publicly proclaim that Mr. Jack Tagert was a man worth having.

"I'm ready."

"Excellent." The duke waved his hand, beckoning the minister forward. "Let's begin."

Lady Avesbury produced a simple gold band from her reticule, and the minister cleared his throat, glanced down at the book in his hand, and began. "Dearly beloved, we are gathered here together..."

A few minutes later, it was done.

Judging from her husband's scowl, she was an unhappily married woman.

He'd fallen victim to the classic parson's trap, one the duke and duchess had helped spring. Or was it an arranged marriage? No, more a scheme cobbled together on the fly and neatly tied up with a pretty bow, rather than the carefully crafted alliance more commonly known among the *ton*.

Cunningly executed, regardless.

Cogs, what kind of marriage had he allowed himself to be steered into? How steep a price would he pay that he might be allowed to put his life on the line in the pursuit of a deadly, venomous beauty? All while guarding a woman, now his wife, who seemed hell-bent on putting her own life at risk to catch the very same creature.

"Keep her safe, or I'll peel off strips of your flesh to fish for kraken on the Vauxhall Bridge," Black growled after kissing his sister goodbye on the train platform and handing her into a private compartment. No doubt the impending task of informing Cait's mother of her daughter's precipitous marriage and immediate honeymoon rendered him grumpy and irascible.

"Safe. Your sister? Is such a thing possible?" Jack asked. Annoyance simmered as it coursed through his veins. "It's like you've never met her. The word simply does not apply. Given her proclivity for all things poisonous and deadly, it'll be a miracle if I survive the honeymoon, let alone the wedding night."

A low blow, reminding Black exactly what his sister would be up to later this very evening? He didn't care. In for a penny in for a pound. Their marriage might be arranged, but they'd both agreed it would neither be celibate nor faithless. Warmth flooded his body at the anticipation of sharing her bed.

"If you had only—"

"You dragged her into this. She followed me." Jack jabbed a finger into Black's chest. "Who trapped who?"

True, a wife as an agent suited him. He himself had proffered the idea. But his stomach sank at the idea that *any* unmarried Queen's agent would have served Cait's cause equally.

No, he revised his position, the moment he'd attached himself to the vampire case, he'd become her sole target. It burned that the duke valued him so little that Jack was easily presented to a favored agent's sister for social and career advancement.

His words found their mark, rendering his new brother-in-law speechless. But Black was not a man to cross. Jack backed away from the glowering agent onto the train, unwilling to turn his back and present an easy target for a knife.

He landed on a red velvet-covered bench opposite his wife. Dragging in a lungful of damp, spring air, he released his breath slowly, conscious that he did not wish anger to color the start of his marriage, regardless of his feelings.

As the train pulled away from the station with great huffs and chuffs and a screech of iron wheels upon steel tracks, Cait ventured a smile. "Is it too much to hope that the frown carved into your stoic face is due to a deep-seated worry that the duchess herself oversaw the packing of our trunks?"

Not trusting himself yet to speak, Jack lifted an eyebrow.

"All new attire, selected by tailors and dressmakers on Bond Street with only our measurements from which to work." She removed her gloves and unpinned her hat, then set both beside her reticule.

Such glorious hair. Dark waves twisted into submission and fastened in place. Resentment battled with a certain sense of gratification that he could soon see it cascade free about her bare shoulders.

"Will my corsets be plain cotton?" Cait mused aloud. "My stockings of itchy wool, my every gown no more than serviceable? Or will there be miles of ruffles, ribbons and beads stitched onto low-cut gowns?" She leaned forward, eyes wide. "Perhaps they packed you striped knee breeches and an orange, paisley cravat? Or maybe waistcoats of yellow silk with embroidered, blue butterflies?"

He huffed a laugh. Impossible not to warm to her game. He kicked up the corner of his mouth and added a new level of heat, all while wondering at the transformation of his earlier ire. "More to the point, were they informed that we were newlyweds? Or did they believe I required a flannel nightshirt and you a high-necked cotton nightgown?"

Her cheeks colored, but she rose to the occasion. "Better an indecent scrap of satin trimmed with lace?"

An image of Cait in his bed crept to mind, one where he wasn't fighting to save her life. One where she encouraged his eager explorations with soft sighs and sharp cries as he peeled away soft layers of silk to—

"Which reminds me." She fell back against the cushions. "We know so very little about each other. I've married a man who once trained to become a physician, then worked alongside cryptozoologists, but holds no degrees nor commands any laboratory space. Care to explain? Or shall I make up wild stories when asked?" The grin that stretched her mouth took on a playful air. "A different one each time, I should think. The sight of blood makes him ill. He can't stand the sound of patients screaming. There was an incident in the laboratory involving a pteryform—" she clamped her lips together, then whispered, "but I'm not to speak of it."

He laughed. "My training is, upon occasion, useful in the field. But neither medicine nor flying creatures proved a true calling. Jack of all trades, you'll recall. All skills have served me well as a Queen's agent." He narrowed his eyes. "I note similarities to your own arrival at Lister Laboratories."

His wife tipped her head, acknowledging a certain truth. "True. I'm a self-taught poison expert with little interest in pursuing a formal degree or permanently ensconcing myself within laboratory walls."

"I've a similar aversion to close walls and missions afford me an opportunity to locate things people do not want found." He gave a half shrug. "A product of my childhood. A father with addictive tendencies and mother determined to present the perfect façade. Mix in a spoiled and misbehaved brother intent upon self-destruction, and my upbringing was a proving ground for self-preservation." Much of which also applied to Angela, traits which had unfortunately caught the duchess' attention.

"And the constant travel keeps you from close familial contact?"

"There's that. Though I happen to enjoy travel, field-work in particular."

"Have you found your aim with a rifle more accurate than holding a scalpel?"

That sobered him.

"Sorry," she murmured. "That was insensitive. Nothing is amusing about your prognosis."

"If also true. Or, rather, it was. I already experience occasional double vision." He ran a hand over his eyes. "For now, it comes and goes. Exhaustion does not help." Time to shift from fact to fiction. He didn't want her pity. "At the baths, we'll require a cover story."

"We were instructed to be ourselves."

"Inasmuch as is possible." He crossed his arms, let amusement ripple over his face. "Would you inform the world that we met across a cadaver? Spent a London evening together following the trail of a venomous creature? How you suffered a near-fatal bite, then slept off the effects in my bed?"

"Certainly not!" She snapped her mouth shut, then tapped her lips with a fingertip. "I've noted a greenhouse perched upon Lister's rooftop. Perhaps we met there?"

"No." He shook his head. "We can do better. An omnibus. You climbed aboard the wrong one and found yourself far from your stop. I escorted you home."

"Unacceptable. I do not require a chaperone, nor would I make such a mistake." She twisted her lips. "An omnibus. You stepped on my hem and tore my dress, making me miss my stop. Then you walked me home, apologizing profusely."

He barked a laugh. "Are you ever wrong?"

"Rarely. Hen's teeth are more common."

"Very well," he snorted. "A ruined gown it is."

"Now, about my brother, why the hostility? In the morgue where we did not meet, you and Lord Thornton were clearly concealing your prognosis from him, so it's not that he's threatened to terminate your status as an active agent."

"Not yet. But if—or when—he finds out, he'll see my status as an active agent terminated."

Cait lifted her eyebrows and spread her hands. "You dislike your new brother-in-law because..."

His fingers tightened about his arms. A wife would know about her sister-in-law. "During my recent mission abroad, he had the audacity to help the duchess arrange and execute the marriage of my sister, Angela, to an Icelandic nobleman."

Cait frowned. "That's a problem because?"

"He knew my objections to her becoming a societal liaison." Jack closed his eyes for a moment. From all reports, his petite sister, often compared to a china shepherdess with her rose-bud mouth and bright blue eyes, had been a smashing success during her first Season. Many had offered for her hand, but she had refused them all.

He had wanted better for her than a life in service, bearing the children of a man the Crown feared. When word of her impending marriage had reached him, he'd wrapped up his foreign assignment and hurried back, but she'd been gone before his feet even touched British soil.

"Whatever for?" Cait stiffened. "Such marriages are arranged by the duchess, that a woman might serve the Crown, but are not forced."

"She was relocated to a cold, remote island with only three months of official training. That's very little preparation, even for a societal liaison. Moreover, her marriage exposed her to direct and immediate danger. That floating castle that nearly tipped into the sea? She was on it. She could have died."

"Yet didn't," Cait pointed out. "I like her already. She and I both have brothers who are peas in a pod." His bride rolled her eyes. "And such similar stories. I nearly died to earn my chance at becoming an agent." She spread her hands wide. "Then married, that I might undertake a mission with no training. But I'll learn."

His sister possessed little in the way of skills, though her determination knew no bounds. "You're different. Stronger."

An eyebrow lifted. "More deadly?"

"Of a certainty."

"Yet my brother objects." Cait huffed, then fell back against her seat, arms crossed. "So predictable. Men. Both of you think your sisters delicate flowers, incapable of strong, independent thought or action though evidence to the contrary has been staring you in the face your entire lives. She knew what she was doing, have no doubt."

"As you did?" He narrowed his eyes, disliking the oily feeling that slid down his back insisting he'd been caught like a rat in a trap.

"As I did."

His nostrils flared. "As we're on the topic, what, precisely, made you agree to marry me? Beyond retaining your access to the hallowed halls of the Lister Institute?"

Chin lifted, she met his gaze. "A yearning for adventure. Travel. I'm done chaining myself to a laboratory bench and missing all the fun."

A dull ache settled into his chest. "The man himself didn't factor in?"

"You need to ask?"

He stared back, silent. Waiting.

"Well, if I'm to be brutally honest..." Her narrowed eyes swept over him from head to toe. "I had every expectation that I was marrying an intelligent man. But it's entirely possible my judgment was unduly swayed by an expert kiss and little else."

With that, her lips pursed, and she turned her head to glare at the dark shapes outside rushing past as the train rattled and swayed its way north, leaving Jack to contemplate the quagmire that threatened to suck him under.

His heart wanted to trust her, but life experience worried that disappointment lurked beneath the surface. Either way, it seemed the next move would be his.

CHAPTER ELEVEN

T HOUGH EXHAUSTED BY HOURS of stony silence and frosty politeness, Cait swore the blinding brilliance of the Grand Menwith Hotel could wake the dead.

Their arrival had been delayed due to the midair collision of a pteryform and dirigible outside London. Track clearance had taken hours ensuring that their journey north to the Harrogate station felt nothing short of interminable.

Even then, reaching their final destination had involved a long carriage ride and an unsolicited lecture delivered by a fellow passenger. By the time the vehicle rolled to a stop, she considered herself an expert on the history and mineral content—iron and sulfur—of the hot springs that welled upward to fill the spa's baths.

The hotel burned coal gas at a rate rivaling any London hotel. Light pooled beneath gas lamps lining its circular drive, splashed across the entryway, and flooded every corner of the marble-paved and gilt-encrusted lobby.

Lord Aubrey and friends had spared no expense.

White-gloved staff descended upon them in a flurry of activity. Dazed, damp and disheveled from the eventful day, Cait crossed the plush red carpet following a uniformed attendant assigned to lead the newlyweds to their suite.

She clutched her reticule and its precious contents.

How many hours had passed since she plated the double immunodiffusion biogels? She counted fifteen. By daybreak, results would be definitive.

At which point, she would have to make a decision.

Could she trust Jack enough to tell him the complete and unedited truth when no one—not Logan, not Janet, not her mother—knew the full extent of her secrets? Or, if she were being brutally honest, not even herself? Her heritage was a patchwork of parts that didn't quite piece together to make a whole no matter the efforts she'd made to stitch them together, bit by bit.

Her near perfect health. An inexplicable resistance to toxic substances of an organic nature. A biological father who reportedly hailed from the subcontinent of India. A man whose name Cait's mother could barely pronounce. A traveler forever on the move amidst gypsies and carnival performers. A man who, in all likelihood, had left British shores long ago. What exactly about his immune system set him, and therefore her, apart?

As the basis for her own research, she longed for

specifics. But the need to know was deeper, less cerebral and more visceral. Who, exactly, was she? *What* was she?

Every time she caught a glimpse of a caravan, or the striped and pointed peak of a circus tent, she had inquired after her father—only to be met with blank stares or the quick shake of a head.

Which was why—when no one was looking—she'd snatched up a flier nailed to a pillar at the train station pinpointing the exact location of Professor Grimaldi's Floating Cabinet of Curiosities. Tethered nearby, out on the moors, there wasn't a chance she'd leave Yorkshire without a visit. With or without Jack in tow.

Leading her back to the questions of how much she ought to reveal to her new husband. He already knew she was an aberration, but the gulf of resentment stretching between them gave her reservations.

Both of them were on their own quests. Both refused to accept their current circumstances. He sought to save his eyesight without losing his livelihood. She wanted more than ceaseless toil in a laboratory. Adventure. Travel. To better understand her gifts.

She snorted.

They needed each other.

For now, she pushed all concerns and doubts aside.

Doors were thrown open, arms waved. A bellboy bustled past with their trunks. The newlywed suite included a sitting room, washroom, dressing room and *two* bedrooms. A small comfort that there was no need to confront a complete and total loss of personal privacy.

Yet.

Grateful, she submitted to the deft fingers of a maid who helped her undress and bundled away her rumpled clothing —all while a steam maid unpacked.

The silk of a lace-edged nightgown skimmed over Cait's skin and a tall glass of water was pressed into her hands. "Drawn directly from the Menwith Well itself just this morning. Will that be all, ma'am?"

Cait sniffed the water, wrinkling her nose at the smell. "The sulfur is strong."

"Good for the hair and skin," the maid extolled. "And most excellent at resolving blockages of the bowels."

"Lovely. Just the thing a bride needs." She set down the glass. "Thank you."

Lips twitching, the maid dipped a curtsy and departed.

Cait slipped a hand over the whisper of barely-there silk, a nice touch on the duchess' part, but... Aether. This was her wedding night, and she was bone-tired, not to mention tied in knots over the unknowable mindset of her new husband.

Should she go to him? Would he come to her?

She dropped her head into her hands. Eyes closed, she sighed. This was not at all a promising start to a successful union.

A soft knock sounded.

She straightened and pulled her shoulders back. Any delays would only extend the torment. "Come."

The door opened. In a heartbeat, all fatigue evaporated.

Jack was a sight to behold. Tousled locks above dark eyebrows and the rough scruff of a beard. A landscape of texture that made her fingers ache to explore. All taken in before her eyes drifted away from his face and fell upon the black brocade robe wrapped about his torso, fabric perfectly cut to emphasize his broad shoulders and narrow hips and provide a tantalizing view of the hair scattered across his chest.

He slipped a finger beneath the lace at her shoulder, sending a shiver across her skin. "Everything I could have hoped for and more."

With that, his lips met hers in a slow, bone-melting kiss. A soft and tender exploration, full of seductive promises. She rose onto toe-tips and leaned forward, sighing in encouragement, but he didn't drop his hands to her hips, gather her close or nudge her toward the bed.

Cait fell back onto her heels and looked into his shadowed eyes where ambivalence flickered.

"Not prepared to make the marriage binding?" she ventured, refusing to step backward. To indicate in any way that such an outcome was acceptable.

"Not tonight. We both need to rest." But neither did he retreat. Instead, he caught a tendril of her hair between his thumb and forefinger, toyed with the curl at its end. Then his hand touched upon the bandage at her neck. "The bite?"

"Healing. Nothing to worry about." She trailed a finger downward, over the rough hair on his chest, parting the folds of his dressing gown, hooking upon the sash at his waist. With a gentle tug, the knot fell free and the two halves opened.

Nothing disappointing lay beneath, save the trousers that

hung low upon his hips. And even they were admirably tented. A broad, muscled chest above ridged abdominal muscles flattened into an enticing vee, one that kept redirecting her eyes to the rather large promise of his male anatomy.

Cait hummed her appreciation.

Once there'd been a boy who worked for his father in a bookshop. Months had passed in harmless flirtation, until she'd arrived one afternoon to find the store empty and his father away. They'd made excellent use of a closed sign and a back storage room. She regretted nothing. But he'd been just that. A boy.

Before her stood a man.

"This was to be a real marriage." She shifted a hair's breadth closer to wrap her arms about his neck, letting the silk-covered tips of her breasts brush against hard muscle. Her blood began to warm, her toes to curl. "We had an agreement."

"One I've no intention of breaking." With a growl, his hands caught at the small of her back and dragged their hips flush. Pressing all that was hot, heavy and insistent between them. A new ache bloomed low in her groin. "But I won't be used, then tossed aside and ignored."

"You wish to renegotiate?" She kissed the corner of his mouth, soft lips and rough bristle. A perfect contrast.

He nipped at her ear lobe, eliciting a sharp gasp. "I want to discuss the underlying assumptions causing tension between us."

"The animosity between you and my brother?" A hollow

above his collarbone beckoned but, regretfully, she needed her mouth for words. "My exasperation on behalf of all over-managed sisters?"

"Why I object to serving as a convenient groom, one indistinguishable from any other unmarried agent, in pursuit of your career?"

Her palms drifted downward over his arms, savoring the shape of powerful muscles. "How I might feel a bit like a pawn in a game of revenge?"

"Point taken. Perhaps it should come as no surprise that an impromptu wedding conducted with alarming alacrity has created problems." He slid the lace strap from her shoulder and the thin fabric fell way, exposing the entirety of one breast to his view. "Beautiful," he whispered, then bent to sample its soft rise.

Her head fell back and she closed her eyes in sweet anticipation as he neared its taut peak.

Then the heat of his body was gone.

Her eyes flew open.

"Regardless, our differences must be resolved." A hardness entered his eyes. "Separate living arrangements are not an option. As trust is the basis of any good relationship," he drew the two halves of his robe together, "and something we've not earned yet of each other, this must wait."

"It's our wedding night," she breathed, conflicted. Or was it confused? "You don't want to consummate our marriage?"

"Want?" He laughed, low and bitter. "Not at all. I'd like nothing better than to toss you upon that bed and take us both to the edge of ecstasy and beyond, but first we must come to terms."

"Terms." His touch had reduced her mind to the reasoning capabilities of a bowl filled with pudding.

"A telegram preceded our arrival." He stalked to the door. "To ensure our compliance with her orders, the duchess pre-arranged for us to participate in a full range of restorative spa treatments. Immediately. Our working relationship begins tomorrow when the baths open at six in the morning. Sleep. We'll discuss our marriage later, when time and opportunity permit."

Final words with an exit punctuated with a firmly shut door.

Sleep?

Sleep?

Little chance of that now. So much for a wedding night.

Cait flopped onto her bed. Alone. Where the hours crept at a snail's pace toward dawn. At some point, she dropped off into a fitful slumber only to snap awake to the clanging of a steambot's bell.

⊰❖⊱

How WAS it his bride managed to look so rested this morning?

Garbed in red and black striped bathing attire with an oversized bow tied at her back, her regal bearing somehow managed to make the ruffly, puffy-sleeved, froufrou garment fashionable. Only the bandage at her neck beneath upswept hair hinted at the recent assault.

Jack had caught a glimpse of himself in the mirror, razor in hand. There were bags beneath his eyes that could hold the entire contents of his pockets. Which might be useful, given the difficulty of concealing his weapon beneath the tight fit of his ridiculous bathing costume. Not that he ought to complain. One glance at him had sent blood rushing to Cait's cheeks. A response that had fired his own blood.

No matter their differences, the magnetic pull between them was strong. A promising sign.

Together, they padded down the long hall, each pretending to focus on the riveted back of the rolling steambot as it led them through a maze of corridors before throwing open a final door and waving them into the Turkish bath.

A man wearing loose pants, an embroidered vest and a maroon fez consulted a clipboard, found their names and nodded. "The baths are open to mixed couples for one hour." He handed them both towels. "Please proceed through the bath chambers. When you reach the end, your therapist, Ceyda, will escort you to your treatment room."

One hour, perhaps two. That would satisfy the duchess' commands. Then they would be free to seek answers of their own.

Lord Saltwell had been a known womanizer. Men had been castrated. A loose woman killed for a portion of her brain.

Would they manage to link his brother and his band of

morally corrupt friends to the venomous woman of London here, hours north, inside a spa dedicated to carnal hedonism?

They might.

Though the connections were tenuous, Aubrey's stupidity and self-centered behavior knew no bounds.

Moorish arches soared overhead and lamps with leaded, colored glass hung, suspended from long chains. Every last surface was glazed or tiled, though the patterns were hard to discern beneath the billowing clouds of steam. The hot scent of eucalyptus met his nose as he watched the soft cotton of his wife's bathing costume grow damp and cling to her skin.

At the far end of the room, another couple lounged. Quite enamored of each other, given their entwined limbs and roving hands.

He ran a hand down Cait's back, then caught her hand to draw her to a nearby bench built for two. Reclining, he teased, "Can you feel the tension melting way? Muscles relaxing, pores opening?"

"As if a lady would admit to possessing such things as pores." She sat, leaned back. But the steam failed to work any magic. Her silence lasted all of a minute. "It's true, our meeting was fortuitous. But I had no intention of marrying the first available agent. I do have standards."

"As do I. Revenge did not factor into my decision to speak wedding vows." He closed his eyes. "And, upon reflection, I cannot hold Mr. Black entirely at fault. My sister waited to launch her campaign to become a societal liaison while I was out of the country for a reason. She has a devious streak."

Cait snorted. "And you expected my brother to ask your permission to give away your sister's hand?"

He popped an eye open. "No. I expected to be informed of her decision in a timely manner that I might deliver input. His silence was underhanded, if not out of character."

"Your sister made her own decision, as did I. Though I suppose there is a certain poetic justice to our marriage." His wife sighed. "Is it possible to move past our suspicions of each other?"

"Shall we try?" Tired of her distance, both mental and physical, he scooped her legs upward to drop them across his thighs, before slipping an arm about her waist.

For a moment she stiffened, then sighed in capitulation, relaxing against him. "Terms?"

"Fidelity was agreed upon, but I also wish for loyalty."

"To the Crown or to you?"

"To each other. Before the Crown." Personal loyalty. Such an abstract concept. In his life, few had proved steadfast, Angela among them. Until she'd married without launching so much as an invitation in his direction.

"Does that encompass personal secrets?" Cait twisted her poison ring.

Was she conscious of her habit? Every time the topic of secrets arose, her thumb swept over the black stone of her omnipresent ring.

Jack tipped her chin upward and met her gaze. What wasn't she telling him? Ought he worry? *He couldn't protect what he didn't know about.* "I'd prefer there be none, but I'll settle for no lies."

Cait gave a short nod, then took a deep breath. But whatever she'd been about to say was forestalled by the arrival of new patrons.

The door opened and Lord Churlton leaning upon a cane and wearing naught but a towel about his waist shuffled inward. Wisps of white hair sprang from a scalp spotted with age. At his side was a young woman, similarly clad. Bathing attire, it appeared, was optional.

The gentleman dropped onto a nearby bench. His female companion nestled close, and Lord Churlton's hands began to wander. "That you, Tagert? Never thought to see Aubrey's brother here." He waggled his eyebrows at Cait. "Wife or..."

"We married a few days ago," he answered, contemplating Lord Churlton's patronage of the spa accompanied by one of his many hussies. Fertility treatment? Ha! He already possessed half a dozen children. His visit here was nothing more than an indulgence in carnal hedonism.

The gentleman squinted at Cait's neck, eyeing the bandage. Then barked a laugh. "Had your wife partake of a treatment? Smart move. But don't be so quick to dismiss the wondrous effects it can have on male anatomy. If it can keep me standing—"

"We've a schedule to keep." Jack stood, depositing Cait upon her feet. "Good day, sir." He tugged his open-mouthed wife along as laughter, both masculine and feminine, followed them.

In the next room, a long, narrow pool awaited. A vigorous massage and scrubbing would have preceded their entry into the plunge pool in a traditional Turkish hamman. However, here in Britain, it appeared prudery had won out.

"Lord Churlton spoke of the treatments," Cait resisted. "We should go back and ask—"

"No."

"Jack, I'm no delicate flower." She yanked her hand away and glowered. "My ears can handle lewd commentary. If he's willing to detail the process, the effects of this treatment, we ought to let him speak. Better to arrive at our appointment informed."

"Fine." He pinched the bridge of his nose, willing away the beginnings of a headache. "You're right, I'm being over-protective." *Of his wife's non-existent sensibilities.* Though he managed to bite off those final words, his voice was, regretfully, sharp. Years of acceptable behavior in the presence of ladies had been drilled into him, not something that could be overcome in the space of mere hours or days. "We'll wait here, float for a bit until they catch up." Jack dove into the pool and swam its length. Quickly, for the icy shock drove the air from his lungs.

When he surfaced and turned back, she stood ankle deep, arms wrapped across her chest. "It's freezing!" she called.

"The better to improve your circulation." A dare he called from the far end of the pool. "Consider it your first physical challenge as an agent."

Not to be outdone, Cait proceeded down the stairs, but stopped waist-deep, shivering and gasping for breath. "This is torture."

Jack dove. Several strokes later, he surfaced before her and grinned. "Not up to it?"

She pulled a face and plunged into the water. Only to surface milliseconds later, sputtering and cursing as water streamed in rivulets from her hair. "I hate you."

Laughing, he slipped arms about her waist and gathered her against his warmth. "Now about those terms, are we agreed? The past is past. From now on, loyalty to each other first. No lies. And all mission-relevant secrets must be shared."

"Only under the condition that you not block me from participating in any part of our assignments, citing feminine sensibilities as a convenient excuse."

"Done."

"Excellent." She dragged in a shuddering breath, pushed at his shoulders. "This is torture. Please tell me there's a warmer room where we can wait for Lord Churlton."

"The very next chamber." He let her go, following far enough behind to admire the curves revealed by clinging cotton as she sloshed through the cold water and lunged up the stairs. A few minutes later they were wrapped in thick towels and reclining upon chaises in a room hot enough to send billows of steam toward the ceiling. "Better?"

"Much," she exhaled the word on a sigh of relief. "Tell me, what do you suspect led your brother to invest in this spa?"

Mission-pertinent details.

Jack blew a long, slow breath through his teeth. "Friendship." He filled Cait in on Aubrey's ties to Carruthers, to Dr. Oakes. "Money."

"You think his sudden interest in matrimony is related?"

"Most certainly. What better promotion than to strut about like an oversexed rooster expecting a dozen eggs to hatch?"

"With a smirk and a suggestive nod at his spa." She snorted. "Nudge-nudge, wink-wink."

"That's about the sum of it." He let his gaze fall upon the bandage at her neck. "Your turn. What is it you're not telling me that I ought to know?"

Cait shifted upon the chaise, wrestling with some internal dialogue. How much would she reveal? What level of trust had he earned?

With a decisive tug, she peeled away the damp gauze of her bandage, exposing the mark at her throat. The skin was puckered and twisted. But also pink and new. All but fully healed.

He gaped. "That bite felled several men twice your size. You should have died."

With a deep breath, she began, "My immune system acts faster and more decisively..."

"Than most humans."

Cait looked away. "I prefer not to cast myself as 'other'. That path invites narrowmindedness."

Standing, she abandoned her towel and paced to the doorway, beckoning him into the next room, one warm enough that beads of sweat broke out on his forehead.

In the morning light that slanted through a window, she

turned over her forearm to reveal a faint crosshatching of scars and puncture wounds.

"Drugs?" Jack swore as memories of his father's weakness for opium stabbed a knife into his heart.

"It's not what you think." She caught at his arm. "I'm not an addict, seeking to set my mind adrift. I use my unique biology to study toxins."

"Study?" He leveled her a look demanding a detailed explanation.

"Their precise effects. How my blood neutralizes biological poisons. I've evidence that it's a kind of protein. Imagine if it could be produced in large enough quantities to save another's life. Do you have any idea how many people die each year from snake bites alone? If I could develop an antivenin—"

"By letting snakes bite you?" His eyebrows slammed together. "Is that what these marks are from, fangs?"

"A few," Cait admitted. "I've managed to catch a few snakes in the countryside..." She waved a hand. "There have been many projects. Should you wish to needle my brother, ask him about the time I borrowed his weapon."

"You didn't."

"I did." A playful look danced upon her face. "Pufferfish are no longer a threat to me."

He blinked. "That's insane."

"It's not. I can demonstrate if you'll hand me the TTX pistol you've strapped beneath your suit." She held out an open hand and crooked her fingers.

"Not a chance. Continue."

She rolled her eyes. "I'm always careful to start with a low dose, gradually building my resistance. Unfortunately, that not-a-vampire's bite was a complete envenomation. Not a controlled experiment, but a full-on, frenzied attack. It's the closest I've come to—"

"Death."

"That." She pressed a hand to the scar at her neck. "Suffice it to say, I expect I *am* immune."

Jack's mouth opened, shut. "I've married a delusional woman." He shook his head, took a step back. "You intend to hunt her, recklessly, under the assumption that you're invulnerable."

"Because I am." Cait turned her back on him and stalked into the next chamber.

"I won't allow it," Jack said, close upon her heels. A suffocating heat poured from the walls.

She threw up her hands and kept walking. "So much for our agreement. For our partnership."

"I won't work with a reckless agent." Cold words, calculated to cut through the haze of her anger.

"Fair enough." She drew up short and threw him a glare. In this third heated chamber, temperatures approached those at the gates of hell. Steam rose from the wet cloth of her bathing costume. "What if I offer you proof of my immunity to her venom?"

He pulled a face. "How could you possibly?"

"We'll return to our suite before our appointment. I'll show you the double immunodiffusion biogels that tell quite the tale." She turned on her heel and stalked away. "Where's the exit?"

"Double what?" He strode along beside her. Finally, a cooler room. "Is that what you had in your reticule? The reason you were clutching it so tightly?" Not once had she relinquished her hold on that silly purple bag the entire train ride. He'd written off her tight grip to mere irritation.

Stupid of him.

"As it so happens, yes."

He sighed. "Fine. Let's go have a look."

No point in standing about, arms crossed and throwing each other glares waiting for Lord Churlton and his floozy.

There was nothing worse than a delusional partner. Better to ignore the duchess' commands and reschedule their treatments *after* interviewing the lusty lord.

"Mr. and Mrs. Tagert?"

A dark-haired woman wearing a gold-embroidered, green kaftan with flowing chiffon sleeves stepped into the doorway before them. "I'm Ceyda, your therapist." She took their angry frowns in stride. "Not to worry, many of our visitors have difficulty relaxing upon their first visit to the baths. My treatments are designed to help couples... unwind. If you'll follow me."

Despite her claim of a Turkish name, the woman's English was flawless. No doubt a moniker carefully selected for her role, part and parcel of a pretense supporting the illusion they had stepped into a building erected upon the far-flung eastern lands of the Ottoman Empire.

Skirts swirling, the woman turned and floated down a hallway.

"It seems proof must wait," Cait whispered. "You'll simply have to find a way to trust me." A bit too eagerly, she moved to follow Ceyda.

"Blind faith won't work." Jack caught his wife's arm and locked eyes. "If needles or vials filled with unidentified substances are involved in this treatment," he hissed, "you are *not* to test them."

"I would never." The blaze from her eyes suggested she might kick her husband in the shins. "Did you learn nothing about proper experimental protocol?" Shoulders stiff and square, she followed Ceyda down a hallway, muttering about the lack of mandatory laboratory hours for medical students.

Why worry about a pituitary adenoma when his wife might bring about his demise long before Thornton could attempt surgery?

CHAPTER TWELVE

YET MORE COLORFUL TILES adorned the walls and arches of the private room into which they were ushered. At its center was a large stone slab draped with toweling, a table of sorts wide enough for two. There was a sink. Shelving holding additional towels. A glass-fronted cabinet containing an array of oil-filled glass bottles.

But no medical implements or machinery of any kind.

Nothing suspicious leapt out at him.

"Robes, towels, nudity. All are acceptable," Ceyda informed them, waving toward a privacy screen standing in the corner. Beside it, a pair of dressing robes hung from hooks. "The choice is yours."

"For?" Cait inquired.

"Your massages, of course."

Was that all? Impatience reared its ugly head. The duchess and her instincts. So far this trip north was nothing more than time wasted when they ought to be monitoring the gaslit streets of London.

But the sooner this was over, the sooner they could return to the privacy of their own rooms. There, he prayed, his wife's jaw-dropping revelation would prove to be fact. Only then could he give in to the desperate need that clawed at him and drag his wife to the marital bed.

Irritated, he lifted an eyebrow and waved her toward the screen. "Ladies first."

"I think not." Arms crossed, she slitted her eyes.

Across the room, Ceyda selected a bottle of oil from the shelf.

"This won't work," he murmured, "if you don't at least pretend to cooperate. Set our disagreement aside."

"Fine." Cait didn't budge. "You first."

"Very well." Tempted as he was to strip bare without prelude and dare her to do the same, there was the matter of his concealed TTX pistol. He stepped behind the screen and divested himself of wet clothing in exchange for a dry linen towel. With much reluctance, he placed his weapon upon the floor.

Stretching out upon the bench, he forced his mind to their assigned task. This "treatment" had, at the very least, led them through a warren of rooms deep into the inner sanctum of the spa. If there were secrets to be uncovered, they would find them here. Behind locked doors.

They'd return later. After midnight, lock picks in hand.

Warm oil and soft hands moved across his shoulders. "So tense," Ceyda commented.

"Cait?" He patted the space beside him, wondering at her sudden prudery. "It's just a massage."

She eyed the woman, uncertain.

"Arrangements were for you both," Ceyda purred, moving hands slick with jasmine-scented oil across his back. "But if you would prefer not to remain and participate, I can return your husband to you when he's more... relaxed."

"No. I'll stay."

Was that a note of possessiveness in her voice? Jealousy? A primitive part of his brain rejoiced. Regardless, it motivated her into action.

He dropped his head onto his arm, watching, as his wife's shadow shifted behind the screen. He imagined her studying his weapon, envious. The moment they returned to London, she would demand one of her own.

"When will we meet with the doctor?" he asked.

The duchess herself would be spreading the news of their marriage as swiftly as possible. His mother would be livid. And, should any connection to the venomous woman exist, his brother would fume until he belched coal dust.

Would Aubrey linger in London? Rush north to forestall their investigation? Or would he merely laugh, gleeful while his younger brother's scandal was discussed and dissected by sharp *ton* tongues?

"Perhaps tomorrow or the day after. Though I ask myself," Ceyda's voice was a low hum as her fingers dug into his shoulders, "why does a man of such strength and obvious virility have need of such a consultation? Are you first-born, keen to extend the family line?"

Second. Though there were certain family expectations.

Keen? To bed his wife? Most certainly.

But children? That rather put the cart before the horse.

However, if Cait was indeed injecting herself with all manner of toxins, such was another topic to discuss. What passed through a mother's bloodstream passed into her unborn child's.

"Or perhaps you're concerned about your wife's ability to conceive?" Ceyda crooned as her hands gripped his biceps, her mouth strangely close to his ear. "No worries. That can be addressed, though you'll have to decide if another's life is worth the price of the one you would create."

Unease crept into his stomach. "What do you mean by—"

Pain stabbed into the muscle of his shoulder. Two sharp pinpricks. Followed by a sudden rush of warmth.

Shit. Fuck. Damn.

He'd been bitten.

Another venomous woman existed?

With no medical equipment in view, he'd stupidly thought them safe.

"Cait!" he cried, rolling. Pushing at Ceyda, he tried to sit up and found his muscles unwilling to cooperate.

"It's best if you remain upon the table." Her voice was firm, her hand pressing forcibly down upon his chest. "The initial effects spike within the first twenty minutes. Hold still. Don't fight it."

His mind leapt to the neutered existence of one unfortunate London publican. *Not a chance.* Focused upon each other, they'd walked right into the den of a viper. Stupid. Stupid. Stupid.

A buzzing swept through his veins as he managed to throw the woman's hand away. His bare feet hit cool tile, and he staggered, reaching out to steady himself upon the wall.

"Don't move!" Cait barked. "Not another step!" The TTX pistol was in her hands and pointed at the venomous masseuse.

Never before had he ever beheld such a sexy, glorious sight. A woman stepping into the fray on his behalf. Her dark eyes flashed. Full lips compressed into a firm line. Midnight hair tumbled, wild and free, over bare shoulders and arms and a most delightful chest.

A stupid grin stretched across his face. She'd opted for the towel, wrapping it tight across the wonders of her generous bosom. A simple tug and he could drop the bothersome linen to the ground to satisfy his sudden and desperate need to see both taut peaks of her glorious breasts at once. To catch them with his lips, each in turn. To nibble and pull and suck until she cried for mercy.

Jack took a step toward her, but the floor dipped and swayed. He caught at the cabinet. Blinked at the flecks of light spun out by the brass lamp overhead. He could *see* spirals of jasmine twist upon air currents. The linen cloth at his waist shifted, slid lower on his hips. Grazed against rampant, straining need.

Everything felt so very right and, at the same time, very, very wrong.

"How dare you bring a weapon into this sanctuary!"

Ceyda threw her hands in the air. "I've done nothing wrong. You *paid* for this."

"Paid for what, exactly?" Cait's demand pounded against his ear drums.

"For the drug." The masseuse flashed a reassuring smile, one edged with a glint of gold.

Cait glanced in his direction. Her words rose on a crescendo. "Did she bite you?"

He slapped a hand to his neck, surprised. "She did." Aether, how had he already forgotten? "It's nothing." Nothing mattered, save convincing Cait to put her hands on him. All of him. Anywhere and everywhere. He let the corner of his mouth curl up. "But perhaps you'd best check."

*R*ELAX, *he said. It's just a massage, he said. What could possibly go wrong?*

Great aether, Ceyda had bitten her husband. Her partner. *Bitten!*

But this was not the dark-haired woman who had attacked her, launching from the shadowy corner of a hired crank hack. Not only was her hair a light brown but her face betrayed no sign of recognizing Cait.

Two such women existed? One in a spa, the other ravaging the streets of London. Were there *more* like her?

With great effort, Cait relaxed her grip on the pistol, dragged in a deep breath, and reminded herself that people *paid* for this so-called treatment. Paid to be bitten, to be drugged. While the woman in London was vicious and bloodthirsty and deadly, this one might well be reasonable. Killing one's clientele, after all, did not ensure repeat business.

Jack would be fine.

She was counting on it.

Ever so slightly, she lowered the pistol.

What, then, stood before her, garbed in the trappings of the Ottoman Empire?

Fascinated, Cait tipped her head, studying the woman's facial features. Completely human. All female. Save for a slight bulge at the corners of her jaw. It could be nothing. Or it could be everything.

"You call it a drug, yet you *bit* my husband. This is not a standard medical technique."

"It is not." Ceyda's hands dropped, twisted about each other before her chest. "I was hired to provide a unique experience. Aren't you curious? Come. Join him." The woman's movements grew sinuous and weaving as she crept closer to Cait. "A little nip is all it takes. With a little help, all inhibition melts away." She crooked a finger. "Look at your husband. How ready he is for you."

"It's the venom." Casting her mind back to the London attack, she could recall nothing but pain and panic and a rising awareness that she might not survive. She took a step back.

"Not all of it," Jack all but hummed the lust-filled words. "You're beautiful. And I'm rather enamored of how steadily you're holding my weapon. Though I can think of other things I'd rather have those fingers wrapped around right now."

A rather forward comment from a man who couldn't manage the slightest buss of a kiss in a London pub without embarrassment, who refused to bed his wife the night of their marriage on moral grounds.

A quick glance away from the venomous creature informed Cait that a rather prominent portion of Jack's anatomy did indeed desire attention.

"If it's the worry of bearing children," the woman hummed, reaching out for Cait, "a tiny nip is all it takes to make your worries melt away."

Doubtful. She suspected she would be immune. Though testing that hypothesis at this very moment would be unwise. One agent with a clouded mind was problem enough.

They—she—needed to capture this woman, tie her up, transport her back to London for questioning and study. So much for visiting the floating cabinet of curiosities. Two darts would render Ceyda dead weight. A massive inconvenience with Jack not in his right mind and no idea how long the venom's effects might last or, aether forbid, what side-effects might develop.

Somehow, she would have to manage. She needed clothing. A steam carriage or a private dirigible. A servant amenable to heavy-handed bribery.

"In small doses, it's an aphrodisiac?" Cait struggled to buy time as her mind raced.

A drug delivered by a venomous beauty in the private luxury of an exclusive spa, one promising to unleash erotic fantasies. Yes, she could see how many would be tempted to sample its effects. How many, she wondered, later regretted their words and actions?

"For men. But for women, it's a different blessing." The woman smiled, and a flash of gold gleamed along the edge of her canine teeth.

An implant?

Cait felt her jaw slacken. *Dammit*. The woman was nothing more than a laboratory-created siren. A bewitching plaything for the wealthy whose entire purpose was to function as a human hypodermic syringe.

So much for discovering a new sub-species. Or even an interesting human variant. Disappointment splashed over her, cold and wet, followed by a touch of shame. Was that not what she was herself, human with a streak of something more? Hiding in plain sight while she worked to unlock the secrets of her unusual biology, levering her discoveries to her own advantage?

Yet there was a key difference. Cait strove to preserve human life, not to destroy it.

The London murders must be stopped, any murderous venomous beauties locked away where their mouths could be pried open and studied, the venom and implant analyzed.

Therein lay the novelty. How had some mad scientist accomplished this feat? Surgical procedure aside, a clue to the origins of the venom lay tucked within her reticule. While dressing this morning, she'd peeked at the biogel plates and stood open-mouthed in wonder.

This venom shared biological properties with that of

Naja naja, the spectacled cobra. Many venoms would, given the large number of species within the genus. Yet, to her knowledge, no cobra's bite had ever demonstrated aphrodisiac effects. Then again, most snakes struck to disable their prey, not to lull them into the stupid stupor now exhibited by her husband.

If the women weren't truly venomous, but instead reliant upon an implant, that meant that there was at least a new species of snake to locate, to identify, to study. Project potential. That brightened her mood.

"What happens at higher doses?" Cait suspected Jack's mind would be addled for hours yet. "Say, if you were to bite your victim and hold tight?"

Out of the corner of her eye, she saw Jack take a step, trip over his own feet and drop onto the stone table. Hard.

"Much as I want you alone and all to myself." He spoke slowly and with effort. "There's a nagging voice in the fog of my mind that insists you shoot her. Just a dart or two. Hold back on the third. Explaining a dead body to the hotel staff is an inconvenience we can do without."

"Enough." Ceyda's eyes grew cold. "It's clear you've entered my sanctuary with ill intent and under false pretenses." She took a step backward, reaching blindly for the door handle behind her. "I want you both to leave. Now."

A harsh reminder of the immediate need to subdue and capture this woman, without Jack's assistance and endure the complications that would follow.

"Agreed. Alas, you will be accompanying us." Cait

squeezed the trigger and—*Snap! Whoosh!*—the TTX pistol discharged its dart on a hiss of compressed air.

Ceyda fell against the door, sagged and slid to the ground, mouth agape. "You shot me!"

"So I did. I've questions, but they'll need to wait a few minutes." With the masseuse temporarily disabled, she rushed to Jack's side, frowning. "Symptoms? Tell me what's wrong."

"Not a thing." He grinned, slipped a hand up the length of her bare arm. "Everything is perfect. Especially you."

She swatted his hand away and pressed her own to his chest. Beneath her palm she could feel his heart skipping and leaping. All while his lungs worked to drag in great gulps of air. "Cogs. Your cardiovascular system is being put through its paces. Too fast and hard."

"Hard is the word for it." In a heartbeat, his arms wrapped about her waist and flipped her onto the table beneath him.

Warm, solid muscle rippled and shifted, pinning her in place. All of it worthy of careful exploration. If only circumstances were different.

"Jack." She kept her voice calm and measured, not a hard task when they had an immobilized audience of one sagged against a nearby wall. "Stop. We have a task to complete."

But her reasoning fell on deaf ears.

"I need you badly." He nibbled at her earlobe, nuzzled at her throat. "I've never been so aroused, so desperate for a woman."

"Jack! Not here. Not now." She shoved at his shoulders. "Stop it. We'll lose our positions if you can't focus."

"Oh, I'm very focused." He shifted, tugged at the towel wrapped about her with his teeth. "But if it's the position to which you object..." He rolled, and she found herself atop him, straddling his arousal.

Gears and pins, he felt good.

She stifled a groan.

Drug-addled, she reminded herself. Not alone. And, eventually, people would come looking for Ceyda.

One must do what one must. "This is not the place and not the time for bedding your new wife."

He thrust against her. "Are you so very certain?"

"If I can't have your assistance, I'll have your compliance." She pressed the muzzle of the TTX pistol to his chest. "Point blank. Not much chance I'll miss."

The manner in which his eyes widened and his hands fell away was quite gratifying. "Fine. I'm listening."

"Good." But she didn't move the weapon so much as an inch. "You've been bitten, albeit lightly, by a woman with fangs. We need to question her." She paused a moment, let his muddled brain process this statement. "Do you wish to help?"

"Yes."

"Then keep your hands and your mouth and all your other body parts to yourself." With that, she climbed from the bench. Interrogation called for sturdier garb than thin towels. Quickly, she pulled on a dressing gown, belted it at her waist. Passed Jack the second.

She crouched before Ceyda, now a crumpled heap of green satin and outrage. The petulant expression on her face did not bode well for a successful interview.

"You work for Dr. Oakes." A flat statement meant to establish a baseline for their conversation.

"I've nothing to say." The woman stared over Cait's shoulder, her jaw tight.

"Is he the one who did this to you, installed those fangs of yours?" She waved at the woman's mouth, careful to keep her hand out of striking distance. Someone needed a clear head. "Have you been forced into his employ? We can help."

"I need no help," the woman hissed, her eyes narrowed to a harsh squint. "Work is steady here, the pay excellent. You'll regret this," Ceyda spit. "Both of you. There is always a need for spare parts."

"Spare parts." Cait's voice was calm despite an increased pounding in her ears as her blood pressure rose a notch. If they located the local coroner, would they find deaths that matched those in London? She'd bet her career on it. "Such as a stray pituitary gland? A pair of testicles that have wandered off?"

Behind her, razor-sharp laughter tinged with outrage burst from Jack's throat.

Cait sighed, half turned to glance at Jack. "We'll have to transport her to London, question her there. Any chance you can—"

"London?" Ceyda cried. "Absolutely not!"

"Stop!" Jack lunged, eyes on the masseuse, half-sliding across the tiled floor, reaching for—

Cait spun back around.

"Kraken!" She swatted Jack's hands aside. "Let me." A suicide attempt was not an outcome she'd anticipated.

A tiny nip promised euphoria to a man, something as-yet undefined to a woman, but a substantial dose was deadly, and the woman had bitten her own lip, deeply. Blood ran over her chin, dripping onto golden embroidery. Carefully, Cait pulled her lip away, easing artificially sharp canines from rapidly swelling flesh.

But the damage was done. The woman's eyes rolled back as her entire body shuddered, convulsed.

"Shit." Jack locked eyes with Cait. "Is there any hope?"

"With a full envenomation? It's possible she's developed a mild immunity, built up tolerance to the venom she must regularly swallow, but if she's emptied the entire contents of her glands into her bloodstream..." She leaned closer to palpate the slight swellings behind the woman's ears. "They're a pair of good-sized glands." Prying open the woman's mouth, Cait peered inside. "One connected to enhanced teeth by a sizable duct."

He swore. "How long does she have?"

"I'd guess some twenty minutes. Longer if she's extremely lucky." Her pulse spiked and a cold sweat broke out on her forehead.

Could she? She'd never tried it before. Not even on rats. She dragged in a deep breath. Life and death scenarios had always been stories told by her brothers, not a part of her current reality.

But she was an agent now.

This would not be the last crisis.

"What is it?" Jack asked.

"There's a small chance my blood could save this woman, though transfusions always carry risks." Cait ran to the cabinetry and flung open the doors, dug through drawers with shaking hands. "Not a single piece of useful medical equipment!" she cried in frustration. "Without a syringe—or needles or tubing—"

It was hopeless.

"There's nothing we can do." Jack swore again. "We'll have to summon help. Perhaps they possess an antidote." He caught her arm. "Ceyda tripped, fell, bit her lip. This was a horrible accident. That's our story and we stick to it. Agreed?"

"Unless someone looks inclined to harvest our spare parts." She dragged the dying woman away from the door, then cracked it open to yell. "Help! Please, come quickly!"

Seconds later, two nurses rushed into the room and dropped to Ceyda's side, exchanging worried glances as they checked her pulse, her respiration.

Assuming the role of a hysterical young bride, Cait shed crocodile tears and stuttered out the details of a most unfortunate accident all while flapping hands at the masseuse as she twitched and moaned upon the ground.

"Help her!" Cait cried.

"There's no protocol for this." Wide-eyed, the nurse addressed her coworker. "Dr. Oakes isn't due back until tomorrow. What do we do? The circus floated away three days ago."

"Do you mean Professor Grimaldi's Floating Cabinet of Curiosities?" Cait asked.

"Does it matter what you call that carnival of freaks?" the second nurse said, wringing her hands. "I'm afraid not even Dr. Thrakos could help. There's no cure."

Save the possibility of her blood. But to offer such a procedure, to force it upon Ceyda who had chosen to end her own life rather than be transported to captivity in London...

"A floating attraction?" Jack stood behind Cait now, skimming his hands over the silk of her dressing robe. Over her arms, cupping her elbows, then finally setting upon her hips. "Dr. Thrakos?"

"The surgeon who works in the clouds. Creator of—"

"Hush," the other nurse interrupted. "Such information is not for guests." The woman stood and, with a light touch, urged them toward the door. "Please, sir, if you and your wife would return to your rooms. I'm certain management will wish to compensate you. Follow the corridor to your left, then take a right through the red door."

"I can't feel her pulse!" the other nurse cried.

There was nothing Cait could do now, and it would be impossible to argue in favor of transporting Ceyda's body to London. She left them to their resuscitation attempts.

Cait wrapped a supportive arm about Jack's waist, draped his arm over her shoulder, then led him, staggering, from the room. "Now might be a good time to make a dramatic exit from the hotel citing irreparable mental distress," she whispered. "Send word of our failed honey-moon to a certain duke and duchess and request aid."

"Yes. But we're not returning to London ourselves. Not yet." The backs of Jack's fingers brushed over the rise of her breast. "Would my bride care to visit Professor Grimaldi's Floating Cabinet of Curiosities?"

"She'd like nothing more."

CHAPTER THIRTEEN

"W E MUST ALTER OUR appearance," he'd slurred. "Mr. and Mrs. Tagert would never chase after a disreputable floating circus."

"Were this not a component of an active investigation, your wife would disagree." In a flurry of activity, Cait had buzzed about their rooms, madly stuffing strange items into a small valise. "As it so happens, she's one step ahead of you."

With that, his fate had been sealed.

Eyes fixed on the horizon, Jack clenched his teeth.

Traveling under the influence of venom that left him sympathetic with Priapus, god of fertility, meant that the remainder of his day would be one of complete and utter torture. Not since the age of fourteen had he been in such a state.

Only a few firing neurons in his higher brain centers kept him from tossing Cait from the clockwork horse into a hedgerow and having his way with her on the side of a country road.

"Are we there yet?" An irritable question, half-groaned and instantly regretted, for Cait shifted in the saddle before him and the soft swell of her backside produced a new and even more delightful friction.

A low and throaty laugh floated back at him. She knew what she was about and found his torment amusing.

Why was it he continued to play the gentleman when all evidence suggested his bride was as anxious as he was to consummate their union?

He ought to have tumbled her onto the thick feather mattress the night of their wedding. Instead, the knowledge that he'd been one of many agents under consideration for the position of "husband" had made him petulant, and he'd insisted upon waiting until they came to an understanding.

Stupid of him.

Stupid. Stupid. Stupid.

The word repeated in his head, over and over, with each iron hoofbeat.

With his heart hammering against his ribs and propelling hot blood through his veins and arteries at blistering speeds, they'd left the hotel in a snit, noses so high in the air they risked altitude sickness. Staff had zipped and zoomed about, trying to appease the brother of their titled investor, each worried their job was on the line. All while an undertone of tension buzzed and maids whispered into each other's ears.

A steam carriage carried them back to Harrogate— during which he'd sat upon hands that had developed a distressing tendency to wander unbidden. They'd sent a cryptic telegram to the Avesburys, another to Black, then boarded a train bound for London. Their trunks would arrive, but they would not. For the small valise they'd carried into a first-class compartment had contained garments with a coarser weave, brighter color and looser fit, permitting them to step back onto the platform as Mr. and Mrs. Swinton. That couple was on country holiday and keen to ogle the exhibits of Professor Grimaldi's Floating Cabinet of Curiosities.

Inquiries had pointed them north and, with all due speed, they'd hired a clockwork horse built for two. Though his mind was now much clearer, Cait cited venom intoxication and insisted upon holding the reins. She'd climbed astride, forcing him to sit behind her with his hands upon her hips. Thus precipitating his prolonged, excruciating torment.

"We've many miles to cover yet." The vixen glanced over her shoulder, eyes flashing with amusement. "Would you care to pass the time by viewing the biogels?"

"Or we could stop. Rest at that barn in the distance. Make use of its hayloft." His body pleaded with her to consent.

"Tempting." She laughed. The red scarf tied about her neck to hide the scar left by her attack fluttered in the breeze. "But your bride expects both understanding *and* an apology before she considers the possibility of consummation."

"Very well." He held out a hand. "Science on horseback."

She unhooked the reticule from the belt at her waist and

handed it to him. "Your heart is pounding against my back. Are you certain hayloft activities wouldn't burst an artery in your brain?"

Something else might well burst in the meantime. Three long hours had passed since the venomous masseuse bit him. How much longer would this insanity last?

He yanked the drawstring open with his teeth and pulled out two biogel plates, each marked with a name. Three holes were punched in each. Beside the holes, he saw faint ink marks embedded within the biogel. On one plate, two white lines curved around one hole. The other plate showed—he squinted—nothing. "As I never ran with the laboratory rats, you'll need to explain."

"Such rudeness." She jabbed him with her elbow. "The ability to reveal what the naked eye can't see will propel medicine through the next century." Cait wriggled against him. "As you exhibit promise as a husband, I'm inclined to let your comment slide."

He groaned. "I could begin to demonstrate my regret now. A prelude, if you will, to the more intimate pleasures I could provide." He leaned forward, murmuring the words against a bare expanse of her shoulder where the ruffles of her blouse had been crushed and tugged aside by the leather straps of his holster. "Provided you promise not to point my own TTX pistol at me again."

Her answering laugh promised nothing, save that a quick roll in the hay would only begin to satiate the desire that burned through him. "I'll return it later, when I'm convinced the effects of the venom have worn off," she said.

"Shall I explain what unseen mysteries are revealed by the biogels?"

He pressed a soft, open-mouthed kiss against her skin, resisting an urge to bite when she fell backward against him, tipping her head to provide him with better access. "Please do."

"One well—hole—in each plate received a sample of my attacker's venom. A second well on each plate received diluted cobra venom. The variable is introduced into the third well of each plate—a sample of my serum in one, Mr. Acker's in the other."

"You have access to a cobra?" That caught the breath in his lungs. "An actual, live cobra?"

A vision of her coiling the poisonous creature about her shoulders, allowing it to slither and slide across her skin sent a pulse of lust through his blood.

"I do, one recently acquired. Though I've yet to use its venom to challenge my immune response."

"Meaning you've yet to let the cobra bite you?" The question emerged as a fascinated hum.

"Focus." She slapped his thigh. "Look at the white line. This forms when an immune reaction takes place between two substances."

Recalling the scars—the punctures and lines—upon her forearms, he glared at the biogels and grappled with the implications. On the plate marked "Cait", a curved line of precipitate arced between the two venom samples. There were no such lines on the other plate marked "Acker".

"You count this as proof that you are immune not only to

the venomous woman, but also to the bite of a cobra?" Incredulous, his voice rose with each word.

"Yes."

His wife, mistress of poisons. It worried him. But he'd be lying if he didn't also admit the edge of danger it presented excited him.

"Moreover," she continued, "while my blood reacted to both samples, Mr. Acker did not react to either of them."

"If the London attack has rendered you immune, that suggests," he forced his mind to wrestle with the medical implications, "one of two possibilities. Something or someone else bit Mr. Acker. Or his immune system has failed to render him resistant to the woman's venom."

"Likely the later, given our venomous masseuse bit her own lip in an attempt to take her life. Such an act implies she knew herself not to be resistant to large quantities of venom."

"She was prepared to die before betraying her employer's secrets."

"Secrets which may be on that biogel you hold," Cait added. "When two substances are unrelated, the white precipitate forms two lines that cross like an X."

Not at all what he held in his hand. "But when they join in a curve?"

"Then the two samples are similar, if not identical substances," she said. "Based on these results, a zoologist would declare both species members of the same serpent family, elapidae."

He slid the plates into her reticule and clipped the bag onto the D-loop of the wide leather belt encircling her waist.

That left his hands free for exploration. A quick glance about informed him they were quite alone. Unbitten, she might not share his hyper-aroused state, but drugs weren't necessary to spark the chemistry that flowed between them.

"So if our not-a-vampire walks and speaks and is, to all appearances, a young woman, she is either an undiscovered, undocumented subspecies or..." He walked his fingers upward over the clasps of her belt, stopping to toy with the topmost fastening, the one nestled just beneath her breasts.

"Or someone has implanted the venom glands of a cobra-like snake into at least two young women and," she leaned back, ever so slightly, into his arms, encouraging his explorations, "altered their teeth to function as fangs."

"Meaning?" Flames of lust licked across his skin. He cupped her breast, drew his thumb over its gentle curve, delighted that only a single thin layer of cotton separated her nipple from his caress.

Her breath hitched. "Meaning we must locate and speak with this Dr. Thrakos."

Astride, her skirts were hiked almost to the knee—all that much easier to slide a hand beneath their hem and onto the silk of her stockings. Stocking turned into the smooth skin of her thigh and still no material stayed his hand—only fading willpower. "No underwear?"

"Whomever packed my trunk forgot to include them."

He hissed, uncertain if such was a curse or a blessing.

A cluster of brightly patterned balloons appeared on the horizon above a distant field. Professor Grimaldi's Floating Cabinet of Curiosities. Soon Jack would be expected to climb from this clockwork horse. And walk. With a persistent erection that had his cods aching. He prayed they wouldn't turn blue and fall off before he had a chance to bed his bride.

"One thing bothers me." Cait shifted in the saddle, turned and caught his lips for an all-too-brief kiss that nonetheless threatened to stop his heart. "Not once has a cobra's bite ever been reported to produce an aphrodisiac effect, not even at low doses."

"Perhaps this Dr. Thrakos altered the cobra's venom somehow?"

She blew a long breath. "Unlikely. Venom is a complicated protein."

"Or discovered an unknown cobra? For this venom was—is—most effective." His blood boiled and seethed with throbbing need. "Though I hasten to add it only served to enhance my attraction to you, to lower barriers. Not to conjure it out of thin air."

"That is very much the correct answer." She turned away, then rocked her hips. Laughed when he groaned. "Now all I require is an apology."

"I am deeply, deeply sorry to have doubted you and your science. It won't happen again."

With a twitch of the reins, the clockwork horse turned off the road. The barn rose up before them, its grounds deserted.

"Cait?" Only the cage of his ribs kept his heart contained.

"I expect the farmers have abandoned fieldwork in favor

of visiting the floating circus. It's time to settle things between us."

"Now?"

The clockwork horse clopped into the barn, gathering in the margins of their world. Overhead, a hayloft beckoned. "You want to wait?"

Hell no. "There's no telling what effects the drug might produce. I don't want to—"

"Hurt me?" Cait scoffed. Directing the horse to the ladder, she downshifted the lever to full stop. "You won't. I'm not some delicate, fainting ninny. If it helps," she snorted, "consider it your duty to the Crown." She slanted him a teasing glance. "What kind of agents would we be if we fail to explore the full extent of the venom's potency, to understand exactly what draws men and women to the Menwith Spa?"

"So romantic." An aggrieved edge sharpened his voice, but his cock throbbed, reprimanding him for daring to lodge a complaint.

She shrugged a single shoulder. "You missed your chance for lace and candles and a scattering of rose petals last night."

With that flippant comment, Cait reached for the rungs and pulled herself from the saddle. She hitched up her skirts and climbed, treating him to flashes of tantalizingly bare skin. "Coming?" she called.

Soon, he hoped.

Jack dropped to the ground, snatched up a nearby

blanket as a concession to comfort, then, stiff with need, followed.

Sunlight streamed through an open window in the loft. A gentle spring breeze stirred the air and sent dust motes dancing. And, though winter had depleted the stores, more than enough hay remained to serve as a mattress.

Most importantly, they were alone. For the first time, his fading peripheral vision was welcome, for Cait was all he wished to see. Tossing the blanket onto the hay, he hooked a finger over her belt and dragged her close.

"If I must lose my weapon to another agent," he slid the leather straps of his holster from her shoulders, lowering it carefully to the ground, "at least it was to my wife. Perhaps the only acceptable outcome."

"Wife?" Cait asked, a teasing note in her voice as she rose onto toe-tips and nipped at the edge of his chin in challenge. "You mean partner."

"Both."

His mouth came down on hers, expecting soft sweetness, finding instead hot desperation. Her fingers, equally impatient, tore at the buttons of his waistcoat, of his shirt, pushing the fabric away on a greedy quest for bare skin.

There would be no slow exploration. Not this time.

That suited him.

A fusion of bodies. A melding of shared desires and goals. A final pledge to irrevocably join their futures.

With the flick of his fingers, he released the clasps of her belt, tugged the soft cotton blouse from her waistband and yanked it upward.

He shucked his own garments, all the while admiring the view. Cait in a hayloft, bare to the waist, her breasts on glorious display. But enough looking. He bent to claim the hard gem of a single tip.

Blood thrummed through his ears at her gasp and deep in a dark corner of his mind, a feral voice growled.

His.

REASON TOLD her to wait until they found an inn, to wait until the fever sparked by the venom released Jack from its grip. But forced proximity and her husband's wandering hands conspired to drive her mad. Add to that the frustrations of an uncertain union during an investigation requiring trust and teamwork...

Well, when a viable solution presented itself in the form of an empty barn, Cait seized opportunity. Better to address such distractions now.

The tug of his mouth at her nipple shot molten heat straight to her core. Upon the clockwork horse, the tease of his lips and fingers had made reasoned thought difficult. Here, complex thoughts resisted organization and flat out refused to coalesce.

More, her body cried.

Hands buried in the thick mass of Jack's hair, she held him tight to her breast. Head thrown back, she could only gasp, breathless, as his tongue and teeth worked magic, concentrated pleasure teasing forth tortuous need.

Cool air met the wet tip of her breast as he straightened. She opened her mouth, but any objection died in her throat when his fingers dug into her hips, spinning her around with a gentle—if insistent—push toward a waiting pile of hay.

She bent, grabbed the blanket, spread it wide. Behind her, two thumps sounded—boots landing upon boards. Cloth whispered. Not wanting to miss another moment of her husband stripping to his skin, she turned to watch.

Wide shoulders. A tapered waist. Ridges upon his stomach that made her mouth water. Features she'd admired while he wore a towel, leaving only the lower half of his body to her imagination.

His hands were at his waist, but she stayed their movement, pushing them aside to allow herself the pleasure of unfastening his trousers, of sliding her hands inside his undergarments to cup—if only partially—the stiff, throbbing rod that rose beneath.

Air scraped past his teeth. A muscle jumped in his jaw. Then, as she gave a gentle squeeze, a groan ripped from his throat and a desperate eagerness filled his eyes.

Muscles rippled across his shoulders as he caught her wrists, tugged them free to wrap her arms about his neck. His mouth clamped down on hers, all while walking her backward. Memories of the pump house balustrade, of its stone wall surfaced, but this time no interruption threatened. Not a single barrier remained.

Drawn to him in a grim morgue, fascinated by his easy acceptance of her presence in a coroner's office, captured by his willingness to operate outside of society's strictures. His ability, his readiness to live in the moment had sealed her attraction. Conducting interviews in a Covent Garden pub. Sweeping her from a London gutter. Pulling her back from near death in his own bed. Marrying her on a moment's notice for both expedience and love.

Love?

No, not yet. But there was passion and devotion. A corner of her heart belonged to him.

And in that corner a tiny niggle worried. Was this no more than the effects of the venom?

No. They'd spoken their vows with clear minds and full commitment. Such worries had no place tossing such melodramatic obstacles between them.

She brushed them aside.

A hayloft suited them.

Jack lowered her onto the blanket, tossed up her skirts, gathered fistfuls of her ruffled hem about her waist.

On his knees, he spread her thighs, dipped down between them. She'd read of such things before, wondered, but—she cried out as the flat of his tongue stroked and teased —written words had failed to capture the blinding pleasure.

Yet two days of unsatisfied desires had already pushed her to the brink. She didn't want caresses or slow, measured strokes. Not today. Hands fisted in his hair, she shoved him away.

With ragged breaths, he met her eyes. "No?"

Control. She wanted to shatter his. "Inside me. Now."

"Cait, I'm balanced on a knife's edge."

"Let go and give in, I'm begging you."

With a growl, he pushed his trousers to his knees. Cait caught a brief glance of impressive girth before he was devouring her mouth, swallowing her cries, all while hooking arms beneath her knees, opening her to a most welcome invasion.

His stiff erection brushed across her curls, slipped lower, thrust inside. Deeper and deeper. Tight. Full.

Satisfaction and delight ripped through her.

Complete. Perfect in every way.

Save he wasn't moving.

She dug her hands into the hay, seeking purchase, finding none.

Her eyes few open. Caught a dark flash of uncertain anguish in his gaze.

"Stillness as torture?" Her body cried out for friction. Her voice pleaded, "Stop holding back."

"As you wish."

His first thrust was long and deep. But slow. His second, only a fraction quicker.

"Harder." A demand, not a request. "I'm not made of spun glass." Her hands found a post, wrapped about them. She arched her back. "Faster."

She watched his face as relief transformed into a concentrated fierceness. Dark eyes looked back at her, revealing depths never before divulged.

When he moved again, all gentleness was gone.

"Vixen." There was a sharp nip at her neck as he shifted, released a knee to plant a hand beside her shoulder. Then his thrusts came faster. Each gathered more momentum, driving her deeper into the hay with each relentless plunge. Over and over.

Heel dug into the floor, she pushed, lifting her hips to his, absorbing his strength, urging him onward.

A roar tore from his throat as he surged impossibly deep, then notched himself higher. An angle she'd yet to experience. One that dragged his length over her most sensitive peak.

"Aether." The word a hoarsely whispered keen. "Jack."

Another shift. A slight tilt. And a new summit with unexpected heights approached. Sounds escaped her throat, not words, as tension gathered, coalescing in the space between heartbeats, then snapped free, spiraling upward and outward as a delicious pulsing exploded between her legs.

"Cait!" A shout. A heaving thrust. Once, twice more, as his own pleasure detonated, a turbulent wave that swept him over, then under into sweet oblivion.

Still pulsing inside her, Jack gathered her close and rolled onto his back. Her limp weight landed atop him as their chests heaved, fighting to satisfy the demands of heart and lungs for air.

Slowly, sense and reason returned. She'd never felt so very alive. Satisfaction washed over her and with it a kind of peacefulness and inexplicable connection.

His fingers brushed aside fallen and tousled hair. "I trust you won't be delivering a negative report of my performance to the duke."

Laughing, she gave him a pinch. "I won't be reporting anything and you know it. What happened in this barn, stays in this barn." She propped herself up on an elbow. "Did that wear off the effects of the venom?"

"Don't belittle this moment." Jack stroked a finger down the side of her face, one that delighted her skin. The light in his eyes was soft. "That was more than scratching an itch, Cait. There's not another woman I'd prefer to call my wife."

Not exactly an endearment. Their lives had only just begun to intertwine. True, the bond between them was stronger now. Forged first by ambitions, tempered by mutual pleasure. But it was too soon for saccharine declarations.

"And partner." She pressed a kiss to the hollow of his throat, and felt his cock throb against her hip. "So soon?"

"I credit the beauty of my bride, not the lingering effects of the venom as the cause of a certain urgency and resilience reminiscent of adolescence."

She pushed upward, straddling him. Enjoying the bright look that lit his eyes, the pulse that jumped at his throat.

"Are you suggesting…"

"We *are* newlyweds." As she bent to kiss him, his adept hands, once again, demonstrated mad skill.

⁂

SOMETIME LATER, sprawled atop warm wool and crushed hay, Jack stroked his hand over the curve of his wife's waist, over the flare of her hip. At long last, the effects of the venom were behind him. Six hours of potency, by his estimation.

Beneath shadows cast by the barn's roof and nestled in scratchy hay beside a woman he was lucky enough to call his wife, deep satisfaction wrapped around him. When was the last time he'd felt so relaxed, so untroubled?

He couldn't recall.

"I must know." He lifted her hand, smoothed a thumb over the black stone of her poison ring. "Is there anything inside?"

"A piece of orange fungus. Poisonous, I'm told. Once it glowed a blue-green color at night, but that faded over the years. Now it's nothing but a relic of my natural father." She shifted. "Your turn. Tell me about your family," she prompted. "You've dropped hints that worry me. And fore-warned is forearmed."

His mother and brother alone were a lot to swallow.

"All my life I've dealt with lies and half-truths," he began. "My father worked hard to indulge his addictions, hiding behind a veneer kept polished by my mother. At the end, his death was more relief than tragedy. When she wasn't making excuses for her husband, my mother executed calculated schemes designed to install her son among the *ton's* elite—all while he resisted with deceitful and dishonor-able behavior."

"What of Angela, your sister?" Her voice was a whisper.

"Ten years younger than me, her birth was a surprise. Mother mostly ignored her, but I kept close watch. At some point, we became a unit, spying on our own family, exchanging information about the truths and lies that shaped both our private and social lives. Marriage was her exit plan. We had a list, carefully vetted. Then..."

"She upended it all with an unexpected choice, shattering your confidence in her decision?"

He sighed. "Her letters indicate no regret."

"Then trust her to know her own mind."

"I'm trying." He pulled her close, kissed her forehead. "Back to our situation. Is it possible for a snake to kill itself with its own bite?"

"No." Cait's fingers danced over the hair upon his chest. "They're immune to the venom of their own species. A fact consistent with the venom gland in Ceyda's mouth as a functional implant." Faint lines appeared between her eyebrows. "An odd choice for a host. A reptile to human biograft is unlikely to be sustainable."

"Yet in keeping with the seductive illusions presented by the Menwith Spa." He agreed that the woman's body, but for her death, would eventually have rejected the implanted tissue.

Same for the woman he'd all but caught in his brother's library who still stalked London's streets. Unless that venomous creature was real?

Cait was an agent now. And his wife. There was no need to keep her in the dark and every reason to enlighten her. "Still, there's one other possibility. Has your brother ever mentioned CEAP?"

"*Seep?*" Her head rocked upon his biceps. "No."

"It's an acronym. C.E.A.P. It stands for the Committee for the Exploration of Anthropomorphic Peculiarities, a shadow board seeking to study animals with human-like characteristics, creatures such as selkies or cat síth."

The appearance of creatures long-thought imaginary or extinct—kraken, pteryforms and dragons, to name a few—had spawned the field of cryptozoology. Why wouldn't the same processes and evolutionary principles apply to humans? Cryptobiology, really. Not that he had any first-hand experience with such humans, but Cait's sister-in-law was rumored to be half-selkie.

"Or is it the other way around?" his sated and well-tumbled wife suggested, accepting the concept without argument. "Humans with animalistic traits? In Hindu mythology, there are mythical beings, naga and nagini, who are half human, half cobra. But they are usually benevolent, not murderous."

An interesting perspective that sent a shiver down his spine. "Henceforth, I shall sleep wearing my holster and weapon."

He stood, offering his wife a hand. *Wife.* When they returned to London, every aspect of their lives would be turned upside-down and given a good, solid shake. Chief among them, their expectations.

But all that must wait.

It was time for them to be about their task. First things first. They had a rented clockwork horse to turn in and a floating circus to investigate.

He pulled on his shoulder harness, slid the TTX pistol into place.

"You'll not let me keep it?" She winked, pulled up her blouse, righted her skirts.

"A woman immune to the bite of snake-women would rob me of my only defense?"

She smiled, satisfied on an entirely different level. "There's that."

"Though I'm certain plenty of non-venomous threats lie ahead. Given the alacrity with which Ceyda ended her own life, Dr. Thrakos is unlikely to be cooperative or forthcoming. So we stick together, work as a team." He locked eyes with Cait. "No unnecessary risks."

"I've no death wish." Cait moved to the ladder, began to descend. "But if there's venom involved, I'm going in first."

A loophole he was certain she would, given the chance, exploit at the first opportunity.

CHAPTER FOURTEEN

THEY JOINED A SMALL, gaping crowd meandering past a handful of colorful tents dotting the edge of the field. Each canvas-clad, striped structure promised a wonder within. Peer at a five-legged goat. Shake hands with a towering giant. Watch a man juggle sharp-edged sabres. All a tantalizing taste of what one might expect to find floating overhead.

"Tug the bearded lady's goatee!" a sign offered.

For the real attraction hung in the sky, suspended by a motley collection of colorful balloons. Some were striped. Some fringed. Round, peaked or oblong. Cait tipped her head back, admiring the complicated confusion of buildings and baskets that bobbed and swayed from ropes and nets lashed to the various balloons.

"See your fortune in a crystal ball!" declared a placard.

Connected by a maze of ladders, stairs and rope bridges, platforms of varying heights supported structures of dubious, haphazard construction. A large propeller jutted from one side of the combined assembly. Crooked chimneys sprouted from roofs. Windows glinted in the fading afternoon sunlight. Many of them would be exhibit halls. One an engine room. Others living quarters. The whole of the assemblage was secured to the ground by ropes too numerous to count.

"Catch the two-headed snake by its tail!" a banner proclaimed.

Only one tether mattered to visitors. A sturdy cable ran from the lowest platform of the floating circus to the ground. Attached to it was a basket with a modest hot-air balloon and a dedicated winch. The only obvious route into—or out of—the floating circus. Cait watched as the wicker shuddered, as an engine puffed smoke, heaving and hauling its cargo upward. Both excited and fearful, its passengers gripped the edges, some hollering with delight, others losing all color as the ground receded beneath their feet.

"Tonight only!" cried a man wearing a red-sequined tail-coat and a towering top hat. In his hands, a roll of tickets. "Unparalleled phenomena await above!"

Including, she hoped, one Dr. Thrakos, the surgeon who worked in the clouds. Worry knotted her stomach. A man who would create the likes of Ceyda would not be on display, only his creations. She and Jack would need to seek him out.

Finding him was their primary objective, for he would possess the answers to many of their questions. Under-standing the what and how of these venomous women was critical, but not for one moment did it slip Cait's mind that Dr. Thrakos might also answer Jack's burning questions about the astonishing procedure used to remove the pituitary gland of that poor woman left for dead on Holywell Street.

Nor had she any intention of leaving before speaking with any snake-handlers. Not just about Ceyda and her ilk, but about a certain snake charmer known to have traveled through Scotland and England some twenty-some-odd years ago.

"Here." Jack slid a warm meat pie into her hands. "Eat. Replace some of the energy we burned." Mischief glinted in his eyes. "A long night stretches before us and perhaps, later, a soft bed beneath us."

"Beds." She shrugged. Winked. "I suppose they have their uses."

He laughed, and her heart swelled. Here, in the windswept Yorkshire countryside, she'd uncovered a new, lighter side to her husband. One she much enjoyed.

"I'll buy us some tickets," he said. "Sooner we go up, the sooner we're down."

There was much to admire about the man she now called husband. An intelligent and progressive mind. His dedication and perseverance. His strength and his most talented hands. He was a man likely to, one day, tumble her head over heels into love. She pressed a hand to her stomach, wondering at her good fortune.

For now, however much she wished to dreamily contemplate their future, their focus must be directed at acting upon behalf of the Crown. The London murders must be stopped.

Every clue they could pry from Dr. Thrakos' lips would be critical.

Hungry, she bit into the savory pie and considered the many divisions of the circus above. Scientists with secrets tended to set themselves apart. A few of the substructures beneath the smaller balloons held promise.

Jack was back. "Come. We're in the next basket." He tucked her hand in the crook of his arm and drew her close. "While efficiency is always a priority, I've learned the circus floats onward at midnight. I suggest we add 'stowaway' to our list of activities and hitch a ride. At dawn, we'll catch a train to London from York."

Nothing but turmoil—of all kinds—awaited them in London. But there was a venomous murderer on the loose. They needed to return, soon, and with information.

"So much for a bed." They were more likely to spend the night huddled on a coil of ropes beneath a tarp. Still, they could share body warmth. She threw him a coy glance. "Upward then."

A short-skirted—all ruffles and striped stockings—beauty with a tumble of golden curls sat atop the basket's edge, swinging her legs and waving customers onward with a flourish. "All aboard!"

Tickets were collected, the engine roared to life, and they lurched into the sky. Below, the expanding vista was stunning. Field after field rolled outward—some dotted with sheep, others bright with spring plantings. Beside a lake crouched Ripley Castle, an ancient stone pile marking the outskirts of the town.

Thud.

The basket slid into a slot, and their circus host leapt from its edge to thrust a fringed parasol above her head. It sprung open with a *pop.* "This way!" she proclaimed, throwing open the door before marching off.

Wooden slats beneath Cait's feet creaked and gaps provided a glimpse of the distant ground.

Worse, the edge of the platform was guarded only by lengths of rope tied about flimsy wooden posts. A barrier easily missed without working peripheral vision. A risk that only now entered her mind.

"Careful," she warned Jack, catching his hand to draw him away from the edge. "It's a long way down."

The path led through a hall of mirrors. Cait smiled at their joined reflections—tall, short, thin, fat. They stepped out onto the edge of a circus ring that invited guests to join in the spectacle. Before them swirled a riot of activity. A band played while poodles danced. Flaming swords were brandished and swallowed. One-armed, a strongman hoisted seated guests overhead.

Curiosities one and all, but not of the variety they sought.

Those were advertised by an overabundance of signs pointing every which way to a multitude of stairs and suspended pathways. Ignoring *ANIMAL ODDITIES!*, she grabbed Jack's hand and tugged him toward *HUMAN CURIOSITIES!*

At a line of booths, spectators gaped at conjoined twins, a young boy sporting a tail, a horned and hoofed midget, and the promised bearded lady. They kept moving until Cait stopped short at the sight of the stall marked *AYLA, THE SNAKE DANCER.*

She squeezed Jack's hand, expectant.

Then sighed heavily.

"Disappointing," she said. Other spectators gawked while Cait frowned at the woman dressed in harem attire as she undulated upon a small stage. "All but one of her snakes are harmless, save the common adder."

"From the disdain in your voice," Jack replied with a hint of amusement in his own, "am I to assume you are immune?"

"You are. It's a viper native to Europe and Britain. Easily sourced with a bite that's seldom fatal. Not the best of pets."

"Pets," he repeated flatly. "We'll revisit that comment. I'm quite certain they're not meant to live in houses."

She only laughed.

"Onward?" he suggested.

"No." She tipped her head. Without friends or acquaintances in London, weeks had passed since she'd indulged herself in trawling for feminine gossip. "She might know something, but with a man present..."

"Understood." He dropped her hand. "I'll go snoop around. See what locked doors and roped off corridors I can discover."

She hesitated. "These rope-lined walkways are treacherous."

"I'll watch my step."

Doubt twisted her lips. "Be careful."

"Ten years an agent. I'll be fine." He left without giving her a chance to counter that his situation had changed.

Cait joined those who stood watching the harmless grass snake slither and twist about Ayla's arm as she rolled her hips seductively for a largely male audience.

Was it the woman's bare midriff that drew their eyes? The diaphanous material of harem pants that revealed shadows of long, shapely legs? The low cut, tight and cropped blouse beneath thin veils?

She very much doubted it was the limbless reptile.

"Come closer," the snake dancer called to her. "Meet my friend." As the woman extended her arm to welcome her new audience member, the snake slithered over her wrist and locked its eyes upon Cait. "Don't be afraid."

"Of a harmless grass snake?" She held out her own hand, inviting the reptile onward.

The five-foot-long, green and yellow beauty accepted, twining about Cait's arm to abandon her mistress. Onlookers backed away, made their excuses and departed for the next— and perhaps safer—spectacle.

"She's rather sweet," Cait said, stroking the reptile's smooth scales as it slithered upward about her shoulders. "Do you ever perform with the adder?"

"Are you mad?" Ayla asked. All seductive pretense fell way. "He's for display only. The nasty creature is—" She snatched up Cait's hand, ogling her ring. "But you know poison, do you not? Or if you don't, you shouldn't be wearing a black nagamani around here."

"A nagamani?" She glanced down at the ring. For the

first time ever, the stone embedded in the bezel had drawn attention rather than the compartment that rested beneath it. She'd thought nothing of the stone, save to value it as part of the ring, the sole item of her father's that had come into her possession. And that word. *Nagamani.* Could it be all this time, she'd worn a stone sacred to the mythical semidivine beings known as naga?

"A snake stone," the woman elaborated. "Taken from the head of a cobra, it protects its wearer against poisonous snake bites."

"Mere myth." An impossible fantasy, if perhaps one perpetuated by snake charmers. Ineffective as an antidote. Though a thought rose unbidden—could it be a symbol worn by those like her? Those with inexplicable immunity to venoms? "It was given to me by a man known as Kālūnāth. Have you heard of him?"

"No, I'm afraid not. Was he an amateur snake charmer like yourself?" Ayla snorted. "For my pet has taken to you like no other."

"I'm told he was." If her father had been here, it was before this woman's time. But might there be others like him? Like her? "Have you known anyone else to wear such a stone?"

"I'm afraid not. I've only heard the stories." Ayla reached for her snake.

But the grass snake hissed, making a decided preference known. The dancer hesitated to reclaim her animal and, as Cait had more questions, she permitted the snake its continued exploration of her hair. "You're floating in a circus known for its curiosities. If not snake charmers, have you ever encountered their inverse, say a woman with fangs of her own?" She pulled aside the colorful scarf wrapped about her neck.

A gasp. "You met one." The woman drew back, eyes on Cait's scar. "And sampled her venom. Why are you asking?"

Sensing the woman's imminent retreat, she wasted no time. "I need to speak with Dr. Thrakos."

"No." Ayla shook her head and began forcibly unwinding the snake from Cait's neck. "I want no part in this. None. Professor Grimaldi has since banned all of his human projects."

"Where can I find him?" she pressed.

"You can't. Not even if he's here. And shouldn't want to." Snake in hand, the dancer turned away. New onlookers approached. She began to dance again. "He works alone, lives apart. But if it's his handiwork you wish to view, visit the animals. The poor creatures ought to be put out of their misery."

Dismissed and ignored, Cait drifted slowly along the pathway, pondering Ayla's words. Was it possible that Dr. Thrakos sought to create a nagini? That what began as a circus attraction proved so successful, he'd sold the results, the women, to the likes of bored, rich gentlemen?

The solitary Dr. Thrakos would have to be found.

CHAPTER FIFTEEN

"WHAT ON EARTH is that?" Cait whispered the soft words into his ear. She wrapped a welcome arm about his waist and drew close.

What was it?

The stuff of nightmares.

Every animal on display brought back memories of time spent at his family's country home where his brother had first discovered a love of torturing his younger brother by releasing such things as wriggling spiders and damp frogs into his bedroom. Such abuse had continued until Jack purchased a large egg nestled in shredded paper and tucked inside a domed wooden box.

"A dragon's egg," he'd informed Aubrey. "Likely to hatch at any moment and remove a finger. Do you dare touch it?"

It was, in fact, a cleverly painted ostrich egg. But the threat of losing a precious body part had kept his brother away that summer.

Such were the childhood proving grounds of a well-developed peripheral vision and an acute sense for ill intent. Skills that had served him well as an agent. Here, he keenly felt the loss in his vision, several stories above the ground, where the creak of timbers and the snap of ropes and flags in the wind had prevented his ears from warning him of Cait's approach.

"A three-headed rattlesnake from the desert southwest of the United States of America," he answered Cait aloud. "Triple the venom, if you're willing to believe the sign."

"But you're in doubt?" She bent to peer through the glass-plate window at the scaled creature, watching. "All three forked tongues flick."

"Note the fine stitches—sutures, if you will—nearly hidden beneath the golden bands billed as collars?"

Beside them, two young men pointed. Whispered and sniggered, then moved on to the next oddity.

"Real, if surgically created in a laboratory?" she suggested. "But not found in the wild."

"Given the venom present in the two snake-women's mouths, it's tempting to think so. But look closer."

"Are those..." She inhaled sharply. "Two of the three heads are stuffed and mechanized. You can see gears rotating beneath the skin." Her lips twisted. "How many others are similarly counterfeit?"

"Many. Though there is a microcephalic sheep and a one-eyed parrot. Some, however, are like this poor creature. Brace yourself." Jack cringed as he drew her along.

"A cat with hooves?" Pain laced Cait's voice.

Staring at the creature, his stomach turned again. He'd had to force himself to evaluate the surgeon's work. "Not a natural state, but the grafted feet exhibit wound healing at the sutures."

"The poor thing. To inflict such suffering, to allow it—" Shaking her head, Cait looked away, visibly troubled. "All of this is horrible. It does, however, establish that this Dr. Thrakos possesses the necessary skills to implant venom glands and ducts into the mouths of human females."

"Ducts that end at canines altered to serve as fangs."

"Quite an abnormal dentistry practice." She shuddered.

"Did the snake dancer provide any useful information?"

"She did." A strange look crossed her face. "The mention of venomous women made Ayla skittish. She did inform me it was impossible to meet with Dr. Thrakos, that he might not even be aboard. Then pointed me in this direction to view his creations."

"I can imagine why." He led her away to stand beneath the shadow of a balloon. Here a balcony overlooked the colorful chaos of the central ring.

Colorful.

Cait's mere presence brought a long-lost vibrance back into his life and made him long for a future with her always at his side.

Tipping up her chin, he kissed her simply because he wished to do so. She nipped his lower lip as he pulled away, shooting a bolt of desire straight to his groin, tempting him to drag her into a deep shadow, hitch up her skirts and give in to the desire that curled through his chest, showing her feelings that he couldn't yet put into words.

But work must come first.

Together, they scanned the haphazard chaos before them.

"We can dismiss the smallest balloons," he said. "The structures beneath are too small to hold a laboratory. Logic suggests one of the mid-sized balloons with independent structures lashed to the sides of the circus. Adjacent, yet apart. Care to guess which one houses his so-called surgical practice?"

"The unimaginative blue one with the attached escape dirigible."

"A basic model." He nodded agreement. "Glider class with patagium wings. Retrofitted to carry a propulsive engine that would permit him to travel as far as London without much trouble." He offered his wife an arm. "Shall we?"

But it was Cait who looked after his safety, who kept him from plummeting to the field below as he cursed his failing vision. As they picked their way across hanging bridges and crooked ladders, she warned of missing slats and rungs. Pointed out rope railings as they traversed narrow ledges.

By the time they reached the door to the gondola beneath the faded, blue balloon, not a drop of adrenaline remained in his system, and the fine hairs on the back of his neck failed to send a shiver of warning across his skin.

Still, the lack of a lock up on the door sounded alarm bells.

"Cait, don't—"

Too late. The door swung inward.

Pffft.

A fine mist coated his face. "What—"

The room tipped, he stumbled and the floor rushed up to smack him in the face.

"AWAKE AT LAST." A bright, white light flicked across Jack's eyes, momentarily blinding him. "Mere trespasser or thief, I've yet to decide, though your lovely companion claims you merely dropped in for tea and conversation. I remain unconvinced, though I've put the kettle on."

Jack pushed himself into an upright, seated position and blinked. His eyes burned. He blinked, cursing. He'd adjusted to a blankness about the edges of his vision, but this blurriness was new. He prayed it wasn't permanent. Squinting, he stared at the face that swam before him.

An older man with snarled teeth and a wild expression etched into weathered skin. All framed by a shock of white hair that lay flat against one side of his head but stood straight up upon the other—layered in jagged clumps as if he used a serrated knife as a comb.

"Cait?" He reached for his weapon—and found his holster empty. Stood, only to find all forward movement blocked by iron bars.

Shit.

He spun about.

A cage?

"Over here." A tremor shook her voice. "I'm fine. For now."

The faint overhead blue-white glow of a Lucifer lamp revealed her seated form, if not the details of her face.

What was wrong with his eyes? Panic leapt into his throat. But no, the symptoms were wrong. This was *not* the tumor's doing. Something—a chemical-laced oil—had been sprayed into his face, into his eyes.

A damp cloth was thrust into his hand. "Wipe them."

The thousand pricks of pain eased and his vision cleared, though it brought nothing akin to relief.

Time slowed as he took in the scene before him.

Living quarters occupied one end of the gondola. At each side, a door. One through which they'd entered. A second that presumably led into the small glider-class dirigible they'd observed from above.

The rest of the space was given over to Dr. Thrakos' unorthodox pursuits.

Overhead, dried bits of animals dangled from strings. Open-topped boxes of all sizes were lashed to the walls and filled with an assortment of clockwork components. Misshapen and deformed embryos floated in jars, a collection housed inside a cabinet with a secure door as a concession to the floating nature of this—dare he call it such—laboratory.

Jack's was not the only cage, merely the largest. Most were empty, though a trio of beady-eyed snakes stared back at him, unblinking, from behind the glass of a terrarium.

A shudder ran down his spine.

All the clutter surrounded a central surgical suite where more modern equipment rested. A fume hood, an incubator, and a bright overhead light above a jointed metal table, one folded into the approximation of a chair. There sat Cait, her wrists and ankles clamped in place by iron manacles.

"Let her go." His words emerged with such coldness they all but froze the air they touched.

"We'll discuss that." The scientist didn't bother to look at Jack as he measured out dried leaves into a teapot, poured boiling water over them, then left the tea to steep. "Traipsing into the 'restricted' section of the circus, breaking into my home? Did it never occur to you that to do so was to trespass?" The man sighed. "Everyone wants something from the great and powerful Dr. Thrakos, so few wish to give anything in exchange."

"You've already taken my weapon."

"A safety precaution. As is the cage. Queen's agents are tricksy customers." Dr. Thrakos crossed his arms. "Shall we start with what brings the two of you here?"

Cait answered. "We need information about the women with fangs."

"You've run across more than one of them?" The scientist shook his head. "Bad luck, that. I expect you had a narrow escape from one encounter."

"You made them," Jack accused.

"Made?" The man tipped a hand from side to side. "I suppose you could say I created Ceyda, but only the one woman. Proof of concept and all that."

Jack frowned, untangling the scientist's words. "Are you informing us that the other woman was formed by nature, not man? That a snake-woman actually exists?"

"Fully assembled." Dr. Thrakos grinned, turning back to Cait. "I expect you've visited the Menwith Hotel and Spa where they keep my artificial construct. Were you afforded a chance to view my work?"

"We were," Cait replied. "Most impressive, though the glands do create a slight bulge."

"An unfortunate effect, I agree." He sighed. "Alas, the venom glands require a living incubator, otherwise they degrade with startling speed. She's a pretty thing, Ceyda. Much more appealing to men—and women—than the alternative."

"Alternative?" Jack asked.

"Well, snake form." The scientist clucked his tongue. "All in the interest of reproductive health."

"On that note, testicles have obvious procreative properties," Cait said. "But what is so special about the pituitary gland? Why construct a medical device to extract it with such targeted elegance?"

Jack grabbed an iron bar of his cage, steading himself as his lungs ceased to inflate, frozen in anticipation of the answer.

"Elegant. Medical device." Dr. Thrakos smiled. "How lovely to have my genius recognized for what it is. But the programing I was instructed to write?" The man shuddered. "A nasty piece of work to slip inside such a contraption of precision, but how does one reuse unlimited research funds?

She's released it upon young, healthy women, I gather?" He nodded. "Of course she has. And *that* would be what brought you here." The scientist frowned, his gaze turned cold and sharp. "You want to stop the murders, don't you?"

"Yes." Jack kept his gaze locked on the man's rheumy eyes. "Who is she? What—exactly—is she?"

"We live in an age of many curiosities." The scientist's eyes grew pensive. "One never knows what might crawl out of the depths of the sea, emerge from the interior of an ancient wood, or flap across the skies. Not to mention those creations handcrafted by man." He turned toward the terrarium, pride glinting in his eyes. "Which can add levels of interesting complexity to our natural world."

Worry slithered down Jack's spine. Dr. Thrakos' sanity was not at all certain. "Does this naturally venomous woman possess a name?"

"Of course. Helena." The scientist poured a cup of tea, passed the delicate teacup upon its saucer through the bars. "I've no milk or sugar. My apologies."

"Helena," Cait repeated, her words a gentle prod. "No last name?"

"Not one I intend to share. Helena arrived at my door about a year ago, seeking my aid." He tapped his chin. "But back to the question of what she is. The answer is most interesting."

"Nagini?" Cait speculated.

"Ooo. Someone knows her snake mythology." The scientist unclamped one of Cait's wrists to hand her a cup of tea. "But no. She claims to be a lamia."

"Lamia," Jack repeated. "A different snake creature, also half human, but of Greek origin. A vicious seductress."

Dr. Thrakos waggled his bushy eyebrows. "Fitting, wouldn't you say?" He drew up short. "Unless you've not yet sampled the venom?"

"Recreational use of the venom is irrelevant to our investigation," Jack said. He wasn't about to share his experience.

"Oh, I beg to differ," Dr. Thrakos replied, lips twitching. "On the whole, working with cultured venom glands is proving quite lucrative. The poison has many uses."

"There have been *murders*," Cait drew the scientist's attention away. "Few survivors. I—"

She broke off at Jack's hiss of warning, but too late.

The scientist might be mad, but he was, unfortunately, quite brilliant.

"Survivors?" The scientist's eyebrows rose, reaching for his receding hairline. "Yourself included? A woman? Helena only ever bites a woman to—" He whipped the scarf from Cait's neck, stared at the gnarled, pink scar tissue. "You survived a full envenomation? How?"

"I nearly didn't." Cait's hand shook and the teacup rattled upon its saucer. She lowered it to her lap. "Swift application of medical intervention saved me."

"No," Dr. Thrakos disagreed. "I very much doubt that." His gaze swept over her. "Dark hair. A skin tone suggesting gypsy heritage. And yet—" He snatched up Cait's hand, dumping warm tea into her lap to stare at the poison ring upon her finger. "A nagamani, the very one I last saw upon a man's hand two decades past. Could it be you're a daughter of Kālūnāth?"

Cait's breath hitched, her eyes widened.

Shit.

She'd finally found a man who might be able to answer all her burning questions, to draw back the veil that concealed the details of her heritage. But something predatory and calculating had entered the scientist's eyes.

"Absolutely not," his wife lied. "My father is a Scottish businessman."

"I doubt you believe that any more than I do. Which presents," Dr. Thrakos snapped Cait's wrist back into the restraint, then crossed to a workbench, "a rare opportunity."

Jack's hands tightened upon the iron bars of his cage. Strong, well-set iron bars. But—perhaps as a concession to weight—the roof and floor were constructed of wood. Not a perfect prison. Given time, he could break free.

Starting now, with a distraction.

He leapt into the air, slammed his boots against the boards beneath his feet. The dirigible shuddered, but the floor of the cage bowed. *Shit.* A trap door?

Dr. Thrakos spun about. A wide, snaggle-toothed grin twisted his mouth. "You're not the first guest to object to those accommodations. And while it's true that you're a prime specimen of manhood, you are not particularly unique." The scientist waved at the control panel. "Cooperate, or I won't hesitate to lighten the load with the pull of a lever."

"Don't," Jack growled. "We've caused you no harm. We only came for answers. Let us go."

"I will." Dr. Thrakos flapped a hand as he turned toward the terrarium. "Eventually. Once you've made restitution for breaking and entering." He lifted the lid. "Behold my creations, my *morphophidia*."

"You replaced the venom glands of a common adder?" Cait's voice shook with the effort of drawing the madman back into conversation.

"Such brilliance!" the mad scientist exclaimed, then frowned. "A shame, really, that you work with a Queen's agent. You would have made the perfect assistant. At least this once, however, you can lend a hand. Or an arm, as it were."

"Leave her alone." Jack twisted at the bars that kept him from Cait's side. Not so much as a hint of give.

The mad scientist ignored him, rambling on. "*Morphophidia* are a much more portable and biddable, if less appealing, way to store and incubate the venom. Quite successful. But my mistress is a jealous and vengeful creature." Dr. Thrakos attempted to catch a serpent about the neck with a mechanical grasping claw. Missed. "Not to mention dangerous. But if I were to possess an antivenin, my work would be much safer on all fronts, would it not?"

"There's no need for the snake," Cait pleaded. "Let me loose. I'll help."

"Ah, would that I could trust you." The mad scientist caught one of his creatures. He pulled it free of its cage, hissing and writhing.

Then dangled it above Cait.

"Absolutely not. Do not set that creature free upon my wife!" Jack howled, stomping upon the floor.

"There is no other way." Dr. Thrakos shrugged. "With a few pints of her activated blood, I no longer need worry."

Shit. The madman was going to allow the transformed snake to bite his wife? Bleed her to study the venom's effect?

An image of Cait upon his bed struggling to breathe rose to mind. Venom aside, most women only possessed some nine pints of blood. The loss of more than four pints in too short a time frame would push her too close to death. The man was insane. Would he go too far?

"It won't work," Cait said. Confident words, but Jack heard the underlying tremor.

"That scar upon your throat informs me otherwise," Dr. Thrakos said. "The snake-charmer's daughter who survived Helena's bite will be resistant. Nonetheless, we'll begin with only one *morphophidian*, a single dose of venom to gently re-excite your immune system. Step by step, we'll tease out the marvel of your blood. Won't that be interesting?"

A rhetorical question, for a woman strapped to a chair and a man locked in a cage could not be expected to participate in reasoned discourse, no matter the fine china involved. With polite conversation at an end, all pretext of manners dismissed, it was time to act.

He reached for his boot, found his knife missing. Disappointing, but not surprising. Though it ruled out the possibility of plunging a knife into the scientist's back from a distance.

He moved his hand to the hem of his trousers. The wire cable was still within. He ripped a few threads and pulled it free. Now all he needed was for Dr. Thrakos to step close enough to—

"Let me go," Cait yanked at the restraints. "We'll study the outcome together. Two scientific minds will make faster progress than one."

"If you were more cooperative, I'd consider it." Dr. Thrakos let the snake flick its forked tongue over Cait's skin, let it grow familiar with its prey.

"No!" Jack jumped. Yelled. Slammed his boots again onto the floor. Again and again. Anything to distract the man, to draw his attention away from Cait. But the scientist was focused upon one thing, and one thing only. Jack didn't even merit a heated glare.

"As you're both keen to be on your way, we won't waste any more time." Dr. Thrakos released the snake, dropping it upon Cait's lap.

It slithered forward, paused, then sank its fangs into her arm, flooding her system with venom.

Not a peep escaped her lips.

She caught Jack's gaze, gave the slightest shake of her head.

She was fine. Or convinced she would be. And didn't wish for him to risk his life on her behalf.

But men such as Dr. Thrakos always pushed and pushed and pushed, until they caused damage beyond repair. And she'd been so very, very sick after encountering Helena.

She might survive one bite without repercussions. But

three, possibly in close succession? No matter how much he trusted her assessment of her tolerance for venom, fear wound through his gut, tied itself in a knot and yanked.

The *morphophidian* lifted its head and the madman caught the snake returning it to the terrarium. "We'll wait an hour, see how you do. In the meantime," Dr. Thrakos lifted a green-glass atomizer and turned, "your companion will rest."

Jack lifted a hand. Turned away. Held his breath as— *pffft*—a fine mist drifted into his cage. But his lungs and diaphragm would not be denied. On a forced inhalation, a sickly-sweet and vexingly familiar scent filled his nostrils.

"HE'S IN A CAGE!" Cait protested. The ire that threaded her voice was not at all manufactured. "What trouble could he possibly cause you?"

Twice now, a misting oil had been applied to eyes that were already failing. The pain and panic written on Jack's face when he'd woken from the first exposure had twisted her heart.

The oily mist had caught them both. When she'd woken, Cait had found herself strapped to this chair, trapped inside a room where various horrors hung upon hooks driven into the ceiling and walls.

She'd been captured, taken as a prisoner after little more than a full day as an agent. Alone, save for Jack's unconscious presence, terror and humiliation had twined and twisted in her chest as she'd screamed. But, muffled by walls, drowned out by circus music, and buffered by the wind, her cries for help had gone unanswered.

"The hassles I endure to pursue my work are legion," the mad surgeon complained as he approached. "Why else install a trap door?" He pointed the atomizer at her face.

Cait held her breath, refusing to give in to the tiny voice that hoped for oblivion.

Contemplative, his lips pressed together forming a flat, annoyed line. "No." He shook his head and set aside the bottle. "There's so much more to be gleaned from a conscious patient. Tell me, *paidi mou*, how do you feel?"

She glared at him.

"Still quite spirited." Dr. Thrakos smiled, smug. His fingers landed upon her wrist to check her pulse. "Elevated, but no more than one might expect of a woman caught and detained. So many ignore the *DO NOT ENTER* signs, then act surprised when they find themselves deprived of their freedom." He clucked his tongue. "There's no chance, *paidi mou*, that I would set you free unexamined. I've never met another with talents like Kālūnāth Sapera. How fortunate for me, for science, that he found great favor with the ladies. Tell me, have you met any of your half-siblings?"

The implication that her father was—had been—promiscuous and fertile was unsurprising. But Cait's inebriated mother had only divulged a first name. "Sapera?"

"Were you told next to nothing of your origins?" Dr. Thrakos tapped his chin. "Snake-charmer. Is that all you know?"

Of her father? Very nearly.

As she'd aged, grown wise to the secrets her mother hid from her, Cait had taken note of the strange ring with the black stone that made her father frown.

Instinct connected the ring with her biological father. And, when she'd lifted it from her mother's dressing table to claim it for her own, she'd hoped the long, silent look they'd exchanged across the breakfast table might lead to revelations. But her father had merely risen and pressed a kiss to Cait's forehead. "Do try to stay out of trouble," he'd whispered.

Too late for that.

She and her brothers had already established a secret laboratory in the cellars... and once Logan joined their number, trouble hadn't been far behind.

"I know plenty," Cait replied. No matter her hunger for details, she refused to be drawn into a conversation where she spilled her secrets, hoping for a few scraps of information in return.

"Yet not of lamia," he pointed out. "A narrowness of focus upon a single culture is always a mistake. India and Greece. Gods and goddesses. Snake-charmers and snake-women. Might you be diametric opposites? A fascinating thought. Regardless, you're a hunted woman."

"For what, my pituitary gland?" Cait swept her eyes across the room, letting her gaze rest upon the various clockwork parts that littered his workbench. The effort it took to keep from glancing at her husband's crumpled form within the cage was enormous, but she would not hand the mad scientist any more ammunition than he already possessed.

"What device did she commission from you in exchange for samples of her venom gland?"

Their situation was dire. Should the *morphophídia* be set upon her in quick succession, delirium would follow. Blood loss would make her situation worse. This might be her only chance to learn about the contraption.

Dr. Thrakos' eyes darkened. "I cautioned Helena against hunting in London, but she will pursue her grandiose plans. Failure has only made her more resolved. She tries for another child, a problem given—" He waggled a finger. "Ah, but you have distracted me, *paidi mou*."

"Fertility?" she pressed. Four London men were missing two of their most-prized possessions, and Lucy Cooper a portion of her brain. "Is the pituitary gland involved?"

"Why else make such an effort to collect it?" Dr. Thrakos waved a hand. "But enough of that, I wish to discuss the marvels of your immunity, not her reproductive concerns." He dragged a fingertip across the fine mesh of white scars on her forearm. "These suggest a number of tightly controlled and self-inflicted studies. To what other poisons have you proven invulnerable?"

Cogs and pins, did he think she'd give him reason to keep her as a *long-term* laboratory rat?

"The restraints, Dr. Thrakos. I'll list them all, if you'll remove them and free my—"

"Husband?" He chuckled. "Don't look so surprised. A gold band, as yet unscratched. The proximity of the Grand Menwith Hotel and Spa. The bite at your neck. Married off to a Queen's agent, were you? A most excellent plan.

Save it failed." The mad scientist turned away, plucked another hissing *morphophidian* from its cage. "From your perspective, that is. From mine? It's worked out quite nicely."

Once again, a flicking tongue explored the taste of her skin.

"It's too much," she objected. "My system needs more time to recover."

"Does it? I detect no effects from the last dose of venom, so we'll press onward." He dropped the snake in her lap.

The snake coiled, lifted its head, then struck.

Cait clenched her fists and bit down against the pain of a second envenomation. Poison coursed through her system, spreading a prickly warmth across her chest, down her arms and legs. All of it followed by an ache that gripped the muscles of her neck with pointed claws.

"Much more of an effect this time." Dr. Thrakos' hand was back at her wrist. "And yet your pulse is only mildly elevated." His voice was a distant murmur. "Most impressive."

"Too soon," she gasped. "Please. Not again."

"We'll wait a few minutes," he conceded, "monitor your response."

Tap. Tap, tap, tap.

A distant sound, one that called to mind skeet pigeons, beaks against glass. Could a floating circus receive such targeted missives?

"I'd wondered if another letter might arrive." Dr. Thrakos crossed to a window and a cool breeze drifted across

Cait's face. He retrieved the skeet pigeon, loosed the canister from the bird's ankle, and teased out a scroll of paper.

The room tilted, spun. Cait blinked. *Kraken.* Was it past midnight? Was the circus on the move?

A heartbeat later, Dr. Thrakos loomed over her, his voice low and threatening. "You have made my clients very unhappy, Mrs. Tagert. Fascinating as you are, without funding, there is no research." He was gone. Then back. "Tricky, balancing such scales. Unfortunately, they do not tip in your favor. I must accelerate our experiment, bring it to a final conclusion, and swiftly. Rest assured, I will utilize all data collected."

Cait whimpered as, again, a *morphophidian* dropped upon her lap.

Coiled. Rose. Struck.

Yet more venom ran through her veins, followed by a blistering heat. Everything ached. Muscles. Joints. Even her eyeballs throbbed as the lights overhead grew too bright.

Then a needle pierced her skin at the crook of her arm. A rubber tube appeared.

"No." Her voice emerged as a distant whisper as she tried to wrench her arm away and failed. "Please." She turned her head, watching her lifeblood stream away, flowing steadily into a glass bottle set upon the floor. "That's too much."

"And yet so little." A note of disappointment colored the mad scientist's reply. But no sympathy. "It is with great regret that I must bring an end to your honeymoon. By death you soon will part."

No. This was not how it ended.

She refused to believe it.

"Jack," she called, focused on her partner, her only hope of escape. "Wake up."

But her lips barely moved.

CHAPTER SIXTEEN

J ACK WOKE TO THE SOFT creak and groan of wood and
steel. Beneath him, the gondola's floor rocked and
swayed. The circus was on the move, floating across
the moors. It must be past the midnight hour.

He breathed a silent curse as he tugged the hem of his
shirt free and wiped his eyes. Only then did the horror
before him swim into focus.

His wife fettered upon the surgical table. Dr. Thrakos at
his desk scrawling notes into a leatherbound journal.

"Cait?" he called softly.

Her head lolled in his direction. She blinked, but failed
to respond.

All color had drained from her face, emptied by a length
of rubber tubing that ran from her arm into a large glass
bottle. More than half its volume filled with blood.

"That's enough blood," Jack growled at the mad scientist.
"Stop. Now."

"A missive," Dr. Thrakos waved at a skeet pigeon without lifting his eyes from his work, "from London dictates otherwise."

"You intend to drain her?" Jack caught at a bar as the room tilted.

"Dry." The madman snorted, dropped his pen and spun in his chair to meet Jack's acid stare. "Though it was not my intent to play the role of vampire, the part comes naturally enough."

"Have you no empathy? You answer to a cold-blooded murderer."

"Murderer, yes. Cold-blooded? No. I assure you, Helena is, mostly, human." Dr. Thrakos rose and began to collect his notes, adding them along with a few odds and ends to a leather satchel. "And her actions are justified. She seeks restitution for a wrong perpetuated by a so-called gentleman."

"Lord Saltwell?" he asked. "What crime did the man commit?"

But Dr. Thrakos flicked a hand, dismissing him. He placed a metal-clad case upon his laboratory bench, snapped open its latches and raised the lid. Cold water vapor rolled forth. Mechanical grasping claw in hand, he began to transfer the *morphophidia* into it, one by one.

A telling move.

The mad scientist was gathering his most precious possessions, preparing to leave. There was no chance he and Cait would walk free. If he took no action, Cait's bloodless body would follow his own to the fields below and the madman would board his glider-class dirigible departing, most likely, for London or Menwith.

Time to utilize a swift, if extremely risky option. Calculated insanity, really.

He squinted at the fetters snapped about Cait's wrists, focusing on the locks that held them closed, judging them easily broken with a solid strike. But first, he needed to escape his cage.

Time to separate a few iron bars from their floor bolts.

It was the labor of a few minutes to free two small, metal cases from compartments hidden inside his boots. One contained powdered ammonium nitrate and salt along with other additives. The other, powdered zinc.

From the first case, he fashioned two small mounds of the powder adjacent to the bases of the iron bars. Ever so carefully, he added zinc to each pile. Then added dry paper twists containing black powder to ensure the fire caught and held.

"What do you think you're doing?" Dr. Thrakos shouted.

With an evil grin, Jack saluted him with the neglected cup of cold tea left within his cell. "Leaving."

Dipping his fingers into the liquid, he scattered droplets upon the powder. Green flames burst to life in a most spectacular reaction.

"Open flames? Fool! This gondola is built of wood! You'll kill us all!"

"You've already delivered a death sentence." Jack splashed more tea upon the chemicals and sent more flames dancing. Beneath the burning powder, splinters of wood glowed orange.

Spitting expletives, the mad scientist strode with purpose across the cabin. Not, however, as Jack had hoped, to retrieve a bucket of water. Instead, he reached for a lever upon the control panel and pulled.

Shit.

He'd meant for the fire to spread, if not in this particular manner. Flames licking at his feet, Jack grabbed at the solid iron bars and braced.

Clang. An unseen mechanism engaged. *Clunk. Thud.* Gears ground as they turned. *Thunk.* A bolt pulled free and the floor of the cage dropped away.

Wind rushed inward, tossing a swirl of sparks into the air. Beneath him stretched nothing but inky darkness studded with pinpricks of light.

Hiss.

A spark caught upon the dried fur of what might once have been a rat.

Snap.

Another spark landed upon a wicker basket.

Whoosh.

A sheet of paper caught fire.

Dr. Thrakos howled his displeasure.

Jack yanked at the two bars he'd targeted with his chemical fire. Loose, but not enough. He kicked at the charred wood, sent flaming fragments falling into the sky.

"Jack?" His name a strangled but welcome sound on his wife's lips.

Still alive, thank aether.

He intended to keep her that way.

The flames spread, already at a point from which there was no return. Dr. Thrakos cranked open the door leading to his escape dirigible, threw in his satchel, the case holding the *morphophidia*, then dashed to Cait's side. The madman ripped the tubing from her arm, pulling the needle free. He grabbed the bottle of her blood then, sparing her not so much as a hasty glare, made his escape, abandoning them to their presumed deaths.

Flames were climbing the walls, time was running out.

With another yank, a bar pulled free. Jack let it fall through the gaping hole beneath him. Wedging his shoulder into the gap, he shoved. Again and again until, with a horrible creak and a wrenching sound, the second bar shifted an inch.

But it was enough.

Snap!

He fell onto the floor of the gondola, rolled and jumped to his feet, then rushed to Cait's side. Grabbing the nearest solid object, he set about smashing the padlocks at her wrists and ankles.

He tossed her over his shoulder and spun about. There, his knife and pistol upon the mad scientist's desk. Above a shelf holding stacks of notebooks. All about to be lost to the flames.

With two great strides, he reached the desk and quickly collected his weapons. Was there time to look? This might be his only chance. He snatched a notebook from the shelf.

For the first time Jack had cause to thank his horrid brother for his fluency in Greek. One-handed, one after the other, he dropped notebooks to the desk, flipped through a few pages, tossed them aside.

Until he found one with most promising entries. Clockwork. Sharp knives. Pincers. Among other mechanisms that hinted at the concept behind the pituitary extractor.

Whoosh! The ceiling exploded into flame. Overhead, something snapped and the floor lurched beneath his feet.

Shouts of "Fire!" met his ears.

Time had run out.

One last thing—the message sent to Dr. Thrakos via skeet pigeon lay in a paper coil upon the desk. He tossed the missive onto the open pages of the notebook, snapped it shut and rushed for the door.

Smoke billowed around him as he crossed a rope bridge, landed upon a small platform. All about him, bridges, ladders and walkways of all kinds lifted and fell away. The circus was separating into discreet sections and floating apart —the only way to avoid the threat of the flames that had engulfed Dr. Thrakos' laboratory.

Heart in his throat, Jack turned, searching for escape and found a single option. A small dirigible nearby, still docked. But the path to it was unclear. He surged forward, praying he wouldn't misstep and send them both plunging to the fields below. Slats rattled and creaked beneath his feet as he ran, jumping from platform to bridge. Turning left, then right. The air cleared as he drew closer. Almost there.

Thud!

A man dropped from the air above, landing on the platform before him. It was the sabre-juggler carrying a coal scuttle. He barely spared them a glance as he dashed past into the small aircraft.

Jack followed, darting into the gondola. A much smaller space than the mad scientist's laboratory. A single Lucifer lamp hung overhead. A table and chairs. Two pallets upon the floor. The bare rudiments of what passed for a kitchen.

A small, frightened girl huddled in a corner leapt to her feet, ran to the sabre-juggler and threw her arms about his legs. Half-turning, she stared at him with frightened eyes. Tufts of fur sprouted—lynx-like—from her pointed ears, and a long, furry tail peeked from beneath her skirts.

The hands that held the girl close each bore six fingers.

Not his place to inquire.

"Why are you here?" The man disentangled the girl and began shoveling coal into the firebox. "Guests were to have left hours ago."

"Over our objections, Dr. Thrakos insisted we stay. The fire interrupted his plans."

The man's gaze caught upon Cait's limp form. He spat upon the floor and cursed the scientist's name. "Lay her down, then help. It's a shit engine, barely works."

Jack tossed the notebook to the floor, eased Cait onto a pallet, then dropped to his knees. Tearing a strip of cloth from his shirt, he bound her arm to stem the flow of blood— the abrupt needle removal had left its mark—and she needed every last drop.

He couldn't lose her. Not when they'd only just found

each other. Emotions clogged his throat. Fear. Denial. And what he thought might be the beginnings of love.

"Cait?"

She moaned, but didn't open her eyes.

"Stay with me," he whispered. "We have a monster to hunt."

Two fingers pressed to her throat assured him her pulse was steady, if too fast. She'd hold. The mad scientist hadn't managed to steal enough of her blood that Jack needed to consider a hasty landing to search out medical assistance.

His palm against her forehead revealed a fever. A reaction to the venom—had Dr. Thrakos set all three *morphophídia* upon her?

What he wouldn't give to wrap his fingers around that man's throat and squeeze. But to do that, the mad scientist would first have to be caught.

With a growl, Jack stood. Time to depart this smoldering pile of kindling in the sky and point their vessel in the direction of London.

He nodded to the little girl, then crossed to the engine. The sabre-juggler was placing wood atop a layer of coal. Jack snatched up a rag, drenched it with paraffin and added it to the pile.

"Matches?" he asked.

"All gone," the man answered, digging through a box.

Fire. The gods laughed, for midst the brewing conflagration, they needed a flame. Outside, he could see flames licking their way along floor slats, creeping ever closer.

Jack shifted, prepared to retrieve a burning plank.

But the man lifted a sparker. Metal scraped. Sparks flew, caught upon the rag and ignited. He slammed the firebox doors. "Cast us off!"

The gondola tilted sideways, pulled by the failing framework of the platform. *Creeeeeak!*

Quickly, Jack untied one rope, then the next, holding tight to the dirigible as he tossed away the final tether.

Free.

Jack and the man stared at each other. There was nothing more to do while they waited for water to boil, for steam pressure to build.

"The fire started in the laboratory?"

Jack nodded. "It did."

"Go." The man turned away to add more coal to the fire. "See to your woman. There's water in the bucket. We'll talk later."

Seated upon the pallet, Jack gathered Cait into his arms as they drifted into the night sky. When she stirred, he dipped a tin cup into the pail, held the cool liquid to her lips.

"Try to sip," he said, relieved when she did so.

"Snakes," she murmured, her eyes still closed. "All three. One after the other."

That rat bastard.

Enough venom to kill a grown man several times over. "We're safe now." From the evil scientist, if not entirely beyond harm's reach.

"Skeet Pigeon," Cait whispered. "From London. Saw you grab."

The note. With one hand, Jack flipped through the pages

of the notebook he'd confiscated, found the slip of paper and read the words written in an unfamiliar handwriting aloud.

Eliminate agents. Operation at risk. Destroy all evidence. Return any assets.

At the root of all this misery was a snake-woman with aphrodisiac venom, one with a vendetta. She'd made an excellent start establishing herself on these shores where there was no shortage of men and women willing to smoke, swallow or inject any number of mind-altering substances. Ones who wouldn't recoil at the thought of a deadly creature nibbling and nipping at their neck in pursuit of certain hedonistic pleasures.

He brushed a thumb over the two puncture marks left by Ceyda as he cast his mind back to his own, personal experience. Such a tiny nip, yet the effects of the venom had manifested in mere minutes and persisted for hours before fading without any noticeable or long-term side effects.

No need to advertise such a sexual stimulant, it would sell itself. Carefully controlled and offered only to those with deep pockets, it would also be wildly profitable.

Which explained the substantial numbers in his brother's account books.

Several hours removed from London, the Grand Menwith Hotel and Spa was a luxurious destination. Its practitioners and patrons easily managed. But once introduced to its pleasures, demand would increase. Hence the portable *morphophidia*. A much more practical venom source, easily carried about London. Had that been the plan all along, to establish a center, then meet the demands of addicted clients within the city?

His head throbbed. Much as he'd hoped to find another explanation, there was no denying the fact that Aubrey was in deep, that the money flowing from the spa into his family's coffers was tainted with the blood of the London murders.

What role did this lamia named Helena play? Had she sent the note by skeet pigeon? Was she a part of the greater plans? Or had she introduced an unforeseen and chaotic factor by stealing out in the dark of night onto London's streets with an agenda of her own?

One way or another, Jack would see his brother and friends answer for their actions.

But first, they needed to return to the city to catch and cage a myth before any more damage could be done. And, near as they must be to York, the fastest way home was by steam train.

Such would require landing, the purchase of tickets, an explanation for their shocking appearance. All made more difficult by Cait's need for rest—and above all else—fluids.

A faint light crept into the sky. Dawn arrived.

Perhaps there was another travel option.

The sabre-juggler reached for the blowdown valve. A moment later, the engine sputtered to life and its propellor began to turn. Mobility restored, the man picked up a spyglass and began to scan the still-dark sky, hunting, no doubt, for other members of the floating circus.

Easing Cait back onto the pallet, he crossed the gondola.

"Jack," he offered his name with a nod. "My wife, Cait. Thank you for taking us on board."

"You left me little choice." The man snorted, lowering his spyglass. "I'm Torkel. My daughter Adie." He fixed Jack with a keen eye. "Most who visit Dr. Thrakos don't leave as they came."

"Nor has my wife," Jack said. "She'll survive, but it was a near thing."

Torkel's face twisted. "The man is evil. After my wife died, he stole away my child while I worked. Poked and prodded at that tail of hers. Now she won't speak, not to anyone."

"She's hulder?" A calculated guess. Fairy folk in the British Isles weren't known for sporting tails whereas the Norwegian folktales often portrayed them as their own race.

The man nodded, then spoke with sad longing. "I'd leave the circus behind, return now to our people but..."

"The cost."

Another nod.

"Take us to London, and I'll help you travel home, if that's what you want."

Suspicious, Torkel's eyes narrowed. "If you'll pardon my own assessment of circumstances, you don't look to have two shillings to rub together."

Bending, Jack slipped his knife from his boot to slash open the hem of his trousers. Pound coins fell into his palm. He counted them out upon the console panel, noting surprise, then growing interest on Torkel's part.

"Twice that when we land," he said, "and enough to

travel in a Captain Oglethorpe airliner—first class—as far as Sweden."

"London it is." Torkel adjusted the dirigible's heading.

"If you agree to a wild plan to speed our voyage, I'll double it again."

Torkel gaped. "What plan?"

Jack held out a hand, crooking his fingers at the spyglass. The juggler passed it over. Eye pressed to its lens, Jack sighted the distant skyline of York, then took in the train tracks below them. Ones that—a quick glance at the compass on the instrument panel confirmed—led straight to London.

"The morning train heads south soon. Is this vessel equipped with a harpoon anchor?"

CHAPTER SEVENTEEN

CAIT WOKE TO THE SOFT pat of a tiny hand upon her face. A small, bright-eyed girl with fur-tufted ears stared down at her. Morning light poured through the windows of an unfamiliar gondola. A quick glance about informed her they were alone.

"Adie?" Drifting in and out of a fever dream, she'd somehow caught hold of names while Jack negotiated a ride south, before fading back into oblivion.

The girl nodded.

Overhead, feet stomped upon the roof.

"What's happening?" Cait pushed herself upright upon the pallet, relieved to find that the walls no longer wavered and rippled about her. The venom's effects were diminishing. Though a lingering fever indicated she was far from fully recovered.

The child pointed at the ceiling, made a throwing motion.

"Putting in anchor?"

Adie nodded. Offered Cait a half-eaten biscuit.

"No." Her stomach rebelled. "I'd best stick to water. But thank you."

Why were the men tethering down? Certainly not on her account. Jack knew better than to drag her into a hospital. Unless he believed she'd lost far too much blood?

Not so. She'd be fine.

Cait staggered onto her feet, lurched toward a control panel and braced herself upon its broad surface.

Well, perhaps in a few more hours.

Through the wide, narrow window above the helm, Cait gaped at the train that steamed beneath them. They couldn't possibly mean to—

She scanned the board, flipped a likely switch and was rewarded with the sounds of two men working to crank something spring-loaded. A tension cannon?

"Jack?" she called into the speaking tube. "This is a bad idea. What if you—"

Thwump. The dirigible leapt in the air. *Hiss.* A harpoon trailing a silver cable shot through the sky. *Thwack.* Its point lodged in the roof of a freight car. Under new power, the gondola jerked forward, nearly causing her to lose her feet.

Shouts and cheers rang out overhead, then two victorious men scrambled down the side of the gondola and jumped back inside, tugging goggles from sooty faces as the door slammed behind them.

Broad smiles stretched their faces. Male bonding. She'd witnessed it too many times to count. The undertaking of exciting—no matter how ill-advised—actions invigorated men.

Not that she disapproved. She herself often gambled on narrow odds. For sometimes, such risks resulted in a triumph.

Jack scooped her into his arms and spun her about, pressing a fervent kiss to her lips. "We did it! London in less than three hours!" He set her down, gently, upon her feet, supporting her when she swayed.

"You shouldn't be up." He steered her toward a chair. "Sit."

"I'm a bit woozy, that's all," she protested as he wrapped a blanket about her shoulders despite the blaze in the fire box. "Blood loss is slowing the clearing of toxins." She glanced out the window. "Won't the engineer object?"

"Most likely." The prospect didn't seem to dim Jack's enthusiasm. "I'll ratchet down later to arrange for your brother to pay an exorbitant fee for aid rendered to Queen's agents."

"Fee?" She lifted her eyebrows. "A fine is more like it." But Jack only laughed. Even Cait had to admit the expression upon Logan's face alone would be worth the cost.

"We will celebrate." Torkel lit a kerosine lamp. Above it, he hung a kettle. Tea for guests upon all dirigibles, a tradition begun by the first aeronaughts in defiance of the risks posed by the giant hydrogen balloons suspended above their heads. Helium and, later, aether, had removed much of the risk, if not the tradition.

"We have time to speak now." Torkel passed out sturdy,

earthenware mugs. "About your unfortunate visit with Dr. Thrakos." His gaze fell upon Cait. "What brought you to the Floating Cabinet of Curiosities?"

She answered. "We were hoping to learn more about a particular project of his involving venomous women."

"Ah, the snake-women. There's not much to tell. Dr. Thrakos always works apart. Occasionally for the circus, mostly for himself. About a year ago, a woman arrived. Though docked not far away, we only caught a few glimpses."

Cait leaned closer.

"Dark hair, average height," Torkel shrugged, "unexceptional, save for the scales my wife claimed covered her legs."

"Scales?" Jack pressed.

"I couldn't say. The woman never mingled, never performed or never put herself on display. And she didn't stay long."

So much for begging Torkel to meet with a sketch artist.

"Did she ever return for a visit?" Cait asked.

Torkel shook his head. "A few months ago, a few of our prettier performers disappeared. Whispers spread among the women that Dr. Thrakos had lured them away. A simple dental procedure in exchange for a promise of riches."

Toilet traps. Simple? Installing glands and teeth that might kill the bearer at any moment?

Torkel continued. "It was whispered that all but one woman's body was found dead upon the moors, their mouths naught but gaping, bloody holes." A final horror that nailed the coffin shut.

Cait shuddered. It was a story to haunt nightmares.

Jack asked a few more questions, but there was nothing more Torkel could add. The sabre-juggler left them to their tea and returned to the helm, adjusting various dials, stoking the fire and watching for tunnels. Before their trip was over, it was a good bet they'd have to cut bait and fire the harpoon anchor cannon at least once more.

"We still know so very little about Helena." Cait sighed. "A mythological creature originating in Greece. Pale. Dark hair. Gold-rimmed gray eyes. Legs possibly covered in scales."

"Did he say nothing more when I was," Jack cringed, "out?"

"Oh!" She sat up straighter. "He more or less confirmed that Helena uses pituitary glands to enhance her own fertility. Extract or consumption," she shook her head, "he wouldn't elaborate."

"Relevant." Jack grimaced and set aside his teacup. "Even if it is information capable of curdling milk."

She brightened. "He did mention meeting my biological father, commented upon his inexplicable appeal to the ladies, hinted that I might have yet more half-siblings. And I have the entirety of his name now. Kālūnāth Sapera."

"It's something," he said.

"It more or less confirms the obvious. The sapera is a twirling snake dance performed in India... and a name given to Indian snake charmers." She shrugged. "I've read so many books. But tell me, how on Earth did you manage to free us?"

As he recounted his daring scheme, her mouth fell agape.

"I managed to grab a single book from the mad scientist's shelf." He handed her a leatherbound notebook, the only physical spoils of their adventure.

"I've not yet have time to study it closely, but…"

Cait cracked the notebook open upon her knees but, as it was all in Greek, could do no more than study the sketches and diagrams as she flipped through the pages to alight upon—

She gasped. "Designs for the pituitary extractor?"

"Rudimentary plans." He grinned. "But all neatly laid out and guaranteed to set the Thorntons agog. Let's hope he and his wife can make sense of them."

Shouts rang out from the train below. Loud whistles blew. The train slowed.

"Rest now." Standing, Jack smoothed a hand across her hair, then pressed a soft kiss to her lips. A comforting peace engulfed her, steadying and calming her pulse. "If you wish to resume our hunt upon reaching London, you'll need every ounce of strength. I'll fix things below with the engineer."

THE QUIET WOKE HER.

No engine rumbled. No wind rushed past air rudders. Nothing clattered or clanged or whistled or slammed.

There was nothing but silence and the thick, soft cloud upon which she floated.

Cloud?

Cait cracked an eye open.

Mattress, she amended. One her husband shared. Fully clothed, he slept beside her. Another first for their marriage.

Holding silent and still, she mapped the features his coal-dusted face. Dark eyebrows arched. Lashes fanned outward upon cheeks. A tiny scar marked the corner of one eye. A long nose bent ever so slightly at its bridge. Full lips surrounded more by beard than scruff.

But he was no angel in repose.

An arm shot out and caught her about the waist, and a moment later, she was beneath him, pinned to the cloud by the heft of his weight and the gleam in his eyes.

A fallen angel, perhaps, for he set about scraping his teeth up her jaw to murmur in her ear. "Dragged once again to my bed but, this time, not a soul in London knows we're here, and I've not a whisper of guilt about having my way with you. We needed sleep, and now we both need something else."

His stiff, swollen member pressed against her thigh leaving no doubt as to what he had in mind.

"We're filthy," she objected half-heartedly, squirming. "Hay. Sweat. Soot."

"Don't care. I want you anyway." He tipped her face away, and the wonder that was his mouth slid down the column of her neck. "And the sheets are already ruined."

Point taken. Was this a step up from their tumble in a barn? With heat pooling between her legs, she was half-tempted to hike her skirts and let him slip inside her without preamble. But, much as she wanted him, she wanted something... more. A chance to look at him, to feel him. All of him.

"Clean first," she insisted, pushing at his shoulder.

He heaved a long sigh. "If you insist..." He rolled again, hauling her off the bed and onto her feet. He spun her about, unfastened her waistband, and shoved the mass of her ruined skirts to the floor.

"Where are we?" She unhooked her bodice, tossed it aside, then set about adding to a growing pile of clothing destined for a rag bin.

"Welcome home, wife."

What with a brief courtship involving a murder investigation, an expedited marriage of convenience, and an all-but-deadly whirlwind of a honeymoon, Cait knew nothing about her husband's holdings.

Save this wasn't the Albany.

"Home?" Stripped down to her undergarments, she turned, taking in the large, airy room as she plucked free the last of her surviving hairpins. Unadorned white walls, curtainless windows, a bare floor. Nothing but a bed that only began to fill the space.

"Your husband is the owner of a newly-built Langston townhome, suitable for a wife and family. Were you not aware?"

"How would I be?" A pin slipped from her fingers, dropped onto the floor and into a fraught silence with a faint ping. "Contrary to your stubbornly held conviction, I did not set out to trap *you* into marriage. I only wanted to be involved in a case." She sighed. "True, when my brother told me only married women might pursue a career as a Queen's agent, I might have begun to hatch plans, but..."

"Any agent would have done." Hurt, quickly hidden, crossed his face.

"Yes. No." She glanced away, shame-faced. "Not *any* agent. I'd spent all of two weeks in London, at the Lister Institute. Precious little time to meet anyone, let alone encourage any kind of courtship."

"When I became a convenient option."

"Is that all you can focus upon? Plots, plans, machinations of all kinds? Can an agent not allow for a bit of serendipity in his life?" Anger simmered. "Who carried me home to their apartment? Whose family betrayed us to the gossip rags?"

"Me and mine."

"An unfortunate beginning," she huffed, "but I thought we'd moved beyond this. We came to terms. Agreed a marriage suited us both."

"For many reasons." His words were grudging.

"You want to hear them spoken aloud?" She poked him in the chest. "Yes, you're a high-ranking agent with field experience. Yes, your knowledge impressed me in the morgue. Yes, I was quite pleased that the first agent who stalked into my first case was a tall, handsome gentleman."

"Don't forget available."

"Not only that, but willing to marry the likes of me." She wouldn't leave this grudge swirling in the air between them, poisoning their partnership. Fisting her hand in his shirt, she tipped her face upward and met his hard gaze with equal grit. "But if you've changed your mind, we could end this. If not an annulment, there's divorce."

"I want nothing of the kind." He trailed a finger across the edge of her jaw. "Why would I give up a stunning, smart and strong-willed partner? I only wanted more of a—"

A love match.

Aether. As plain as black ink upon paper, she could read it on his face. "I want that too." She surprised herself with her words. Love wasn't a requirement she'd set for marriage, but now that it was within her grasp? Yes, she very much wanted it.

"With me?"

"With you." She swallowed, then, heart thumping, stepped onto unsteady ground. "It's a lot to ask of three days, extraordinary though they've been."

"It is." He closed his eyes. "Is there a chance?"

Her heart jumped, fluttered as she lost another piece of the four-chambered organ to him. She reached up and brushed her fingers over the roughness of his jaw. "Every chance."

At that pronouncement, he bent to press a hard, quick kiss to her lips. "Then, as my wife, you will need to tour the premises."

"Such as the basement?"

"Eventually. Much as I know you'd like to assess the furnace surrounds for herpetological colony possibilities—a proposition which will make hiring staff difficult—we should start with the bathroom." He pulled his shirt over his head with a single hand, grinning when her gaze snagged upon his torso. He backed away. "A modernized townhome possesses modern amenities—all newly installed."

"And in need of testing?" She pressed a hand to her chest, enjoying this playful side of her husband. "Such words of endearment."

Jack laughed. "Experimentation, the way to my wife's heart."

She opened her mouth to ask something about the depth of the tub, but his hands fell to his waistband and, a heartbeat later, her question was forgotten as the presence of a naked man—*her* naked man—refocused her priorities upon a more enticing benefit to their marriage.

One they'd already enjoyed. Still, explorations had been limited in the hayloft, half-dressed as they were. Full nudity —with her husband's rampant interest on display—was an entirely new experience.

Heat rose to her cheeks. All that had been inside her, would be again, as soon as—

"Come. I've a mind to investigate the uses of one household appliance in particular." With the devil in his eyes, he caught her hand and tugged her into an adjoining bathroom of grand proportions. One fixture held his undivided attention. "The possibilities are endless, wouldn't you agree?"

In a marble-lined corner stood a magnificent shower. Ringed by a fencing of perforated pipes, adorned with knobs and valves to shunt hot and cold water this way and that, it was crowned by an enormous shower head.

"For washing up?"

"For more than that." With a few twists of his wrist, water cascaded from rings of pipes overhead. He dragged her into its midst.

"Jack!" Her cry was a sharp protest at the cold water that poured down upon them, dousing hair, soaking her shift until it clung to her, translucent.

"It'll warm." Hooking his fingers about the garment's straps, he slid them down her bare arms, dragging the neckline's edge of wet ribbon and lace to the pebbled tips of her nipples. Eyes dark, he let it hang there as he lifted his gaze to hers.

"Shall we conduct our first experiment?" His voice grew full of promised pleasure as the water grew warm. "Fully assess the rewards of involving such a contraption in marital relations?"

Steam billowed upward. Her finger traced a path across the damp hair upon his chest. "Will the pipes stand up, one wonders, against the force required to elicit an explosive finish?"

"I'll take that as a yes." A final tug dropped her shift to the floor.

Then his mouth was on hers, working its magic, both scattering her thoughts and narrowing them. There was only him. Her. And wet, warm pleasure.

Soap skimmed over skin as they explored each other's shapes. Her hands slid over broad shoulders roped with muscle, an impressive chest and a tapering waist before they finally reached the prize beneath.

An intake of air scraped over his teeth as she cupped him, wrapped her fingers about his hard length and gave a none-too-gentle yet encouraging squeeze.

"Vixen." His hands caught her hips and spun her about, pulled her back against him. One hand lifted the weight of a breast, while the other slid over her belly, slipping into the cleft between her legs to toy with the swollen nub begging for attention. All while water streamed down them.

It was heaven.

It was also torture.

Edging ever closer to a peak, her hips flexed. Rocked against his erection. It was too much and not enough.

She turned in his arms, nipped at his chest. "Phase one assessment?"

"Full marks." He gripped her chin, tipped it up to extract a deep kiss. Tongues tangled. Lips were nipped. "Phase two?"

"Please." She hitched a leg up alongside his thigh. "I need you."

His hands captured hers, lifted them overhead—and wrapped her fingers around a pipe. "Hold tight." He hooked an arm beneath her knee, then, as their eyes caught and held, pushed into her. Slowly. Inch by inch. Until he was fully seated.

"Jack," she whispered.

At first he took her with long, deep strokes—both of them keeping an eye on the piping surround. When it proved firmly anchored, his thrusts quickened, each one more vigorous than the last. If the bolts that fixed their modern waterfall groaned or strained, they couldn't be heard over the cries and shouts that accompanied the rushing current that pushed them careening over the edge.

Wet, chests heaving, they slid to the tiles beneath, wrapped in each other's arms. Warm water continued to fall in a steady downpour as their heartbeats pounded and, eventually, slowed.

He pushed the wet mass of her hair to the side, kissed her. "Were we successful?"

"Very." Smiling, she stroked a hand over his face, doing her very best to memorize its satisfied, relaxed lines, an uncommon state. "Yet only a first effort. A good scientist will seek to both replicate results—and improve upon them."

But later, for even now she caught a hint of strain about his eyes. Certain warning that a headache simmered below the surface. They needed to visit Lister Laboratories posthaste, locate Lord and Lady Thornton and set the notebook in their hands. The sooner the penned drawings revealed their secrets, the better.

"One of many delightful discoveries." He traced his finger over the tiny skull and crossbones tattoo upon her ankle, eyes dancing.

"You like it?" She grinned.

"I do. Though I think you have it backward, wife." His smile softened. "You're the cure, not the poison."

Her heart soared. "Best keep me close."

"Always." Alas, the water grew cold. "And it's time for

reality to intrude." He stood, pulled her to her feet and turned off the water. "And we—well, you—face a conundrum." The corner of his mouth kicked up. He toed her sodden shift. "As the household's first and only female occupant, what *will* you wear?"

CHAPTER EIGHTEEN

Wicked of him, perhaps, to take so much delight in the vision his wife presented. Barefoot, garbed in one of his shirts, and wrapped in his dressing gown, Cait was not at all happy with his proposition for the day's activities.

Her frustrated agony was completely understandable.

But in the aftermath of their sudden, unanticipated wedding, not a single domestic issue had been addressed. As their travel trunks had been sent to the Albany, his wife was left without, well, much of anything.

Skeet pigeons had been launched. One to Cait's mother. A second to her maid, Janet, with a desperate plea for clothing.

And, after much gnashing of teeth, a third to Black, informing him of their return.

"Carte blanche," he teased as she paced.

"I've no interest in shopping." Cait's eyes narrowed as

she turned to face him, notebook held hostage in her arms. "Besides, I wish to be present when you question Lord Aubrey. He is, after all, my new brother-in-law."

"He'll admit to nothing, and there's not enough evidence to escort him to an interrogation room."

"Yet." She drummed her fingers on the notebook.

"Moreover, my mother is a misery. News of my marriage is bound to have her as unbalanced as a flywheel without counterweights." His wife was a wonder among women, but the inability to locate her name within Debrett's would have sent the dowager viscountess into a fit of the vapors.

No need for Cait to bear witness.

"Dress," he continued. "Promote Janet to housekeeper so that she might set domestic matters in motion." He tugged on his coat. "Your mother is of most value for her society gossip."

"We've been in London for two weeks," Cait huffed. "Her efforts are mighty, but renewing old acquaintances in London is proving difficult to impossible."

"Still, with her ear to the ground, she might have heard rumors. A lamia is bound to draw attention. We might as well engage her assistance."

"Nothing like questioning your own mother about a, possibly Greek, woman who might be moving among the *ton* peddling a promise of enhanced fertility and heightened eroticism." She rolled her eyes. "I can't wait." Cait let her gaze slip downward over the buttons of his waistcoat to settle upon the fall of his trousers. "Your own capabilities will be drawn into question."

That pricked beneath the cravat. "Only your opinion holds weight." He wrapped his arms about her. With the mad scientist's notebook trapped between them, he claimed a slow, soft kiss. "I don't recall any complaints, enhanced or otherwise."

She stomped upon the floor. "You're leaving me behind. That's my complaint."

"Briefly. I need to spur my brother to action. Kick the hornet's nest, as it were. We'll meet at Lister Laboratories, hunt down Thornton and set him to cracking the secrets of this notebook."

"I'll hold you to that promise. Which is why it's staying with me." She tucked the volume in question securely under her arm. "Four hours," she warned. "Be there, or I'm transforming the front parlor into my laboratory."

Visions of faces pressed to the bay window, mouths agape, while his wife handled deadly creatures with careless disregard flashed through his mind.

"You would turn our home into the neighborhood sideshow?"

Her quiet smile was anything but demure.

"Four hours," he agreed.

CHAOS HAD OVERTAKEN Jack's family's townhome, a fact that did nothing to improve the growing headache expanding inside his skull.

Workmen tromped up and down the stairs, hammers,

trowels and paint cans in hand, while the steam butler rushed about, swatting at various overworked cleaning bots. One zoomed past, brooms twirling so fast its engine emitted thin curls of smoke, rather defeating the frantic efforts.

"Lord Aubrey and my mother?" he inquired.

"Up." Emsworth's iron chest heaved. "Up. Up. Up." Bellows that served as lungs creaked as they forced the word out over a metal reed. "Up. Up. Up."

The turmoil centered around one particular suite of rooms where walls were being relocated and re-plastered. Paint, judging from the various splotches applied to said walls, was not yet decided upon. In the midst of it all stood his mother. At her side, a woman holding fabric swatches prattled on about color palettes.

"Drastic alterations," he interrupted, eyebrows raised, "are traditionally yielded to the new viscountess."

"These will be my rooms," his mother countered, dismissing the woman with the wave of a hand. "Lady Mildred's taste is entirely too provincial."

He knew a moment's pity for his future sister-in-law. "No quiet, retiring country life for you?"

"Certainly not," she huffed. "Much instruction will be required to establish a country bride's position in London society. A situation," his mother planted her hands on her hips, "that your recent behavior has not at all aided."

"Many apologies, Mother, for my inconvenient existence. Is Aubrey about? We need to have words."

"Aubrey," her voice was thin and sharp, "has withdrawn to his club for the day."

Jack nodded, turned to go. But his mother's hand shot out and fingers dug into his arm.

"Do you know how I was informed of your marriage? Your mother-in-law drove that knife into my chest. Stood in my parlor, nose so high she would have drowned in a rainstorm, and informed me that the Duke and Duchess of Avesbury had witnessed your vows."

"It was a small, impromptu ceremony. The only other guest was my colleague, Mr. Black."

His mother's eyes hardened. "The three people responsible for driving my daughter into the arms of a foreigner, into exile." Air scraped into her lungs over clenched teeth. "How could you?"

Jack pried his mother's fingers free. "Angela chose her husband fully aware of the life that waited for her beyond our shores." Of the tasks that lay before her. "As for myself, I assure you, I am quite content."

"Impossible." Mother sniffed. "Your bride's lineage is tainted on both sides. Her mother strayed and her natural father is unknown. Not that any of my set find ourselves surprised, given her mother's disastrous first Season."

Trouble awaited Cait in London society. While he wasn't at all certain she would care, Jack found himself questioning the origin of the smoldering hostility glinting in his mother's eyes.

He tipped his head. "Who is Mrs. McCullough to you?"

"Trouble." She sniffed. "She defined indiscretion. Always the coquette, forever wandering off into dark corners out of her chaperone's line of sight. Your father wasn't the only gentleman she attempted to lure into her snare."

Making any future family gatherings a true treat. *Wonderful.*

"When scandal broke, no one was surprised." An unpleasant smile tugged at the corners of his mother's pinched lips, suggesting a similar fate awaited him. "Caught in a linen closet with a footman. The next day she married a Scottish entrepreneur and was banished from London. Both Mr. Black and your wife are products of that unhappy union."

Interesting and most informative. But the tale altered nothing of the depth or the intensity of his feelings for Cait.

Time ticked steadily onward, but his brother's club, Sharp's, was only a few streets away.

"I must go."

"You can claim coercion," his mother called as he strode for the door. "It's grounds for dissolution of marriage."

He kept walking. "Not a chance. Goodbye, Mother."

With the headache's onset, the edges of his vision had closed in, forcing extra attention and vigilance to weave through the crowds of pedestrians thronging the streets.

"Pardon me. Excuse me."

Twice, he bumped shoulders. Crossing a street, he narrowly escaped having his toes flattened by carriage wheels.

Dammit. The effects upon his peripheral vision had worsened since he'd left London.

He slid inside the quiet of the club and exhaled his relief.

Reflexively, he pinched the bridge of his nose, but it no longer served to force the headache into abeyance. His only hope lay in the contents of a mad scientist's laboratory notebook. And in the chase.

Cage a lamia.

Imprison a mad scientist.

Locate the pituitary extractor.

The list of tasks drove him onward.

Step one: bait his brother.

He rolled his shoulders, addressed the doorman. "Lord Aubrey?"

"In the clocktower, sir."

A three-story climb. During which he steeled himself for the unpleasantness to come. At the room's entrance he paused. Stepping into the room would only further limit the field of his vision. Instead, he leaned against the doorway, watching.

Across the room, an enormous clock face—both window and timepiece—marked the hour. Light pouring through its leaded glass illuminated the faces of three suspects. His brother, Oakes and Carruthers. Curious. He wouldn't have thought Sharp's would welcome an untitled physician as a member, but there sat the three old school chums, heads tipped together, in heated discussion.

Well, two of them conferred. Carruthers was too soused. Eyes closed, his head wobbled upon the fist that propped it up. At any moment, he might topple from his chair. His companions, used to such behavior, ignored him.

From the intensity of their conclave, it would appear that

a number of disturbing skeet messages had reached their aviaries. They would know about Ceyda's death, that the floating laboratory was no more than ashes scattered across a distant field.

He was betting that they also knew where to find a London-dwelling lamia. One who could leap from windows, scale walls and disappear deep inside shopping arcades.

Unless they'd lost control of a most valuable commodity. At the very least, they would need to aid Dr. Thrakos, help him establish a new facility that he might continue to culture glandular tissue and place it within living hosts, be they serpentine or human. The continued operation—and profitability—of the Grand Menwith Hotel and Spa depended upon it.

It was that, or theirs would become yet another failed venture. For without living incubators to generate and deliver ever more venom, their most valuable commodity would stagnate.

An unexpected undertaking requiring additional outlay of capital that, from the expressions contorting their faces, the threesome hadn't thought to save for a rainy day.

Aubrey lifted his head, caught sight of Jack in the doorway. Forcing an expression of nonchalance, he rose to cross the room.

"Congratulations," his brother said, customary smirk fixed in place. "Your marriage almost drove Mother to murder. When the Duchess of Avesbury's name was dropped, I am convinced that only thoughts of bloodstains on a prized carpet kept her from swinging the teapot at your mother-in-law's head."

"I'm not here to discuss my marriage." Jack met his brother's gaze with a look that made most men back away. He'd give Aubrey one chance. "When I left to work abroad, the family coffers were running dry. Now they overflow. Explain."

Aubrey stiffened. "Right to it, then. I'll return the favor. It's none of your concern."

"That's where you're wrong," Jack said as his brother began to turn away. "I've been to your luxury hotel. Availed myself of its facilities. Met a fanged masseuse. Your business plan is unsustainable."

Let Aubrey wonder how much he knew. Would his brother slip, reveal Helena's role in this enterprise? How long would she suffer the partnership of these men before taking her venomous talents elsewhere—if she hadn't already?

Helena's words at his brother's engagement ball had spoken of vengeance. Yet her every action pointed toward another goal: reproduction. The London murders weren't personal, weren't revenge, but a quest for fertility, one following a gruesome logic. Testicles for a male partner. Pituitary glands for herself.

Had her efforts met with success?

"You owe me. Much. That woman cost me a pretty penny." Aubrey glared. "Wanton destruction of my property, but not, I hear, before enjoying a nip or two." He leaned close and mocked, "Such an upstanding agent of the Queen. I hope your balls turned blue and fell off."

Painfully accurate, but he'd long since stopped responding to Aubrey's jabs. "Turn the lamia in, or I'll see you and your partners take equal responsibility for the London murders."

"I've no idea what you're talking about." Aubrey lifted his chin. Challenge glittered darkly in his eyes. Did his fingers—regrettably out of sight—curl into fists?

"I wonder," Jack replied, "will Dr. Oakes be equally reticent when I pose the same question to him? What of Carruthers? Will he spill all under influence of alcohol? After all, I've yet more questions for him concerning his father, Lord Saltwell, and his visit to Menwith. Beginning with, why did you send a lamia to murder your father in Aubrey's library?"

Aubrey's eyes slid away. "We had nothing to do with that."

Not exactly an answer. Not guilty of the crime, perhaps, but his brother knew something. When the truth came out, how central to the crimes would his brother be? He sighed. Family was family.

"If you help me catch Helena," Jack began, "I might be able to—"

"Excuse me." A gentleman pushed past them, stopped short to scan the room. "On your feet, Oakes!" His voice vibrated with anger. "You had no right to interfere. None."

There was a collective gasp as the gentleman raised his arm. In his hand was a pistol.

A chair scraped back. Dr. Oakes stood. "You put her very life at risk. Five is enough, wouldn't you say?"

"It was not your decision to make!"

"Or hers?"

Whatever their argument, it didn't promise to end well.

"Don't do this." Jack edged toward the man. "There are more civilized ways of handling disputes."

"Civilized?" Wild-eyed, the man swung his arm to point the muzzle at Jack. "What he's peddling is anything but civilized. It's dishonest and morally corrupt. He had no right."

Back to that, were we?

Both hands raised, Jack angled his head, trying to catch a glimpse the man's ankles without losing sight of the pistol. With a quick hook of his foot, he could sweep the man's feet out from under him, drop him to the floor. But as he shifted, the edge of his vision blurred and, for the briefest of moments, Jack could swear the man had four feet.

All which moved. At once. Swiftly.

Shit.

He lunged, reached for the armed gentleman. Missed.

Bang!

The glass clock face shattered into a thousand shards, all raining to the street below, sharp-edged and deadly. Gears and pins caught, shuddered and groaned. Vibrations shook the walls, the floor. Men leapt to their feet, shouting.

Oakes cowered behind a chair as the armed gentleman advanced on him.

Jack ran, reaching. He caught the gentleman's coat, yanked hard.

But a moment too late.

"A wife has a duty to provide her husband with heirs!"

Bang!

"He's hit!"

Oakes clutched his chest, shocked that a bullet had found him. Beneath his hands, blood spread across the white field of his shirt. He blinked, staggered and fell backward against the giant clockwork mechanism.

There was a loud creak, then together with the remainder of the clock, Oakes tumbled from the gaping hole in the club's wall. From below, screams rose to meet their ears.

Dammit.

So much for questioning the doctor.

Jack kicked away the spent weapon, rolled the gentleman onto his stomach and pinned him in place with a knee. Cursing, he stripped the cravat from his neck to bind the man's wrists.

A glance behind told him that in the commotion Aubrey and Carruthers had bolted. He'd catch up with them later.

And while he'd not be late to the Lister Institute, he would be tardy for his appointment with Cait. Meeting with Thornton would have to wait. He had a man to question.

CHAPTER NINETEEN

"Y{ou did what?}" Cait pressed her hands to her ears, lifted them, certain she'd misheard. But no, there was nothing amiss with her hearing.

Impossible. Decades had passed. How could such a connection still exist, one strong enough that Mother simply—

"Called in a favor. Foolish of me, I suppose, to have expected another outcome." Her mother stood beside her directing a steady stream of footmen as they traipsed past, carrying hatboxes and trunks in an efficient and organized manner, a general executing a long-planned invasion.

Alert for a skeet pigeon announcing her daughter's return, Mother had arrived at Cait's new door a scant few minutes after Jack's departure and stepped into the town-house with a gleam in her eye.

Cait had expected reprimands. A long-winded lecture on observed proprieties in society. Tears of regret and remorse that the entirety of the *ton* had not witnessed her wedding.

Anything but smug satisfaction.

A mood that had arrived along with a bundle of clothing —combinations, stockings, shoes, corset, bustle, petticoats, underskirt, green and white striped bodice with a matching overskirt—and persisted as her mother brushed and pinned Cait's hair into a jaunty upsweep.

With her daughter once again presentable, her mother had thrown open the doors, admitting her troops.

"Another outcome?" Cait echoed.

Her mother glanced at the servants, then beckoned her into the parlor where they stood, for there was not so much as a stick of furniture in the parlor.

"When I requested aid in finding you a husband," her mother began, "I rather anticipated that you would be presented with a selection of suitors. That a period of courtship would be followed by a proper wedding. But Eudora always was one to take immediate and decisive action." Her mother flapped a hand. "Regardless, it's done."

Cait's ribs grew tight, as if there was not enough air in the room to fill her lungs. "Eudora?"

"Well, Lady Ravensdale, if we're to be precise." Mother clucked her tongue. "Though it's been a few decades. Such an effort, remembering to address her as one does a duchess."

"Lady Ravensdale, Duchess of Avesbury?" Cait's voice rose, climbed into the aether. "You're friends with the Duchess of Avesbury?"

"Friends might be stretching it, though there was a time I

would have called her one. During our first Season, she set her eye on the duke and... well, suffice it to say she owed me a favor."

Cait gaped. "And you called it in."

Such was a revelation that cast the entirety of her time within the Italian Gardens in a new light. It explained much. Rather deflating, really, to learn it was not her intelligence or skill that had induced the duchess to advocate for the marriage, but obligation.

On the other hand, it was a relief to know that Logan himself—via an overinflated sense of duty—had not reported the overnight shenanigans following her encounter with the not-a-vampire.

"Mind you, I asked Her Grace to smooth the damage done." A cloud lowered, damping the sunlight of her mother's earlier cheer. "Not to force your hand. I wanted you to have a choice. If such was not the case, I failed."

Though her mind reeled at the implications, Cait could not allow her false belief to stand.

"You did not," she said. Her mother had launched endless campaigns to see her daughter well-established. An uphill battle Cait had sabotaged at every turn. It was time to call a truce. "I entered into this union of my own free will. I *chose* it."

"Did you choose a husband or a career?"

Without a moment's hesitation, she answered, "Both."

"I'm glad to hear it." Her mother's lips pursed. "For everything with that woman is a double-edged sword. Don't think it has escaped my notice that all my children now serve

Queen and country, a state of affairs that suits both the duke and duchess quite well." Her mother drew a deep breath. "Well, then. You have married higher than I expected. I can only hope that your marriage, albeit rushed, will be a happy one, unlike my own."

Was that what worried her mother? Parallels certainly existed. An indiscretion followed by a swift marriage. Save her mother had married a man with a wandering eye who was interested only in the size of his bride's dowry.

Cait might not have married for love, but there was mutual respect, a commitment to both their careers, an undeniable physical attraction. And every hope it might someday be more.

She smiled. "It's off to a promising start."

And that was when she noticed. Her mother's smile had slipped, just the tiniest amount.

"There are other past connections you ought to know about," her mother said. "Yesterday, I took great pleasure informing your new mother-in-law that, after so many years apart, we would once again be keeping company." She clucked her tongue. "Watch your step about her, she's a snake in the grass ready to strike, unprovoked."

Twice now, she'd been warned. "How fortunate I'll quickly grow immune." Cait hesitated. "Does she know my natural father?"

Her mother bristled. "Cait..."

"On my honeymoon, I met a man who knew him." She lifted her hand, the one upon which she wore the poison ring. "He called the stone a nagamani and named me daughter of Kālūnāth Sapera, snake charmer."

Color rose in her mother's cheeks. "Well. Now you know more about the man than I do. He never mentioned a surname. Our affair was a brief one." Her chin trembled, ever so slightly. "He gave me that ring. Foolish of me to think it meant something. When I returned to the carnival next evening, his tent was gone..."

Leaving behind her expectant mother.

"There's nothing more you can tell me about him?" Cait's voice was hushed.

"He was kind and funny and," her mother reached out and caught her hand, "left me with an incredible daughter." She rubbed her thumb over the nagamani. "But, no, other than this ring."

"I have it on good authority that Lady Aubrey will be entirely focused upon her eldest and any future heirs his bride produces." Cait squeezed her mother's hand. "So if Lady Aubrey has no other secrets with which to sharpen her knife, I'll manage."

"None. Not that she'll give you any trouble. If anything, the shoe is on the other foot." A sly smile once again stretched itself onto her mother's face. "Oh, the tales I could tell. Most of them old and dusty. Many no longer relevant, but some... well... the measures Lady Aubrey took to secure the title of viscountess would curl the ends of any man's mustache."

"All stories I'd like to hear." Time to dip her toe in the

water. "A woman who hovers on the edge of society hears much."

"And sees even more." Her mother grinned.

"Perhaps you might be of aid?" Cait gave her mother a knowing look.

"Oh?" Light danced in her mother's eyes. "How might that be?"

"We, the Queen's agents, are interested in finding a certain woman, possibly of Greek ancestry, thought to be peddling a fertility treatment. She may or may not move among the *ton*. Have you heard any whispers?"

"I can't say that I have. But my network is not as established as it once was. Why the interest?" Her mother's eyes widened. "Is *she* the vampire?"

Cait cringed at the term, yet declined to clarify or elaborate. "This stays between us. It can go no further."

"Please." Mother scoffed. "Our family overflows with secrets. Your brothers, sneaking all about. You, experimenting with aether-knows-what in the basement. People eye our family and speculate about all manner of things, but have they ever confirmed a single rumor? No." She crooked her fingers. "Ask me. Your secrets are safe."

As the footmen filed out of the townhouse, Janet stopped in the parlor doorway. "The spectacled cobra is in the sitting room with the southern exposure. Unless you'd like the cage moved, that's the last of it, ma'am."

Janet met her eyes, not her mother's, a tacit statement that her maid wished to answer to a new mistress. Gratitude filled her heart.

"Does the role of housekeeper suit?" Cait asked.

Janet all but bounced on her toes grinning. "Very much. Thank you."

"You'll need to hire all new staff. Loyal individuals capable of keeping all manner of secrets."

With a nod, Janet began to turn away.

"Wait," Cait called. "Will you join us?"

Between the three of them, Janet was the most versed in traditional remedies and lore.

"Of course." It was impossible for her housekeeper's eyes to grow any brighter.

"On my honeymoon, I learned the name of the woman who attacked me: Helena. She's connected, if only indirectly, with my brother-in-law, Lord Aubrey. His friend and personal physician, Dr. Oakes, and Stephen Carruthers, the new Lord Saltwell, are also involved." Cait took a deep breath and filled them both in on the specifics, making mention of the drastic measures the venomous woman had employed to enhance her fertility. "From what we gather, Helena is desperate to bear a child. We expect the murders will continue until she achieves her goal."

"Castrations." Her mother turned a shade of green. "Testicular extracts and brain glands with a side of venom. All necessary for her to conceive? That is quite the witch's brew. Disgusting."

"If such items were commonly required for conception," Cait agreed, "it would certainly curtail London's population."

"So the venom of her bite—" Janet blushed.

Her mother laughed. "Is a stimulant at low doses, one that enhances a man's libido and performance."

"What of a woman's?" Janet asked.

"Presumably the same, though we don't know for certain." She touched the scar at her throat. "I can speak only to the pain and illness of attempted murder involving a *large* quantity of venom."

Twice. Though a less dreadful experience the second time at the hands—or, rather, snakes—of Dr. Thrakos.

"Snakes and fangs." Janet shook her head. "The things men will do for a roll in the hay."

Cait's face blazed.

"A story told throughout the ages." Her mother snorted. "Our best odds at locating this monster are to trace her whereabouts via those who pay handsomely for her personal service, for a nip at the neck before a four-legged frolic."

A point of frustration.

"Unfortunately, we were unable to acquire a list of names." Their hasty exit from the Grand Menwith Hotel had negated any chance to access the records room.

Irritating, the paucity of clues.

Wait.

"We heard a rumor hinting of scales upon her legs." Cait looked to her maid. "Have you ever heard of such a thing outside of fairy tales and legends?" Not that they necessarily need dismiss actual snakeskin as a possibility.

"On a human?" Janet tugged at her ear. "No, never. There is, however, a dreadful skin condition that bears a certain resemblance to reptilian skin."

"Treatable?"

"Possibly," Janet answered. "I couldn't say for certain."

"If I had a horrible skin condition," Cait mused aloud, "I would consult a pharmacist known for his skill at compounding creams, salves, ointments, and emollients."

Her mother frowned. "London is a very large city."

Cait tapped her lips. "Many of the attacks took place near Covent Garden, near the theaters."

That cheered her mother. "T. Everly and Company. A most excellent apothecary. They cater to actresses, women who must make the most of their faces. It's said they sell a cold cream that erases ten years from a woman's face." Her mother stroked a finger across her cheek. "But there's little chance the chemist will divulge any information about a client. To do so would ruin his reputation."

"But he would keep written records," Cait countered. Plans churned inside her head. "Detailed notes and receipts. And I'm not due at the Lister Institute for two hours." Time enough for a brief shopping trip before she—and the note-book tucked inside the reticule clipped to her belt—were due at Lister Laboratories. "Hats and gloves, Mother. We've shopping to do."

PARASOLS ALOFT, mother and daughter traversed the pavement side by side, both of them in their milieu, projecting an air of mystery and purpose as they strode down the street. Like her daughter, Cait's mother on a mission was an unstoppable force.

They turned a corner and came upon the apothecary Mother deemed most promising. Above its store front, gold lettering proclaimed T. Everly & Co.

Wide glass-paned windows displayed tall canisters and carboys filled with colorful liquids of unfathomable use. A bell sounded as they stepped through the door. Inside, gleaming wooden shelves stretched from floor to ceiling. Stacked with tinctures and teas, soaps and lotions, and row upon row of labeled bottles containing all manner, there was *materia medica* that promised to cure countless aliments.

"How may I help you today, ma'am?" asked a man from behind the counter.

"Are you the famed Mr. Everly?" her mother asked.

"I am."

"Excellent." Her mother glanced sideways, as if to assess the chances that another might overhear, then leaned closer. "I'm in a bit of a quandary, Mr. Everly." She kept her voice low. "A stubborn patch of dry skin refuses to heal. Quite frankly, it reminds me of something I viewed in the Reptile House at the zoo, if you take my meaning." She gave a dramatic shudder. "I chanced to overhear whispers between two women praising a new formula you developed for an actress aimed at curing such a condition. Tell me my ears have not failed me."

The chemist beamed. "They have not."

"And the key ingredient?" Cait nudged, assuming the

role of doubting Thomas. "I won't have my mother paying for snake oil."

"Never." The chemist drew up, offended. "Shark liver oil has proven benefits."

A green tinge colored her mother's face. "You would have me consume shark liver?"

"Not at all. The oil is highly refined, then added in its purified form as one of many ingredients in the lotion. All topically applied, I assure you."

"But the smell!"

The chemist turned, plucked a bottle from a shelf behind the counter, then set it before her. He uncorked it, then lifted an eyebrow. "Do you detect an odor?"

Her mother leaned forward, sniffed. "I do not."

"Exactly as it should be."

"But will it hold up in warmer temperatures? In the limelight?" Her mother leaned forward. "Might you whisper the leading lady's name?"

He resisted. "I'm afraid I cannot divulge that information."

A chemist with principles.

Cait lifted a cake of scented soap from a tiered stack, studying its floral wrapping while her mother continued her efforts to draw forth the woman's name. If anyone could crack him, it would be her mother.

Without a name, they'd only managed to confirm the possibility that Helena performed on stage. Not enough to hone their search.

She drifted away, examining various wares displayed

beneath the glass-topped counter, all while side-eyeing a curtained entryway set behind it. It would be a moment's work to step into the back room. Save for one impediment.

"May I help you?" a young, female assistant inquired.

"No, thank you," Cait answered. "I'm merely accompanying my mother."

The door's bell jingled, and the assistant moved away.

It was the only opening she was likely to get.

With all eyes directed elsewhere, Cait slipped behind the counter, then the curtain.

Gone was the polished wood and gleaming glass. Here, the inventory-laden shelves were of rough-cut wood. Against the wall stood a large copper distillery. Overhead hung bundles of fresh and dried plants. A long worktable supported multiple items including a brass scale and pill-making machine, long-necked flasks and lidded crocks. Dark, purple liquid bubbled over a Bunsen burner in a glass beaker.

All fascinating, but she required a name, not a product. Certainly, a customer deserved her privacy—unless she was in the habit of murdering innocents upon the street.

Which was why only the leatherbound ledgers held her attention.

Without hesitation, Cait opened one after another, searching for a record of sales that linked names to treatments. She found none.

Only page after page of recorded formulas.

She focused on the creams, ointments and emollients—on those which included shark liver oil as an ingredient.

On the opposing page, neat columns noted dates of sale alongside an alphanumeric code. Three formulations compounded within the last month matched her search parameters: #782A, #9B62 and #Q293.

Mr. Everly took his promises of discretion quite seriously.

Lips pinched together, she fought the temptation to hurl the ledger across the room and instead concentrated on what little information she could extract from the notions scrawled beneath the formulas.

"Miss? You can't be in here." The shop attendant had found her.

Cait didn't look up. "Apologies, but I need to—"

Ichthyosis vulgaris. Dry, thickened and scaly skin. Face not usually affected. A condition that can be made better or worse by exposure to sunlight. Symptoms often improved by a warm, humid environment. The only treatment, attempting to hydrate the skin. Urea. Lactic acid. Propylene glycol.

She committed the notations to memory.

The attendant's palm landed on the open book, blocking the inked words from view. "No. This information is both private and proprietary. Please leave."

Strong words.

Privacy was a given, but the choice of the word "proprietary" was an odd one for that of an assistant. What value could an employee place upon such information?

The assistant's thumb strummed over the edges of the

ledger, rifling its pages. A rather well turned-out assistant, at that. A dress of superfine wool. A crisp, white apron. But most telling was the apron's lace edge. Not the kind formed upon a steam-powered loom, but a handmade variety of Princess lace from Belgium.

This woman had aspirations far beyond her current station, a goal the woman confirmed with a quick glance at Cait's purse.

For the right price, she would set aside her employer's principles.

Cait could work with that. "Miss—" she prompted.

"Smyth." Her eyes grew bright and animated as she prepared to negotiate.

Cait nodded. "I have reason to believe that one of your clients is suffering from a medical condition that adversely affects those with whom she comes into close contact."

All true. Those who had lost their testicles or pituitary glands hadn't survived the experience. All save one.

"Is that so. Might this be related to," Miss Smyth lifted her hand to peruse the formula beneath, "a certain skin condition? Perhaps ichthyosis?"

"It is."

"I'm afraid you're mistaken. That's not a communicable condition." Miss Smyth smirked at Cait's misstep and reassessed the value of such information. The price notched higher.

Crumbling mummies.

"Nonetheless, I need to speak with her directly."

"Mr. Everly keeps the names of his clients close." Miss

Smyth spoke with gravity, her voice stressing the unscrupulous nature of Cait's request. "There's a small notebook he keeps tucked into his coat pocket. Occasionally, while working in the stillroom, he removes it to work in his shirtsleeves."

Ah, so that was to be the game.

"How much?" Cait asked.

"Fifty pounds," Miss Smyth replied, shrugging a shoulder when Cait gaped. "Your request risks both my livelihood and reputation."

She snapped her mouth shut. "Done." An outrageous sum, but if it led her to Helena's door? Cait would pay it. Somehow. "But only if you provide me with all *three* names and any known addresses."

"Agreed. The store closes at nine." Miss Smyth gave her a knowing look. "There's a small courtyard around back..."

And payment would be required upon receipt.

"I'll meet you there." Cait inclined her head. "Until then."

She slid from behind the curtain back into the store. Now to acquire the necessary funds and send an agent to collect the information.

Her next undertakings required expertise and equipment that could only be found at the Lister Institute. Delivering the notebook into the hands of a competent neurosurgeon was her first priority.

Jack's habit of pressing his fingers against his eyes was a constant and worrisome reminder that, millimeter by millimeter, the tumor stole his vision and threatened their future. Moreover, she required a few hours in her own laboratory. Torment at the hands—snakes—of Dr. Thrakos presented a unique opportunity she refused to squander.

Cait was so focused that, as she swept her mother out the door, the whispered and derisive words of two nearby ladies who stared at her in open horror, "Is *that* who he married? A lab rat?" barely pricked her skin.

She was a Queen's agent now and above such malicious gossip. Shoulders back, chin up she marched down the street with pride and purpose.

CHAPTER TWENTY

"H E STOLE FROM ME," Mr. Garlock protested. "I was within my rights!"

"I'm afraid the courts do not recognize murder as an acceptable form of vengeance."

Anger bubbled and seethed deep inside Jack's chest. Word of the shocking death of Dr. Oakes buzzed through high society, a fact that would carve frowns into the faces of his superiors. Worse, the doctor's death stole away Jack's best chance to force a relatively sane man of science to answer his many questions about Helena and the nature of her poison.

The temptation to corner Aubrey and apply thumb screws to encourage and hasten his brother's answers grew with each passing moment.

With a firm grip upon the shackles that bound the man's wrists behind his back, Jack marched Mr. Garlock behind the gurney transporting his victim's corpse through the morgue entrance. A few feet inside Lister Institute, he steered his prisoner into an interrogation room.

There, the torture of sitting upon a battered chair for ten minutes in a bleak, windowless room broke Mr. Garlock. The man was terrified and rightly so.

"Physicians take an oath to do no harm!" he shouted as Jack entered, closing the door behind him.

"And how did Dr. Oakes betray your trust?" He suspected he knew the answer and braced for details of the man's impotence.

"I was advised that he was an expert in the field of," Mr. Garlock all but spit the next word, "fertility."

"Was Dr. Oakes unable to provide a satisfactory treatment for your flagging virility?"

"Excuse me!" The man drew up, offended. "It's my *wife* who cannot conceive."

Of course it was.

Cait would roll her eyes, snigger.

He fought back a smile.

Apart only a few hours and already he missed her. Years of working alone, preferring it that way, and he'd fallen fast and hard for a career-minded woman, one who'd crashed headlong into his life, irreversibly complicating everything.

Yet in a way that made him long to spend years at her side, not a mere handful of weeks or months. Deteriorating vision would end his days in the field just as hers began. The tumor might not kill him, but it would render him blind, then slowly steal his virility. He did not care for the bleak picture Thornton had painted.

The best solution was to oust the menace lodged in his skull. Surgery, with its many risks, loomed. Locating Helena and the mad scientist she patronized were his best chances at increasing his odds of survival.

A shame Cait was not here, that she might bring her keen and unmatched insight to the questioning process.

Or was she?

He pulled out his pocket watch, cringed at the time. He was late to their meeting with the Thorntons. His decision to visit Sharp's—an all-male stronghold—had immeasurably twisted the afternoon hours into a knot he had no choice now but to untangle.

Time to focus, that he might wrap up this interview, hand the man over to another agent for processing, and hunt his wife down.

"You already have five children." Jack frowned. "Not a situation suggesting fertility is a problem."

"All my wife has managed so far is to produce a passel of daughters." Mr. Garlock crossed his arms. "We wish for a son."

Cannot conceive.

The very problem that Helena reportedly faced, and the reason she'd turned to Dr. Thrakos for aid.

If Mr. Garlock had not paid to enhance his own virility...

Jack narrowed his eyes. "And Dr. Oakes promised..."

"A fertility treatment for my wife!" The man pounded on the table. "Yet all that time, he knew." Fury filled his eyes. "Knew that my reinvigorated efforts to father a child would come to naught."

Helena struggled with her own fertility. So much so, she'd turned to murder in an effort to conceive.

Men had lost their testicles.

A woman her pituitary gland.

Jack all but cringed as he asked, "What, exactly, did Dr. Oakes do for Mrs. Garlock?"

The man turned puce. "It's more what he did *to* her, to countless ladies." Leaning forward, he snarled. "I caught her red-handed. Gathered around the table with her friends, taking tea. Nibbling on little cakes. Discussing society weddings. Frivolous nonsense. I was about to call a greeting from the doorway..." He glanced away.

"Until?" Jack prodded.

His shoulders tensed. "My wife reached beneath the table to produce a trinket box. Not one I'd seen before. When she opened it, a white fog billowed out and cascaded to the floor. Inside were four vials. Each woman counted out coins from their purse, stacking them in a pile, then took a vial. They toasted each other before tossing back a strange, yellow-colored fluid."

"Toasted," Jack repeated. "To what exactly?"

"To keeping the cradle empty." Mr. Garlock's eyes blazed. "Shameless, all of them betraying their wedding vows."

"Did you confront her, your wife?"

"I did." He crossed his arms. "After dispersing the tea party. Their husbands will all be hearing from me."

Not any time soon. Outside communications were forbidden to those in Lister holding cells.

"And her reply?"

"My wife claimed it was an elixir, a method to temporarily prevent conception, introduced to her by none other than Dr. Oakes. Tears and pleas followed. She claims she's not yet ready to bear another child and begged me for more time." His lips flattened. "She will have it. Divorce is more commonplace these days."

The man's quest for a son at the expense of his wife's health left a sour taste in Jack's mouth. "That may be within your marital rights, yet you confronted her physician with deadly force."

"I care not how fleeting the drugs' effects might be, a physician has no business salting the field, as it were." His lips flattened. "Wives, all of them, yet thrilled to avoid their duty to bear children. That defies a husband's fundamental rights!"

He pinched the bridge of his nose, willing away the growing ache between his eyes. The man could take up such legal squabbles with his barrister.

Jack's primary concern centered upon the contents of that refrigerated box. One that held several vials containing a consumable drug aimed at suppressing the negative effects—as perceived by the ladies—of conjugal relations, no bite to the neck required.

A twisted kind of logic emerged.

A venomous woman unable to conceive due to the poison she consumed with every swallow. Did the venom force her, a lamia, to practice a reproductive strategy involving the harvesting of human reproductive organs to boost both her and her partner's fertility? With the final act a nip to the neck to send her lover into a sexual frenzy?

If so, it was an ingenious twist of marketing to sell that very venom as a male stimulant and a female contraceptive, capitalizing on her biology. A bite for the men, direct into the blood stream. Ingestion for the women.

"Did Dr. Oakes himself provide her with the vials, directly, that is?"

The man threw his hand in the air. "One presumes."

Jack dug deeper. He pushed and prodded, but the man knew no more.

"Your address?" he asked. Mrs. Garlock would need to be interviewed, the contents of those vials confirmed.

He ordered the man to a holding cell, then took to the maze-like halls of Lister Institute, burrowing deeper into the research wing that housed those men and women who worked to unlock the mysteries of human biology.

His first stop, the Department of Neuroscience.

Lady Thornton glanced up as he entered the office she shared with her husband. "You're late. Not that it matters, as your wife filled us in on all the particulars." She lifted the notebook he'd rescued from the floating laboratory, tapped a page. "Sebastian is in the laboratory taking inventory, then we're off to Clockwork Corridor to procure any additional parts and pieces necessary to attempt a reconstruction of this device. The notes appear to detail an early version, so if you can catch the lamia—"

"You will be the first to study the pituitary extractor," Jack promised. "Where is she, my wife?"

"Off to her laboratory."

He hesitated, unwilling to be rude.

"Go." Lady Thornton waved a hand, her eyes drifting back to the pen and ink drawings. "Catch your venomous murderess and her collaborators, place them under lock and key. You can regale us with all the details later."

Minutes later, he marched into the Department of Pathology and stopped short. A long hall stretched before him. Which door was Cait behind? Whose laboratory had she joined? Was this even the right department? Building?

"Two days married and you've already lost track of my sister?" Black materialized beside him. "Returning to London in a singed dirigible tethered to a rail car is quite a dramatic end to a honeymoon." He slapped Jack on the shoulder—hard—pushing him down the hallway. "Wise of you to send a skeet pigeon, warning me of the impending railway bill."

"I thought so." Now was not the time to spar. "Will you direct me to her research laboratory? There is much to share."

"I would hope so, given a key suspect plunged to his death from a clocktower." Black's visage darkened. "What exactly did you find floating above the moors?"

Jack shook his head. "Take me to Cait. Easier for us both to debrief you at once."

"Very well." Black strode to a door secured by multiple bolts and an iron bar and placed his hand upon a biometric gel pad to verify his identity.

Jack shook his head slowly. Was there anywhere in Lister the top agent was denied entry?

A red light blinked green and a toothed gear rotated. *Click. Scrape. Snap.* Black heaved the heavy door open and beckoned Jack to follow.

"It's about time," Dr. Whitby grumbled, setting aside a pipette. "Married? A Queen's agent? Primary investigators are to be informed when their students are tapped for service to the Crown."

"There were—*are*—pressing circumstances," Black replied. "Is she here?"

"Given her unauthorized absence and complete lack of progress on the TTX project, not for much longer." Thin-lipped, Dr. Whitby crossed his arms. "Unless I am provided with a detailed explanation."

Silent, Black offered nothing save a long, unyielding stare.

The scientist sighed, then tipped his head. "In the back room. With the Haimatos Separation Machine. She hooked herself up to it, claiming the procedure is of vital importance to her new duties as a Queen's agent."

Black shifted his gaze to Jack, eyebrows raised.

"That may well be," he offered. "Our unconventional honeymoon involved a number of poisonous, fanged creatures."

"Of course it did." Jaw tight, Black led the way to a small, windowless room.

There, Cait reclined upon a padded bench, her face pale and drawn. Though dressed for a stroll through Hyde Park, the tasseled and fringed edge of her sleeve had been yanked into a bunch above her elbow. Fashion and taste swept aside to connect her vein to the Haimatos Separation Machine. The internal centrifuge of the device spun, whirling and humming, as her blood passed into the contraption via a length of rubber tubing.

His gut twisted. "It's far too soon, Cait."

"I disagree."

"We agreed—" Black began.

"Hear us out?" Her voice rose. "I have my reasons."

Black glowered. "They had best be outstanding."

"They are." Battle won, she caught Jack's gaze. "I have news!"

Jack braced himself, praying he would be as enthusiastic.

"My mother and I found traces of the lamia's recent past in Covent Garden, near the theater district."

He nodded. "Hub of most of the attacks."

"Remember the mention of scales upon her legs?" Cait's eyes danced.

He nodded.

"A woman involved in the theater would treat rough skin with a cream or an ointment—and my mother knew of a place with a reputation for catering to leading ladies! Turns out the chemist compounds a special emollient to treat a skin condition called ichthyosis vulgaris for three women."

"Who are?"

"He refused to say." She grinned. "But, with a little bribery, I convinced his shopkeeper it was worth her time to delve into his coded notes after hours—one of them must be our lamia. The shop closes at nine."

Pride swelled his chest. "Excellent work."

"That's twice you've used that term." Black lifted a finger. "Lamia?"

"A beautiful half-woman, half-serpent creature of Greek mythology reputed to seduce young men then later feed on their flesh," Cait answered. "Some accounts mention a thirst for blood. In short, a lamia is a folkloric monster on par with a vampire or succubus. Ours happens to be hunting men and women upon the streets of London with an aim toward reproduction."

"Part cat. Part seal. Why not part snake?" Black fell back against the closed door. "Speaking of our not-so-mythological lamia, there were two more attacks while you were on your honeymoon." His brother-in-law grated out the last word. "Another man, castrated. A second woman, bitten. Pituitary removed. Both left for dead."

Shit.

"Thornton conducted the autopsy of the woman's brain," Black said. "Seemed particularly taken with the find-ings—chemical cauterization, sharp blades and the like. He thought you would deem those particulars of interest." He side-eyed Jack. "What is it you and Thornton are keeping from me?"

A potentially career-ending brain tumor.

"Nothing of great import," he lied. The double vision and headaches were manageable. For now.

Black exhaled with force. "Fine. What more did you

learn in Yorkshire?"

While his wife's blood flowed in and out of various tubing, Jack delivered a succinct account of their experience with Ceyda at the Grand Menwith Hotel and Spa. Though it pained him to report the physiological effects of the venom upon male anatomical structures, he did so. Black's eyes rose to study overhead light fixtures as a deep crimson colored Cait's cheeks.

He omitted mention of a certain hayloft, choosing to highlight instead the floating circus, their time spent imprisoned within the airborne laboratory, and their subsequent escape.

"Dr. Thrakos may be here in London," Jack finished. "Have agents search for a glider-class dirigible with patagium wings—singe marks on the port side—retrofitted to carry an oversized propulsive engine."

Rigid, Black nodded.

During the second half of his narrative, the agent's expression had tightened, and he now drew in long, steady breaths. For a moment, his dark gaze focused upon his sister.

"So first a lamia, then snakes modified to carry the same poison glands. Multiple exposure events inside forty-eight hours?" He shook his head. "Rats, you promised me, would be your research subjects. Not yourself." Teeth grinding, he waved a hand at the dark fluid that coursed through the machine. "Yet your recklessness proceeds apace. How you're still alive..."

"Rats," Cait scoffed. "Even if you drained one dry, you'd be lucky to collect thirty-five milliliters of blood." She rolled onto her side to adjust a dial and peer through a small glass window. "Setting aside the complications of interspecies transfusions, one rat—or even ten—wouldn't generate nearly enough antivenin from my plasma to save an adult human, even if I did have a vial of Helena's venom with which I might inoculate the beady-eyed creatures."

A muscle jumped at Black's jaw. "If CEAP was to catch wind of your unusual capabilities—"

"Were you not listening?" She twisted a knob and the humming and whirling began to subside. "I neither encouraged the lamia to bite me, nor the mad scientist to set his *morphophidia* upon me. I will not, however, fail to take advantage of recent events, however traumatic. I can easily spare one hundred milliliters. We can't afford to be caught in another situation where a supply of antivenin might mean the difference between life and death."

An artery throbbed at Black's temple. "You expect a confrontation?"

"No agent worth her salt would fail to prepare for one." Cait swung her legs over the side of the table and pulled the needle from her arm. She held Jack's gaze as she spoke her next words. "It's the only hope of saving the next person she attacks." Concern filled her eyes.

His heart hammered against his ribs as he closed the space between them to brush his fingers over her face. A brief caress before he reached for cotton to press into the crook of her arm, flexing her elbow to stem the flow of blood.

Was it too soon to have fallen in love?

Traditions, after all, were not for them. There'd been

flirtations, but no flowers. Instead, they'd moved straight to danger and drugs.

"I've new information myself," he told Cait.

Her eyes sharpened. "About Aubrey?"

"Not yet." He ground the words out. "He managed to slither away during the aftermath." Jack recounted the incident at Sharp's and Mr. Garlock's assertions. Cait gaped, wide-eyed as he shared the details about the wife's tea party. "If the venom negatively impacts female lamia fertility—"

"It circles us back to the question of Helena's presumed infertility," she said. "Her first goal is to conceive a child." She closed her eyes. "It all keeps circling back to fertility. Explain the pituitary gland again?"

"As an organ, it has a poorly-defined yet clear role in glandular diseases and a nebulous influence upon reproduction," Jack said. "What if Helena—or the Lamian race, if you will—has a primitive understanding of its connection to the proper functioning of the female reproductive system?"

"With very real, practical applications?" Cait tapped her lips. "You're proposing that, as a consequence of constantly swallowing the venom produced by their modified salivary glands, lamiae suppress their reproductive abilities, such that their own pituitary glands' excretions are not sufficient to overcome the inhibition. Thus, to reproduce—"

"They must collect and administer a pituitary extract to stimulate their own reproductive cycle," Jack finished.

"Female pituitary glands to augment female fertility?" Black looked like he'd swallowed a live frog.

"It's known as organotherapy." Cait grimaced. "The

treatment of a disease state using an extract of the same organ procured from a healthy animal, in this case humans."

Jack lifted a finger. "Close. Organotherapy is an antiquated term. The focus now is upon the secretions that glands produce, then release into the blood stream. To date, isolated glandular extracts have been used to treat a number of diseases. For example, it's established fact that extract of cock's testicle can, not by consumption, but by injection into a man's veins, elicit an extraordinary rejuvenating effect."

Still a bit green about the gills, Black snorted. "You're proposing the lamia cultivates a chosen partner, then follows the extract with a nip from her venomous fangs to ensure enthusiastic consummation."

Jack's face burned. "Yes."

"Whereas a woman can use the venom to suppress fertility." Blood rose to Cait's cheeks, and she moved the conversation along. "Delaying unwanted motherhood that she might enjoy relations, marital or otherwise, without worry."

She stood, opened a glass window set into the Haimatos Separation Machine, lifted out the flask within, then crossed to a workbench. Carefully, she pipetted a clear, yellowish fluid into amber glass vials.

"To summarize," Black began, "we believe this creature arrived upon our shores, established herself as an actress, providing her easy access to randy men. Failing to conceive with ease, she seeks out her fellow countryman, Dr. Thrakos, a mad scientist without moral compass who is known for his mechano-surgical creations. He devises a pituitary extractor, enabling her to collect the gland with relative ease."

Nodding, Jack took up the narrative. "In exchange, she allows him to culture cells from a biopsy of her venom glands. Together, they devise a scheme to enrich their coffers. They approach Dr. Oakes, a physician with many clients among the *ton* and friends such as my brother and Carruthers, who agree to invest in their scheme."

"Together, they enter into business," Black said. "The Grand Menwith Hotel and Spa, complete with a manufactured venomous massage therapist."

"Whilst Dr. Thrakos constructs *morphophidia*, snakes who can be milked for their venom. A side venture peddled to women who no longer wish to bear children."

"A plausible scenario." Cait opened a small, metal canister. Cold fog wafted forth from its interior as she inserted two now-sealed amber vials filled with antivenin beside a glass syringe. "Once Helena conceives, the murders may well stop. At least for some nine months."

"Making her impossible to trace," Black grumbled.

Cait snapped the container closed and clipped it to her belt. She gave Jack a confident nod. "Shall we hunt a lamia?"

Jack caught her hand, drew her close and kissed her forehead, resisting the urge to fully embrace her in the company of her brother.

His wife was immune. Not so him. Or any other.

The kit she'd prepared might well save the life of the next person Helena attacked. His wife, always planning two steps ahead. *His.* Was it wrong to take such pride in her when he'd done nothing to win her hand? A thought to explore later, once this investigation was behind them.

"By now my brother will have poured Carruthers from his carriage and, one hopes, returned home." He tucked Cait's hand into the crook of his arm.

"Time to introduce your bride to your family?" Mischief danced in his wife's eyes.

He pulled a face. "It won't be pleasant, but, with any luck, Aubrey will spill everything in an attempt to save his own hide." Dipping his head, he caught Cait's lips with his own.

Black cleared his throat.

The top agent had fingers and thumb pressed to closed eyes. Two days past, Jack would have delighted in the discomfort Black was forced to endure at their display of connubial bliss before him, however odd the context.

Now, Jack was only mildly amused. One of many indications that he'd lost his heart to the man's sister.

"I'll set agents on alert for Dr. Thrakos and his dirigible." Black reached for the door handle. "They can also comb through Dr. Oakes' finances. With luck, he's left a paper trail." He eyed Jack's TTX pistol. "Cait, stay close to Tagert. If this lamia knows you're immune to her venom... well, there are other, more direct ways to kill."

"If you're so worried," Cait leveled her brother a look, "there's an easy solution. You know my aim is as good as yours."

With a great, put-upon sigh, the agent unstrapped his holster and weapon. "Welcome to the agency." He held them out to his sister. "Try not to get yourself killed."

CHAPTER TWENTY-ONE

WHILE HER HUSBAND stormed up the staircase in search of Lord Aubrey to ensure that "not at home" was not a polite euphemism for "your brother wants nothing to do with you", Cait followed Emsworth, the family's steam butler—a particularly arrogant model—into his mother's parlor, curious to gauge her reaction.

"Your daughter," her mother-in-law's voice clipped as she poured tea, "is pliant and sweet. Which is all very well. But she must begin as she means to go on, by insisting that Aubrey attend to the time. Punctuality is of utmost importance. Particularly when there are a number of details that need to be settled before the wedding."

"Agreed. It's entirely unacceptable that our children have yet to return from their afternoon drive." The woman seated across from Lady Aubrey pinched her lips. "I will speak with her."

At the doorway, Cait cleared her throat.

"You." The soon-to-be dowager-viscountess glared.

"Me," she agreed, omitting even the politest of nods. "Mrs. Tagert will suffice as a form of address. No need to pretend to intimacy, even in a familial setting."

Icy eyes stared back at her. "I suppose I ought to be glad you favor your mother in looks, that your walking dress is of current fashion. However, all that gadgetry strung about your waist offers little hope for your behavior."

"I can assure you that I *will* disappoint," Cait replied. The words, spoken aloud, chased away a certain lingering tension, leaving behind a lightness. She drew her next breath with ease. "I'm much less compliant than my mother ever aspired to be." She paused while the implied threat registered. "But such is a topic for another day. We must speak with Lord Aubrey. Immediately. Is he often late when not browbeaten into obedience?"

Lady Aubrey sniffed. "Already you overstep, making demands."

"All on behalf of the Crown, I assure you."

"Mother," Jack stepped into the room. "Enough. Where is Aubrey?"

"Out. Driving in the park with his fiancée as befits a gentleman, an example the two of you ought to follow." Lady Aubrey's lip curled. "Alas, my hopes for Jonathan are forever dashed. Do make an effort to ensure all future reports of your exploits find themselves buried in the newspapers beside the current price of kraken ink."

A smirk tugged at Cait's lips. When news of her eldest's

business dealings with a seductive, snake-like woman broke, it would most certainly be headline material, deserving of a font two inches tall. The only thing that could save her mother-in-law was the discretion of the Queen's agents.

"Neither of you are welcome here," Jack's mother snapped. "Take yourselves elsewhere."

Cait laid a hand upon Jack's arm. "They were both expected for tea, but are late."

"How late?" he asked the other woman, his voice tight.

"By some thirty minutes." Worry shifted Lady Mildred's mother onto the edge of her chair. "Is something wrong?"

"Very much so. My brother frequently tempts fate, and this time he has gone too far. I suggest you take steps to shield your daughter from the fire and brimstone that will soon rain down upon him." Jack gave a short bow. "We'll return later."

"Explain yourself, Jonathan!" His mother's glare threatened to throw off sparks and set afire the hand-knotted silk rug beneath their feet.

"Remember how I advised you to let me inspect Aubrey's investments?" Jack's eyebrows rose. "You ought to have agreed."

Their departure was hastened by an indignant steam butler who knew where his gears were greased. Rolling at top speed down the hallway, he threw open the front door.

"You certainly know how to drop the temperature in a room." An inappropriate delight buoyed her steps. "Steam from the teacups froze midair and crystalized into snowflakes."

Jack snorted. "I learned the technique at my mother's knee."

"Are we to chase after Lord Aubrey?" She frowned. "Hyde Park is three-hundred or more acres in size."

"I suggest we pay a visit to my brother's inebriated friend, Carruthers, the new Lord Saltwell."

"Who has, by now, sobered?"

"If the death of Oakes hasn't done the job, we'll try a bucket of water. It's time to revisit the question of what, exactly, his father was doing in my brother's library." Outside on the pavement, he offered his arm. "We'll walk. His townhome isn't far."

Afternoon was fading toward evening. Though quieter than most neighborhoods, Mayfair was not without its traffic —or overconfident young gentlemen steering steam-chaises with more power than control. As they were prone to take corners on two wheels and without warning, Cait accepted his escort as they crossed the street.

"If he's uncooperative, I've heard tell of a truth serum." Cait nudged him with her elbow. She'd won a TTX pistol today, but knew the Queen's agents carried many other toys up their sleeves, tucked in pockets and sewn into seams. "Veritasium, I believe it's called?"

He clicked his tongue. "Always tempting, but not sanctioned for use on a British citizen."

"Officially."

"You say that with entirely too much enthusiasm." Jack slanted her a look. "We'll start with a thorough dunking in cold water."

"I suppose it'll have to do." She gave an exaggerated sigh, then winked. "To review, Carruthers is the only son and heir of the deceased Lord Saltwell, over whose body Helena was crouched."

In the library during Lord Aubrey's engagement ball. At which Jack had exploded an ice sculpture. Cait grinned, wishing she'd witnessed the event. Would she have noticed Jack's sleight of hand, followed him down that hallway? She liked to think so.

"Correct," he said. "Bitten on the neck, with the surrounding tissue rapidly swelling." He pressed his lips together. "A mistake, in retrospect, letting Dr. Oakes oversee his care while I chased after the lamia."

"With no antidote," she pressed a hand to the case at her hip, "it would have changed nothing. Would you agree that, unlike the other murders, the attack upon Lord Saltwell was not only targeted, but personal? Was there any indication that she intended to remove his testicles?"

Jack flinched.

"No knife in hand?" Cait pressed.

"None that I observed." He glanced over his shoulder at his family's now-distant townhome. "But..."

"Your brother or Dr. Oakes or the steam staff might have removed anything Helena dropped." She nudged at various possibilities, no stone left unturned and all that. Only son and heir did not rule out a multitude of bastards. "How many children did this Lord Saltwell produce?"

"Via his mistresses, a dozen or more, all healthy." Jack

confirmed her suspicions. "But his wife was plagued by still-births. Only one child came into the world screaming."

"He sought no new marriage to redouble his efforts at producing an official and legally sanctioned spare?"

"Not a possibility," Jack answered. "His wife still lives, tucked away in the countryside. Otherwise, I'm sure he would have placed that on his agenda. The survival of his direct family line falls to Carruthers, who has, incidentally, produced a male child. Moreover, his wife is expecting."

"An older gentleman with a taste for the ladies could easily be lured into a library for a *rendezvous* with a young lady and the promise of restored, youthful virility." Cait rolled her eyes at the recurring theme. "But instead of a therapeutic nip followed by a romp on settee, he dies gasping upon the floor."

"An ignoble death," Jack said. "And one he did not expect. His final words were, 'I didn't know. I swear it. She is evil. Her blood polluted.' All of which suggest he knew his attacker and, quite likely, what she was."

"His own son, along with Lord Aubrey and Dr. Oakes, had been in business with the lamia for over a year..." Cait tapped her lips. "Discovery of their deeds seems likely, but—"

"Perhaps Lord Saltwell discovered his son's business venture and demanded a percentage? A steady supply of venom? That, as a result, the triumvirate decided Lord Saltwell was a liability?"

"And condemned him to death by lamia?" Cait paused

for thought. "It's a possibility. But this Helena doesn't strike me as a team player, a woman to follow orders."

I didn't know.

Cait mulled over the man's final words. "Lord Saltwell arrived in the library, alone. You heard no shouts, no calls for help?"

"None."

"And all members of the triumvirate were present in the ballroom, enjoying themselves, seemingly unconcerned."

"Yes."

"When, lured by promises of sexual favors and unburdened by moral scruples, Lord Saltwell slips away to the library."

"But it's a trap."

"Sprung by your brother and his business partners—"

"An unlikely scenario, given the venue," Jack interrupted.

"What if Helena acted on her own, went rogue, so to speak? What better way to sow chaos and scandal? Imagine the headlines!" Cait swiped her hand through the air before her. "The London Vampire strikes in the heart of Mayfair! Lord Saltwell murdered in the midst of frolicking *ton!*"

"It certainly would send a message," Jack agreed. "It would explain why my brother and his friends staged a vampire hunt through Covent Garden. Deadly serious business concealed as whimsical jest. Perhaps they found her, renegotiated terms."

Cait nodded. "Then arranged to complicate your life, leaking false news to the press."

"Aubrey *was* uncannily calm the next morning." Jack narrowed his eyes. "But if he hoped to occupy my time with something other than chasing after the London Vampire, he failed miserably." He stopped abruptly, swinging Cait about to catch both her hands in his. "Little did he realize his efforts would only redouble our own. Even his efforts to curtail my movements with matrimonial claims failed for I am utterly besotted with my talented and lovely new wife."

"And I with my husband." Beaming, she lifted onto her toes and pressed a quick kiss to his lips, uncaring of who might be among the strangers strolling the evening streets of Mayfair. "Are we here?"

His eyes sparkled. "We are. Ready to conduct your first interview of a suspect?"

Cait slanted him a look. "Please, I have three brothers."

He laughed. "As an agent, then."

"I can only hope he'll be uncooperative. I'd very much like an excuse to see him molder in a Lister Interview room for a few hours."

Together, they climbed the stairs.

Entered.

And elbowed past the steam butler who claimed, "Lord Saltwell is not at home."

But their feet proved faster than a mechanical servant's ability to latch onto the stair's hoist mechanism. Within seconds, she and Jack were knocking on doors, calling out for Carruthers. He wasn't behind door number one, but when they threw open door number two—

"Again?" A tousled head half-lifted from a pillow, then

fell back. Naked as a newborn beneath a thin sheet, the new Lord Saltwell lay sprawled on his bed. His voice held a note of protest, but the tenting of the bedclothes at his groin indicated female company was both expected *and* desired. "Oh, it's you. Did someone else die? I'm going to need fortification before we talk." He rolled, reaching for a glass upon the bedside table.

Jack snagged a dressing gown from the floor and threw it at Carruthers. "You'll cover yourself in the presence of my wife."

"Wife?" The man grinned. He balled the cloth at his waist. "Nobody thought you'd go through with it. Congratulations." He raised the glass, then tossed back two fingers of the amber-tinted drink. "Apologies, thought you were my—er—"

"Wife?" Cait echoed, raising an eyebrow. "Don't most of the married *ton* slip in and out of each other's bedrooms via adjoining rooms?" She spoke while crossing the room, reaching for one particular door handle. "Shall I see if Lady Saltwell will join us, or were you expecting someone else?"

"My wife is some four months along," Carruthers complained. Unconcerned, he shoved himself from the bed onto his feet. The sheet fell away exposing a rampant erection and—as her eyes snapped upward—a raw, inflamed patch at his neck where puncture marks dotted his skin. At his throat, shoulder—all along his arm—were tiny pinpricks of scar tissue. Evidence of repeated venom-tipped fang punctures. "Like many in a loveless marriage, she prefers I occupy myself with another partner for now. So much so that she herself selected my mistress and installed her in the guest room."

"A woman by the name of?"

Carruthers shrugged the dressing gown over his shoulders, tied it at the waist. "Helena."

Cait gaped.

All this time, the venomous woman had been in Mayfair? Mixing business and pleasure, nipping this man's neck yet confining her hunting grounds to her old neighborhood. Was he aware of his mistress' reproductive efforts? Unconcerned? Too enamored of her bite to care either way?

Snapping her jaw shut, she caught Jack's gaze, then quipped. "Virility, fertility, paternity."

"Rather a theme of late." Jack pulled his TTX pistol from its holster. "We clear the wife's room, then locate Helena." He shot a narrow glare at Carruthers. "Stay here."

Gripping her own weapon, Cait threw the door open and hurried through the connecting bath and dressing rooms. "Lady Saltwell?"

The viscountess' suite was empty. The bed was neatly made. No ashes littered the hearth. And the underlying smell of a cleaning agent permeated the air. All serving to highlight two incongruencies. A trinket box upon a dressing table was askew. The door of a wardrobe was ajar.

Cait flipped up the lid. Empty. "I can think of only one reason a lady might pocket all her jewels: to finance an escape." She turned on her heel, reached for the handle of a wardrobe. "Are there gowns missing from her—"

She gasped as a body tumbled out onto the floor.

Thunk.

Jack dropped to one knee, pressed his fingers against the throat of a young woman.

"Dead?" An unnecessary question judging from the vacant eyes that stared up at her.

"Very," he said. "But still warm."

Cait leaned closer, drawn by a certain familiarity of the woman's features. "Corpse candles! That's the apothecary's assistant!" She pressed a hand to her chest where her heart gave a great thump, then took off, racing. Bending, Cait plucked a crumpled paper from the woman's fingers. A receipt for a jar of lotion marked T. Everly and Company. "She played me false. Miss Smyth must have known who the chemist's customer was all along and," she swallowed, "came bearing gifts to warn Helena?"

"If she had thoughts of blackmail, it was a most fatal decision." Jack tipped up the woman's face. A dark crust ringed the edges of a ruined nose. "I would venture to guess we'll find her pituitary has been removed."

That drew Cait up short. "And in Lady Saltwell's room, not Helena's. Could there be two lamia working together? One married to Carruthers, the other serving as his mistress?"

He swore. "That or we're looking at a hostage situation."

A few tense moments of searching turned up nothing else. Not that she'd held much hope of discovering they'd conveniently left the pituitary extractor behind, a murder weapon which they might haul back to Lister for examination.

They burst into the hallway, throwing one door open after the other, searching for lamiae. But all were empty.

Hazy-eyed, Carruthers emerged from his suite. He waved a glass, sloshing its refreshed contents. "What on Earth are you doing?"

"Where is Helena?" Jack demanded. "Which is her room?"

Carruthers pointed to an open door. "That one. If it's empty, well, she's my paramour, not my prisoner." He tossed back his drink.

"And you last saw her when?" Cait asked.

From beneath heavy-lidded eyes, his gaze oozed, like the slime that seeped through sewers, over her body's form. Was it the influence of the venom or the nature of the man? Both? Impossible to know.

She snapped her fingers in front of his face.

"We know what the venom does. Its effects upon you are, regretfully, obvious." She flicked the lapel of his dressing gown aside. "And at least one of these bite marks is recent."

His grin spread. "Three hours, give or take?"

Cait rolled her eyes. Trust a man to be proud of his staying power, no matter its exogenous source. "Your wife, where is she?"

"With the children in the nursery? Or perhaps she's gone out." A shoulder lifted. "Who can say? Her advancing pregnancy seems only to increase her desire to be out and about, serving on one committee or another."

"Think harder, Carruthers," Jack yelled, already halfway

up the stairs. "There's a dead woman on the floor of her bedchamber."

"Dead?" Carruthers stared at the empty glass in his hand as if surprised to find it so, then turned and careened back into his bedroom.

Hitching up her skirts, Cait ran after Jack to the upper floor.

"Deserted," he informed her. "No child, no nursemaid."

"Dying embers in the grate," she noted, turning about. Push toys and blocks scattered upon the carpet. An abandoned cup of tea upon a table. A shawl draped over the back of a rocking chair. All signs of recent occupation. "That's odd." She frowned. "A cradle *and* a cot? They're expecting their second child, correct?" She lifted a ring of teething pegs, eyeing the deep gouges left by a coping child.

"Yes. Their son is nine, perhaps ten months old."

"Yet judging from the rumpled linens, both beds appear to be in use." Rifling through various bits of baby clothing deepened her sense that something was off. The two stacks of diaper clothes confirmed it. "Two sizes," she said. "One pile folded for a three-month-old, the second for a child nine months or older."

"Carruthers did mention *children*, plural." Lines appeared on Jack's forehead. "Would a wet nurse care for her own child in an employer's household?"

"Unlikely." Cait looked about, bewildered. "But if so, her own child would, necessarily, be of the same age or older. Not younger."

She stepped into the nursemaid's room. A single bed. A

washstand. A foot stove. A chest of drawers. A pier glass. A chair and writing desk placed beneath a window to catch the light. Standard furnishings, but all items were of high quality.

Particularly the bedding.

She holstered her weapon, then tossed aside the bedcovers, pressing a hand to the mattress. "Feather-filled," Cait announced. "Not horsehair or wool. Lady Saltwell's nursemaid lives in great comfort, an uncommon state for most servants."

"Clothes are missing from their pegs." Jack peered beneath the bed. "And there's not so much as a carpet bag in evidence." He swore. "Gone. We must have missed them by mere hours."

"Could all three have left, together?" Cait stalked from the room. "Lady Saltwell selected her nursemaid, as would be expected. But to hire her husband's mistress? It simply isn't done. Which begs the question, who was Lady Saltwell before her marriage?"

"A former actress?" Jack followed her. "One who met Helena in Covent Garden."

"Perhaps both of them traveled to England from Greece, together?"

"Or all three?"

Aether, a trio of lamiae?

Cait ran down the stairs and found herself gasping for air. High fashion wasn't suited to all this running—the corset nipped in her waist to an excessive degree, leaving her short of breath. As a Queen's agent, a wardrobe overhaul would be in order. "One snagged a husband, then hired her friends into lives of relative luxury?"

"It tracks," Jack said. "Carruthers was known to favor the burlesque and Covent Garden was his stomping grounds." He leapt over the railing to land outside the gentleman's door. "Your wife," he yelled, stalking back into the bedroom. "You met her where?"

The prone form upon the bed didn't so much as groan.

He rolled Carruthers onto his back, slapped his face and repeated the question. But the man was insensate, useless.

"Jack." Panting, Cait pointed to an open—and nearly empty—bottle of laudanum on the bedside table. There would be no reviving their suspect for questioning, not for several hours.

He swore. "Drink and drugs."

So much for direct answers.

"We interview the downstairs staff." Cait pivoted, exited the room. "Steambots might be mute and steam butlers uncooperative, but kitchens are never fully automated. The cook or a maid will know something, and perhaps even be able to point us in Lady Saltwell and company's direction."

"Go." Jack tugged a punch card and a message canister from his pocket. "Black needs to be informed of the situation. I'll send a skeet pigeon from the aviary, then meet you below stairs."

CHAPTER TWENTY-TWO

A S FAST AS HER FEET would carry her, Cait
descended. In the foyer, the steam butler rolled
from one end of the hallway to the other,
clanging his annoyance.

"Not at home. Not at home. Not at home."

"I must speak with Miss Helena." Cait addressed the
steambot, uncertain how else to politely identify the lamia in
hopes of receiving a rational answer. "Might you point me in
her direction?"

"Not at home. Not at home. Not at home."

Alas, it appeared there was a glitch in his programing. A
quick smack to the steam servant's forehead did nothing to
reset or alter his behavior. Perhaps he'd torn a punch card?
But such did not—yet—number among her skills. A deficiency to be addressed at a later date.

Cait dodged past the useless steam butler, pushed open
the green baize door and rushed down into the kitchens

where she dropped both hands onto the large wooden table and stood, gasping. From now on, she needed stop wearing corsets. A least, not ones with steel boning.

An open-mouthed cook stared at her, blinking, as raspberry jam dripped from a spatula she held. Cait had interrupted the preparation of a Victoria sponge.

A face—that of a young maid—peeked out from around the edge of a door.

"And who might you be?" the cook inquired. "Rushing in here, unannounced and unaccompanied?"

"Apologies," Cait wheezed, "for my abrupt intrusion. The steam butler is stuck in a loop, insisting no one is at home. We've located Lord Saltwell, but need to speak with Lady Saltwell, her nanny and Miss Helena." She pulled back the edge of her jacket to reveal the TTX pistol strapped in place. "Immediately."

"They left," the maid said, wide-eyed. "About an hour ago."

The cook frowned. "And how would you know such a thing?"

"I saw their boots pass the window," the maid replied, lifting her gaze to the short half-windows that permitted a grimy light to leak in from the street. "It's me that polishes them. Miss Helena went one way. Lady Saltwell and Nanny the other. They left about an hour ago with the pram."

"One child?" Cait asked. "Or two?"

Tight-lipped, the servants exchanged a look.

Cait waited, letting the grinding of the nearby steam

mixer's gears fill the air as it worked to knead the dough that would be tomorrow's bread.

"I know there is more than one child in that nursery," she said. "Why?"

"I'm not at all certain we ought be answering your questions." The cook looked down, spread the jam carefully over the golden cake. "Without permission of our employer."

"Just now I found a dead shopgirl stuffed in your lady's wardrobe," Cait said. "More agents are on their way. Expect your employment here to come to an abrupt termination."

That dropped their jaws.

"Now, if you'll answer my questions," Cait pressed. "Unless you prefer to do so at the Lister Institute. Why is there more than one child?"

The cook swallowed, set aside her spatula. Placed the second sponge atop the jam, dusting the top with a handful of sugar.

"Well, then, we might as well enjoy my most recent efforts over household gossip." She lifted a knife. "Katie," she addressed the maid. "If you'll serve tea?"

The maid measured leaves into a teapot, then lifted the kettle from the stove to pour boiling water over them.

"Those three have an arrangement," the cook said, cutting slices, lifting them onto plates. "Unconventional. Worse, it's immoral. I said as much when I was made aware."

"But they pay double for us to look the other way," Katie added, setting the teapot on the table before them. "Milk? Sugar?"

"Yes, please. One lump." Cait looked back to the cook. "The lady, the nanny, the mistress. And two children."

"Gentlemen often interfere with maids once the bloom is off the bride." The cook set a plate before Cait, passed her a fork. "Lady Saltwell does her best to steer the lord away from the staff. Not an easy task with such a randy one."

Was that why the Lord Saltwells, past and present, had been targeted by a lamia? Did such creatures always choose fertile men with excessive sexual appetites? Cait snorted. Not that such criteria narrowed the selection of prey, even if one limited the pool to male members of the peerage.

The cook continued. "Lady Saltwell herself arranged for another woman to take her place in her husband's bed."

Odd, but if one wished to keep one's spouse at home...

"The nanny?" Cait took a bite of the sponge, closed her eyes in appreciation, contemplated offering her a job. Pending the outcome of inquiries, of course.

"One might think," the cook answered. "But it was Lord Saltwell the elder who was overly fond of that particular woman's company, if you take my meaning. He was a frequent visitor to the nursery. Soon after the birth of his grandson, he had another bastard son on the way."

Cait wrinkled her nose. "So the nephew of the nanny's son is under the nanny's care."

"It's utterly baffling, what the gentry get up to." The maid set a cup of tea before her. "And both Lady Saltwell and the nanny are expecting. Again."

Goodness, such rampant fertility.

"That's awfully fast." Cait straightened. "And what of Helena's role?"

"Installed in our household days after the wedding." The cook lowered her voice. "Our lady arrived already expecting their first child."

"And Helena has been in and out of the new Lord Saltwell's bed ever since." The maid flushed, looked away. "More than once I've entered my lord's bedchamber—as duties require—and found her beneath his sheets."

Cait sipped her tea, then set the cup down. "Two children in the nursery," Cait tapped on the table before her. "One the current Lord Saltwell's legitimate heir, the other his unacknowledged bastard brother."

"Babies are precious things." The cook lifted an eyebrow. "The more in a household, the better. Or so Lady Saltwell informs me."

"Is her husband aware of the particulars?"

The cook shrugged. "Hard to know. Our lord spends his days moving between various addictive pleasures."

"And Helena, is she also expecting?" She took another bite of the wondrous cake.

The maid shook her head. "Not yet, a situation that seems to upset her. Of late, she's been in Lord Saltwell's bed more than she's been out of it." Another blush. "Not that he's objecting."

Yet bedsport was not the creature's aim.

After a year of infertility, Helena's failure to conceive must have triggered her murderous rampage through the streets of London. She'd taken to injecting her already randy and fertile lover—Carruthers, the new Lord Saltwell—with testicular extract before eliciting further arousal with her potent venom. All enhanced by her own use, consumption or otherwise, of a young woman's pituitary gland.

Yet still failed to conceive?

All horribly fascinating, but none of this information brought her closer to apprehending the lamia. Or the nanny. Or, given the body in her wardrobe, Lady Saltwell herself. The three of them sounded complicit, which suggested—

"Did Lord Saltwell happen to meet his wife at a theater?" she asked.

The servants glanced at each other.

The maid leaned forward. "There were rumors—all hushed—that she did once tread the boards and bask in limelight."

Cait set down her fork and leaned forward. "Would you happen to know which theater?"

Eyes wide, the maid looked to the cook. Both shook their heads.

A distant pounding echoed down the stairs. A door burst open and the steam butler exclaimed loudly, "Not at home. Not at home! NOT AT HOME!"

"Agents?" the cook asked.

Among the voices overhead, she recognized Logan's. Definitely Queen's agents. They'd made impressive time.

"Yes." Cait rose. "I'm afraid that's my cue to assist. Have you any idea where the three women may have gone, as a group or individually?"

"They frequent Hyde Park." The maid twisted her

hands. "Though sometimes they take the children to the zoo."

That perked her ears. "The zoo?" Perhaps they enjoyed reptilian company?

The maid bobbed her head even as her eyes skittered to the doorway, where Jack now stood.

"Any leads?" he asked.

"Possibly." Cait laid a hand on the maid's arm. "Any chance the children have a favorite animal?"

"An Egyptian crocodile. Lady Saltwell claims staring at the beast's teeth is the only thing that will calm Master James. He's having a horrible time with teething, chewing on everything he can wrap those tiny fists about."

Cait's breath caught. "Behind the exhibits there are laboratories."

"Twenty minutes by crank hack." Jack held her gaze, his mind leaping to the same conclusion. "That's the fastest we can reach the Reptile House at the Zoological Gardens."

Wooden joints, nails and screws groaned in protest as the crank hack took the corner on two wheels. Jack had promised the driver a gold sovereign if he travelled at top speed, the wisdom of which he now questioned. In a heartbeat, they traversed the bridge crossing Regent's Canal and careened left. The wheels slammed back down onto the road, a final test of the vehicle's structural limitations.

Ahead, the rooftops of various zoo buildings rose among

treetops. In mere minutes, they would reach their destination. Beside him, Cait tugged gloves onto her hands and adjusted the angle of her hat, the better to masquerade as a casual visitor out to see the exhibits with her husband.

They'd verbally tossed Black a sketchy outline of their discovery, of their destination. A few hasty questions and answers had followed, then they'd departed the townhome in a rush, leaving Black to organize reinforcements.

Three women. Two children. Two pregnancies.

What on Earth had been going on in Carruthers' townhome?

The man himself might wish to attribute his wife's and mistress' persistent interest in bedsport to his own virility and sexual prowess, but from an outside perspective, he'd been manipulated. Was he aware of what his father had been up to in the nursery? Jack doubted it. He rather suspected Carruthers had spent the better part of his marriage in a drug and venom-induced haze.

"Do you think all three women are lamia?" he asked Cait.

"Quite likely," she replied. "Two rotating in and out of his bed according to gestation. A third preferring to seduce the elder Lord Saltwell for reasons as yet unknown. Regardless, they weren't there for fun and recreation."

"That household does seem to be where the lamia first sank their teeth into London society, only later hatching a plan to sell their venom."

"At which point they drew your brother, Dr. Oakes and Dr. Thrakos into their scheme."

He pulled a face. "But why take up with Carruthers in the first place? There are plenty of wealthier *ton* to prey upon."

"His 'patronage' of theaters." She ticked items off on her fingers. "His title. His pre-existing abuse of alcohol. All make him an easy target."

"But fail to address the question of 'why Carruthers'," Jack pointed out. "Insofar as I am aware, he engendered no bastards—there's no preexisting evidence of his fertility. Only of his father's."

"An excellent point."

This whole situation was bizarre.

The hack came to a sudden stop. Or rather, the driver pulled so hard on the hand break that its iron banded wheels skidded along the drive, throwing sparks.

Jack handed the promised treasure to their driver and, moments later, they strolled into the Reptile House.

A soft afternoon glow of sunlight struggled to percolate through soot-dusted rooflights such that overhead chandeliers contributed more than their fair share to the general illumination. Ferns dripped fronds from hanging baskets, and potted palms dotted the room.

In the center of the main hall, low walls topped by domed, iron cages surrounded larger reptiles, including a solitary and forlorn crocodile hunched beside a small, stagnant pool of water. At the sides of the room, spectators gathered behind brass handrails and before enormous sheets of plate glass.

They both spotted Lady Saltwell at the same time,

strangely still amidst the moving swirl of other visitors, as she watched a bright orange snake slither its way up a twisted tree branch.

Cait's hand tightened upon his arm, her chin lifted. "That's an African bush viper." Her voice was a hoarse whisper. "A snake with retractable fangs. Perhaps she's bitten her own lip too many times and is seething with jealousy."

He snorted softly, shaking his head.

Lady Saltwell rested one hand on the gentle swell of her stomach, the other on the handle of the pram. The child within seemed equally entranced with the snake on display. He turned his head, looking upward to his mother, with a wide grin upon his laughing face—one that displayed a shocking amount of teeth for an infant of only nine months.

Not just incisors, but—

"Do you see that?" he asked.

"Canines," Cait said. "Uncommonly sharp ones at that. One might even call them—"

"Fangs," he finished.

Hissssss.

The sound came from their right. A woman in plain dress holding an infant. The nanny sounding a warning?

Lady Saltwell's head snapped up. She met Jack's gaze.

For a moment, time stood still. Lady Saltwell's eyes flashed, cold and hard, and her lip curled as if she might bare her teeth. Then she turned, pushing the pram with both hands toward a distant exit.

A classic split maneuver. Two women, two agents.

"Go." Cait let go of his arm. "I'll grab the nanny. Do not

let Lady Saltwell bite you." She turned and pushed through the crowd, all elbows.

Every instinct screamed at him to guard his wife. But she was immune. A fact he reminded himself of with each step as he pursued his own quarry. Protected. Invulnerable. Safe.

He, on the other hand, was not. The reason Cait had assigned him the task of chasing a visibly pregnant woman pushing a large child in a pram. Not that such slowed Lady Saltwell. Her increasing speed was hindered only by the length and weight of her bustled skirts.

He'd eat his left shoe if she wasn't also a lamia.

Behind him, Cait let out a cry of distress.

Heart in his throat, Jack glanced over his shoulder.

"Stop that woman!" Cait cried. "She stole my baby!"

A feint. And one that worked.

An older woman holding a sturdy parasol stepped in front of the nanny. *Thwack,* she snapped the steel core of the parasol down upon the brass railing blocking the nanny's advance. "That's far enough."

Others responded, surrounding the nanny. A top-hat-wearing cane-carrying gentleman. Two little girls in short skirts joined hands. A group of young men.

Cait had cornered her prey while his was still on the move.

Pride filled his lungs.

With renewed effort, he dashed about the corner, searching the interior of the building for his own lamia. But there was no sign of Lady Saltwell or her pram. How far could a pregnant woman and nine-month-old child possibly travel in mere minutes?

But they had disappeared.

In the distance, a new round of shrieks erupted.

Cait.

He turned, moving in an all-out sprint.

Jack burst back into the main hall in time to watch the nanny—now wielding the gentleman's brass-topped cane—smash the pane of an exhibit. Sharp pings sounded as shattered glass rained down.

The crowd recoiled.

Someone cried, "Snake!"

And everyone turned, scattering toward the exits as a light gray viper with black zig zag marks slithered across the black and white checkered floor.

Jack ran toward Cait, dodging both spectators and the snake's winding trajectory.

The nanny leapt into the display case, clutching a now-screaming baby, and ignoring the escaped viper's serpentine habitat companion. She kicked open a small door in the back of the enclosure and jumped, disappearing from view.

With equal nonchalance, Cait had ducked beneath the brass handrail and climbed into the display case in pursuit. The remaining viper took advantage of her crouch to strike, sinking fangs deep into her hand.

Shit.

Jack's heart gave one great thud, then stopped as he landed on the cage floor beside her. Twice now extreme measures had been necessary to keep her alive, and *this* was a new breed of snake.

"How bad will your reaction be?" Straight and to the point, lest she soon not be able to answer.

"I doubt I'll react much at all." She grabbed the snake at the base of its triangular head, squeezing to pry its fangs loose. "It's but an Asp Viper." She gave it a great shake. "Common to much of France. Nothing special, we met long ago during a family visit to the continent."

Short for, "I'm immune to the snake that killed Cleopatra."

Was he gaping?

Yes, but at least his heart had begun to beat again.

From a bag at her hip, she pulled a mesh-like draw-string pouch.

"Go." She waved at him, urging him past. "We need to catch the nanny. I'll secure the viper, then follow."

Jack ducked through the door and dropped into a narrow access hallway, searching for any signs of the nanny's escape route.

A door marked "no entry" caught his eye. Not quite shut, it had caught upon the latch. As a door might when one attempted to carefully and quietly conceal one's exit.

TTX pistol at the ready, he nudged it open. Heat blasted outward, lifting hair from his forehead. There was a roar of flames and the clang of machinery.

Inside, a series of conveyor belts, power shovels and steambots worked to feed coal into a huge furnace. Valves hissed and spit as pipes carried cool water in, hot water out.

Such was the boiler room, source of the heat that kept the Reptile House at a comfortable temperature for the more tropically adapted serpents.

The room was empty of humans. And lamia.

Cait appeared at his side, weapon drawn. "Any sign of her?"

"Not even the cry of a distressed infant could cut through this din."

Together, they moved through the room, searching in vain.

But there was something about the equipment. Or was he seeing double again? He pinched the bridge of his nose and closed his eyes. Sweat broke out on his forehead, between his shoulder blades. This was not the time for everything to go sideways.

Cait pressed a hand to his arm. "What's wrong?"

He opened his eyes. "For a moment I thought, but..." He squinted at the metal contraptions before him.

There were two hulking furnaces. Surely the zoo did not require the function of both at once.

"She left." Cait pointed at a second door set in the wall, an emergency exit, and gave a gentle tug at his elbow. "Let's go."

"Wait." Jack tugged her toward a hulking heap of metal, one with rusted edges and angles, pressed the back of his hand against its metal surface. "Cold and unused. Why leave behind an old furnace?"

"It must weigh a ton..." But doubt narrowed her eyes.

He grasped a worn handle, one that was conspicuously

rust-free, twisting and pulling. Without the slightest of squeaks, the great iron door swung open on well-oiled hinges.

Instead of impenetrable darkness within, a distant, faint light beckoned—from below. Plunging through the base of the not-so-abandoned furnace was a duct wide enough to accommodate the breadth of a man's shoulders. Welded to the side was an iron ladder.

"A secret underground hideaway!" Excitement lit Cait's eyes as she bounced on her toes.

He pressed a finger to his lips. "Shh."

From an inside coat pocket, he produced a decilamp. A few shakes activated the bioluminescent bacteria. Much as he wished to offer his wife the thrill of first descent, she was a new and untrained agent. He would go first.

Taking care not to let the leather of his soles tap against the rungs and announce their arrival, he climbed down into what one might best describe as a cellar. Various bits of old machinery were stacked into towers that leaned against the rough walls.

Cait dropped onto the ground beside him.

Given they'd landed in storage, he'd guess this was the back door. Rule number one, always have a secondary exit.

Which, of course, meant there was a front door.

He could hear the murmur of voices. Would they find both the nanny and Lady Saltwell hidden within?

Step by step, backs against the wall, they edged closer.

CHAPTER TWENTY-THREE

GREEK?

They were speaking in Greek.

But of course they were.

Cait forced herself to analyze the words that the women hissed and spit at each other. But she struggled with the translation. Her working vocabulary began and ended with the bare basics necessary to pass Lister's entrance exams, a project she'd set herself in a misguided attempt to keep up with Alec and Quinn.

The volume of the conversation rose, growing heated enough to upset at least one baby who let out a loud, objecting wail.

"Please, ladies." Dr. Thrakos interrupted their squabbling. Metal clanged and glass clinked. "English please. I agree with the infant. Your Greek is positively archaic and hurts my head."

"You've ruined everything, Helena," a woman accused.

Her voice lost none of its edge as it sliced back into proper English like a razor. "There was no need to harvest yet another pituitary. In. My. Home."

Jack mouthed her name: *Lady Saltwell.*

"There was every need. But isn't that just the problem," Helena snapped back. "Your home. Your husband. Your money. Everything is yours, yours, yours."

Helena, the woman who attacked me in the carriage, Cait mouthed back.

Jack's eyes grew wide. *She's also the woman who escaped through the garden at my brother's ball!*

He reached into his pocket and tugged out a telescoping rod of dull silver. At its end, a tiny mirror. One with just enough surface to allow them to catch a glimpse of activities around the corner.

Cait squinted at the looking glass.

Shrunken heads!

A secret laboratory, fully equipped and land-based! All this time it had been tucked beneath the Reptile House of the London Zoo, beneath the feet of countless visitors as they gasped at the serpentine exhibits overhead, blissfully unaware of the true horrors below.

Dr. Thrakos bent over a laboratory bench, twisting the knobs of a machine as a thick, viscous fluid dripped into a test tube. What *was* he processing? At one elbow, a refrigerated carry case, much like the one she had used to transport her cobra, though his three precious transformed *morphophídian* snakes had been moved to a wire cage. Such were quite likely the source of venom milked for ladies wishing to avoid childbirth, yet not something that required processing.

However, on his other side, a tray held an assortment of medical instruments. Beyond that, the most Cait could make out was the corner of a metal gurney. Not unlike the one in his floating laboratory. A shiver ran down her spine. Did this one also sport leather straps? She'd wager in the affirmative, but was a victim bound to its surface?

Jack adjusted the angle of the mirror, providing a view of the quarreling women.

"Hush, sisters," the nanny admonished. "Lower your voices, lest you wake another child." Unbuttoning her bodice, she lifted the fussing baby from the pram to set the infant to her breast. The infant latched on with gusto.

Had she just seen—?

Cait squeezed her eyes closed.

Opened them.

Nope. Her vision was fine.

A trickle of blood leaked from about the infant's lips.

Fangs. And at only three months!

Cait caught Jack's gaze. *They're* all *lamia!*

"Yes, Lord Saltwell is *my* husband," Lady Saltwell hissed back at Helena. "He chose *me.* I was, after all, the first to conceive."

Stripped to her underpinnings—an old-fashioned chemise and a corset with additional grommets and laces to accommodate an increasing pregnancy—she sat upon a low stool, yanking at silk stockings that appeared to be caught upon something.

Impossible not to stare.

The silk pulled away, and Cait cringed at the dry and scaly patches of skin covering Lady Saltwell's legs from toes to knees, disappearing beneath the edges of her petticoats. A flash of sympathy that vanished the moment the woman unscrewed the lid of a squat jar, scooped forth a thick emollient, and spread it over the angry epidermis.

Not so rattled by the shop assistant's death that she was willing to abandon the jar of lotion. She pulled a face and mouthed, *cold-blooded*.

"I am the most fertile, in both body and mind," Lady Saltwell continued, pulling a pair of plain, cotton stockings from a carpet bag. "Without me, you'd still live in a tumble-down hut. Instead, we live—lived—in luxury, built an empire that had London's elite kneeling down before us. All destroyed when you took to the streets of London to perform an outdated ritual hunt."

"And where would you have preferred I stalk my prey?" Helena countered, arms crossed. "In the northern wilds of Scotland? Packed on ice and hauled home by steam train?"

"You ought not have hunted at all." Lady Saltwell huffed. "It is you who drew all the unwelcome attention down upon us. You should have followed the plan. Dr. Oakes would have provided, as he did before."

"Cadavers?" Helena spit back. "Dead from one disease or another? With what chance of success, when my carefully chosen, prime specimens fail to work?" She flapped a hand at Dr. Thrakos. "Had I not located a scientist of our homeland, my daughters would never have been born."

"Fresh extracts naturally provide the most potent effects," Dr. Thrakos said. "This time they will also be free from the effects of any venom."

"Does it matter?" A scoff, a noise emerged from the back of Lady Saltwell's throat. "Conception is only a beginning. Not one of your offspring has drawn breath for more than a few minutes. You proclaim your superiority yet, over and over, the biological failing is yours alone. Enough. Accept that you will produce no queen."

Lady Saltwell pulled on simple ankle boots, then stood to don entirely different attire, a dull brown dress that would turn no heads. Perfect for blending in crowds while evading authorities.

"Sisters," the nanny interjected, her voice soft. "We arrived on these foreign shores with but one purpose in mind, revenge. That has been accomplished, our actions rewarded beyond our wildest dreams. Now we must turn our attention to the future and our homeland."

"If prematurely," Lady Saltwell bit out. "Who is Helena to decide for us the time and place to end Lord Saltwell's life? At the engagement ball of our business partner? With half of the *ton* present? But for her needless drama, the Queen's agents would never have been placed on our trail. She's a fool."

A low moan sounded. Cait's eyebrows drew together. Had they not accounted for everyone in the space?

Jack extended the handle of the mirror yet farther, angling for a look at the alcove beyond the mad scientist. The image reflected back showed two shoe-clad feet upon a gurney, toes pointed toward the ceiling.

She swallowed. Were these the fresh victims to which Dr. Thrakos referred? At least one was still alive. She loosed her TTX pistol and held it at the ready.

"We've discussed this." A steel rod threaded through the nanny's words. She laid her infant back in the pram and buttoned her jacket. "Repeatedly and at length. Lord Saltwell intended to reveal all. To see your marriage invalidated, your children disinherited. Instead, Helena ensured he died knowing exactly what we'd stolen from him."

And what was that? Cait raised her eyebrows at Jack and lifted a palm upward.

Jack shrugged and shook his head. *No idea.*

Lady Saltwell blew out a long breath as she rose, smoothed her skirts and picked up the carpet bag. "Come with us, Helena. It's not worth the risk."

Cait nudged Jack in his side. *TTX darts?*

He readied his weapon, but held up a finger. *Wait.*

"Not without one final effort," Helena pouted. "I'll not abandon my chance at achieving what was thought impossible."

"Ladies." Dr. Thrakos turned, holding a vial of viscous fluid aloft. "How can you begrudge her one more attempt at a miraculous birth?"

Helena snatched the vial from his hand. "How is this enough?"

"I harvested but one."

"Not both?" Helena's voice was petulant.

The madman chuckled. "I left him one stone, a reminder that we're not to be crossed."

"Fine," Helena huffed. She tucked the tube of testicular extract behind her corset, cradling it between her breasts. "Finish with the woman. There's little time to waste."

Woman? Cait mouthed.

Jack stretched his arm out, extending the tiny mirror as far as he could manage.

Suddenly, he jerked backward, catching Cait's hand to drag her back into the storage room. Pain from the asp's bite surged, but only mildly so. A small price for renewed immunity.

"It's Aubrey and Lady Mildred," he breathed into her ear. "Gagged and bound upon the gurneys. Laid out as if for—"

"Surgical sacrifice?" she whispered back, lifting her weapon. "I'll target Lady Saltwell and Dr. Thrakos. You aim for the murderesses." The pinched expression upon his face worried her. "Unless your eyes..."

"They're fine."

She pressed a finger to the crease between his eyebrows. "What are you not telling me?"

"It's a headache, nothing more." He pulled her hand away, dropping a quick kiss upon her palm. "By now, I've every expectation that your brother will have the building surrounded. One dart each to slow them down—I'll not risk the lives of the unborn, lamia or otherwise."

Cait nodded. "Let's move."

They slid sideways down the hallway, took aim, and fired.

She hit her targets. Lady Saltwell in the shoulder, the mad scientist in the hip. Jack's first dart caught the nanny's upper arm, but Helena spun away, and his second missed its mark.

Kraken claws.

There was a blur of motion.

Helena, almost too fast for human eyes, struck Jack upon the head. A moment later, a horrible screech assaulted her ears as an arm wrapped about her neck with preternatural strength.

Cait kicked and clawed as Helena yanked her backward into the laboratory leaving Jack in the dim hall, motionless upon the floor, blood trickling from his mouth.

With her lungs deprived of oxygen, only Cait's mind could scream.

"Go," Helena ordered her sisters. "Take the children and flee. They are first priority."

Lady Saltwell and the nanny had been quick to jerk the darts free. Regretfully, the poison scarcely slowed their movements. Lady Saltwell pulled open a door—what must be the front entrance—and the nanny pushed the pram through.

Gone.

And there was little hope that Logan would recognize either of them.

"You," Helena hissed in her ear. "The woman who refused to die."

She shoved Cait away, slamming her shoulder into a wall. Flashes of light danced across her field of vision as she slid to the floor, hands at her throat, dragging in great gasps.

Helena dropped both TTX pistols upon the laboratory bench in front of the gaping Dr. Thrakos. "Harvest their organs as well."

"Not the snake charmer's." The mad scientist shook his head, plucked the dart from his leather vest and set it aside. "Antivenin. Remember I explained how—"

"Yes, yes." Helena flipped a hand. "A blood product capable of counteracting my own venom. It's why she didn't die that night in the carriage."

"If anything, her pituitary extract would thwart your efforts." Dr. Thrakos slid his eyes to Jack's prone form. "Even his is of questionable value."

"If we've no use for the woman..." The lamia snatched up a TTX pistol, took aim and fired, once, twice and a third time—three darts into Cait's chest. "There. Problem solved."

Cait collapsed in a heap as a familiar numbness spread across her body.

Cogs. Shot with her own weapon. *Breathe in, breathe out.*

It would be a minute or two before she could move. She slid a glance in Jack's direction and caught the faintest of movements. Good.

"Hurry up," Helena grumbled at the mad scientist. "Or I'll handle the extraction myself."

"No." With a regretful glance at Cait—no doubt Dr. Thrakos regretted losing another chance to bleed her dry— the mad scientist staggered toward Lady Mildred. Though unconscious, she still breathed. "I've made adjustments to the programming cards and want to verify the algorithm."

With an unsteady hand—courtesy of the small amount of TTX poison that had made it into his system—he lifted a brass device resembling an oversized metallic insect and began to fuss and fumble over the cipher cartridge.

There was a strangled shout and leather heels kicked at the metal gurney in protest. An effort followed by a pained moan.

"I imagine it does hurt, Aubrey," Helena snipped. "At least you'll survive. Your bride, on the other hand..." She clucked her tongue. "No worries. You may be partly unmanned, but there are many silly, overbred girls who will overlook such a deficiency in an effort to secure a title."

Lord Aubrey's trousers had been yanked to his knees, exposing hairy legs. Between them, he clutched a thick wad of blood-stained cotton.

Cait cringed.

Jack's brother was wide-eyed and fully awake and clearly in much pain. An entire testicle removed without benefit of an analgesic? A cruel way to treat the lord who'd provided the financial backing for a Lamian-based enterprise.

He was, however, guilty of shielding a murderess, while Lady Mildred, innocent of all wrongdoing, was about to pay with her life.

Beneath her skirts, Cait flexed her fingers and toes, then arms and legs, confirming the full return of movement. Her shoulder throbbed as she braced her arm, shifting her feet in preparation for a mad leap.

From the corner of one eye, she saw Jack move. Though appearing to lay insensate, he was now some five feet closer.

Dr. Thrakos flicked a lever, spreading the sharp-tipped legs of the device wide, then lowered the mechanical insect onto the woman's face with deadly, surgical precision.

This? *This* was the device Jack wished the Thorntons to modify for his personal use?

Then again, the tumor threatened more than just his sight.

A low buzzing began.

Lady Mildred was about to lose her pituitary and her life. Cait snapped her fingers, and Jack's eyes popped open. With a quick tip of her head at Helena, she mouthed, *Now!*

She shoved herself onto her feet at the very moment Jack did the same, both of them rushing at full speed, intent upon stopping the procedure.

Again, the lamia moved like quicksilver. With a twist and a turn, she slithered beyond their grasp, hissing. Cait and Jack crashed into the metal gurneys, sending them careening into the wall. Aubrey roared in smothered pain. Lady Mildred whimpered as the contraption affixed to her face ripped free and fell to the floor. Momentarily safe, if an awful way to return to consciousness.

Howling, Helena snatched up the broken pieces of the pituitary extractor and stuffed them into a canvas bag. "Enough!" With a backhanded swipe, she knocked the cage holding the *morphophidian* creatures onto the floor. Its latch snapped and the lid popped open. The irate serpents wasted no time effecting their escape.

"No!" Dr. Thrakos cried. "How could you? They're priceless!" He dove, scrambling across the floor, reaching for his creations. "Help me catch them, I beg you."

Cait ignored the snakes, concentrating her full attention upon Helena. The lamia feinted left, then right, her movements swift and serpentine as she darted for the door.

As she passed, Cait flung herself onto Helena's back, wrapping her arms about the lamia's neck, praying her weight would slow the woman.

"Jack," Cait cried. "Shoot her!"

The lamia bit her arm.

"Ouch, you monster!" Cait bellowed into the woman's ear. "Have you learned nothing? Your venom is powerless upon me. Jack! Jack?"

With a hiss, Helena spun about, heaved herself backward and slammed Cait into the wall, aiming to further damage her injured shoulder—and hitting her mark. Her left arm was losing strength. Any minute her grip would fail.

Jack sidestepped writhing *morphophidia* and the frantic Dr. Thrakos to lunge for the TTX weapons. He snatched one up, took aim at the lamia's chest and fired.

Zwing. At last the welcome sound of an air-powered dart releasing.

Thwack. The dart hitting its mark.

Helena howled and threw Cait against the wall once more, a final attempt to divest herself of the clinging weight. Pain burst over Cait's shoulder, and she fell.

Canvas sack in hand, Helena fled, slamming the laboratory door closed behind her. Jack threw it open, but she was already gone.

Dammit.

"Help!" Dr. Thrakos howled. "I've been bit!"

He fell to the ground, a deadly dose of venom pumping through his veins and arteries. In the chaos, two *morphophidian* serpents had slithered off to a shadowed corner. But the third had extracted revenge for a life of imprisonment with a fast strike to the mad scientist's arm. Fangs still sunk into flesh, the creature stared at her with slitty, defiant eyes.

Corpse candles.

Jack cursed. "We have to save him. Think of all the information stored inside his skull."

He was right. There really was no choice.

Muttering, Cait grasped the base of the *morphophidian's* head and forced its jaws open, prying it free. With both hands, she gave a sharp twist, breaking its spine, ending its miserable life, and reducing it to nothing more than a curious, uncanny specimen fit for a brief dissection before an afterlife of confinement floating in a formaldehyde-filled jar.

"Pull up his sleeve," she ordered Jack.

He propped Dr. Thrakos against the cabinets and tore his sleeve from wrist to shoulder.

In the distance, she heard shouts ring out.

"Here!" Jack yelled.

"Go," she said. "Find them. I can handle this."

"I'll be right back." Jack ran down the hallway, calling to the approaching agents. "We're down here! Beneath the boiler room!"

All blood had drained from Dr. Thrakos' face, leaving him pale and waxy with a growing sheen of cold sweat. "Heart racing," he gasped. "Breathing... a struggle."

Her sympathy for his plight was in short supply. Still, her pulse picked up its pace. This would be the first time her hypothesis was put to the test.

Oh, how the tables had turned.

Dropping onto her knees beside Dr. Thrakos, she cracked open her refrigerated case and tugged out a vial of antivenin and a syringe. She filled the barrel and tapped the syringe, dislodging air bubbles.

With dead eyes, she stared down at him. "You mentioned half-siblings of mine."

"Will tell you," he wheezed. "If I live."

"I'll hold you to that." She wrapped rubber tubing about the mad scientist's arm and set about locating a vein. "Or I'll find a way to reunite you with your remaining *morphophídia*."

"You wouldn't."

"I'd certainly try." The hollow needle slid into the mad scientist's vein, and she depressed the plunger, injecting every last drop of the antivenin into his system. "In a few minutes," she said, "you should feel a lessening of the bands about your chest, then a slowing of your heart rate."

But her words fell on deaf ears. The mad scientist had fallen unconscious.

Sighing, Cait set about retrieving his escaped creations.

Moments later, hard shoe leather clanged on the rungs of the metal ladder that led downward from the boiler room and agents, chests heaving, burst into the room, her brother in the lead.

"Ten minutes too late for taking Lamian prisoners." Cait sat back on her heels, securing the latch that would keep the two remaining *morphophídia* safe within their cage. She waved her hand. "Allow me to introduce two venomous creatures and their creator, one Dr. Thrakos."

Lady Mildred began to cry, and Aubrey renewed his garbled shouts.

Familiar Romani curses fell from Logan's lips as he took in the scene before him. "Everywhere you go, destruction follows." He sighed. "But at least no one is dead." His eyes darkened as they fell upon the mad scientist. "Yet."

CHAPTER TWENTY-FOUR

"HE ESCAPED?" JACK all but shouted, incredulous. "How? I watched the man pour half a bottle of brandy down his throat."

"Not to mention the empty laudanum bottle on his bedside table," Cait added, frowning. "But it's possible he dumped its contents, then played dead, counting upon us to leave him alone."

Black leveled them both with a narrow gaze. "One way or another, you were fooled. While Agent Jackson stood guard at the new Lord Saltwell's door—in full view of all other doors connecting to his suite—the gentleman managed to climb out a window and shimmy down a rain spout."

Implying complicity with the lamia.

Had Carruthers slipped away to sound the alarm? Would he aid and abet the three women in their flight from British shores? Where on Earth might they have planned to meet?

The three of them stood together—outside of the Reptile House entrance and beneath the night sky—pondering the implications of their discovery and the next steps that ought to be taken.

Jack swore. "How many agents are searching?"

"As many as I can spare," Black said. "Guards watch the entrances to various train stations for his wife and children. For the man himself, they wait at his club and a few of his other known haunts. That's all we have, given your brother refuses to cooperate."

Jack had slid the gag from his brother's mouth. "Where have they gone?"

"You," Aubrey had gasped. "Forever on hand to ruin everything."

"Is that any way to talk to someone who saved your lives?"

"Mildred's." Aubrey had glared. "Not mine."

Further proof his brother cared only for his own skin.

Jack had snorted. "That may well be true. Have you seen the equipment Dr. Thrakos kept on hand?" He'd lifted a glass jar of needles, given it a shake. Metal clinked against glass, kicking up a fine dust of dark material. "Dried blood? Certainly not the cleanest of sharps and sutures. A few stitches might have stopped your bleeding, but chances of an infection are through the roof. Your other nut might yet rot and fall off."

"Fix this," his brother had hissed through clenched teeth.

He'd shaken his head, slowly. "This is far past fixing, though mitigation might yet be an option." He'd dropped the jar of needles onto the gurney. Right beside Aubrey's head for closer inspection. "Carruthers is the reason you're in this mess. *Your* testicle was sacrificed to augment *his* bedroom performance."

Aubrey's face turned puce.

"Time to throw your drunken friend under the omnibus. Name him as the instigator. Tell me everything you know about his wife, nanny and mistress. Begin by telling me the name of the theater in which he met them." Any clue that might hint at where Helena and Carruthers might have arranged to meet.

"Escaped, have they?" Aubrey scoffed. "Let me know when you have them in custody. We'll talk then."

Jack had pushed, but his brother had flattened his lips and refused to utter another word.

"Perhaps if you threatened to remove the last of his family jewels?" he suggested, pinching the bridge of his nose. The headache pounding within his skull threatened to crack it open along its many sutures at any moment.

"Tempting." The corner of Black's mouth kicked up.

Cait snorted. "Or suggest that the slip of a tongue in the presence of a newspaperman might make his life yet more difficult?" Cait tipped her head. "Tit for tat?"

Black lifted an eyebrow. "An act prohibited according to the terms of your employment."

She sighed. "Terribly trying, professional behavior."

Lady Mildred had taken one glance at her fiancé lying beside her, clutching a bloody cloth to his groin with his pants at his knees, and broke into a hysterical keening that only lessened when she was delivered into her mother's arms. An end to their engagement would raise questions, the answers to which, if discovered, might well cause the gossip rags to spontaneously combust.

Aubrey himself was not so fortunate as to secure transport home. Instead, he was en route to a hospital ward beneath Lister Laboratories where he would be shackled to a bed frame and the consequences of his unfortunate amputation addressed.

Thanks to Cait's efforts, Dr. Thrakos—brought down by his own creations who were even now en route to her laboratory—would follow Aubrey on a gurney of his own where measures could be taken to make him speak. Jack had very specific plans to extract all the data he could about the pituitary extractor's design, construction and function.

With no remaining on scene responsibilities, he and Cait were under orders to return home and recover while agents hunted down three deadly lamiae and one misguided lord.

Not that he had any intention of resting. Not while a venomous and deadly lamia, mistress to the complicit Carruthers, and her sisters roamed free.

"For you." Black slapped an envelope against his chest, its seal broken. The top agent made no effort to conceal that fact, nor did he offer a false apology. "A missive from your sister."

With that, Black left them to attend to other pressing matters.

Jack pulled out the paper, read aloud the short message. "All's well that ends well." The note was unsigned.

"Angela?" Cait inquired.

He nodded. "It's her handwriting. As to its meaning..."

He shared a knowing look with his wife. Best to leave the words unspoken.

His sister had either executed her husband as ordered. Or had done the unthinkable and fallen in love. Impossible to know.

But the message delivery?

An olive branch, and likely the only one Black would offer.

As a steady stream of zoo officials in evening attire poured out of crank hacks and carriages, all expressing varying degrees of shock and horror at the egregious events beneath the Reptile House, they slipped away.

He'd given the driver directions to their home. Not that he or Cait would stay longer than it took to effect a change of clothes, to replenish their supply of TTX darts. Then it was back out onto the streets, hunting the London lamiae.

"With Dr. Thrakos in custody," Cait began, "we could abandon the lamia chase and focus upon extracting information from him."

"We could, but he might well resist."

"There are ways..."

"I'd prefer to deliver an actual device, broken or otherwise, into Lady Thornton's hands," Jack said. "Then we question Dr. Thrakos. Better to let the mad scientist ponder his bleak future. That alone will loosen his lips."

"Patience is not a quality I possess in large amounts." Inside the dim interior of their for-hire steam carriage, Cait pressed a hand to his face. "Especially now, when you look as if someone used a hammer to drive a nail between your eyes."

He swept her into his arms and onto his lap, attempting to kiss away her concerns. "Ignore it as I do." Activities other than conversation were at the forefront of his mind. "Or, better, distract me. We've a bit of time to ourselves in this conveyance." He drew a finger over the edge of her rumpled bodice. "Alone."

"True." She unknotted the sad, limp cravat at his collar, slid it from his neck and tossed it aside before pressing a kiss to the hollow of his throat. "It's not as if we could possibly become more rumpled or disheveled."

"Nor are we a stodgy, old married couple tied to convention." He shifted, tipping her backward onto the lumpy seat. Tufts of horsehair stuck out from worn patches. "After all, we've yet to make it to our marriage bed."

"I expect it's overrated." His wife bent a knee and a cascade of ruffles fell to her hip, exposing thin silk stockings that disappeared beneath the lace edges of pink-tinted knickers. "And you did promise we'd pass time in the most interesting and pleasurable ways possible." She crooked a finger.

Lovestruck and fully aroused, he stared. Fighting to focus that he might fix this image of her in his mind—illuminated in flashes of gaslight through glass windows as the carriage rumbled through the streets—should the worst come to pass.

His wife, the very picture of a victorious Queen's agent,

a far cry from a prim and proper lady. Everything he'd ever wanted—needed—and hadn't known.

From her gauze-wrapped snake-bitten hand to the tangled tumble of snarled hair cascading over her shoulders. Even the blood stains upon her bodice, scuffed boots and torn stockings was irresistible seduction, for every detail marked a moment she'd prevailed.

"Jack?" A hint of concern edged her voice.

She was right to worry. His vision struggled and his head pounded. Was it possible that the tumor within his brain could rupture without warning? Yes. Today or tomorrow. Next month or next year. And his life would implode.

Or it might sit there, dull and boring, yet stealing tiny fractions of his vision away day by day.

But right now, they were safe and secure, and he intended to make the most of every moment.

"Aether, Cait. A man needs a moment to admire the beauty of his wife."

"That's long enough." Stern words, belied by the smile upon her face. Leaning forward, her fingers fell upon his waistband. "Come make a closer examination."

In a moment, his trousers were loose about his hips and he fell upon her, like a ravenous wolf.

♦

"FORCED MARRIAGES MAY BE UNDERRATED," he said some time later, sated and sweaty and still wrapped in his wife's arms. "I never would have sought out an eavesdropping, snake-collecting woman with powerful blood on my own."

"Never fear," she laughed against his neck. "Tall, handsome, single and a Queen's agent. You were already within my crosshairs."

"I'm sorry I ever doubted the power of your blood," he whispered. "Most impressive, how it just saved a man's life."

"Only in hopes of saving your vision." She pressed two fingers to his lips when he dipped his head again, smiling. "Stop. We're almost home, and we have monsters to hunt, one in particular. Helena with the pituitary extractor in her possession." With a fingertip she traced the furrow between his eyes. "Your first dart missed."

He winced, then dropped his forehead to her shoulder. The brief respite from confronting the inevitable was at an end. There was no escaping this conversation. Partner and wife, she needed to know.

"Up." She poked him in the chest. "No dissembling. How bad is it, really, your headache?"

With a sigh, he lifted his head. "Bad enough to trigger recurring double vision."

"You took aim at the wrong image?"

"Not exactly." Regretfully, he extricated himself from the tangle of limbs.

As they went about setting themselves to rights, he recounted those close, fast moments in the subterranean laboratory. "My vision was good enough. My mistake was targeting Lady Saltwell first. In the space between the moment when the second dart fell into its chamber and when my finger pulled the trigger, Helena shifted—and my dart missed her by a hair's breadth. Before I could blink, she was in front of me. A second later, she struck my head, pain exploded, and the world went dark."

"She moves with extraordinary speed," Cait agreed. "And fights with an unnatural strength. I can feel bruises forming across my shoulder and back."

He frowned.

"I'll recover." She caught his chin between her thumb and forefinger, glanced from one eye to the other. "I'm more concerned about your head."

"And my pupils?" A concern, as any difference would indicate optic nerve damage.

"Still the same size." Her lips twisted. "For now."

"What will you do with the remaining *morphophídia*?" A blatant change in topics.

"That will depend," she commented. "Those serpents were created purely for venom production, not for direct use upon a patient. They lack control, as demonstrated when delivered by lamia or masseuse into a vein. They may be deemed too dangerous for study."

"It was an excellent scheme. A venom syndicate." Jack waggled his eyebrows. "Gentlemen willing to pay a steep price for the pleasure of a venomous bite and the promise of rampant virility."

She rolled her eyes. "All while their wives and mistresses swallowed monthly doses milked from the *morphophídia* to prevent conception. Round and round it went, with no end in sight."

"An ouroboros."

Her eyebrows drew together. "Is that the snake eating its own tail?"

"It is. Often said to represent the cycle of life, death and rebirth, it's an early alchemy symbol with roots in ancient Egypt and Greece," he breathed out the last word. "What is it, Cait?" Her gaze had become distant.

"How on Earth was I to draw the connection at the time?" She snapped into action, rapping at the roof and calling to the driver. "Thirty-Six Holywell Street!"

The carriage lurched, abruptly changing direction.

"Cait?"

"Alchemy. Magic. Circle." She shifted onto the edge of her seat, eyes glittering. "I knew Helena looked familiar, but I've only now figured out why."

"Not only from the confines of a dark carriage in Covent Garden, I gather?"

She shook her head. "It's no wonder I've forgotten. How on Earth was I to draw the connection at the time? It all leads back to my cobra."

"Your cobra?" Only *his* wife would use such a possessive, a unique woman among the *ton*. He rather looked forward to introducing her—inflicting her?—upon high society.

"Mine." She swatted his shoulder. "Much as he desired to arrange for a photograph depicting 'Eve and the Serpent in the Garden of Eden', the artist from whom I purchased my snake could not find a woman willing to pose nude with the creature."

"Wise, given its poisonous nature."

"But how did he come into possession of the cobra in the first place?" She lifted a finger. "The photographer shared his studio with other artists. Among many charcoal sketches tacked to the wall was one of a dark-haired woman with a distinctive nose, naked but for a twist of fabric wrapped about her waist. She stood, hand extended, tracing a circle upon the ground." Cait leaned close. "There was a serpent wrapped about her neck, tail tucked inside its mouth."

"Helena," he said. "Your snake was once her snake?"

"Cobra venom and her venom cross-reacted with my serum on the biogels indicating immunity," Cait reminded him. "What other woman would handle such a serpent without fear?"

"Besides you, daughter of Kālūnāth Sapera?"

She grinned. "Besides me."

"So you've redirected our carriage based on—?" He lifted his eyebrows.

"There was background in the sketch, but I paid it no attention."

"Focused as you were upon obtaining a cobra."

"Exactly." Her face beamed. "We need to examine the drawing, locate the artist. She was an actress, and Holywell Street is adjacent to Covent Garden. Perhaps he could help us trace her past."

"Where she might even now be taking refuge?"

"We've no other leads." Cait threw up her hands. "Most of the killings took place in and around Covent Garden, save for Lord Saltwell and our unfortunate apothecary's assistant. What if she still rents her old rooms?"

"And this artist might point us to a specific theater—"

"Where her old associates might be able to direct us to her lodgings, the perfect place for her and Carruthers to hide from Queen's agents while they plan their next move."

They turned from The Strand onto Holywell Street, passing the church of St. Mary le Strand. Rumor had it that street took its name from a holy well, one that still bubbled and gurgled in the basement of a tavern, largely ignored, though its water was as clean and as fresh as in Roman times.

Not that clean or fresh were words he'd use to describe any other aspect of this section of London. Tired and tilting half-timbered buildings loomed overhead as hired crank hacks, clockwork horses, and pedestrians clogged the narrow passage. At this late hour, all were here for entertainment of the risqué sort.

"We're here." Cait squeezed his hand.

They alighted before a narrow alleyway that led back to The Strand. Half-Moon Passage, or Pissing Alley, an accurate honorific given the odor that emanated forth. The ancient carved wooden sign, a rather disgruntled looking half-moon who looked down upon them with distaste that gave the passage its name also hung over Thirty-Six Holywell Street, a bookseller's store. One which was, to all appearances, closed.

Cait looked up at him expectantly.

So much for impressing her with the lock picks he slid from his coat pocket. Jack threaded the narrow metal tools into the keyhole of a bolt barely worth the cost of the iron used to forge the padlock.

Click.

The lock fell into his hands, and they slipped inside. Decilamp held aloft, they picked their way past tables and between bookcases and such texts as *An Erotic Philosopher's Lectures.*

"That one caught my eye as well." Cait laughed behind him. "We could take it with us, leave appropriate remuneration behind on the counter."

"Yet another reason to be pleased with my wife. But another time."

Narrow stairways led upward. A dark hallway to a street-facing studio, its door unlocked. Inside, streetlight filtered through windows casting the shadows of props and stools and camera equipment upon the floors and across walls papered with photographs and sketches.

Cait pointed. "There."

The blue-white light of his decilamp illuminated the charcoal drawing.

An expertly drawn sketch, exactly as Cait had described it. Naked woman. Snake. Some kind of magic ceremony in progress. The backdrop, surrounded by hanging curtains was clearly stage scenery, but one he couldn't place. Not even with one eye closed, that he might focus more clearly. The drawing was, unfortunately, unsigned.

"Who's there?" Frying pan raised overhead, a man approached.

"Mr. Dryer?" Cait spun, hands lifted. "We had no idea the building was occupied. Many apologies, but we're in dire need of time-sensitive information."

"You!" the man lowered the cookware. "Snake-woman."

"But not," she pointed, "the only one. Who is she? Where is she?"

He shook his head. "He warned me about your kind."

"Her kind?" Jack asked.

"Slithery and Greek." The man backed away. "Kiss you, kill you. Best avoided."

"I'm neither Greek nor venomous," Cait said. "But this woman is." She tugged at her jacket, giving the man a glimpse of her TTX pistol. "We wish to take her into custody."

"Do you know who sketched this?" Jack asked.

The man nodded. "Waterhouse. He's making a bit of a name for himself these days. Warned me that woman in the picture was up to no good, but that he couldn't prove it. He gave me the sketch as payment for taking that cobra off his hands."

"And where might we find Mr. Waterhouse?" she asked.

The man shrugged. "About."

Jack sighed, pointed the decilamp back at the drawing. "This scenery, can you pinpoint the play?"

Squinting, Mr. Dryer drew closer, nodded. "It's a backdrop from Fay O'Fire. Playing over at the Opera Comique right now as we speak."

CHAPTER TWENTY-FIVE

A S IT HAPPENED, the Opera Comique was but steps
away.

Built upon the grounds that once housed
Lyon's Inn, one of the Inns of Chancery, a former law court
once situated between Holywell and Wych Streets, were
two back-to-back theaters, The Royal Globe Theater and the
Opera Comique.

Not that you could exactly see it, tucked away as it was
behind existing buildings that lined the streets. There was no
grand façade, merely a sign hanging over an unremarkable
street entrance. A steep flight of descending stairs delivered
them to passageways that led them beneath buildings and
into a largely underground theater.

Subterranean.

Suitable for evil, burrowing creatures with small, beady
eyes and sharp pointy teeth.

A category into which she now placed lamiae. But Cait's

thoughts on the matter were decidedly unkind.

City officials wished to demolish the entire area, for both moral and aesthetic reasons. As of the moment, the city had not yet moved on its plans to widen and improve The Strand, but with such a possibility in mind, those constructing the two theaters hadn't over-invested in building materials. Rickety and drafty, descriptive terms most often applied.

"Two tickets for Fay O'Fire," Jack requested.

Judging from a flier pinned to the wall, the play was a romantic opera wrapped about the legend of a ghost.

"The production is already well underway," the man in the ticket booth objected, correctly sizing up their wild and unkempt appearance as trouble. The twitch of his nose and the faint curl of his lip suggested he was eager to turn them away. Good instincts. "Perhaps another night?"

Jack frowned.

"We promised to view my friend's performance and do not wish to offend her with our absence," Cait lied smoothly. "Tonight."

"Friend?" the man's eyebrows rose.

"Miss Tempest." She'd found the name off the flier, choosing one of the leading ladies.

Adoration lit the man's face. "A rising star, isn't she?"

"Let me make our presence more palatable." Jack dropped a number of gold sovereigns upon the counter. Far, far more than necessary. Enough that the ticket-seller could pocket the majority. "A private box, so that we do not disturb the other attendees?"

Relieved to be handed a mutually beneficial solution, the starry-eyed man swept the gold away and pushed two tickets toward them. "Miss Tempest is a true leading lady with a long and brilliant career before her. Enjoy the show."

An usher led them to their plush, velvet seats, then disappeared behind the fall of a curtain.

The stage before them currently supported a lugubrious gentleman plaintively bleating out a dismal song about water —of which the audience loudly disapproved. She eyed the curve of three tiers holding the booing spectators aloft—such manners!—but had little time to take in the beauty of the theater before Jack tugged at her sleeve and tipped his head toward the hallway.

It was time to locate Helena's former colleagues.

They dropped down flight after flight of steep stairs, at last ducking through an unmarked door and into a narrow hallway lined with stage props.

She fell against a wall, gasping. "A moment."

"Is it the asp's bite?" Jack's face scrunched with worry.

She shook her head. "No. It's my boned corset, tightly laced. Suitable only for a leisurely stroll. Not the active pursuit of suspects."

He laughed.

"Excuse me." An indignant man dressed as a demon stomped forward. "You can't be here." He pointed at the door, ordering their exit.

"Many apologies." Jack flashed his holstered weapon. "But we need to speak with Miss Helena. Immediately."

The demon's lips pursed. "Rather popular, tonight,

Helena. But the she-devil and her sisters left our theater company several months ago." He pointed again at the door. "Please go. We don't want any trouble."

"Not an actual denial of her presence." Cait narrowed her eyes. "She's here. Where?"

The demon sighed.

"Listen," she pressed. "We're not here to partake of the substance she peddles, nor to have a polite conversation." She tapped her own TTX weapon. "We're here to remove her from the theater's premises on a permanent basis."

"And what of the lordling?" The demon planted red-painted, taloned hands on his hips. "He promised them a home, but she refuses to vacate the undercroft."

"Lordling?" Jack asked, his focus knife-sharp. "Might his name be Carruthers?"

The demon's lips stretched, revealing a mouthful of pointed teeth. "You know of him. Excellent."

"He's here?" Jack crowded the actor. "At this very minute?"

"He is. Thorn in my side, that gentleman, always pining after her. These past months, we'd hoped we were well rid of him. But he's back, and madness has stolen his mind. He burst into Helena's old dressing room and all but scared Marie to death." His talons pointed a new direction. "I expect you'll find him wandering the vaults, howling her name."

"Vaults?" Cait frowned.

"The Opera Comique replaced an old, medieval pile. An Inn of Chancery."

"Lyon's Inn," Jack said.

The demon snapped his fingers. "That's the one. They knocked it down and hauled most of it away, but left its underbelly behind as foundations. The undercroft—a number of vaulted chambers—is suitable only for the storage of things one wishes to forget. Or lose." The demon's eyes gleamed. "The three sisters had a habit of wandering its passages. Men who followed them never returned."

"Save Carruthers," Cait stated.

"None but him," the demon confirmed.

"What makes him special?"

"Besides his longevity?" He shrugged. "If you search the vaults, perhaps you'll find out. Try not to get lost in there. No one will come looking for you." He pointed. "End of the hallway, down a flight of stairs on your right."

A fairy, a revenant, and a whole chorus of young ballet dancers popped in and out of dressing rooms as they passed, shooting them disapproving or curious gazes as they rushed past.

"Have you seen a man by the name of Carruthers?" Cait asked the fairy.

She frowned and shook her head.

But two women recalled him.

"Had a habit of pinching your are if your back was turned," one grumbled.

"If you're referring to the lordling obsessed with the witches," her friend said, tipping her head. "He headed into the vaults."

"When?" Jack asked.

A half shrug. "Before curtain call?"

An hour past, perhaps more.

A matron clapped her hands, and the entire ensemble rushed to take their positions on the stage while the orchestra struck up a new melody.

Leaving them entirely alone.

At the far end of the hall, beyond the bright lights and chaotic backstage tumble of props and costumes, a dusty, stone archway where modern red brickwork met Medieval mortared stone.

Cait reached into a pouch at her waist and pulled out a handful of TTX darts.

"Stolen from your brother's pockets?"

"Pickpocketing numbers among my many skills." She grinned. "Quite handy."

They refilled the chambers of their weapons, then Jack shook his decilamp to life, ready to light the way. "Ladies first?"

"I'm not a lady." Cait eyeballed the stairs descending before them. "So long as your brother is alive. As he is, by now, in the hands of talented Lister physicians, I've no expectation of answering to anything other than Mrs. Tagert."

"For Aubrey, death by misadventure will always be a possibility." Jack snorted, not bothering to suppress an amused smirk. "Don't tell me you're afraid of a few spiders?"

"Not afraid." She wrinkled her nose. "But who in their right mind enjoys the presence of multi-legged creatures that scurry so very quickly?"

One was bad enough. Clouds of cobwebs filled with them? Well, that pricked the hairs on the back of her neck in dreaded anticipation. Arachnids had a nasty habit of dropping with uncommon speed, swinging from those ghastly threads they spun and landing where you least wanted them.

But traces of pain threaded through the amusement that illuminated Jack's face. His headache was clearly asserting itself, and they couldn't chance a misfire brought about by double vision.

No choice but for her to take the lead.

She rolled her shoulders and adjusted the grip of her TTX pistol. Dropping Carruthers to his knees would be her reward for tolerating the eight-legged beasties. She plunged forward. "Not at all."

At the bottom of the stairs, they found nothing save the long-forgotten props of past plays. Before them stretched the undercroft. They entered a forest of thick wooden columns, an ancient beauty of arched timber. Still, she was wary of what might lie in the shadows. Jack was quick to search its corners, but found nothing of interest.

"If I didn't know better," Jack murmured beside her, flicking blue-white light into the dark, empty chambers on their right, then left, "I'd expect to stumble across three dirt-filled coffins."

"And the drained husks of their victims tossed into dark crevices?"

"Precisely."

Thankfully, not a single long-lost corpse presented itself.

On they moved. With only one decilamp between them, the dark quickly settled back into place behind them.

An entire team of agents would need hours to scour the vast space of the vaults, but with Helena and Carruthers on the run, time wasn't on their side.

Onward they stalked, with one room bleeding into the next and spawning an ever-growing number of storage chambers and passageways.

They were in a labyrinth hunting a monster without a ball of string.

The space was ancient and timeworn. Yet above, they could hear the tap-tap of shoe leather. Were they beneath the stalls? The orchestra? Impossible to know. Modern London's floors covered medieval London's cellars. Old atop the new.

She turned a corner and almost stumbled over the sudden unevenness of the ground beneath her feet. A humid, damp smell rose to mingle with the scent of earth.

Aether, how deep into London clay had they descended?

They turned yet another corner.

She froze.

Before them, the warm glow of lantern light seeped forth from a side chamber. Had they found the lamia's lair?

Jack flicked off his decilamp and drew his weapon. On tiptoes, they crept closer. Cait nudged the door. Not a single squeak issued from its hinges, and the mingled scent of sex and perfume that hung in the air suggested they'd found their quarry. She pushed it open further.

Yes, indeed, they'd found their troublesome lord if not a murderous lamia.

Once again, Carruthers was naked and lounging beneath sheets upon a bed. A pallet upon the floor, in this particular instance, for all that it was covered with silks and satins in a riot of colors. Scattered across the floor were hand-knotted rugs in beautiful geometric patterns, low stools and tables. Overhead, light flickered through the punched holes of ornate lanterns that hung from loops of brass chain.

Much as one might imagine the room of a harem.

Carruthers didn't so much as stir. Asleep then. Or unconscious. A fact likely explained by the empty vial upon a bedside table, one last spotted tucked between Helena's breasts. An empty hypodermic syringe lay beside the vial.

Had they missed Helena by mere minutes?

"Eww," Cait breathed. "That was the extract from your—"

"Stop," Jack interrupted her. "I'm begging you."

A few steps down the hallway, another arched doorway emitted faint light.

"Shall we?" Jack whispered.

She nodded.

They tiptoed away from the insensate lordling and toward the next chamber and peeked carefully inside.

Though neither humans nor lamiae were present, it held a lost treasure.

"Amazing," she whispered and stepped into a space lost to London's skies some five hundred years ago.

CHAPTER TWENTY-SIX

Lanterns hanging from iron hooks driven into the wall cast a flickering dance of shadow and light throughout the austere chamber. Thick timbers weathered with age arched upward to support a wooden ceiling above the smooth expanse of stone below. Stacks of old, cracked barrels lined one wall, long forgotten. A tall cabinet stood beside a broad table. Amongst other items upon its surface—pen, paper, a curved blade and a scattering of herbs—was a carpet bag and a familiar carry case that spoke of an imminent and planned departure.

But the focus of the room was a mysterious pool of water that lay in the center of its stone-paved floor, a remnant of ancient Londinium. Its natural margins lost long ago to the carved stone that edged the pool, framing water so dark its depth was beyond sight.

Two feet? Twenty? Two hundred? Impossible to guess.

As was its source.

Was it fed by the River Fleet or did it well up through a fault in the London clay from low-lying chalk?

Impossible to know. Regardless, this must be one of Holywell Street's forgotten springs.

Of more recent origin was a low altar beside the well.

An iron-framed glass box rested upon its surface, surrounded by a scattering of flowers.

Liquid filled the entirety of the vessel. An aquarium with a lid, though nothing alive moved within. Instead, a single, unmoving object floated—alcohol acting as a preservative?

They stepped closer.

"Aether," Cait breathed at his side. "Any explanation for *that* will require your expertise in cryptobiology."

He closed one eye to compensate for his annoyingly persistent double vision and squinted. "It's a dead—" What did one call such a creature?

"Infant?" Cait suggested, the doubt in her voice justified.

"Well, yes, but..." From the waist upward, the child was undeniably human. A newborn who looked as if it had not survived much past delivery. Possibly because its coiled lower half was a long, scale-covered tail.

"How very ghoulish," she whispered. "One of Dr. Thrakos' creations, do you think? Or is this Helena's child, the one Lady Saltwell belittled as her 'biological failing'?"

He bent closer, then shook his head. "I see no sign of stitching, no other indications that this... child was not born exactly so. Though an autopsy would be required to confirm such a statement."

"But... how?"

"There's a condition known as sirenomelia, a congenital deformity in which the legs fuse during development to varying degrees, a condition some believe supports myths of mermaids. Alas, it's associated with multiple internal abnormalities that are incompatible with life."

"This is more than mere leg fusion." Cait straightened. "And the serpent-like tail suggests fangs, not gills. As befits our lamia."

"Agreed. If, as I suspect, surgical manipulation played no role and, instead, a biological process generated this child, then an extreme deviation from the normal course of human development occurred."

"Do you think she intends to take the infant with her?" Cait pointed at the refrigerated carry case upon the desk. "A quick visit to the zoo to snag the mad scientist's case and acquire a few reproductive ingredients for a final tryst with her lover?"

"Followed by a swift departure from our shores?" He nodded. "Quite likely."

"But where is the... found it!" Triumphant, she pulled a familiar canvas sack from inside the carpet bag, tugging at its drawstring and reaching for its contents with a smile. "It's the pituitary extractor! In pieces, true, but this means..."

Her comment broke his fixation upon the remains of the lamia's child. He looked up, watched as her smile faded and the spark in her eyes dulled, as momentary celebration renewed their awareness that any attempt to remove his tumor courted widowhood.

But to not try, however, would bring about a different kind of end to their partnership.

"There's no rush." He drew her against his side with one arm, hoping he spoke the truth but fearing he uttered a lie. "We'll discuss steps later."

She nodded. "We should go. It's not safe here." Her rigid form resisted comfort. His throat grew dry as the insecurity of his future loomed before them, but what could he possibly say that would raise her spirits? "Haul in Carruthers, send in agents to examine the scene more closely." She pulled away. "Your vision is worrying, and we need to deliver this contraption directly into the hands of—"

"Very well. We'll take the infant with us, head straight to Lister." He turned her about to face the carved, wooden cabinet. "But not before we look inside." He threw open the doors and let out a low whistle.

"Aether," she breathed. "There were so very many."

Each shelf held a row of glass jars. Each alcohol-filled receptacle held a single specimen. Miniature faces. Eyes closed, lips gently parted. Arms, hands, fingers formed without distortions. But at the hips, the torsos became serpent tails.

Many conceptions, many failed pregnancies.

Had any been live births?

"All transformed in exactly the same manner," he commented softly. "Insofar as can be determined by superficial examination. We may learn more at autopsy."

"You trespass," Helena hissed from the doorway, her arm about a certain lord.

Zwing. Thwack.

The moment the lamia spoke, Cait had dropped the bag and the extractor, lined up her shot, and fired.

But Helena moved with superhuman speed. She'd twisted, pulling her lover in front of her—and the dart had passed though the sleeve of a dressing gown embedding in the thick flesh of Carruthers' upper arm.

He howled, eyes full of aggrieved resentment. "How dare you! This is sacred space." Already there was a slight slur to his words, a buckle to his knees as muscles succumbed to tetrodotoxin.

Not a loss, really, but the lamia's lover wasn't their primary target.

Cait kept her weapon at the ready.

"A lord of the land who aligns himself with a murderess will find himself hunted." Jack pulled back his shoulders, keeping his own TTX pistol pointed in Helena's direction. "A woman was killed in your townhome today, a gland extracted from her skull. She was stuffed inside your wife's wardrobe. Your wife, your nanny and your mistress have all fled. You covered for them, then followed." He shook his head. "Yet you expect privacy?"

"Murder?" Carruthers sneered. "Not Helena. You have the wrong woman."

"Would you accuse your wife instead? Or perhaps your nanny?" Jack turned his attention to the lamia. "Care to enlighten us, Helena?"

"I regret nothing," Helena sneered. "The humane approach failed." Her gaze welled with sadness as it fell upon the daughter resting beside the holy well. "My sisters were wrong, mistakes were made." She pressed a hand to her stomach. "The old ways demand respect. When necessary, sacrifices must be made."

"Five men, three women," Jack stated. "At last count. I expect there are more."

Cait all but vibrated beside him, but his extended hand forestalled another dart. Answers. Confessions. He wanted —needed—to know the *why* behind her actions.

"Their deaths were necessary," Helena spat, shifting to brace her now-tilting lover. "All of them. But enough of that. We are leaving all this behind. As you've interrupted my packing, you'll complete it for me." She slid her lips over her lover's neck. "Hand it over, or I'll lighten my load."

The lamia wore a plain gown suitable for travel. Carruthers, however, wore nothing save a loosely belted dressing gown. She'd been elsewhere, preparing to leave when they entered her underground lair.

Had she already made plans to abandon him? How essential was the lord to her reproductive plans?

Regardless, cooperation was the wise approach.

Until a better opportunity presented itself.

Cait lifted the pituitary extractor, dropping it back inside the carpet bag and held it out.

"My daughter as well," Helena instructed, unmoving.

Slowly, Jack lowered into a crouch beside the altar, then opened the water-tight refrigerated case Cait handed him. Inside lay broad swathes of oiled canvas, the kind one might use to transport large biological specimens. He lifted the lid off the aquarium and set it aside. The scent of ethyl alcohol rose into the air.

"Why take a failed attempt back to Greece?" He rocked back on his heels, buying time. How strong was a lamia? How long before she tired of a grown man's weight? Could she be provoked into rash behavior? His next words sought to elicit answers to all his questions. "What value is such a mutant?"

"My daughter is a queen, not a monster," Helena hissed. "She will be buried with respect and reverence."

"I disagree." He tipped his head at the cabinet. "She is but one of many failed attempts."

"Each is a tiny miracle of conception," Helena countered. "But I failed them by ignoring the old ways. Many life forces are required to sustain the development of a *drakonourá*. Traditional rituals must be observed, lest a queen not draw first breath."

Jack lifted the snake-tailed infant from her preservative bath, laid her gently upon the cloth, and—sparing only a moment to marvel at the tangible evidence of myth—carefully wrapped the water-resistant fabric about her, securing arms and tail.

"You prey upon men," Cait said. "Seduction for the purpose of reproduction." Via incremental shifts, his wife advanced upon Helena. "But feed upon the flesh—brains—of young women to sustain your development, a task made easier by the device Dr. Thrakos built. How is that traditional?"

"Who are you, snake charmer, to judge when you know so little of your own heritage?" the lamia sneered.

"I'm resistant to venom." Cait lifted a shoulder. "What more is there I need to know?"

"Oh, my love," Carruthers murmured, his head lolling upon Helena's shoulder. "It's true, then. You killed a woman? In our home?"

"Your home." Helena's voice hardened. "My sister's home. Not mine. Never mine."

"I've offered a million apologies. It's only that—"

"Life is not fair." Insincere, oft-repeated words spoken from between clenched teeth. "My sister fell pregnant first. You required an heir. Hence the marriage. I understand. You are forgiven."

Jack lifted eyebrows. How long had she been spooning the lord such pacifying drivel? Carruthers couldn't possibly believe her, could he?

Yet they'd found him here.

In the lamia's lair. In her bed.

Which begged the question. "Why this family, why Carruthers?"

"Why?" The sharp tips of fangs appeared as Helena's lips parted in a sneering smile. "We came for revenge, stayed because male lamia are as rare as dragon's teeth. And the birth of a *drakonourá* changed everything."

Not to mention aligning themselves with Carruthers and friends brought societal power and the means to acquire riches. At least until he and Cait had paid a particularly destructive visit to their northern operations. But he declined to introduce the topic.

Helena shifted behind Carruthers, directing a narrow-eyed gaze at Cait. His wife had slowly but steadily shifted in the lamia's direction. "That's close enough, snake charmer. Set the bag down."

The holy well kept the lamia at a safe distance from them, but Helena's position before the door also blocked the only exit from this medieval chamber of horrors. She had to be dealt with before they handed over her possessions, lest she lock them in this room, never to be seen or heard from again.

"Revenge?" he prompted.

Helena's smile was cold. "Incest. Taboo in your culture, save perhaps among your so-called royals. What better way to pollute a lineage, to horrify the patriarch who promised our mother much, then abandoned her, their daughters, without care?"

"You—" Carruthers gagged. He shook his head, twisting in his lover's arms. "Are you implying that my father... that we are—"

"Family," Helena finished, her voice ice cold. "Sister with brother. Daughter with father. Infertility surmounted, and the first male lamiae in centuries conceived and born. The merging of lineages has produced the miraculous." Spiritual reverence illuminated her face as she turned her lover's face toward hers. "Together, you and I produced a *drakonourá*, a queen among the Lamian. How could we abandon such goddess-given gifts?"

"You're my... sister?" Carruthers struggled in her embrace.

Adoration fell away. "Half," she spat back, tightening her grip upon him. "As is your wife."

Carruthers turned a queasy shade of green, sputtering. "But... why?"

An untold number of drugs circulated through the lordling's veins and arteries.

Jack offered the simplest of explanations. "Revenge. Reproduction. Money."

Three sisters, three goals.

All but one death due to Helena's efforts to conceive a very specific, rare mythological creature.

No. Not so mythological. The evidence lay all about them.

Lamia. *Drakonourá,* a daughter who would, had she lived, have been a queen among her people, elevating Helena into the annals of Lamian history.

"She killed your father, Carruthers," Cait said. "Peel the wool from your eyes."

"Do you regret delaying your departure?" Jack asked. "How critical is your half-brother to your plans, your final evening upon our ancient soil?" He placed the infant in the case, snapped it closed. Standing, he held the case over the cool, clear water of the holy well between them. "Did you call upon London's naiads to bestow a blessing? Will they help you now?"

"Do not!" Helena screamed, pushing Carruthers before her. A hasty and desperate bargain. "His life for my child!"

An interesting choice. The lamia clearly valued proof of her reproductive abilities above that of the lord's loins. Did another half-brother await her back home in Greece?

From the corner of his eye, he saw Cait balance on the balls of her feet.

Jack waggled the case and taunted, "You prize a dead infant more than her father?"

With narrowed eyes, the lamia spat back, "He is replaceable. I am not."

Helena moved, and Cait squeezed the trigger.

Zwing. Thwack.

Dammit. She'd missed.

Again.

But not for lack of aim.

The lamia was far too agile, too aware, and the second dart landed in the lordling's hip.

Carruthers howled.

"A third dart will kill him," Jack warned.

"Replaceable," Helena repeated, taking a sinuous step forward.

"There's a solution to all this." Cait caught his eye, held his gaze as she waggled the TTX pistol in her grip.

Trust me.

He'd witnessed firsthand her recovery from multiple deadly bites. A lamia. Several *morphophidia*. Not to mention three direct hits by successive TTX darts.

On that matter, he'd managed to pin a dart in Helena herself at the zoo only a few hours past. Much as he hated Cait's plan, it was viable tactic.

He gave the slightest of nods, and his glorious wife lunged, arms wide, flinging herself bodily against the lamia.

Arms wrapped about Helena's waist, Cait planted a heel and twisted, wrenching the lord from his lover's arms and presenting Jack with a clean target.

He tossed the case aside, aimed his TTX weapon and fired—all while Carruthers crumpled to the floor, boneless.

Zwing. Thwack.

Zwing. Thwack.

Zwing. Thwack.

All three darts emptied from their chambers.

Whimpering, Carruthers belly-crawled for the door.

Helena and Cait crashed into the side of the antique cabinet with such force that the jars within slid across the wooden shelving and toppled over the edge. Glass shattered upon the ground, its sharp sounds accompanied by the wet thuds of tailed specimens landing in pools of ethyl alcohol upon the stone floor.

Two darts had struck Cait.

But one had lodged itself in the backside of Helena's shoulder. She leapt to her feet and yanked it free, howling. "If the *drakonourá* within me has been harmed—"

With one hand against the wall to brace herself, Cait lifted her other arm, TTX pistol still in hand.

Thwack.

A third dart struck Lamian flesh.

Slam! The heavy wooden door closed.

Click.

Locked? By Carruthers?

Jack leapt past the well, swearing as he yanked upon the iron door handle. Dammit, they were trapped.

Helena fell sideways, caught herself upon the desk. "Fools." She snatched up the lantern, lifted it above her head, over the spreading pool of flammable ethyl alcohol.

Shit. She meant to set them aflame. Between the alcohol and ancient wood, a task easily accomplished.

"You've made a grave mistake." The lamia's eyes grew glassy, her posture loosened. "Cursed is London." Her fingers uncurled, and both he and Cait dove for the falling lantern.

Cait snatched it from the air, stopping its downward plummet.

But Helena—unsteady upon her feet—refused to die quietly. And Jack had made a fatal mistake, fearing fire and rushing close.

As the lamia fell to her knees, she lashed out, snagged his ankle with talons of iron. She bit through fabric into flesh, sinking her fangs deep into the muscle of his calf.

"No!" Cait cried.

He shoved at the lamia's shoulders, wrenching his leg free, but the damage was done. Tendrils of pain spread up his leg, over his hip, and across his torso, wrapping the entirety of his body in agony. The bite had been no simple nip, but a full envenomation intended to kill.

Flat upon her back, Helena laughed up at them baring teeth in a bloodstained smile. As tetrodotoxin flooded her system, she knocked the lantern from Cait's hand and sent it careening into the pool of alcohol upon the floor. A final diabolical act.

There was a crash, then a whoosh. Fumes filled the air. Greedy for fuel, flames ignited across the alcohol, rushing outward. They clawed at the old wood of the cabinet, then crawled upward with staggering speed to lick at the thick timber beams overhead.

His knees gave out. A slow collapse that stretched, as if time hung, suspended. He watched as the blazing room swirled and twisted around him, gripping his skull as his headache exploded, reaching new heights at the very moment his vision contracted.

"Jack!" Cait's cry met his ears.

Nausea clawed at his innards. He had no memory of landing upon the floor, but her hands were under his arms, pulling him away from the flames, unwilling to admit defeat.

"Antivenin." Her voice all but a shout above the crackle and snap of flames devouring wood. "We still have a vial."

But could she administer it in time? Uncontrolled flames would soon swallow the ceiling. What value his own life if both of them failed to survive its collapse?

Surviving the inferno took priority.

He caught at Cait's sleeve, forcing the words out on a hoarse exhale. "The pool."

CHAPTER TWENTY-SEVEN

PANIC LEAPT INTO her throat.

Venom and fire. Two immediate threats, two obvious solutions.

How to accomplish both simultaneously?

"Antivenin," she huffed, dragging Jack's solid weight over broken glass to the edge of the spring, worrying as she eyed its depths. "You need it now, but the flames—"

Corpse candles, the altar. Hooking her fingers under its edge, she hauled it away from the holy well, muttering as alcohol sloshed against the sides of the vessel on its surface. Overhead, the fire snapped, ravenous, at the five-hundred-year-old beams whilst throwing sparks at the old, abandoned barrels stacked in the corner. Smoke billowed and, with it, the nauseating stench of burning flesh.

Water was the only thing that would save theirs.

"I'll try—" He heaved himself onto his side, rolling toward the holy well.

"No." Too easily, she stopped him with the flat of her hand. "Not yet."

Even if he managed to lower himself into the water, the venom in his system would soon steal his consciousness. If his grip loosened, if his head nodded—

Her fingers flew as she unhooked her bustle, dunked it in the well and tossed the sodden fabric over Helena's carpet bag. She yanked Jack's coat from his shoulders, pulling it free to repeat the process.

"Here's the plan," she coughed. "Water first." She tore a long, wide strip from the hem of her petticoat and wrapped it around Jack's chest, knotting it securely. "Antivenin second."

"If it fails—" he wheezed.

"It won't." No other outcome was acceptable. She unhooked her belt, set the antivenin case within arm's reach. "Three *morphophidia* attacked Dr. Thrakos, and he left the zoo breathing, did he not?"

"Widows are assigned..." he wheezed, "missions."

She fought to keep the tremor out of her voice. "We'll be working those together."

Once they were in the water, she would need access to a prominent vein. She took a firm grasp upon the cuff of his sleeve and ripped the cloth past the crook of his elbow.

Crash. The desk collapsed and burst into flame, well on its way to becoming a heap of embers.

Cait laid beside him, tying the ends of her make-shift strap about her own waist before swinging their legs into the cool water. "Wrap your arms about my neck," she ordered. "Hold on as long as you're able."

Together they slid neck-deep into its depths. She dunked them once—as protection against sparks—but felt nothing beneath her toes, not even the hint of a ledge which might support them. Thank aether the well was narrow. Legs spread, she dug the toes of her boots into the rough walls of the spring and braced her elbows upon the carved stone ledge.

Not an ideal position from which to fill a syringe, but needs must. With shaking fingers that managed to be both hot and cold at once, she unlatched the case.

"Do not... let duchess..." Face pressed to her shoulder, he dragged in air, "tell duke otherwise."

Against her back, she felt the rise and fall of Jack's chest, reassuring despite his slurred words, ones that belonged in a last will and testament, not a conversation.

"Enough dark thoughts." Cait pulled the syringe from her case, screwed in the needle. Disappearance and death beneath a theater was not an option. It wasn't happening. She refused to— "Shit."

Fear reached past her ribs to grip her heart as shards of glass met her fingertips, followed by a certain dampness. Despite the rigid case walls and soft inner lining, the vial of antivenin had shattered. When? Impossible to know. Possibly during a struggle with Helena.

Not that it mattered.

"Cait?" His breath was soft at the back of her neck.

Wood crackled as it blistered the roughly-hewn beams above. A loud snap rent the air, and a chunk of burning wood dropped, crashing onto the floor only a few feet away. A glance told her the fire had breached the ceiling. Or, more accurately, the sub-flooring for whatever theater space lay above.

"Small problem." Her mind whirled. It was impossible to ever fully imagine the details of such a crisis or the strange circumstances under which emergency actions would need to be taken, yet such were upon her. Them. "Change of plans."

Thank aether the syringe was intact.

Her legs shook with the effort of holding them both in place as she splashed alcohol over her own arm. Blinking against the ash that clouded her vision, she slid the needle into her vein, then slowly pulled backward upon the plunger, watching as a deep red filled the glass barrel.

The direct transfer of blood held a multitude of poorly understood risks, all of which revolved around the possibility that a transfusion could make a patient's condition worse, rather than better. Physicians reserved such therapy only for those whose lives careened at ever-increasing speeds toward death.

Conversations with her sister-in-law—and subsequent experiments—indicated that mixing whole blood products from two different, non-compatible individuals carried a high risk of causing red blood cells to agglutinate, to clump. As a result, it was suspected that the reaction had something to do with the presence or absence of proteins on the cell surface of erythrocytes.

Which was the entire purpose to the Haimatos Separation Machine. The device removed whole cells from blood, collecting only the plasma—the yellowish part of her blood that held the antivenin—thus rendering the product safe for all.

The very first test of her plasma with any associated risks had been upon Dr. Thrakos. It had worked. At the time, she'd been downright gleeful to finally have a willing test subject and not the slightest of ethical barriers to prevent her from implementing an immediate investigative case study.

And the outcome had been successful.

Now resentment bubbled up at the memory. A precious vial wasted on a disreputable, morally corrupt scientist. The second vial, shattered. Leaving her without a treatment for the man who had, in the space of days, transformed her existence and stolen the better part of her heart. An organ that now pumped his only hope of survival through her veins.

Her actions here were a forced experiment with far higher personal stakes wagered upon a positive outcome. She prayed that whole blood would not, instead, worsen his condition.

"I need your arm."

But no response came.

"Jack?" Cait twisted, reaching. At the movement, his arms slid from her shoulders, limp. His weight shifted and tugged, all of it now suspended from the make-shift sling wrapped about her waist.

Unconscious.

Her mind suggested that was for the best. Her heart vehemently disagreed.

Plunging her hand into the water, she grabbed at his

wrist and lifted his arm out of the water. Resting it upon the edge of the well, she splashed alcohol over the crook of his elbow and took aim at the dark blue of a prominent vein. The needle slid inward, and she depressed the plunger, mingling her blood with Jack's in a desperate bid to save his life.

Again and again, she repeated the procedure, waiting several minutes between each treatment, alert to any changes in the rhythm of his heart, to the depth of each breath. All while doubt and worry gnawed at her mind and churned in her stomach. She was no physician, equipped with the education and experience to judge Jack's response.

He required sufficient plasma to neutralize the venom, but not so much as to trigger a negative response to her own red blood cells. But what was enough? What was too much?

Impossible to know.

Experimenting upon herself was all well and good. Such tests had been measured, gradual and carefully controlled. But the floating circus had given her a taste of what it meant to be an experimental subject who had not given consent. A terrifying experience, finding herself helpless beneath the hands of a volatile mad scientist driven by whim and impulse with no regard for her life.

She shuddered, pushed away the horror of the memory. The crimes of one Dr. Thrakos would be weighed and measured by the Queen's agents. Justice would be served. If surviving the *morphophidian* strikes meant her blood could save Jack's life here and now, that was all that mattered.

Releasing his arm back into the water, she cupped her

hands over the precious syringe, over the small bottle of alcohol, to keep them safe from the blistering sparks that fell from the beams overhead. She bent her head and closed her eyes, forcing herself to take deep breaths.

Against her back, Jack's chest rose and fell, a regular rhythm, if rather shallow. His heart thumped steadily, if a touch too rapid. All to be expected from a significant envenomation.

There was nothing to do but wait, to watch, to pray her blood was enough save the man she loved.

Time stretched as they hung, suspended in the cool water. Blistering heat from above beat down upon their heads. Her lungs demanded air, even as the fire sucked the oxygen from the room. She kept her breaths measured and shallow, trying not to draw a deep breath of the pollution that churned through the space around them. All while monitoring Jack's vital signs.

"Cait?" Jack's voice emerged as a faint whisper against the damp of her neck.

A tear ran down her cheek. Success?

HE WOKE to smoke and flames and water and waves.

And Cait.

Alive. Even if the pounding in his head suggested his continued existence was temporary.

"Thank aether," she exhaled. "It worked."

There'd been doubt?

"Proven a few hours past, was it not?" he asked.

Her short laugh was rueful. "Under entirely different circumstances." She looked over her shoulder at him, her fire-lit face full of concern. "How does your leg feel?"

"Swollen. Painful. And it hurts like the devil. This was not at all how I envisioned our pursuit of a lamia to end, but..." Were those tears upon her cheeks? He gripped the edge of the holy well, ignoring the pain, and gathered her close with his other arm. "Tell me."

"I was so afraid." She twisted the cloth about their waists that tied them to each other, bringing them face to face.

"What—"

"Symptoms," she interrupted, then ran down a long list of every side effect a snake bite could possibly induce.

Every last one of them negative, save the searing pain in his leg. The persistent throbbing of his head and double vision was all too easily attributed to his pre-existing condition.

"Do I count as a success?" he asked.

"You do." Her lips curved in a faint smile as she smoothed a finger over the furrow between his eyebrows. "The vial of antivenin shattered."

"Then how did you— Blood?"

She swallowed, nodded. "A transfusion."

Risky in the best of circumstances, but here, under such horrid conditions? "How?" His eyebrows shot up. "You used nothing but a syringe?"

"Repeatedly, and with only the roughest of estimates of

how much volume to use." She frowned. "The Haimatos Separation Machine uses a complicated algorithm—"

"You saved my life." He caught her chin in his hand, pressed a brief kiss to her lips. They were bound by more than mere blood. "That matters most." He glanced about at the burning wreckage. "Now we need to escape, that we might share the tale of how we hunted a venomous monster through labyrinthine tunnels and brought her attacks to an end. I want the duke and duchess to know why the lamia prowls London's streets no more."

"You want to write a report for the Department of Cryptobiology." A teasing light came into her eyes. "Do you think they might, given her penchant for underground passages, hypothesize that lamiae are a cave-dwelling subspecies geographically located within the borders of Greece?"

"Emerging to prey upon young men and women in order to sustain their population?" He loved her mind. "Perhaps it's best kept a secret? I shudder to think of the lives that might be lost in the pursuit of lamiae. Worse, even, than dragon hunting."

"The reproductive drive is a strong one. And, according to Helena, Lamian traditions extend back into the mists of time."

He snorted. "Is that what we're calling castration now?"

"Not to mention cannibalism of the pituitary. Which reminds me." Pulling upon the carved stone at the edge of the pool, Cait lifted her head above its edge, casting her gaze about, searching through the haze of smoke. "The pituitary extractor. It's in the carpet bag beneath—"

He followed her gaze to where the desk had collapsed. "Debris and smoldering embers?" he finished. "All is not lost." He spoke the words to comfort them both. Still, the thought of the device smashed to smithereens drove the nail between his eyes deeper. "The Thorntons have Dr. Thrakos' notebook." But the contraption would require modifications. After all, surgical outcomes were only positive if the patient survived. "Try not to worry. We'll look for it after."

After.

Would there be a second act—or ought they label it a third—to this cursed evening?

Overhead, feet stomped and voices shouted in alarm. The Opera Comique was a drafty tinder box and this fire far more than a simple spark. The theater would have been evacuated, the fire brigade summoned. With luck, in time to save lives.

Theirs?

Possibly. If the entire structure didn't collapse down upon them in a giant, raging inferno.

Would that their luck held.

Cait sank back into the cool waters beside him. Distress filled her eyes. "How bad is it, your head?"

"Bad." No point in lying. "There's pain and double vision, as always. Save the pain now stabs rather than gnaws, and my vision has narrowed yet further. All of it accompanied by recurring bouts of nausea."

Deepening concern carved a furrow between her eyebrows. "Meaning? Elaborate and explain, Mr. Tagert." She poked him in the chest. "My medical expertise does not extend much past the physiological effects of biological toxins."

He sighed as they bobbed in the water. "In all likelihood, it's a pituitary apoplexy. I expect the tumor has ruptured, flooding the space in and around the sella tunica with blood, hydrostatically placing pressure upon my optic nerves."

"You need surgery. Immediately."

"It's not deadly." But such a comment side-stepped her question. Unfair. He relented, but delivered the bad news as if he'd merely forgotten his umbrella on a rainy day. "But, yes, it's likely to render me blind on a permanent basis if not addressed."

"Within what? Hours? Days?"

"Impossible to say, but it would be best to presume the timeframe for saving my eyesight is limited."

She dropped her forehead against his shoulder, sloshing the water about them.

"Thornton and his wife, Lady Amanda, are tireless in their pursuit of novel neurosurgical procedures," he offered by way of comfort. "No doubt they've already been to Clockwork Corridor half a dozen times consulting with Nicu Sindel, a master of clockwork mechanisms, with Dr. Thrakos' laboratory notebook in hand. Even now, an equivalent—no, superior—surgical instrument might wait upon a chromium steel surgical tray for my arrival."

Snap. Hiss. *Crash!* More wood fell about them, splintering upon the ground, flinging fiery sparks onto their skin.

Jack extended his arm, dipping them deeper into the water.

"A procedure which, to quote yourself, possesses a high likelihood of mortality." Her voice betrayed her anguish.

He pressed a kiss to her damp and sooty hair. "Should the worst come to pass, please apologize to Angela for the overly protective and primitive instincts that caused me to object to her career choices."

"No. You'll do that yourself."

Crackle. Thud. Pop.

Her head snapped up. "Jack!" She grabbed the far edge of the well and yanked, pulling him with her.

Crash!

A heavy beam fell from above, narrowly missing them.

Water rained from the ceiling.

Rained?

"Help!" Cait cried, her face tipped upward. "Is anyone there? We're down here!"

No answer came.

He added his voice, shouting with her.

Minute by minute, the flames died down, sputtering and hissing from the onslaught of an overhead deluge.

They kept yelling as long, seemingly interminable minutes ticked past.

Then an answering shout, "Someone's in the vaults!"

CHAPTER TWENTY-EIGHT

OUTSIDE, MEN AND WOMEN dressed in their finest thronged the street gaping at the firemen who tromped in and out of the theater's entrance, dragging out the few remaining bedraggled souls who'd managed to become trapped inside.

Amongst whom she and Jack numbered.

Their rescuers had dropped a ladder through the collapsed ceiling down into the vaults. Relieved, she and Jack had abandoned the underground carnage and charred remains of the lamia's lair, clambering from the underground vault and winding their way out into the relatively fresh air of London's streets.

Not, of course, without retrieving the pituitary extractor.

Or, Jack insisted, the case containing the preserved remains of Helena's infant, the *drakonourá*.

She clutched the soggy and sooty yet precious carpet bag to her chest with torn and bloody hands. Jack gripped the case. Battered but not yet beaten, it had been quite the task, dragging away burnt timbers to reach the lamia's luggage, but one should never underestimate the motivation of an anxious wife or a fascinated scientist.

Beside her, Jack swayed.

Cait shot out a hand to steady him.

Here, beneath the light of a streetlamp, his expression was drawn and grim and she didn't care for the pallor of his skin. Was his condition worsening? Had he downplayed the severity of his symptoms? Both?

They needed a crank hack, one that would convey to them to Lister at a swift clip.

As she cast about, a man broke away from a knot of people and rushed toward her. "Cait."

"Logan? Thank aether you're here. But how could you know we—"

"Were involved?" Logan all but rolled his eyes, as concerned irritation replaced relief. "You failed to return home. Nor did you arrive at Lister, where those poisonous snakes await your analysis. Then reports of a raging fire near Holywell Street reached my ears. It wasn't much of a gamble. When my agents disobey orders, disasters usually follow. And here you are, soot-streaked and soaked to the skin." He frowned. "Am I going to learn the two of you are responsible for the fire?"

"It's a long story," Jack said, pressing a hand against the nearby lamppost.

"He needs medical attention," Cait said. "Now." There was no sense in denying the obvious. Deep inside her chest, her heart refused to settle. "The Thorntons are best prepared to assist."

Logan pulled a decilamp from an inner coat pocket, gave it a shake and flicked it into her husband's eyes. "Mismatched pupils." A long string of Romani curses fell from his lips. The ones he always refused to translate. "What—exactly—is wrong with you, Tagert? And no equivocal answers, if you please."

"Rupture of a pituitary adenoma," Jack answered on a sigh.

"That explains all the cagey behavior." Logan shot her a speaking look. "And why the Thorntons have been sending out skeet pigeons trying to reach me."

She stuck out her jaw and lifted a shoulder. As if she'd betray such confidences. "He's my husband."

Her brother gave the slightest shake of his head, then sighed. He pulled Jack's arm across his own shoulder, steadying him. "This way."

A scant few minutes later, Logan handed them both into a steam carriage then climbed in to take the seat opposite. The vehicle jerked into motion, moving swiftly through the streets.

Her brother eyed the carpet bag on her lap. "Might that contain a murder weapon, one pituitary extractor?"

"It does."

Falling debris had half-crushed the brass device, snapping yet more parts and pieces from its frame. Non-functional, yet still more informative than the inked lines of a concept drawing. How much so? Jack was confident of Lady Thornton's clockwork skills. Cait reserved judgment.

"You intend to deliver this device to the Thornton laboratory along with your husband?"

"Immediately." She hated how every jostle, every jolt caused Jack to wince.

"There is to be surgery?"

Cait swallowed.

"As soon as possible." This time Jack answered. "It's the only hope of saving my vision." He winced, pressing a hand to his forehead. "Though the operation carries considerable risk."

"Not that he'll be dying," Cait snapped. Such an outcome was unacceptable. Falling in love was a process, and she was not quite finished.

Lips pressed into a thin line, Logan eyed the silver metal case at Jack's feet. But he failed to ask about its contents.

How very unlike him.

Instead, he cleared his throat, then drew a document from an inner coat pocket and held it out. "About your marriage..."

Unease crept up her spine on tiny, spiky feet and her stomach clenched. *Kraken claws.* Her brother was a weaver of convoluted secrets. But he never hesitated. Such unusual behavior was not to be trusted.

She snatched it from his hand and peered at it in the gloom, frowning. "It's our marriage license, signed and witnessed."

Eyes narrow, Jack plucked the paper from her hand.

Bewilderment crossed his face. "Why has it not been filed with the registry?"

Logan cleared his throat—and Cait's stomach sank.

"The duke and duchess arranged your marriage without consultation," her brother began. "Vows were spoken under duress. As I wished for you to have a choice, a chance for you to back out after your trip north, I withheld the document."

Jack's nostrils flared. "Our honeymoon was a mission, not a lark." Her not-quite-a-husband dropped his voice to a growl. "An agent with a penchant for explosions. Your sister, mistress of poison and mischief. Are you mad? If I die, your sister inherits nothing."

"Nothing." Cait echoed the word, instilling it with threats of dire retribution. "Not even the assurance of my position within the Queen's agents. How could you betray me, your own sister in such a manner? How dare you make such decisions on my behalf!"

Logan was a romantic at heart. Few realized this. But to turn on his own sister in such a manner? To act without consulting her? If a single dart had remained within the chamber of her TTX pistol, she would have fired it, point blank, into his chest.

Beside her, Jack tucked the marriage document into an inside coat pocket, silent.

Unease slithered through her chest, twisting its tentacles about her heart.

Propriety. Position. Lust. Such had defined their beginnings as a couple.

Was that all that was to her not-yet-an-official marriage?

Was she a fool to believe their mental connection, their physical intimacy was more than a primal response to a crucible of shared ordeals?

"The record's office is open tomorrow." Her brother crossed his arms, unconvinced. "If you wish to legitimize your marriage, file then. Now tell me what's in that silver case."

"Semi-human remains," Jack snapped. "A deceased infant that Helena intended to carry home to Greece as proof of her reproductive potential."

"Semi?" Her brother's eyebrows rose. "Explain."

Vexed and miserable, Cait took a deep breath. "In a room on the lowest level of the Opera Comique—an area known as the vaults—there are charred biological remains that will require transportation for further examination."

"Plural?"

"Helena, London's not-a-vampire." Her voice grew cold and emotionless. "She died from an overdose of TTX. There are the remains of other, non-viable offspring also present." Cait dragged in a rough breath. "Elsewhere in the labyrinthine halls of the vaults, you might find Carruthers, Lord Saltwell."

"Might?"

"During the confrontation with the lamia, he escaped, locking us in the room with his mistress."

Logan swept a hand through his hair. "And how did this come to transpire?" He waited, expectant.

Briefly, Cait sketched out an overview of their discoveries. "Alcohol jars shattered during the ensuing struggle. Her death was not particularly swift. At the last moment, she bit Jack." Logan's gaze drifted to the grimy, makeshift bandage twisted about his pant leg. "Then knocked over a lantern."

Logan grimaced, then finished painting the scene himself. "Setting on fire the corpses of her children and, consequently, the theater wherein the lives of everyone attending the play were threatened. Fay O'Fire, with all too realistic elements added." He gave a sharp nod. "I'll send an agent to see all humanoid remains are safely stored in the autopsy suite for examination."

"Excellent," Jack bit out, pinching the bridge of his nose. "To return to more pressing matters, why are the Thorntons looking for you?"

"For the same reason everyone seeks me out," Logan snapped back. "They want something. In this case, permission to drag information from one Dr. Thrakos by way of veritasium."

Fear froze the breath in her lungs. She looked to Jack. There could be only one reason. Not enough detail was contained within the notebook.

Jack yanked at his collar. "Shit."

His vision and any future they might salvage from this mismanaged mess of a marriage were at stake. Heart racing, she leaned forward, prepared to beg. "And you'll grant it?"

"No." Her brother gave her a hard smile. "Drugs are not always the answer. Besides, I foresee no need. You saved the scientist's life when he would have taken yours. Bargain with him." He shifted, fixing his flinty gaze upon Jack. "Promise him anything short of freedom."

Sooty water dripped from the skirts of his all-but-legal wife as she stormed into the prisoner's holding cell. Her eyes flashed. "You owe me."

Dr. Thrakos sat in his bed, propped against iron bed railings with only a thin pillow to keep them from digging into his back. On his lap was a writing desk, in his hand a fountain pen. A shackle clattered at his wrist as wrote a long sequence of digits—Jack squinted—3.14159265359…

Pi.

Bedside, Lady Thornton glowered. "It's no better than doodling. He refuses to cooperate, to provide us with the algebraical algorithm necessary to operate the pituitary extractor with any precision."

Jack caught at the doorframe, steading himself as dread roiled in his stomach. Or was it simple nausea, an effect of blood oozing and seething about inside his skull?

The situation was exactly as he had suspected. They might have caught a madman with the power to save his life, but Dr. Thrakos knew he faced a grim future. He wouldn't part with an ounce of useful information unless offered sufficient motivation.

Dr. Thrakos lifted his eyes and looked squarely at Cait. "I owe you nothing but a name and a location." His lips stretched into a sour and bitter smile. "She's in Paris, your sister Gabrielle. Proprietress of an apothecary by the name of Le Serpent Tordu."

The Twisted Serpent.

Cait gaped at this revelation, a calculated move by the mad scientist to rip away any advantage she might possess. But only for a moment. She rallied, countering, "You attempted to drain my lifeblood."

The mad scientist lifted a shoulder. "You killed my creations, set my floating laboratory on fire, and chased my collaborators from your shores. "

"You knowingly helped a murderess stalk women upon London's streets." Her voice rose with each word.

"For which I am now imprisoned." He shook the chain that bound him to his bed.

Not so much as a hint of remorse colored his words. The mad scientist was a void into which strong emotional appeals would fall and disappear. Only one passion drove him: pursuit of scientific knowledge. Specifically, a desire to discover new life forms.

Jack stepped into the room and lowered the silver case to the floor. Adopting an air of indifference, he crossed his arms and leaned backward against the wall. A chair would have been more welcome, but he refused to reveal any weakness. Not to mention, standing at a distance allowed him to glower without further restricting his narrowed field of vision.

"We found the lamia's lair." He toed the case, scraping metal over tile. "Saw her children. Brought one back."

The mad scientist froze, an obvious tell.

He'd guessed correctly, shooting a verbal arrow directly into the man's weakness, pinning him in place. Jack let a heartless grin stretch over his lips—Dr. Thrakos had never laid eyes upon any of Helena's offspring.

"She's dead, your lamia," he continued, careful to keep a note of boredom in his voice as he leaked details. The mad scientist barely breathed. "No more *drakonourá* conceived or born. Her final act was to set fire to the Opera Comique, a successful effort to destroy her... collection."

Air hissed as it scraped inward over Dr. Thrakos' teeth.

"Only one specimen survived the conflagration," Jack added, finally meeting the madman's intense gaze. "Might you be interested?"

"You seek to barter?" Dr. Thrakos turned the paper over, sketched out a gear and a pin, made a notation indicating precise sizes, then paused. "You stole an old notebook." He lifted an eyebrow. "With the proper inducement, I could—"

Lady Thornton frowned.

"Not that," Cait interrupted. "We've no need of mechanical specifications." She opened the sodden carpet bag, dragged forth the pituitary extractor. Broken. Bent. Missing a piece or two. But largely intact. "I'm certain Lady Thornton will be able to make any necessary adjustments by comparing her reconstruction to the murder weapon."

Wide-eyed, Lady Thornton took the device, cradled it in her hands examining it from every angle. "Without delay."

Dr. Thrakos pursed his lips in a pout.

"You've nothing else to offer?" Jack taunted. "Do the algebraical algorithms escape you? Did too much lamian venom damage the old neurons?"

"There's nothing wrong with my brain." Dr. Thrakos threw down the pen and crossed his arms. "Show me. Prove that you have something to bargain with."

Jack caught his almost-wife's gaze. The slightest of twitches flashed over her lips. A quick nod indicated Cait was in full agreement with the approach.

She dragged a table across the room, and Jack summoned every last ounce of his resolve to bend, to lift the silver case onto the table, all while fighting growing nausea.

He flipped open the latches and lifted the lid. Slowly, he folded back the damp cloths wrapped about the *drakonourá*.

"Real?" Lady Thornton gasped.

Jack nodded. "We believe so, though an autopsy will confirm."

She pressed a hand to her chest."I would have denied the possibility of such a creature existing."

Dr. Thrakos leaned forward, snarling when his shackles clanged. "Bring the creature closer."

He countered. "Prove you recall the mathematics necessary to direct the fine, precise movements of the pituitary extractor."

With a huff, the mad scientist took up his pen and began to scratch out a complicated formula. Lady Thornton nodded as he wrote.

"That's all." Dr. Thrakos dropped his pen. "No more until I'm permitted to examine the *drakonourá*."

They dragged the table closer.

"Such perfection." Awe filled the madman's voice as he swept a fingertip over the infant's tail. "A smooth transition from skin to scale. Helena swore the Lamian queens moved at great speeds upon thick, muscular tails. Such a claim suggests that the thoracic vertebrae must repeat—over and over—as they do in every serpent. Ribs are, after all, necessary for the function of caudal musculature." His head snapped up, eye greedy for more details. "Fangs?"

How annoying that the same question simultaneously sprang into both their minds. Carefully, Jack parted the *drakonourá's* lips. Everyone in the room leaned forward, all held their breaths.

Two tiny white points protruded from the infant's pink gums.

"Amazing," Dr. Thrakos exhaled. "You'll perform a dissection, of course, to study the internal anatomy. To pinpoint the location and morphology of the poison glands. To determine if pelvic structures are present, if the development of lumbar vertebrae is completely suppressed. I *must* be allowed to observe."

"Must?" Jack slid the case across the table, moving it once again beyond the mad scientist's reach. "Convince me." He slid open a cabinet drawer, rummaged about, then laid forceps, a blunt-nosed probe and a sharp scalpel in a neat row upon the table. A teasing temptation. "Provide the complete algebraical algorithm necessary to generate the extremely precise and adjustable mechanistic sequences of the extractor's pincers."

Cait lifted the man's pen, held it out. "And without further delay."

"Fine." Narrow-eyed, Dr. Thrakos glared at them. "But I'll need considerably more paper."

Long, tension-filled minutes coalesced as the mad scientist scribbled, filling page upon page with complicated mathematical formulae that made no sense to Jack but had Lady Thornton snatching up each sheet as the ink dried, nodding and humming and examining the damaged device they'd retrieved from the bowels of the theater as if viewing it in an entirely new light.

All while Cait leaned against the wall beside him, shoulder to shoulder.

"Mission all but accomplished." Her fingers plucked at the holster slung beneath the ruin of her jacket. "The murderess is dead, her scientific accomplice in captivity, and her sisters have presumably fled our borders."

"My brother in custody, one of his business partners dead, the other likely so. With their unique services no longer available, the hotel and spa will likely fail. Questions remain, but not every case can be neatly tied up with a bow." He shrugged, a movement that caused the shoes beneath his feet to squelch. "Is more necessary?"

"I've a final item on my list." The gray tattered ends of Cait's shredded petticoats swept—mopped?—the ground beneath her sagging skirts as she turned to face him. The clothing that clung to them like wet dishrags would need to be burned. Her chin lifted. "A successful surgery."

His heart gave a great thud. Could their unorthodox marriage be saved?

Dr. Thrakos set down the pen. Muttering, he held out the stack of papers.

Lady Thornton paged through them, asking questions and receiving grumbling answers in return.

"Anything could happen," Jack said. The slightest

miscalculation could cause the shift of a sharp edge, leading to a nicked blood vessel. A sliced nerve. A fragment of bone thrust into neural tissue. "Even with the algorithm, a positive outcome is not a foregone conclusion. We ought not depend upon it."

"We," she repeated. "About that..."

They made quite the pair. Both of them hesitating to speak of their feelings for each other aloud in the face of Black's revelation. He hated the man for casting doubt once more upon the wisdom of their marriage. At the same time, he could appreciate the gesture.

Jack tugged the marriage license from his coat pocket and held it out. "File it the moment the registry opens. Even if the surgery ends my days as a field agent, there's no need for your fledgling career to stall."

She took the damp paper with shaking fingers, folding it carefully into a leather pouch at her belt. "I'll not deny my aspirations, but our marriage is—always was—more than a business partnership." A tear ran down her cheek. She brushed it away with an irritated swipe of her hand. "At least to me."

His heart jumped and gave a great twist. Was it possible? Had they fallen in love?

He rather thought they had.

Painted an institutional green, this dull block of a room in the basement of the Lister Institute was not at all a romantic location suitable for the declarations of deep feelings, but a Queen's agent often lived on a knife's edge, and this might well be the calm before another storm.

"Cait." He caught her hand in his, lifted it to his lips. "Whatever happens, know that I could not have chosen a better wife for myself. Perhaps it's why I let your claim on me go unchallenged our first evening together."

"And our marriage of convenience?" She lifted her eyes in challenge, though he glimpsed an underlying current of doubt. "Would you deny the attraction that sparked between us?"

"Never." He smiled softly. "As it turns out, career advancement was but a convenient excuse, nothing but a superficial narration for the duke and duchess." He kissed her forehead. "You are a dangerously beautiful woman, Cait. One I've come to trust with all my secrets, personal and professional."

"A gentleman who ignited an ice sculpture, creating a distraction worthy of newspaper headlines, could not possibly escape my notice or admiration." Mischief gathered at the corners of her mouth. "Intelligent and handsome and wildly good in—" She grinned. "Well, I wouldn't know, would I?"

"Something to rectify," he agreed with an answering smile. Hope dug in and held tight, no matter the pounding inside his head. "Might we be even more to each other?"

"I'll confess." Her cheeks flushed. "My heart has begun to entertain certain aspirations. Do you think—"

"How dare you!" Jack's brother burst into the room clad in nothing but a long, white sleep shirt. Wild-eyed, he snatched the scalpel from the table, pointed it at Dr. Thrakos. "Generous funds were funneled into your research.

Not once were you denied the slightest request. But where was your loyalty the moment a pretty woman bared her fangs?"

"I chose the future of a species over your money-grubbing ways," Dr. Thrakos countered, waving a hand toward the *drakonourá*. "Behold the possibilities!"

"That?" Aubrey's lip curled. He kicked the table, knocking the case and the dead infant to the floor. The accused madman jerked his head backward at the insult. "An abomination. Such a creature should never be allowed to crawl upon the earth. Had I known what you planned—"

"Which is why you were not informed." Dr. Thrakos crossed his arms. "A short-sighted ingrate such as yourself can't possibly understand."

"All my resources went into this project!" his brother yelled, eyes bulging. "All!"

"Aubrey, drop the blade." Jack pushed away from the wall, reaching, ready to stop his brother by force. But the room tilted and shifted.

"Back away!" Aubrey shouted, lashing out, slicing a deep gash into Jack's forearm. "All of you."

He hissed, slapping his palm atop the wound. Hot blood welled between his fingers.

Cait ran to the door. "Guards!"

Lady Amanda scrambled out of the way, dropping the papers she held and drawing her TTX weapon. "Set down the scalpel or I'll fire."

Aubrey lunged at the mad scientist, grabbed the man by

the tangled mess of his hair, pressed the scalpel to his throat. "You'll die for what you've done."

Lady Thornton cursed at the dilemma before her.

"He's already in custody." Jack tried reason. "Dr. Thrakos will never walk free. Don't hurt him. You'll only make things worse for yourself."

"Worse?" Aubrey shrieked. "He castrated me!"

"One testicle," Jack replied, keeping his voice calm even as blood dripped from beneath his hand to the floor. "Children are still a possibility."

There were those among the *ton* with unwed daughters who might ignore other inconvenient facts, though Jack would do his best to warn them away.

"Wrong!" Insanity crept into his brother's eyes. "I will never sire an heir. He wrought irreversible damage in that pit of his beneath the zoo. A roaring infection set in. Amputation of my remaining testicle was required to save my life. Not even your precious Lister physicians could reverse the damage."

Appalled, Jack opened his mouth. Shut it. All while struggling for a response.

Two guards skidded into the room with Cait hot on their heels.

"Sir, drop the knife," a guard barked.

The guards edged close, ready to tackle his brother.

"I wish I'd never laid eyes on your precious snake-woman." Aubrey snarled, glaring at the mad scientist. "Or your cursed laboratory."

Then all hell broke loose.

The guards lunged.

Aubrey slashed the mad scientist's throat.

Arterial blood sprayed.

Lady Thornton fired, her dart finding its mark in his brother's back.

Jack staggered forward, pressed his hands to the mad scientist's neck in a hopeless attempt at saving him while the guards dragged his still-screaming brother away.

Beneath his palms blood pulsed, gushing forth from the carotid arteries midst a horrible, bubbling gurgle sound that told him the man's trachea had also been cut.

Hopeless.

Cait rushed forward, gauze in her hands, but it was already too late.

Jack shook his head. "He's gone."

"Sit." She tugged at his shoulders. "Your face, it's lost all color."

Fitting, as the room blazed a blinding white before his eyes.

"Jack?" Cait's voice traveled the length of a long hallway to reach him. "Jack!"

Then the world went dark.

CHAPTER TWENTY-NINE

Twisting her poison ring, Cait paced in the waiting room outside the surgical suite throwing anxious looks at its doors as nearby nurses cast both curious and sympathetic glances in her direction. Her hands rose, unbidden, to rub the back of her neck, and her mind spun out worst-case scenarios. She was a wreck, brooding over a future without Jack—how could she carry on without the man she loved?—then agonizing over the numerous repercussions that remaining his wife might generate. Would societal expectations rip them apart?

No matter her protests, both the Thorntons had refused to let her stay by his side. Total concentration was an absolute necessity for a procedure that had never before been attempted.

Except by a mythological venomous woman, all with fatal outcomes.

Dread crawled from her stomach into her throat.

Hours had passed since the mad scientist's death. Hours upon hours spent modifying the device to safely extract her not-quite-a-husband's tumor. Consulting with Rankine engineers to examine the algorithm scratched out by Dr. Thrakos. Generating a series of tiny punch cards to fit inside the slot of a miniaturized cipher cartridge. Adjusting critical features of the clockwork mechanism based on novel elements found within the irreparably damaged pituitary extractor retrieved from the bowels of the Opera Comique.

But the worst had been the tests.

Lady Thornton, neuroscientist extraordinaire, had placed the entirety of her completed device atop a squash—a gruesome stand-in for Jack's brain—where it had crouched like an overlarge metallic insect, drills and pinchers ready and waiting.

With the flick of a switch, clockwork had clicked and whirred, executing an extremely precise mechanistic sequence devised to avoid all critical structures en route to extracting the offending tumor.

An observer might have been forgiven for thinking the device a harmless children's toy. But the claw-tipped arms of the contraption were designed to grip a victim's face while a hole was drilled into the base of their skull via the nose, an approach Lord Thornton termed "transsphenoidal".

Her stomach flipped over and shuddered as her mind recalled the horrifying details. Would Jack survive? Would he be the same man?

"Cait!" Her mother rushed into the waiting room, wrapping her arms about her daughter and holding her close.

"Mr. Black tells me there was a fire, an accident at the Opera Comique, that your husband is in surgery!"

"A head injury." She gave the agreed upon answer as the tears that had built behind her eyes finally burst free. The device—its history and function—was classified, not to be spoken of outside agency circles. "He collapsed, unconscious, and has yet to reawaken." She swallowed. "His prognosis is... grim."

She allowed herself to sink into the softness of her mother's comfort. Only when she finished drying her eyes, some long minutes later, did Cait notice Logan's silent presence.

Annoyance dried her sniffles. "Any news?"

His eyes were tired, having passed the hours hunting for the escaped lamiae. "Lady Saltwell and her nanny have vanished."

Her mother sucked in a shocked breath. "Goodness, scandal is about to break amidst the *ton*. Tongues already wag." She lowered her voice. "Lady Saltwell was once an actress who sang at the Opera Comique and..." Realization struck. "The ointment." Blinking, her mother clapped a hand to her mouth.

Logan glared at Cait.

"But for my mother's insight," she defended, "we might never have unearthed our suspect." There was no need to burden her with knowledge of the unfortunate Miss Smyth's end.

"Your contribution was valuable." Reluctant gratitude forced the words past her brother's lips. "However, please keep the details to yourself, Mrs. McCullough, lest your daughter be unable to avail herself of requesting your assistance in the future."

Her mother nodded, wide-eyed at the thought of working, however peripherally, for the Queen's agents.

"The rest you will read in the papers." Logan sighed. "Carruthers, Lord Saltwell, was found in the vaults beneath the theater. Trapped under a fallen beam. His death appears to have been asphyxiation by smoke inhalation. With his wife and child missing, there will indeed be much scandal."

"A missing heir?" Her mother's eyes danced. "Speculation will last for years. Search parties will be launched. In two decades, we can expect fraudulent claims." With her fingers, she made a twisting motion before her lips. "I will not speak a single word."

Gossip would abound, and her mother could sit at the center of it, smug with her secret knowledge.

Even better if she could do so in Lady Aubrey's parlor, with the satisfaction of knowing that—as a grandmother to the future heir of a viscounty—she was the woman's equal.

Provided her marriage endured. Cait pressed a hand to her stomach, sick with worry.

"Have you filed the license?" her brother asked, easily reading her mind.

Curse him for putting her in such a position. Were they still children, she'd kick him in the shins for his high-handed failure to file her marriage certificate. Might still, when no one was looking.

She narrowed her eyes and swallowed the expletive that leapt onto her tongue. "Not yet." First, she needed to be certain beyond all shadow of a doubt that Jack still desired a shared future in light of his brother's inability to procreate.

Rocking backward upon his heels, Logan fixed his gaze upon the ceiling. "Aubrey *will* make trouble for you. Tragic though his injury may be—"

Did he roll his eyes? Cait suppressed a reluctant smile. "It will not shorten his life," she finished. "My societal role would not alter."

"For now. But if you have children, certain adjustments will be necessary."

"Do *not* speak in circles around me," her mother huffed, turning hard eyes upon Cait. "Are you not legally married?" Her voice grew louder with each word.

"There are complications..." How to explain she would have a willing husband or none at all?

Spine stiff, her mother huffed. "The duchess assured me of her steadfast determination to see you respectfully wed."

Logan's eyebrows reached for his hairline. "Tell me it was not you who informed the duchess that Cait was the woman alluded to in the gossip rags?"

"Why would I not?" Her mother bristled. "Her role was bound to be discovered. Someone had to safeguard her future."

For a moment, Logan was speechless. A first. "Never lecture me again about her recruitment," he snapped. "The duke and duchess never let an opportunity to—" He stopped.

"Finish," Cait demanded, her hand shifting toward her holster. If a single dart remained in her pistol, the temptation to skewer him where he stood might have overwhelmed her good sense.

Her brother drew a deep breath. "Via the duchess, your mother may have brought you to the duke's attention, but his precipitous decision to welcome you into the Queen's agents speaks to your skills. You're beyond qualified." His expression softened. "Never doubt that."

She gaped, uncertain how to respond to such praise.

The doors to the surgical suite swung open. Lady Thornton pulled a mask from her face. "All went exactly according to plan." Though her eyes were tired, she beamed. "Your husband is asking for you. Forgive the delay. We wanted to wait until he was awake, that we might fully assess the procedure's outcome."

Heart soaring, Cait rushed to Jack's side. She dropped onto her knees, bedside, relieved at the sight of his lopsided smile, no matter the grogginess that lingered in his eyes.

She examined his head, his face with gentle fingertips. The only evidence of the grip exerted by the pituitary tumor extractor's pointed legs were six small perforations, three on each side, that had been swabbed with iodine and left to scab over.

The surgical wound itself was hidden deep inside Jack's nose where the drill bit had passed from the nasal cavity into his sphenoid, the bone at the base of his skull that housed the gland. The Thorntons had assured her that such was the most direct and least-damaging pathway to access the pituitary. At least, when the device was modified and placed in the hands of an ethical and competent neurosurgeon.

The only evidence that such had taken place was a slightly bloody bandage beneath his nose.

"A near perfect outcome," he said, answering her question before she asked. "A slight loss of peripheral vision in the left eye, but nothing that will keep me from a mission. Once I'm cleared for duty," he amended. "Thornton insists upon three days of bedrest, six weeks of near inactivity, and a full twelve weeks of recovery before I'm allowed to resume an agent's duties."

"Thank aether. I was so very afraid," she snatched up his hands and squeezed tight, "that I might never have the chance to tell you that I've fallen—madly, desperately and deeply—in love with you."

"I'd meant to profess the same moments before my brother rudely interrupted us, bursting in and wielding a scalpel." Stars filled his eyes as he tugged at a loose lock of her hair. His brow furrowed. "But something is wrong. Tell me."

She swallowed, forcing doubt and worry back into her stomach where she prayed the churning acid would dissolve them to nothing. "It needs to be said. In the eyes of *ton* society, I am the worst possible mother imaginable for a future viscount. Registering our marriage is a step from which there is no easy retreat."

"You've not filed yet?" Sadness lined his expression. "Cait..."

Tension drained away. "I had to know." She tightened her grip on his hands. "You're certain?"

"Beyond all doubt." A teasing smile overtook his face,

and a lightness brightened his next words. "It's you who won't be able to escape your brother-in-law. You're certain *you* wish to be *my* wife?"

She laughed. "My willingness to endure him should be viewed as testament to my devotion." Happiness suffused her chest with a buoyancy that felt as if it might overcome gravity.

"Our children will be his heirs." He pulled a face. "Aubrey will be insufferable."

"A decided drawback," she agreed. Her voice, light as it was—as if filled with bubbles—was barely recognizable. "At least *we* won't be saddled with titles."

"Yet," Jack warned, grinning. "Don't underestimate his self-destructive tendencies."

"Your warning is duly noted," she said, then snorted. "Our mothers will fight."

"Like cats and dogs." His eyes danced. "My mother will hate every minute."

"Her discomfort will delight mine." Cait laughed, then lifted an eyebrow and infused her next words with a hint of conspiracy. "All of which we could side-step, at least for a while, by accepting foreign assignments. My brother owes us both. I will force him to file our marriage license this very afternoon, then insist he give us our choice of missions. Someplace warm and sunny. An Italian villa, perhaps."

"Lest he find a poisonous creature beneath his pillow?" Jack tossed her a knowing grin, then hesitated. "But what of your research?"

"The constraints of working within Lister walls rather

dulls the shine of such a career in comparison to the excitement of field work." She leaned forward. "If we miss it badly enough, we could always establish our own secret laboratory in the basement."

"True." He dragged her hand to his mouth, pressing a kiss to her palm. "Are we off to Paris, then, for a proper honeymoon, Mrs. Tagert? After all, we've yet to explore the possibilities of a mattress."

"As soon as you're fully healed." Heart full, she laid her head on his shoulder. "We'll try to slip away. But I place low odds on us leaving British shores without a new assignment."

"Perfect," he answered, pulling her hand to rest against his chest, directly over his heart. "Life will never be dull with you at my side."

EPILOGUE

QUINN TOUCHED A MATCH to the missive informing him of his sister's marriage. When flames began to lick his fingers, he let the wind carry it away in a cascade of sparks to the waves below. Leaning against the railing, he fixed his gaze upon the distant horizon.

Another sibling married. For better or worse, Cait was one of them now, a Queen's agent. A smile tugged at his lips. With quite the courtship tale if he read the grumbling between the lines of Logan's scrawl correctly.

"Mr. McCullough," the man sent to collect him from the docks called. "The train leaves in half an hour. We should go."

At his side stood a dark-skinned woman. Trouble, from the looks of her. She kept her own council, but he recognized the fire in her eyes—the same flames burned in Cait's.

Was she the man's wife? A fellow agent? Both?

Not Quinn's place to ask. This meeting was merely an exchange, the handover of a dull brown envelope packed with information that would orient him to the situation brewing in New York.

He had a few more months, perhaps less, to wrap up this assignment, before the Duke of Avesbury demanded his return to British shores. Time to make use of every minute that remained.

ABOUT THE AUTHOR

Though ANNE RENWICK holds a Ph.D. in biology and greatly enjoyed tormenting the overburdened undergraduates who were her students, fiction has always been her first love. Today, she writes steampunk romance, placing a new kind of biotech in the hands of mad scientists, proper young ladies and determined villains.

Anne brings an unusual perspective to steampunk. A number of years spent locked inside the bowels of a biological research facility left her permanently altered. In her steampunk world, the Victorian fascination with all things anatomical led to a number of alarming biotechnological advances. Ones that the enemies of Britain would dearly love to possess.

www.AnneRenwick.com

instagram.com/anne_renwick

facebook.com/AnneRenwickAuthor

pinterest.com/AuthorAnneRenwick